PRAISE FOR THE NOVELS OF
PENELOPE DOUGLAS

"I read this book in one sitting. *Rival* was as gripping as it was sexy!"
—Colleen Hoover, #1 *New York Times* bestselling author

"Penelope Douglas just keeps getting better and better."
—Samantha Young, *New York Times* bestselling author of
the On Dublin Street series

"Passion and anger simmer on the page, turning love into a battlefield . . . their chemistry is downright explosive."
—*Publishers Weekly*

"Another powerfully written contemporary love story that delivers . . . raw emotions."
—*Booklist*

The Next Flame

A
Fall Away
Novel

PENELOPE DOUGLAS

BERKLEY ROMANCE
NEW YORK

BERKLEY ROMANCE
Published by Berkley
An imprint of Penguin Random House LLC
penguinrandomhouse.com

Aflame copyright © 2015 by Penelope Douglas
Next to Never copyright © 2017 by Penelope Douglas
Penguin Random House supports copyright. Copyright fuels creativity,
encourages diverse voices, promotes free speech, and creates a vibrant culture.
Thank you for buying an authorized edition of this book and for complying with
copyright laws by not reproducing, scanning, or distributing any part of it in any
form without permission. You are supporting writers and allowing Penguin
Random House to continue to publish books for every reader.

BERKLEY and the BERKLEY & B colophon are registered trademarks of
Penguin Random House LLC.

Library of Congress Cataloging-in-Publication Data

Names: Douglas, Penelope, 1977- author. | Douglas, Penelope,
1977- Aflame. | Douglas, Penelope, 1977- Next to never.
Title: The next flame / Penelope Douglas.
Other titles: Aflame. | Next to never.
Description: New York : Berkley, [2017] | Series: The fall away series
Identifiers: LCCN 2016058369 (print) | LCCN 2017004521 (ebook) |
ISBN 9780399584930 (trade paper) | ISBN 9780399584947 (ebook)
Subjects: | BISAC: FICTION / Romance / Contemporary. |
FICTION / Contemporary Women. | FICTION / Romance / General. |
GSAFD: Love stories.
Classification: LCC PS3604.O93236 A6 2017 (print) |
LCC PS3604.O93236 (ebook) | DDC 813/.6—dc23
LC record available at https://lccn.loc.gov/2016058369

InterMix eBook edition of *Aflame* / April 2015
InterMix eBook edition of *Next to Never* / January 2017
Berkley Romance trade paperback edition / October 2023

Printed in the United States of America
5th Printing

Aflame

For the girls . . .
For Juliet, who thinks everyone deserves a white picket fence,
For Fallon, who thinks that if we know what we really want,
then there is no choice,
And for Tate, who knows that fighting with someone isn't half
as satisfying as fighting for them.
Carry on, ladies.

AFLAME **PLAYLIST**

Music inspires the development of my characters and inspires my scenes. Enjoy!

"Adrenaline"	by Shinedown
"Alive"	by P.O.D.
"Blow Me Away"	by Breaking Benjamin
"The Boys of Summer"	by The Ataris
"Breath"	by Breaking Benjamin
"Click Click Boom"	by Saliva
"Girls, Girls, Girls"	by Mötley Crüe
"I Get Off"	by Halestorm
"I Hate Everything About You"	by Three Days Grace
"My Way"	by Limp Bizkit
"Nothing Else Matters"	by Apocalyptica
"She's Crafty"	by Beastie Boys
"Something Different"	by Godsmack
"This Is the Time"	by Nothing More
"Weak"	by Seether
"Wish You Hell"	by Like a Storm
"You Stupid Girl"	by Framing Hanley

Aflame is the conclusion of the Fall Away series, which includes *Bully*, *Until You*, *Rival*, and *Falling Away*. While every book in the series is written to be a stand-alone, *Aflame* will be most enjoyed by those who have read at least *Bully*, as *Aflame* is a continuation of that story.

TATE

Four Years Ago

"Jared Trent," I scolded, "if I get into trouble for the first time in my life, three weeks before I graduate high school, I'm telling my father it was your fault."

I nearly jogged behind him as he pulled me along down the darkened school corridor, the music from the dance like a subterranean hum around us.

"Your father believes in taking personal responsibility, Tate," he pointed out, and I could hear the humor in his tone. "Come on." He squeezed my hand. "Pick up the pace."

I stumbled as he led me faster up the steps onto the second floor, my royal blue floor-length prom dress sweeping the length of my legs. It was nearing midnight, and our senior prom, happening downstairs, wasn't holding my boyfriend's attention. Not that I thought it would.

Sometimes I imagined he simply endured social activities by plotting what he was going to do to me when we were finally alone. Jared Trent had a few favorite people in the world, and if you weren't in that group, then you received a modicum of his attention. If he couldn't be with me, then the only other people he could stand being around were his brother, Jax, and our best friend, Madoc Caruthers.

He hated dances, he hated dancing, and he loathed monotonous chatter. But while his demeanor was meant to push people away, it only enticed them to want to know him more. Much to his delight, of course.

But he put up with it. All for me. And did so with a smile on his face. He loved making me happy.

I jogged to keep pace and held his arm with both hands as I followed him. He swung open a classroom door and held it wide, waiting for me to enter. I pinched my eyebrows together, wondering what he was up to, but I hurried into the room anyway, afraid we'd be caught. We shouldn't be roaming the school, after all.

Once inside the deserted room, I twisted around as he followed me inside and closed the door.

"Penley's classroom?" I prompted. We hadn't stepped foot in this room since last semester.

His mischievous chocolate brown eyes flashed to me before he answered. "Yeah."

I wandered down the aisle between two rows of empty desks, feeling him watching me.

"Where we hated each other," I reminisced in a teasing voice.

"Yeah."

I let my fingertips graze a wooden desktop. "Where we started to love each other," I kept playing with him.

"Yeah." His soft whisper felt like a warm blanket on my skin.

I grinned to myself, remembering. "Where I was your north."

Elizabeth Penley was our literature teacher. We'd both had her for several classes but only for one class together. Themes in Film and Literature last fall.

When Jared and I were enemies.

She'd given us an assignment in which we had to find partners for each of the cardinal directions. Jared ended up being my "North." Reluctantly.

My strappy silver heels—which matched the silver jewels on my nearly backless dress—struck the floor as I turned around to eye him still standing by the door.

And his flat, stoic expression did nothing to hide the dangerous streak. I suddenly felt an urge to climb him like a tree.

I knew he hated suits, but he honestly looked like a devil of the best kind dressed up as he was. His tailored black pants draped down his legs and accentuated his narrow waist. The black dress shirt wasn't tight, but it didn't hide his body, either, and the black jacket and tie completed the look in a way that emanated power and sex, as always.

In the eight months since we'd gotten together, I'd become very adept at swallowing my drool before it seeped out of my mouth.

Luckily, he looked at me the same way.

He leaned against the door, his jacket pulled back from his waist as he slid his hands into his pockets and watched me with interest. His dark brown hair sat across his forehead in elegant chaos like a dark shadow hovering just above his eyes.

"What are you thinking?" I asked when he continued to just stand there.

"How much I miss watching you come into this room," he answered, looking me up and down.

My body warmed, knowing exactly what he was talking about. I'd enjoyed toying with him when I knew he was watching me in here.

"And," he continued, "I'm going to miss how your hand shoots into the air like a big dork to answer questions."

I gasped, my eyes rounding in mock anger. "Dork?" I repeated. I put my hands on my hips and pursed my lips to hide my smile.

He grinned and kept joking. "And also how you huddled so close to the desktop when you were concentrating on a test, and how you chewed your pencils when you were nervous."

My gaze flashed to the side, where his old desk sat behind mine.

He went on, pushing off the door and inching closer to me. "I'm also going to miss how you blushed when I whispered things in your ear when Penley's back was turned." He cocked his head to the side, and I looked up at him as he approached me.

Shivers ran down my arms as I remembered Jared leaning forward over his desk and tickling my ear with his hot promises. I closed my eyes, feeling his chest brush against mine.

"I'm going to miss sitting two feet away," he whispered over me, "and no one the wiser as to what I'd snuck into your room that morning to do to you."

I sucked in a breath, feeling his forehead dip to mine.

He continued, "I'm going to miss the torture of wanting you in the middle of class and not being able to have you. I'm going to miss us in this room, Tate."

Me, too.

The pull was always there between us. Even in a crowded classroom, full of noise and distraction, there was an invisible rope cutting through the space, connecting him and me. He touched me even when he couldn't reach me. He whispered in my ear from twenty feet away. And I could always feel his lips even when we were apart.

I smiled and opened my eyes, his lips now an inch from mine. "Even though you sat behind me, I could always feel your eyes, Jared. Even when you acted like you hated me, I felt you watching me."

"I never hated you."

"I know." I nodded gently, circling his waist with my arms.

The three years he'd made an enemy out of me seemed unbearable at the time. Now I was just glad it was all over. I was grateful that we were here. Together.

But I wouldn't look back on high school as a very enjoyable experience, and I knew he had a lot of guilt about that.

All of Jared's life, he'd suffered abandonment and loneliness. From his horrible father and alcoholic mother. From the neighbors who ignored what was happening and from the teachers who looked the other way.

The summer before freshman year, the parents who should've protected him hurt him nearly beyond repair. His father was abusive, leaving permanent scars, and his mother couldn't be there for him.

So Jared decided alone was best. He shut everyone out.

But with me, he went a step further. Several steps, actually. He sought revenge.

I was his best friend at the time, but he'd thought I'd abandoned him as well. It was a culmination of too many bad things happening in too little time, and Jared couldn't be forgotten about anymore. He wasn't going to allow it.

I was the one he could treat badly to feel in control again, and so I became his prey. All throughout high school I suffered at his hands.

Until last August, when I came back from my year abroad.

When Jared pushed, I started pushing back. The world turned upside down for both of us, and after more shit than I care to remember, we found our way back to each other.

"We have a lot of good memories in this room." I pulled my head back and looked up at him. "But there is one place where we don't have good memories . . ."

I slipped out of his arms and walked for the door, reaching down to slip off my heels. "Come on," I urged with a backward glance and a smile.

Swinging the door open, I darted out into the hallway and bolted, running.

"Tate!" I heard him yell, and I spun around, jogging backward as I watched him come out the classroom door. His eyebrows were pinched together in confusion as he watched me.

I bit my bottom lip to stifle a laugh before I whipped around and started running down the hallway again.

"Tate!" he called again. "You're a runner! This is an unfair advantage!"

I laughed, excitement energizing my arms and legs as I lifted my dress and hopped down two flights of stairs, racing down the hallway toward the Athletics Department.

I could hear the thuds of his large body gaining on me. He was jumping stairs, and I squealed with giddy fright as I hurled open the locker room door and ran away from his gaining advance.

Hurrying to the third row of lockers, I collapsed against the little metal doors, my heavy breaths stretching the bust of my dress as I dropped my shoes.

I'd left my long blond hair down, but I'd had my best friend, K.C., blow it out and fix it in loose, wavy curls. Given the exertion, I was tempted to shove it away from my face, but Jared loved my hair down, and I wanted to drive him wild tonight.

The locker room door opened, and I fisted my hands, hearing him approach.

His soft steps rounded the corner as if he knew exactly where to find me. "The girls' locker room?" he asked, discomfort written all over his face.

I knew he'd be timid, but I wasn't letting him off the hook.

I took a deep breath. "The last time we were here—"

"I don't want to think about the last time we were here," he cut me off, shaking his head.

But I forced it again. "The last time we were here," I emphasized, "you threatened me and tried to intimidate me." I walked over and grabbed his hand, leading him back to the spot against the lockers where we'd had our confrontation last fall. I leaned backward, taking his waist and leading him in close, so he hovered over me.

"You pushed into my space and hovered just like this," I whispered, "and I ended up being pretty damn embarrassed in front of the whole school. Remember?"

I laid it all out on the line for him. We couldn't be afraid to talk about it. We'd have to laugh, because I'd done enough crying. We'd face our fears and move on.

"You were mean to me," I pressed.

He'd come in after I'd showered, rushed my teammates out of the room, and issued a few threats as I tried to stand tall dressed in nothing but my towel. Then some students came in and snapped pictures of us, in which nothing was happening, but being nearly naked with a boy in the locker room didn't look so great to everyone in school who saw the pictures.

Jared's eyes, always soft with me now, always holding me close, turned heated. I clutched the lapels of his jacket and melted my body into his, wanting to make a good memory here.

His face inched closer to mine, and my breathing faltered as I felt his fingers glide up the inside of my thigh, clawing my dress higher and higher.

"So we're back to where we started," he whispered against my lips. "Are you going to hit me this time like I deserve?"

Amusement threatened, and I could feel the corners of my mouth turn up.

I slid out of his shadow, hopped up on the center bench behind him, and stood over him, loving his wide-eyed expression as he turned around to face me. Placing both of my hands against the lockers, now behind him, on either side of his head, I bore down, crowding his space as I leaned in close.

"If I ever lay my hands on you," I whispered his same words to me from all those months ago, "you'll want it."

He let out a quiet laugh as his lips grazed mine.

I cocked my head, playing with him. "Do you?" I prompted. "Want it, I mean?"

He cupped my face with both hands and begged, "Yes." And then he snatched up my lips. "Hell yes."

And I melted.

I always melted.

CHAPTER 1

JARED

Kids are crazy.

Batshit, certifiably, without-a-brain-in-their-head crazy. If you're not explaining something to them, then you're reexplaining it, because they didn't listen the first time, and as soon as you explain it, they ask the same damn question you just spent twenty minutes explaining the answer to!

And the questions. Holy fuck, the questions.

Some of these kids talked more in one day than I have in my entire life, and you can't get away from it, because they follow you.

Like, take a hint, you know?

"Jared! I want the blue helmet, and Connor had it last time, and it's my turn!" the half-pint blond kid whined from the track as all the other children climbed into their go-kart cars, two rows of six each.

I tipped my chin down and inhaled an aggravated breath as I gripped the fence surrounding the track. "It doesn't matter what color helmet you have on," I growled, tensing every muscle in my back.

Blondie—what the hell was his name again?—scrunched up his face, getting redder by the moment. "But . . . but it's not fair! He had it two times, and I—"

"Get the black helmet," I ordered, cutting him off. "It's your lucky one, remember?"

He pinched his eyebrows together, his freckled nose scrunching up. "It is?"

"Yes," I lied, the hot California sun beating down on my black-T-shirt-clad shoulders. "You wore it when we flipped in the buggy three weeks ago. It kept you safe."

"I thought I was wearing the blue one."

"Nope. The black," I lied again. I really had no idea what color he'd been wearing.

I should feel bad about lying, but I didn't. When children got more reasonable, I could stop resorting to rocket science to get them to do what I wanted them to do. "Hurry up," I shouted, hearing little go-kart motors fill the air. "They're going to leave without you."

He ran for the other side of the gate to the shelves of helmets, snatching up the black one. I watched as all the kids, ranging in age from five to eight, strapped themselves in and shot each other excited little thumbs-ups. They gripped their steering wheels, their thin arms tense, and I felt a grin pull at the corners of my mouth.

This was the part that wasn't so bad.

Crossing my arms over my chest, I watched with pride as they took off, each kid handling his or her car with increasing precision every week they came here. Their shiny helmets glistened in the early summer sunshine as the tiny engines zoomed around the bend and echoed in the distance as they sped off. Some kids were still pushing the pedal to the metal for the entire race, but others were learning to measure their time and assess the road ahead. Patience was hard to muster when you just wanted to be in front the entire race, but some quickly caught on that a good defense was the best offense. It wasn't just about getting ahead of that car; it was also about staying ahead of the cars already behind you.

And more than just learning, they were also having fun. If only a place like this had existed when I was that age.

But even at twenty-two, I was still grateful for it.

When these kids first walked through my door they knew next to nothing, and now they handled the track like it was a walk in the park. Thanks to me and the other volunteers. They were always happy to be here, full of smiles, and looking to me with anticipation.

They actually wanted to be around me.

What the hell for, I didn't know, but I was certain of one thing. As much as I complained or escaped to my office, struggling to scrape up just a little more patience, I absolutely, without a doubt, wanted to be around them, too. Some of them were pretty cool little shits.

When I wasn't traveling and working the circuit, racing with my own team, I was here, helping with the kids program.

Of course, it wasn't just a go-kart track. There was a garage and a shop, and lots of drivers and their girlfriends hung out, working on bikes and shooting the shit.

Godsmack's "Something Different" played over the speakers, and I looked up at the sky, seeing the sun beat down, blinding me.

It was probably raining back home today. June was big on summer thunderstorms in Shelburne Falls.

"Here," Pasha ordered, shoving a clipboard into my chest. "Sign these."

I grabbed it, scowling at my black-and-purple-haired assistant from under my sunglasses as the go-karts roared past.

"What is it?" I unclipped the pen and looked at what appeared to be a purchase order.

She watched the track, answering me. "One is an order for your bike parts. I'm just having them shipped to Texas. Your crew can sort through it when you get there in August—"

I dropped my arms to my sides. "That's two months away," I shot out. "How do you know that shit's still going to be there when I get there?"

Austin was going to be my first stop when I went back out on the road racing after my break. I understood her logic. I didn't need the equipment until then, but it was thousands of dollars' worth of parts that someone else could get their hands on. I'd rather have it here with me in California than three states away, unprotected.

But she just shot me a glare, looking like I'd put mustard on her pancakes. "The other two are forms faxed over from your accountant," she went on, ignoring my concern. "Paperwork to do with establishing JT Racing." And then she peered over at me, looking inquisitive. "Kind of vain, don't you think? Giving your business your initials?"

I dropped my eyes back down to the papers and began signing. "They're not my initials," I mumbled. "And I don't pay you to have an opinion about everything, and I certainly don't pay you to get on my nerves."

I handed over the clipboard, and she took it with a smile. "No, you pay me to remember your mom's birthday," she threw back. "You also pay me to keep your iPod fresh with new music, your bills paid, your motorcycles safe, your schedule on your phone, your flights booked, your favorite foods in your refrigerator, and my personal favorite: I'm to call you thirty minutes after you've been forced to go to some function or party and give you a dire excuse as to why you need to leave said social gathering, because you hate people, right?" Her tone dripped with cockiness, and I was suddenly glad I didn't grow up with a sister.

I didn't hate people.

Okay, yes. I hated most people.

She continued, "I schedule your haircuts, I run this place and your Facebook page—I do love all the topless photos chicks send you, by the way—and I'm the first person you seek out when you want someone to yell at." She planted her hands on her hips, squinting at me. "Now, I forget. What *don't* you pay me to do again?"

My chest inflated with a heavy breath, and I chewed the corner of my mouth until she took the hint and left. I could practically smell her smug smile as she made her way back to the shop.

She knew she was priceless, and I'd walked into that one. I might take a lot of sass from her, but she was right. She took a lot of it from me, too.

Pasha was my age and the daughter of the man I co-owned this bike shop with. Although the old man, Drake Weingarten, was a racing legend on the motorcycle circuits, he chose to be a silent partner and enjoy his retirement in the pool hall down the street when he was in town or in his cabin near Tahoe when he wasn't.

I liked having this as a home base near the action in Pomona, and I'd found I actually took an interest in the kids program he sponsored here when I started hanging around the motorcycle shop almost two years ago. When he'd asked if I wanted to plant some roots and buy into this place, it was the perfect timing.

There was nothing left for me back home. My life was here now.

A cool, little hand slipped into mine, and I looked down to see Gianna, a bright-faced brunette I'd grown pretty fond of. I smiled, looking for her usual cheery expression, but she squeezed my hand and brushed her lips into my arm, looking like she was ten kinds of sad instead.

"What's the matter, kiddo?" I joked. "Whose butt do I need to kick?"

She wrapped both of her little arms around mine, and I could feel her shaking.

"Sorry," she mumbled, "I guess crying is such a girlie thing to do, isn't it?" The sarcasm in her voice was unmistakable.

Oh, boy.

Chicks—even eight-year-old chicks—were complicated. Women didn't want to tell you what was wrong flat out. Oh, no. It couldn't be that easy. You had to get a shovel and dig it out of them.

Gianna had been coming around for more than two months, but just recently she'd started in the racing club. Out of all the kids in the class, she had the most promise. She worried about being perfect, she always looked over her shoulder, and it seemed as if she always figured out how to argue with me even before she knew what I was going to say—but she had it.

The gift.

"Why aren't you on the track?" I pulled my arm out of her grasp and sat down on the picnic table to meet her eye to eye.

She stared at the ground, her bottom lip quivering. "My dad says I can't take part in the program anymore."

"Why not?"

She shifted from side to side on her feet, and my heart skipped when I looked down and saw her red Chucks. Just like the ones Tate wore the first time I met her when we were ten.

Looking back up, I watched her hesitate before answering. "My dad says it makes my brother feel bad."

Leaning my elbows down to my knees, I twisted my head to study her. "Because you beat your brother in the race last week," I verified.

She nodded.

Of course. She'd beat everyone last week, and her brother—her twin—left the track crying.

"He says my brother won't feel like a man if I race with him."

I snorted, but then I straightened my face when I saw her scowl. "It's not funny," she whimpered. "And it's not fair."

I shook my head and grabbed the shop cloth out of my back pocket. "Here," I offered, letting her dry her tears.

Clearing my throat, I got closer and spoke in a low voice. "Listen, you're not going to understand this now, but remember it for later," I told her. "Your brother is going to do a lot over the years to feel like a man, but that's not your problem. You got that?"

Her expression remained frozen as she listened.

"Do you like racing?" I asked.

She nodded quickly.

"Are you doing anything wrong?"

She shook her head, her two low pigtails swinging across her shoulders.

"Should you be afraid to do something you like just because you're a winner and other people can't handle that?" I pushed.

Her innocent storm blue eyes finally looked up at me, and she tipped her chin up, shaking her head. "No."

"Then get your butt on the track," I commanded, turning to the go-karts flying by. "You're late."

She flashed a smile that took up half her face and shot off toward the track entrance, full of excitement. But then she stopped and swung back around. "But what about my dad?"

"I'll handle your dad."

Her smile flashed again, and I had to fight to hold back my own.

"Oh, and I'm not supposed to tell you this," she taunted, "but my mom thinks you're hot."

And then she twisted around and darted off toward the cars.

Great.

I let out an awkward breath before glancing over to the bleachers where the moms sat. Jax would call them cougars, and Madoc would just call them.

Well, before he was married, anyway.

It was always the same with these women, and I knew some of them enrolled their kids simply to get closer to the drivers and riders who hung out here. They showed up in full hair and makeup, usually in heels and tight jeans or short skirts, as if I was going to pick one and take her into the office as her kid played outside.

Half of them had their phones in front of their faces to look like they weren't doing what I knew they were. Thanks to Pasha's big mouth, I knew that while some people used their sunglasses to disguise that they were staring at you, these women were zooming in with their cameras to stare at me close-up.

Super. I then and there made it another part of Pasha's job description not to tell me shit I didn't need to know.

"Jared!" Pasha's bark boomed over every other sound here. "You have a phone call on Skype!"

I cocked my head to the side, peering over at her. Skype?

Wondering who the hell wanted to video chat, I got up and walked through the café and into the shop/garage, ignoring the faint whispers and sideways glances from people who recognized me. No one knew me outside of the motorcycle world, but inside it, I was starting to get a name for myself, and the attention was always going to be hard to deal with. If I could have the career without it, I would, but the crowds came with the racing.

Stepping into the office, I closed the door and rounded my desk, staring at my laptop screen. "Mom?" I said to the woman who was a female version of me in looks.

Thank God I didn't look like my dad.

"Aw," she cooed, "so you do remember who I am. I was worried." She nodded condescendingly, and I leaned down on the desk, arching a brow.

"Don't be dramatic," I grumbled.

I couldn't tell where she was from the furniture behind her. All I saw was a lot of white in the background, so I assumed it was a bedroom. Her husband—and my best friend's father, Jason Caruthers—was a successful lawyer, and their new Chicago apartment was probably the best money could buy.

My mother, on the other hand, was perfectly recognizable. Absolutely beautiful, and a testament to the fact that people do take advantage of the second chances they're given. She looked healthy, alert, and happy.

"We talk every few weeks," I reminded her. "But we've never video chatted before, so what's up?"

Since I had quit college and left home two years ago, I'd been back only once. Just long enough to realize it was a mistake. I hadn't seen my friends or my brother, and even though I'd kept in touch with my mother, it had been only via phone and text. And even that was kept short and sweet.

It was better that way. Out of sight, out of mind, and it worked, too, because every time I heard my mother's voice or got an e-mail from my brother or a text from someone back home, I thought about her.

Tate.

My mother leaned in close, her chocolate hair, same as mine, falling over her shoulders. "I've got an idea. Let's start over," she chirped and straightened her back. "Hey, son." She smiled. "How are you doing? I've missed you. Have you missed me?"

I let out a nervous laugh and shook my head. "Jesus," I breathed out.

Aside from Tate, my mother knew me better than anyone. Not because we'd shared so much mother-son time over the years, but because she'd lived with me long enough to know I didn't like unnecessary bullshit.

Small talk? Yeah, not my thing.

Plopping my ass down in the high-back leather chair, I placated her. "I'm doing fine," I said. "And you?"

She nodded, and I noticed the happiness that made her skin glow. "Keeping busy. There's lots going on back home this summer."

"You're in Shelburne Falls?" I asked. She spent most of her time

about an hour away in Chicago with her husband. Why was she
back in our hometown?

"Just got back yesterday. I'll be staying for the rest of the summer."

I dropped my eyes, faltering for a split second, but I knew my
mother saw it. When I looked back up, she was watching me. And I
waited for what I knew was coming.

When I didn't say anything, she egged me on. "This is the part
where you ask me why I'm staying with Madoc and Fallon instead
of in the city with my husband, Jared."

I averted my eyes, trying to look disinterested. Her husband
used to own the house in Shelburne Falls, but he gave it to Madoc
when he married. Jason and my mother still stayed there when they
were in town, and for some reason my mother thought I was interested.

She was playing me. Trying to get me intrigued. Trying to get
me to ask about home.

Maybe I didn't want to know. Or maybe I did . . .

Talking to my brother had been easy these past two years away.
He knew not to pry, and he knew I'd bring up anything I felt like
talking about. My mother, on the other hand, was always a time
bomb. I always wondered when she'd bring it up.

She was in Shelburne Falls, and it was summer break. Everyone
would be there.

Everyone.

Instead, I rolled my eyes and leaned back in the chair, determined not to indulge her need for playing games.

She laughed, and I looked up.

"I love you." She chuckled, changing the subject. "And I'm glad
your disdain for small talk hasn't wavered."

"Are you?"

She tipped her chin up, her rich eyes sparkling. "It's comforting
to know some things never change."

I gritted my teeth, waiting for the bomb to detonate. "Yeah, I love you, too," I said absently and cleared my throat. "So get to the point. What's up?"

She tapped her fingers on the desk in front of her. "You haven't been home in two years, and I'd like to see you. That's all."

I had been home. Once. She just hadn't known it.

"That's it?" I asked, not believing her. "If you miss me so much, then get your ass on a plane and come see me," I teased.

"I can't."

I narrowed my eyes. "Why?"

"Because of this." And she stood up, revealing her very pregnant belly.

My eyes grew wide, and my face fell as I wondered what the fuck was going on.

Holy shit.

I felt the vein in my neck throb, and I just stared at the ski slope running from her neck to her waist, and . . . and it couldn't be real.

Pregnant? She was not pregnant! I was twenty-two. My mother was, like, forty.

I watched her flatten her palms on her back and slowly lower herself back down into a sitting position. I licked my dry lips and breathed hard.

"Mom?" I hadn't blinked. "Is this some kind of joke?"

She offered a sympathetic look. "I'm afraid not," she explained. "Your sister is due to arrive within three weeks . . ."

Sister?

"And I want all of her brothers here to greet her when she does," she finished.

I looked away, my heart pumping heat throughout my body.

Holy shit, she's fucking pregnant.

Sister, she'd said.

And *all of her brothers.*

"So it's a girl," I said, more to myself than to her.

"Yes."

I rubbed the back of my neck, thankful that my mother was light on the chatter, so I could process this. I had no idea what to think.

She was going to have a baby, and part of me wanted to know what the hell she was thinking. She'd been an alcoholic for about fifteen years while I was growing up, and while I knew she always loved me and she was ultimately a good person, I'd also be the first person to burst her little bubble and tell her she had sucked as a parent.

But the other part of me knew that she'd recovered. She'd earned a second chance, and after five years sober, I guessed she was ready for it. She'd also been a perfect surrogate mother to my half-brother, Jax, when he came to live with us, and she had an amazing support system now.

Just one that hadn't included me since I'd been absent.

Her stepson, Madoc, and his wife, Fallon; Jax and his girlfriend, Juliet; my mother's husband, Jason; the housekeeper, Addie . . . everyone was there for her except me.

I shook my head clear and turned back to the screen. "Jesus . . . Mom, I . . . I'm . . ." I was stammering badly. I had no clue what to say or do. I wasn't touchy-feely or good with this kind of stuff.

"Mom." I swallowed and looked her in the eye. "I'm happy for you. I never would've thought—"

"That I wanted more kids?" she cut in. "I want all of my kids, Jared. I miss you very much," she admitted. "Madoc and Fallon are watching over me, since Jason is finishing up a case in the city, and Jax and Juliet are being wonderful, but I want you here. Come home. Please."

I cleared my throat. *Home.*

"Mom, my schedule is . . ." I searched for an excuse. "I'll try, but it's just—"

"Tate's not here," she cut me off, dropping her gaze. My pulse echoed in my ears.

"If that's what you're worried about," she explained. "Her father is in Italy for a few months, so she's spending the summer there."

I tipped my chin down, inhaling a hard breath.

Tate's not home.

Good. My jaw hardened. *That's good.* I wouldn't have to deal with it. I could go home and spend time with my family, and it could be done with. I wouldn't have to see her.

I hated to admit it, even to myself, but I'd been afraid of running into her. So much so that I hadn't gone home.

I ran my palm down my thigh, ridding myself of the sweat that always came when I thought about her. Even though I'd left to make myself whole, there was still a piece of me that seemed forever hollow.

A piece only she ever filled.

I couldn't see her and not want her. Or not want to hate her.

"Jared?" My mother was talking, and I evened out my expression.

"Yeah," I sighed. "I'm here."

"Listen to me," she ordered. "This isn't about why you've been away. This is about your sister. That's all I want you to think about right now. I'm sorry I didn't tell you sooner, but I . . ." Her eyes fell, and she looked to be searching for words. "I never know what you're thinking, Jared. You're so guarded, and I wanted to have you to myself to tell you this in person. You never find time to come home, however, and I've waited as long as I can."

I didn't know why it bugged me that my mom had a hard time talking to me. I guess I'd never really thought about it, but since she'd put it out there, I realized I didn't like that I made her nervous.

She took a deep breath and looked at me, her eyes kind but serious. "We need you," she said softly. "Madoc will be the one playing with all of her toys with her. Jax will be climbing mountains with her on his shoulders. But you're her shield, Jared. The one who will make sure she is never hurt. I'm not asking you. I'm telling you. Quinn Caruthers needs all of her brothers."

I couldn't help it—I smiled.

Quinn Caruthers. *My sister.* She had a name already.

And hell yes I was going to be there for that.

I nodded, giving her my answer.

"Good." A relieved look crossed her face. "Jax emailed you a plane ticket."

And then she clicked off.

CHAPTER 2

JARED

Two Years Ago

I love mornings like this. Mornings when I wake up first, and I can just watch her sleep for a few minutes. The smooth, glowing skin of her chest rises and falls with her shallow breaths, and I know that if I slide my fingers up her back, underneath her tank top, I'll feel her sweat. She overheats when she sleeps.

I relax into the chair by her window, watching her soft pink lips purse as she starts to stir. Her long, slender neck calls to me, and I'm desperate.

Fucking desperate never to leave her. Wanting never to do what I know I have to do right now.

Tate holds my heart, and I could choke trying to swallow and bury my need for her.

I try to remember the good things. The things that will keep me alive in her heart while I'm away. The rainy nights in my car. How the skin of her neck tastes different from the skin of her lips. How hot she gets under the sheets.

How I hate sleeping alone now.

Her phone starts vibrating on her nightstand, and I tighten my fists, knowing that everything is about to fall apart.

When she wakes, I have to hurt her.

Her head turns to the other side, and I see her eyes flutter open, her body coming to life. She inhales a deep breath and slowly pulls herself to a sitting position. She notices me right away and holds my gaze across the room. A small smile dances across her face until she sees me not smiling back.

I nod to her phone, hoping she'll answer it and give me a minute. Heat floods my chest, and my heart pounds. I need to be able to do this. For her, and for me.

For our future together.

She looks at her phone, swiping her thumb up and down the screen, and then back up at me. "They made it," she whispers. "They're in New Zealand."

She's talking about Jax and Juliet. I'd driven them to the airport yesterday, and they must've been texting to let her know that they arrived safely. I probably had the same text, but my phone was in my duffel bag at my feet.

"Where are you going?" she asks, noticing the bag.

I drop my eyes but look up again, determined not to be a fucking coward. "I'm leaving for a while, Tate." I try to keep my voice soft.

Her eyes turn worried. "ROTC?" she asks.

"No." I lean forward, resting my elbows on my knees. "I . . ." I let out a breath, speaking slowly. "Tate, I love you—"

But she throws off her sheets and starts breathing hard, already knowing where this is going. With her long blond hair pulled back into a low ponytail, I can see the realization written all over her face.

"Jax was right," she rasps.

"Jax is always right," I admit, wishing I could keep doing what I'd been doing for the past two years. Just take her lips, turn off the lights, and shut out the world.

My brother can voice what everyone else is afraid to face, and he knows me like he knows himself. I'm unhappy, and I can't use Tate to hold me up anymore.

"*Continuing like this . . .*" I shake my head. "*I'd make you miserable.*"

My brother knows that I hate ROTC. He knew without my telling him that I hate my life in Chicago. I hate school. I hate the apartment. I hate feeling like I'm a lost puzzle piece.

Where the hell did I fit?

And since Tate had overheard Jax and me the other day, now she's on to me, too. It's time to own up.

Fuck up, own up, and then get up.

Her eyes shoot to mine, and I can see the tears pooling there. "*Jared, if you want to quit ROTC, then quit,*" she cries. "*I don't care. You can study anything. Or nothing. Just—*"

"*I don't know what I want!*" I burst out, yelling so I won't cry. "*That's the problem, Tate. I need to figure things out.*"

"*Away from me,*" she snaps.

I stand up, running a hand through my hair. "*You're not the problem, babe.*" I try to soothe her. "*You're the only thing that I'm sure of. But I need to grow up, and it's not happening here.*"

I'm twenty, and all I know about myself is that I love Tatum Brandt. Two years ago I thought that was enough.

"*Here, where?*" she prods. "*Chicago? Shelburne Falls? Or around me?*"

I clench my jaw and stare out her French doors. I just want to grab her and keep her. I don't want to leave.

But I can't do what she wants me to do. I can't quit school to find myself and be around her at the same time. What do I do? Stay home all day, wander the city, take on odd jobs as I explore my options for who knows how many years while she comes home every day from her classes, which keep her life moving forward?

I hate to put it like this, but the raw truth? My pride can't take it.

I can't be the deadbeat boyfriend doing shit with his life as he figures himself out while she's there to see it.

But I will come back. I'll always want her.

She sits on the bed where we've slept next to each other for nearly ten *years. The bed where I've made love to her countless times, and I feel like a candy-ass right now. I'm a fucking coward because I need to leave, and a coward because I don't want to. I feel myself giving in.*

But I clear my throat and meet her eyes, pushing forward. "The apartment is paid up for the school year, so you don't have to worry—"

"A year!" she cuts me off, shooting out of bed. "A fucking year! Are you kidding me?"

"I don't know what I'm doing, okay?" I admit. "I don't feel like I fit in at college! I feel like you're moving a hundred miles an hour, and I'm constantly trying to catch up!"

She shakes her head at me, unable to believe what's happening.

I steady my voice, speaking firmly. *I have to do this.* "You know what you're doing and what you want, Tate, and I'm . . ." I steel my jaw. "I'm fucking blind. I can't breathe."

She turns away to hide tears I know are falling. "You can't breathe," she repeats, and my stomach knots. *Did she think that this didn't hurt me, too?*

"Baby." I pull her around to face me. "I love you." I look into her storm blue eyes. "I love you so goddamn much. I just . . . I just need time," I plead. "Some space, to figure out who I am and what I want."

Her eyes search mine as she lowers her voice. "So what happens?" she asks. "What happens when you find the life you're looking for?"

I straighten my back, taken by surprise. *There was no future without her in it. She had to know that.*

"I don't know yet," I admit. *I didn't know where I'd end up, what I'd be doing, but she was mine. Always.*

I would be coming home again.

She nods. "I do," she says, her voice turning clipped. "You didn't come in here to tell me you'll be back. That you'll call or we'll text. You came in here to break up with me."

She pulls away and tries to turn around, but I catch her. "Baby, come here."

But she brings her arms down, severing my hold. "Oh, just get out!" *she shouts, looking up at me with fire in her eyes. "You cut off everyone* *who loves you. You're pathetic. I should be used to this by now."*

"Tate—"

"Just leave!" she shouts and walks for her bedroom door, yanking it *open. "I'm sick of the sight of you, Jared. Just go."*

I shake my head, narrowing my eyes on her. "No," I argue. "I need *you to understand."*

She lifts a defiant chin. "All I'll ever understand is that you needed to *live a life without me in it, so just go and do that."*

"I don't want this." I search for the words to get her back. "Not like *this. I don't want to hurt you. Just sit down, so we can talk. I can't leave* *you like this," I press. Why can't she understand? I'm not leaving her. I'm* *coming back.*

But she shakes her head. "And I won't let you stay. You need to be free? *Then, go. Get out."*

I swallow the hard lump in my throat and watch her. What the hell's *happening? Regret races through my brain as I think that maybe I* *should've done this differently. Sat her down and eased into it. But I don't* *know how to do that shit. I don't know how to be gentle.*

Fuck, I'd blindsided her. Even though we'd been distant the past week, *I knew she wasn't expecting this.*

After everything I'd done to her over the years, she still doesn't trust me. *She doesn't see that I'm trying to be strong. That I'm trying to be a man. All* *she sees right now is me causing her more pain, and she's had enough.*

"Now," she orders, her tears drying on her face.

I let my eyes fall, and every muscle in my arms tenses with the urge to *charge her. Take her, hold her to me, and will her to melt into me like she* *always does. I have to have Tate in my life.*

She'll wait for me.

And as I grab my bag and leave, I know that I'll be back. I have to do *this, but I will be back for her.*

I didn't even need a year, either. Only six months.

Turns out six months was too long.

"Awesome," Pasha bit out, peering out the window of her first-class seat. "I totally get what they mean by 'flyover state' now."

I ignored her distaste for whatever she was seeing out there and stuffed my iPad into my carry-on, nudging it back under my seat with my foot.

"Cheer up," I sighed. "We have cars and liquor and cigarettes in Shelburne Falls, too. It will feel just like home to you."

She settled back into her seat, and I could feel her little scowl directed at the seat in front of her. "Looking forward to it." Her voice dripped with sarcasm. "I do get to get drunk tonight, right?" she confirmed.

I grinned and closed my eyes against the popping in my ears as we descended. "As long as you are glued to my side, I don't give a shit what you do."

I could hear her short, aggravated breaths, and I wondered—probably as much as she did—why I felt the need to drag her with me. "This is weird," she grumbled. "You're weird. Why do I have to be here?"

"Because I pay—"

"You to," she finished. "Well, someday when you want a kidney, it's really going to cost you, man."

I licked my lips, envisioning an invisible hand pressing on my heart to slow that fucker down. In a minute, I'd be back at home base, and even though Tate wasn't there, I was nervous. Seeing my house, her house next door, our old high school . . . and my best friend, who wasn't talking to me . . .

Jesus, I was a little bitch.

I twisted my head, still lying on the headrest. "Pasha?" I mumbled softly. "What do you want me to say? That I can't chew my food without you these days?" I shrugged. "I'd rather have you around and not need you than need you and not have you."

Her dark eyebrows—the right one adorned with two barbells—knitted together, and she looked over at me like I'd grown a horn. I'm sure she knew it, but I'd certainly never admitted it before. I relied on her a lot, and it was a perfect arrangement, because she liked to be needed. Neglect did that to people.

As much as I liked her dad, he was about as good a parent as my mom was when I was growing up.

Pasha turned out well, though. She reeled me back in when I was drowning and made a lot of decisions for me when I couldn't. She got me out of the pit crew and turned me on to motorcycles, hooked me up with sponsors and investors, and convinced me to buy into the shop. None of this happened over calm and reasonable business dinners—more like her screaming at me to get my head out of my ass—but before I knew it, I had so much shit going on, there was no time to think. She filled my life with noise when the quiet was too dangerous.

I not only needed her, but I wanted her around.

And now she knew it.

She was probably going to ask for another fucking raise.

Jax was waiting outside the terminal even though I'd told him I would text when we were at passenger pickup.

But I grinned anyway the minute I saw him, barely noticing Pasha zoom past us to go outside for a cigarette.

"Hey." I hooked an arm around Jax's neck and pulled him in, dropping my duffel on the floor.

"Hey," he said for only me to hear. "I missed you."

I let my eyes close for a second, all of a sudden weighted down by how long I'd been away from him. We'd kept in regular contact, and even though I'd stayed away only to avoid one particular person, Jax had suffered the price, too.

I was his blood. The only blood he had.

Pulling away, I took stock of everything that hadn't changed. His black hair, styled to look like he'd just run his fingers through it, and his blue eyes were the same vibrant azure as the last time I'd seen him. No scars or bruises that I could see, so I knew he was keeping out of trouble.

Not that Jax got in regular fights anyway, but instinct told me to make sure. He still dressed in jeans and black T-shirts, matching me almost to a tee. I shook my head when I realized he was also taking stock of me, and then he finally relaxed, putting an arm around his girlfriend's shoulders.

"Juliet." I finally looked over, seeing her slip a hand around his waist.

She smiled and then greeted me. "It's good to see you."

I wasn't sure if that was true, but I didn't really care. She and I got along fine, but we weren't—and probably never would be—besties. I had a limited tolerance for mindless chatter, and she seemed to regard me with less and less cordiality as well. Probably because of Tate.

Back in high school, Juliet went by her sister's initials, K.C. When she started dating my brother two years ago, she reclaimed her birth name, and it still took some getting used to for me.

I picked up my bag and looked at both of them. "I hear congratulations are in order," I told Juliet. "Teaching in Costa Rica? You two ready for that?"

Juliet had just graduated with her teaching degree, and since Jax had also beaten the clock and finished college early, the two of them were headed to Central America in the fall. Jax had told me a few weeks back that she had signed a one-year contract, but I hadn't talked to Juliet about it at all.

She turned to look at him, a knowing smile playing on her lips as if they shared a private joke. "There's no adventure too big," she teased, speaking more to him than to me.

I cleared my throat. "So where's our mother?"

Jax stuck his hands in his pockets. "Doctor's appointment."

"Is everything okay?"

"Yeah." He nodded and turned around, starting to lead us out of the airport. "She's perfect. When you get close to term you have to go in every week, apparently. You should see her, man." He laughed under his breath. "She's shopping like crazy and eating ice cream after every meal, but she's on top of the world."

I followed, seeing Pasha walking toward us, having just come back in.

"Why the hell didn't you tell me that she was pregnant?" I prodded Jax.

I knew why my mom had kept it from me, but Jax could've warned me.

He shook his head, smirking at me. "Dude, it's not my business to tell you your mom is pregnant. Sorry." By his amused tone, I could tell he wasn't sorry. "Besides, she really didn't want you to find out over the phone. That's why she's been trying to get you home."

A pang of guilt started jabbing at me from several directions when I thought of all the shit I was going to have to smooth over. Answering my mother's questions, Madoc's silent treatment, and getting reacquainted with my brother . . .

"Um . . . hi." Juliet turned around as we kept walking, looking at Pasha. "Are you with Jared?"

I swung my bag over my shoulder, looking to Juliet.

"Sorry," I shot out. "You guys, this is Pasha." I jerked my chin at the girl next to me. "Pasha, this is my brother, Jax, and his girlfriend, Juliet."

"Hey," Pasha said casually.

Juliet shook Pasha's hand quickly and then turned around, looking confused. I caught her sideways glance at Jax.

"Hi, Pasha." Jax gave her a quick shake and then glanced to me quickly before crossing the walkway to the parking garage. "Why didn't you tell me you were seeing someone, man?"

I let out a bitter laugh but was cut off.

"Aw," Pasha cooed as we headed into the parking garage. "You didn't tell him about us, honey?" And she kneaded my biceps with her hot pink fingernails.

I rolled my eyes. "My assistant, guys." I tossed my bag in the trunk of my old Mustang, now Jax's car. "She's just my assistant. That's all."

Jax swung his pointer finger between us as he walked to the driver's side. "So you two aren't . . . ?"

"Ewwww," Pasha grumbled, disgust written all over her face.

"So you're gay, then?" he shot back.

I snorted, shaking with laughter as I opened the passenger side door for the girls.

Pasha planted her hands on her hips. "How did . . . what . . . ?" she stammered, looking to me accusingly.

I held up my hands, feigning innocence.

Jax narrowed his eyes on her over the hood. "When you think about the women who aren't interested in my brother, it pretty much just leaves the lesbians."

Pasha grumbled and climbed into the backseat behind Juliet. I slammed the door and headed to the driver's side.

Jax straightened, seeing me coming. "This is my car now." He knew what I was doing.

I pinned him with a pointed look. "And I don't ride. I'll wait for you to come to terms with that."

After about three seconds, he realized he wasn't going to win. He finally let out a hard sigh and walked his ass around to the passenger side.

Climbing in, I started the engine and stilled, slowly easing back into the seat. The old, familiar rumble of the engine reminded me of a time so long ago. Back when I was the king of a small pond. When I thought I knew everything.

The long, late-night drives, my music filling the small space, as I planned my life around Tate and how I was going to torment her in the only universe that mattered.

An image of her flashed in my mind, walking to school. Her back would straighten when she'd hear my engine coming, and I'd blow past her, seeing her hair whip in the wind in my rearview mirror. I almost wished she was in town this summer.

I'd give almost anything to make her feel me again.

Not to mention, she'd turned my best friend against me. He wasn't talking to me, and I knew it was because of her.

I buckled up. "So let's have it," I told Jax. "Where's Madoc?"

He hesitated, speaking softly. "Around," he caged. "He commutes to his summer internship here in the city, but he's still staying at his house in Shelburne Falls."

"Good." I nodded, remembering that it was early Friday afternoon. "I'm going to hit his house before we go home."

"Dude," Jax urged as I drove out of the garage. "I don't think Madoc's going to be up for—"

"Screw it," I gritted out. "It's been two years. I'm sick of his bullshit."

CHAPTER 3

TATE

Summer breaks no longer exist once you reach college. Maybe you start taking a summer class, or you pick up a summer job, or you have a reading list or an extra credit to earn, but free time slowly starts to ebb away, and before you know it, you're doing one thing a day that you like and fifteen that you hate.

Welcome to adulthood, my father would say.

I should be grateful. All in all it wasn't so bad. Opportunity abounded in my life, and anyone else would be gracious and appreciative. My education would secure my future.

I had it made. I'd be a doctor someday. Maybe close to home. Maybe far away. I'd undoubtedly marry and have children. The house and car payments would come. The stock portfolios to ensure a comfortable retirement. Maybe I'd have a time-share in the Bahamas. I'd laugh at my children's school plays and hug them when they were scared.

My patients would hopefully bring a feeling of worth into my life. I would help some and lose others. I was prepared for that. I would comfort many and cry with a few. I would take everything in stride and with the knowledge that I did my very best.

My professional life would be devoted to curing illnesses. My private life would be the dutiful spouse and mother.

Patients and patience.

And up until two years ago, I was excited for all of it.

I had wanted all of it.

"There you are." Ben took my hand, brushing a kiss on my cheek. "They've been paging you for five minutes."

I smiled, placing a hand on his chest and leaning in. "Sorry," I whispered, kissing him again, gently on the lips this time. "I couldn't exactly drop the bedpan, could I?" I joked, pulling back and setting my charts down at the nurse's station.

The corners of his bottom lip turned down at the disgusting thought. "Good point," he acquiesced.

"Besides," I continued, "I'm a woman worth waiting for. You know that."

He lifted his chin and hooded his blue eyes. "I'm still deciding," he taunted.

"Ouch." I laughed. "Maybe Jax was right after all then."

His face fell, the humor gone. "What did that guy say about me now?" he grumbled.

I grinned, pulling my blue scrub shirt over my head, leaving me in my white tank top. "He said that you're awesome," I teased.

Ben cocked an eyebrow, knowing better.

Jax, my ex-boyfriend's brother, didn't like anyone that tried to take his brother's place in my life. Good thing I didn't need his approval.

I shrugged and kept going. "But he does think that I am far too much for you to handle."

His eyes bugged out, and he smiled, challenge accepted. Sliding his hand around the back of my neck, he stepped up and crashed his lips down on mine.

The warmth of his body surrounded me, and I relaxed into the kiss, savoring the hunger I felt rolling off of him.

He wanted me.

I might not be reeling from need of him, but he made me feel in control, and I definitely liked that.

Pulling away, he smiled like he'd just proved a point.

I licked my lips, tasting his Spearmint gum. Ben always had a flavor and taste I could pin down. Mint or cinnamon on the lips, cologne on the clothes, Paul Mitchell in the hair . . . and it occurred to me that I didn't really know what he smelled like without all of that. Cologne preferences change over time. So do shampoos and breath mints. What would he smell like on my pillow? Would it change or always be constant?

He gestured to the black container and package of wooden chopsticks on top of the counter. "I brought you dinner. It's sushi," he pointed out. "Salmon is supposed to be, like, some super brain food." He waved a hand in front of us. "And you've been burning the midnight oil, so I thought you could use it."

"Thank you." I tried to act excited, knowing it was the thought that counted. I hated sushi, but he didn't know that. "But I'm actually about to get off work. I thought I told you that."

He narrowed his eyes, thinking, and then they went wide. "Yes, you did." He let out a breath and shook his head. "I'm sorry. Your schedule changes so much, I forgot."

"It's okay." I unwrapped my messy bun, feeling instant relief as the cursed bobby pins were removed. When I wasn't working at the hospital—giving sponge baths and administering Band-Aids—I was at the library getting ahead on my reading list for my fall classes, or at the Loop, blowing off steam. I was a hard girl to pin down lately, but Ben rolled with it.

"I can still eat it," I offered, not wanting to be ungracious. "And now I don't need to worry about dinner, so you see? You really are a lifesaver."

He grabbed hold of my waist and pulled me in, kissing my forehead and nose, always gentle.

Ben and I had been seeing each other for about six weeks, although most of that time was long-distance. During spring break, we were both home, and one day I'd lost control of my car on a rainy, slick road.

And I'd slammed right into his car. As it was parked at a curb right in front of him and all of his friends. *Yeah, great moment.*

But I played it off. Got out of the car barking at him about his lousy driving and that he better have good insurance or I was calling the cops.

Everyone laughed, and he asked me out.

We spent some time together, went back to school to finish the semester, and reconnected when we came home for summer break.

Since we'd gone to high school together and actually had a date senior year that ended pretty badly, it was kind of fun to catch up after so much time had passed. We got to know each other, and I enjoyed the time we spent together. It wasn't pedal to the metal from day one. Ben was slow.

And calm.

It was always when *I* was ready. Not when *he* was ready.

And I was nowhere near ready yet, so that was a relief.

And the best part? He wasn't intense. He didn't get angry or rude. He didn't have problems that would make me unhappy, and I didn't have to worry that he would have so much of a pull on me that I would make decisions based on him.

He never pushed or challenged me, and I liked that I dominated the relationship. I never took advantage of it, but I knew I was the one in control. It was comfortable, but more than that, it was easy. I was never surprised with Ben.

He was safe.

He'd finished his bachelor's degree in economics at UMass in May and would be going on to graduate school at Princeton in the fall. I'd be heading to Stanford for medical school, so we were looking at more time apart. I wasn't sure if the relationship would continue, but right now, I was content to keep things light and easy.

He'd already hinted to me that I should move to New Jersey with him and apply to medical school there or somewhere at least in the vicinity. I'd said no. I'd compromised my college plans once— for a good reason—but I was sticking to the plan this time. Come hell or high water, I was going to California.

"Will you be at my race tonight?" I asked softly.

"Aren't I always?" he answered, and I knew there was a sigh that he'd held back.

Ben hated that I raced. He said he hated the crowd, but I knew it was more than that. He didn't want the girl he was dating racing the boys while he sat on the sidelines.

But even though I liked Ben, I wasn't quitting the Loop, either.

Wisely, he never asked me to stop—just suggested—and I expected that he thought it was something I would grow out of or give up when I went off to Stanford.

But I wouldn't stop for anyone or anything. I wouldn't stop until I was ready.

Madoc whined about my safety, my father chided me about the car costs when I needed parts or repairs, and at least a dozen assholes made snide remarks when I climbed into my car every weekend to race against them.

But none of it made a difference. That's the beauty of knowing your own mind. No one tells you what you can and can't do. Once you're sure of something, it really is *that* easy.

"I'll meet you at the track, then." I circled his neck and leaned in for a kiss, his gentle lips leaving a feathery kiss on mine. "I need to shower and clean up after I leave here."

He leaned over, nuzzling my ear. "And then after the race, you're mine, right?"

I could hear the playfulness in his voice, but my heart still skipped a beat anyway.

Mine.

A shiver ran down my arms, and I closed my eyes, feeling a hot mouth move across my cheek and then his breath glide over my lips.

I want to feel what's mine. What's always been mine.

Heat fanned across my face, and need gripped me low in my stomach. His lips brushed mine, never taking, just teasing, and I inhaled a shaky breath as excitement burned under my skin after so long.

It wasn't Ben.

It wasn't his lips or his breath that I dreamed about.

I want to touch you.

I pushed up on my tiptoes, pressing my body into his and pulling him close. *Jared.*

And just like that, I melted at his memory.

"It's too late to beg," Jared whispers as his hand threads through the back of my hair, gripping it tight as he pins me against the wall of the janitor's closet. "This is what you get when you eye-fuck me in the middle of class."

I squeeze my eyes shut and squirm as he pushes his hand down the front of my jeans and dips his fingers inside me, bringing the wetness back out to swirl around my clit.

"Oh, God," I whimper, my breath shaking as I clutch his shoulders. "Jared."

He leans in, and I can feel his breath hot across my lips. "I want you naked, Tate," he commands. "Everything off. Now."

I brushed my nose against his neck, smelling Ben's exotic cologne instead of Jared's woodsy body wash with that hint of spice I still remembered.

I lowered myself back down to my feet, releasing Ben.

Dammit.

Why did the memory of him get me more excited than anyone else could in the flesh? Ben treated me better. His easy demeanor was no threat to me. There were no expectations, and the conversation was safe.

But old habits die hard.

I craved dirty words and rough hands, possessiveness and everything that wasn't Ben's style. I missed being the breath in someone's body and being craved like water.

It was dangerous, but that was young love, and once I had been nearly consumed with it.

"You okay?" Ben asked, looking concerned.

I gave him a casual smile. "I'm fine," I assured him, leaning in for a quick kiss. I might not feel the fireworks with Ben that I wanted yet, but there was no rush. Never any pressure.

I pulled back to say good-bye, but he dove in for another quick peck on the lips before walking away down the hallway, leaving me smiling at his easy attitude.

After logging out on the computer, I jogged to the locker room for my backpack and keys, dumping my scrub shirt in the laundry basket which left me in my super-stylish matching blue pants.

The wind was calling, and I couldn't wait to get outside. I could already feel the chills of anticipation running through my body.

I sent a mass text to Madoc, Fallon, Juliet, and Jax, letting them know I'd be skipping dinner to tweak a few last things on my G8 before the race tonight. I'd meet them at the track.

As soon as I walked through the automatic doors, I broke into a run and couldn't help the laughter that escaped. I'm sure I looked ridiculous, giggling like a child.

But I loved my damn car. It was fast and hot and all mine.

I'd had my Pontiac G8 since my senior year of high school, and I would admit it only to myself, but it owned more of my heart than Ben did right now. Driving was like a drug. Climb in, sit down, shut up, and hold on. It was the only time in my life when I felt like I was moving but also didn't need to work to accomplish anything. I was going places but not really getting anywhere. For hours on end, I'd drive and listen to music—lost in my own head—but I always seemed to find myself, too. My shower used to be the one place I'd escape to. Now it was my car.

Sliding into the driver's seat, I threw my backpack—loaded with some books and a change of clothes—onto the passenger seat and set down the sushi I was probably going to give to Madoc. I started the car, rolling down the windows and jamming up the music. Saliva's "Click Click Boom" raged out of the speakers, vibrating off my body, and I inhaled the sweet, early evening summer air. It was a little after five, but the sun still shone bright in the sky, and the warm breeze blew through the windows, tickling my hair.

I tightened my hands around the leather wheel, cruising down the two lane highway well over the speed limit and feeling so much more alive behind the wheel than I did anywhere else. This was the one thing I did with my time that I loved.

It wasn't always like that. Two years ago I was connected to everything, each day built the foundation for a tomorrow I couldn't wait to jump into. But now . . .

Now I couldn't help the fear that crept in when I thought about what would happen when I finally got to tomorrow. When I was done with school, when I was a doctor, when I achieved the future I'd worked for . . . what then?

For some reason, driving—racing—kept me connected. Connected to a time when my blood ran hot under my skin and my heart craved more life.

Always more.

Sticking my arm out the window, I smiled at the gush of wind pushing against it as the air blew between my fingers. Cranking up the volume, I inhaled an excited breath as my stomach dropped with the increased speed. I loved those butterflies.

I got back to the house quickly, even though the last thing I wanted to do was get out of my car. But I reminded myself that the wind was waiting for me later on tonight, and it would all be good when I was on the track.

I had a lot of work to do before I left, though, so I parked the car along the side of Madoc's house and grabbed my phone off the seat, instantly feeling it vibrate in my hand.

Peering down, I saw Juliet's name. "Hey," I answered. "Did you get my text?"

"Did you get mine?" she burst out, sounding excited.

I narrowed my eyes in confusion as I climbed out of the car. "No, but I saw you called." I swung my backpack over my shoulder and slammed the door shut. "I just got off work, so I haven't checked my messages yet. What's up?"

I rounded the stone staircase, jogging up the steps to my private entrance. Jared and I used to keep a room here, and I still used it from time to time. Madoc and Fallon were like family, and I'd needed a place to escape to while the entire downstairs of my house was being repainted.

"Where are you?" she asked, and I could hear her excited breathing.

"I just got home." I unlocked the door and dropped my backpack inside, switching the phone to the other ear.

"At Madoc's?" she rushed out.

I nearly laughed at her urgency. "Alright, spit it out. Is something wrong? Did Katherine go into labor or something?"

"No," she shot back. "I . . . I just need you to stop and listen to me, okay?"

I groaned. "Please tell me Jax didn't hack into Ben's Facebook and flood it with gay porn again," I said, kicking off my shoes and walking toward the private bathroom.

"No, Jax didn't do anything," she answered, but then continued. "Well, he kind of did. We all did. I should've told you, and I'm sorry," she rambled, "but I didn't know he was going straight to Madoc's, and I didn't want you to be ambushed, so—"

"What is going on?!" I shouted, pushing open the bathroom door.

"Jared is at Madoc's house!" she finally cried out.

But it was too late.

I'd already halted.

A lump stretched my throat as I stood there, locking my eyes with his dark ones staring at me through the bathroom mirror, her warning coming a second too late.

Jared.

"Tate, did you hear me?" she yelled, but I couldn't answer her.

I tightened my fist around the doorknob and glued my teeth together so hard my jaw ached.

He stood at the mirror, with his back to me, and every muscle in his naked arms and torso was steel-rod tight as he leaned down on his hands and held me with a hard stare.

He didn't seem surprised to see me. And he definitely didn't look happy.

I inhaled short, shallow breaths. What the hell was he doing here?

"Tate!" I heard someone shout, but all I could do was watch as he straightened and picked his watch up off the counter, fastening it to his wrist as he held my eyes the entire time.

So calm. So cold.

It was like a razor cutting through my heart as I resisted a need to rush him. Maybe to hit him or maybe to fuck him, but whatever it was I was going to hurt him. I cemented every muscle in my body to keep myself in check.

He wore fitted black pants that hung low on his waist, his feet and torso were bare, and his hair was chaos, like he'd just towel dried it.

Our childhood tree filled his back in a stunning black tattoo, and I looked over his shoulder and arms to notice a few new ones.

My stomach shook, and I tightened my abs to resist it.

It had been so long.

His black clothes, his black moods, his nearly black eyes . . . My heart pounded like a drum, and I gritted my teeth, feeling my core tighten.

He looked exactly like he had in high school. Gone was any trace of his ROTC days in college. He was a little more muscular, with more angle to his jawline, but it was four years ago all over again.

I tipped my chin up, seeing him grab his belt off the counter and turn around, walking toward me.

"Tate?" Juliet pressed in my ear. "Tate, did you hear me? Hello?"

He stepped up to me slowly, threading his belt through the loops, and my chest was on fire. My heart couldn't possibly beat any faster, and I hardened my eyes and expression as he stopped a few inches in front of me and hovered.

"Tate," Juliet yelled, "I said that Jared is at Madoc's!"

And the corner of Jared's lips tilted in a smile, telling me he'd heard her futile warning.

"Yes," I answered, clearing my throat as I glared up at him. "Thanks for the heads up," I told her.

And I brought the phone away from my ear and clicked End Call.

His arms worked, fastening his belt, but he didn't break eye contact. Neither did I. This was natural for Jared. Hover, make me cower in his shadow, threaten with just his presence . . . but it was all in vain.

Because that's just how well I knew myself now. No one dominated me.

I kept my voice calm, trying to sound bored. "There are about twenty other rooms in this house," I pointed out. "Find one."

His eyes turned from threatening to amused, and it was the exact same look I got in the lunch room the first day of senior year in high school when I'd decided to fight back. Jared always got a rush out of challenging me.

"You know," he started, reaching behind the bathroom door and pulling out a white T-shirt. "I smelled you as soon as I stepped foot into the room. Your scent was everywhere," his velvety voice sent chills over my skin as he continued, "and I thought maybe it was just leftovers from our time here, but then I noticed all your shit." He gestured to the beauty products on the bathroom counter and then threaded his arms into his short sleeves and pulled the shirt over his head.

So he'd come here not knowing he'd find me. At least he wasn't planning anything, then.

He patted his pants pocket and cocked his head, smirking. "I hope you don't mind, but I borrowed a few of your condoms."

My hand suddenly ached, and I realized I'd been squeezing the doorknob this whole time. I didn't know if I was angry that he was referring to my sex life or insinuating plans about his own, but the asshole hadn't changed. He was waiting for me to react.

The condoms were leftovers from a year and a half ago, the last time I had sex. They were probably expired anyway.

"By all means." I plastered a tight smile on my face. "Now, if you don't mind . . ." I cleared the doorway, waving my arm wide and inviting him to get the hell out.

A million questions raged through my head. Why was he here? At this house? In my room? Where was his little entourage I'd seen him with on TV and YouTube when I'd given in on lonely nights and Googled him?

But then I reminded myself that Jared Trent wasn't a part of my life anymore. I didn't need to care about him.

He brushed past me, grazing my arm, and I started breathing through my mouth, because the smell of his body wash messed with my nerves. With my memories and a time when I was completely his.

I couldn't stand here with him. Not in this room.

I'd never let Ben stay the night when I crashed here, and no one knew, but Jared's and my homecoming photo still sat in its frame, hidden in the dresser drawer. Along with the charm bracelet he'd given me senior year. I'd wanted it out of my house but not gone. Not yet.

This room had played a crucial part early on in our relationship. It was the first space, away from our parents, that was ours— where we could do what we wanted and act the way we chose. To wake up next to each other, to shower together, to make love without fear of who would hear us, to stay up all night talking or watching movies . . . Whether it was the bed, the floor, the shower, the wall, or the bathroom fucking counter, every surface had a memory of him attached to it.

I still couldn't face the fact that I loved being in here, and what's more, I couldn't face the fact that I had never let Ben—or anyone else—stay in here.

It didn't matter, though. It was my room, and I didn't need to explain anything.

I crossed my arms over my chest and watched him clip his wallet chain to his pants and tuck his wallet into his pocket. I glanced over, seeing his duffel on the bed, a few clothes—all black, gray, or white—strewn about.

"Make sure you take everything with you when you leave," I ordered, sliding off my socks and tossing them into the hamper by the door. "This is my room now."

"Absolutely," he said smoothly, and then finished in a hard voice, "Tatum."

I straightened, suddenly feeling the first spark of excitement under my skin—outside of racing, anyway—in a long time. I hated being called "Tatum," and he knew it.

We were back there again.

I looked over at him, tilting my mouth into a smile. "Tatum?" I repeated. "Those are tactics you come home armed with?" I asked.

He turned his head, eyeing me over his shoulder with a stern expression.

I laughed. "The players might be the same, Jared," I said, untying my scrub pants and letting them fall down my leg, "but the game has changed," I warned.

His deep brown eyes flared just slightly as his gaze swept down the long legs that he used to love and back up to my lacy, white underwear.

I turned to step into the bathroom, but I stopped to regard him over my shoulder. "This isn't high school," I said, eyeing him playfully. "You're way out of your depth."

And then I slammed the bathroom door, cutting off his view.

CHAPTER 4

JARED

'd been played.

Of course, my mother's pregnancy had forced me back home, but I should've been warned instead of lied to.

Tate wasn't in fucking Italy.

She was staying with Madoc and Fallon, which Jax should've told me when I'd insisted on coming here first.

But no, he'd let me trail my ass upstairs to shower and clean up while we waited for Madoc to get home, and as soon I opened the damn door to that room, her smell hit me like a ten-ton tranquilizer. I was almost dizzy.

But then I remembered . . .

No. She wasn't here. She was out of the country. The bed was made. The room was spotless. There was no one staying in here.

I'd put my bag down and started to strip as I walked into the shower, but then I noticed that someone was very much staying here.

The same products that Tate used to use for her hair and face hugged the back edge of the sink counter, and then I saw her brush, clogged with her blond hair.

And that's when I knew.

My eyes fell closed, and I froze.

Tate was home.

She was home, and she was staying with Madoc and Fallon, and I immediately wanted to see her.

Was she okay? Was she happy? What would her face look like when she saw me again?

After so long, I just wanted to see her.

Until I noticed the condoms.

She had a small box sitting in her makeup bag, and they damn well weren't ours. After she'd gotten on birth control in high school, we'd stopped using them.

I pushed away from the sink and nearly ripped off the rest of my clothes, diving into the shower before I broke anything and everything in the bathroom.

I hated her. I wanted to hate her. Why did I still want her?

Fuck!

I kept my head under the hot water for a long time, the loud cascade of heat drowning out my thoughts as I slowly brought myself back down.

The condoms were a trigger—a reminder—that she was having sex with someone else.

I knew that, and she was free to do it. We weren't together, and I shouldn't be upset. She'd never judged me for all the ass I took before we were dating, and her life was none of my business. I shouldn't be mad.

But that didn't stop me. Reason never stopped me from trying to keep her in my orbit. After I got out of the shower, I emptied the box into the toilet and flushed, and whomever she was screwing could go fuck himself.

And that was even truer the second I heard her voice drift in from the bedroom when she'd arrived. I could tell by the one-sided conversation that she was on the phone, and I leaned down, bracing myself on the countertop, knowing she was about to walk in at any second. And then I lifted my head, she opened the door, and . . .

And I held her.

Everything flooded back. Every breath, every kiss, every smile, every tear, everything about her was mine.

Her stormy blue eyes, which have held me captivated since she was ten years old; the heavy rise and fall of her chest, which I'd held flush with mine so many times; and the ten different emotions that crossed her face, each of which had been directed at me at some time or another during high school. They all hit me at once.

I still loved her.

My pulse raced and I could feel it all through my body.

But then she'd stunned me. My natural inclination was to challenge her as I always had, and the words left my mouth without thinking. But she didn't engage. She didn't react.

I was used to Tate's bite. She was a wildcat who pushed when you pushed, but this Tate was on a different level. She was condescending and almost cold. I didn't know this game.

I left the room and charged down the stairs and out the front door, trying to push her out of my mind. She wasn't the reason I was home after all.

My mother. My unborn sister. My friends.

I headed for the garages, having seen Madoc's GTO finally sitting in the driveway.

The house featured four two-car garages, so I went for the open one and stopped at the entrance, crossing my arms over my chest as I glared at my best friend.

"You don't even look for me when you get home?" I challenged, seeing him pause as he pushed a box onto a shelf.

Turning around, he met my eyes with his annoyed blue ones

and arched a brow. "Yeah, that's how it is, isn't it?" His bored tone kind of made me nervous. "Everyone else has to make the first move with you?"

Stepping inside the garage, I kept my stare on him. Madoc wasn't just my friend. He was my family, and no matter what we went through, that never changed. Anger, trouble, differences, and even distance and time wouldn't take my best friend from me. I wouldn't allow it.

"I made the first move," I pointed out. "And the second and third. How many times have I called you, texted, e-mailed—who the fuck even e-mails anymore? But I did it." I inched closer, lowering my voice. "*You* never wanted to talk to me. Why?"

He crossed his arms over his white-T-shirt-clad chest and dropped his chin, looking like he was searching for words. His blond eyebrows dug deep, and I was floored by how different he seemed.

Madoc never shut up. He could vomit story after story and argue any point at the drop of a hat, but now . . .

I shook my head. He was actually speechless.

Or there were things he clearly wasn't sure how to say.

I heard footsteps behind me and turned my head to see Jax slowly stepping into the garage. He hung back and remained quiet, like he was waiting to see what was going to happen.

I twisted my head back around, narrowing my eyes on Madoc. "What the hell's going on?"

Madoc's eyes flashed to Jax, and then he looked at me, letting out a sigh.

Okay, screw this.

I got in his face. "Do you remember when Fallon showed up after high school and left you hanging? You left for Notre Dame and cut everyone off. No calls. No contact. Just gone. We had to track you down. You were our friend and we weren't letting you go. Now I left and you don't even show the same concern for me?" I bared my teeth. "What the fuck is going on with you?"

Madoc ran a hand though his hair and shook his head.

Finally, digging into his pocket, he pulled out his keys. "Jax and I want to show you something."

As much as I hated riding instead of driving, I decided it was best not to challenge Madoc in his own car right now. Since Jax still drove my old ride, I could push him around, but Madoc and I weren't at our old comfort level . . . yet.

He sped out of his ritzy community of upper-crust homes and down the quiet highway, the day's last light still glowing through the trees on both sides of the road. Jax sat in the back, fiddling on his phone next to Pasha, who had insisted on coming—because she was bored—and Madoc still wasn't talking to me. Framing Hanley's "You Stupid Girl" played on the stereo, and I was still clenching my fists over the buzz running through my body after seeing Tate.

As we entered the more populated part of town and Madoc began navigating the residential streets, I figured out where we were going. We passed our old high school and the same street leading in where I used to watch Tate walking to and from school every day. The same corner where I used to catch the ice cream truck with her when we were younger.

And then we turned onto Fall Away Lane, and Madoc pulled to a halt in front of my old house, which now belonged to Jax.

I rubbed my sweaty palms down my pants, praying like hell that this was going somewhere good instead of bad.

But it took only a glance out the window before I noticed it.

I tried to speak, but my chest tightened and my words came out breathless. "What the hell happened?"

Not waiting for them to answer, I climbed out of the car and walked up the incline into the space between our houses. The closer I got, the more I didn't want to face it.

Two cables looped around two branches on both sides of Tate's and my tree and ran into the ground, securing the heavy maple in place. And at the trunk, what looked like some sort of steel brackets cut into the bark on top of and beneath a nearly two-foot slash across the width of the tree. I ran a hand through my hair, stopping mid-stroke as I took in the sight and tried to wrap my head around what could have done this.

"Tate." I heard Madoc's raspy voice from behind me.

But I barely heard him. I approached the tree, running my hand down the jagged trunk to the shallow gash, letting my fingers dip into the cut.

And then the bark bit into my skin as I curled my fist.

"She wouldn't do this." I swallowed down the trembling in my throat.

This tree was us. She would *never* do this. She would never try to cut it down!

"After you left, she went cold," he started, and I felt him approach. "She wouldn't talk about you. She wouldn't come home on the weekends . . ." He trailed off, and I wished I didn't have to hear this.

"I let her have time," he continued. "I remembered how it felt when I lost Fallon. First loves are the worst pain."

Except Tate never lost me. I was coming back for her.

"I came home one day the September after you left," I heard Jax chime in. "And workmen were bringing down the tree."

No. I closed my eyes.

He continued, "But when they sliced into it, she stopped them. She couldn't do it."

"I think she knew you would never have forgiven her," Madoc added. "And she would never have forgiven herself once she got her head out of her ass."

I bit the inside of my mouth to stifle my shaky breath. And then

I opened my eyes, taking in the damage and almost hating her in that moment.

How could she?

"I understood at first," Madoc told me. "I was with you the whole way, man. I knew what you needed to do."

I finally turned around and met his eyes. He and Jax stood back, while Pasha had sat down on the grass with her bag of Sour Punch Bites, playing on her phone.

Madoc continued, "But then she stayed distant—she kept pulling away—and it was like slowly the family was breaking. All of us. She wasn't Tate without you, and without you both, the rest of us had to struggle to keep things together. To feel normal."

I dropped my head back, looking up at the bright green leaves fluttering in the early evening breeze. Aside from the gash, the tree looked healthy. It was repairing, thank goodness.

"After a while," Madoc kept going, "and a lot of persuasion from me, she started to come around. To find her place without you. I think she felt like the fifth wheel all of the time."

"I couldn't be there for you and for her, Jared," Madoc explained. "I don't want to go into it. It's Tate's business, but I had to choose, and I'm not going to apologize for that. She needed me more."

While I had a damn hard time understanding why he couldn't be Tate's and my friend at the same time, I was glad that if he had to choose, he chose her.

Tate had shut me out, she'd kicked me out, and she wouldn't return texts or calls. But then I realized it wasn't just me. She must've been different for everyone.

"There's more," Jax said hesitantly.

I let out an aggravated laugh, shaking my head. *What now?*

They started walking back from where we came. "Take a look in the front yard," Madoc called out, gesturing in front of Tate's house.

I didn't have to walk far. When I spotted the FOR SALE sign on the other side of the driveway, the ache Madoc's story had created in my gut turned to full-blown rage in my head.

"What the hell is going on?" I growled, eyeing the tall white wooden pole planted in the grass that hung the FOR SALE sign in full view of anyone who drove by.

Her house is for sale? My eyes shifted from side to side, the flood of thoughts keeping my feet planted to the same spot.

Jax stepped forward. "Tate's off to Stanford in the fall. Her dad is spending most of his time abroad," he explained and then approached me. "Last week, he decided to sell, since they're both home so rarely. He's buying a house closer to work when he's in the country."

"And Tate was okay with that?"

"She had no choice," Madoc stepped in. "James wouldn't let her spend her inheritance on buying the house from him. She needs it for medical school."

I squatted down, running my hand through my hair. I breathed in and out, trying to stay calm, but this shit was flipping my world upside down. Tate's coldness, the tree, the house . . .

What did I think was going to happen, anyway? That she was going to stay in this house forever? I knew shit was going to change, and I had to accept it. Tate fell away from me, and her life was as it should be. She was moving forward and on track.

But as my lungs filled and emptied, I wished the knots in my gut would hear what my brain was trying to convey.

Tatum Brandt isn't yours anymore.

But then my fists tightened, and I looked up at her house.

And then at our tree.

And then at my house.

And I couldn't accept that.

Even after all the good in my life—my business, my career, and how I'd grown—I was satisfied but not really happy.

I still loved her. I'd only ever wanted her.

"Are there any offers on it yet?" I asked, not meeting anyone's eyes.

"They've had two," I heard Madoc say.

Of course. No one could refuse a *Leave It to Beaver* house like this. The offers would come fast, and there would be plenty.

"James rejected both, though," he continued. "He doesn't seem to be in too big a hurry to sell. That's why Tate's staying at my house for a few days. They're doing some touch-ups inside for new buyers."

I ran my hand through my hair again, ignoring the fact that Pasha now had her full attention focused on me as she stared wide-eyed, eating her candy. There was only one other time she'd seen me really angry, so she was probably damn well enjoying this show.

I looked up at Tate's house. Perfect white with some summer green trim. A big, beautiful porch. Her manicured lawn sprawling down an easy little hill. I remember loving the sight of the lights glowing inside on cold winter nights as I pulled into my own driveway.

And my fucking eyes started burning, and I had to look away.

The backyard where we made love the first time. Our bedroom windows facing each other. The tree that connected us.

I bared my teeth, inhaling a sharp breath. I'd thought nothing would change.

"Jared." Madoc cleared his throat. "We just told you that your girl tried to cut down your tree. The one you tattooed on your back." His hard voice got louder. "That the house she's lived in ever since you've known her is up for sale."

"She's not my girl," I barked.

"She's not anyone else's, either!" Madoc shot back. "Tatum Brandt loves one person. You. She will always love you." His threatening growl was almost a whisper. "She breathes for you, no matter how much she denies it or tries to hide it."

I wanted to believe that was true. That buried inside this new, cold Tate was the girl that still held my heart.

Standing up, I slid my hand into my pocket, my fingers fisting around the familiar round of clay that held her fingerprint. After all this time, I still needed the little thumbprint fossil she'd made as a kid. I couldn't live a day without her.

"You should've come back for her a long time ago," Madoc scolded.

"I did," I growled, lashing out at Madoc. "Six months after I left I came back, and she was with somebody else!"

I inched back, my limp hand releasing the fossil and falling to my side as I looked at his shocked expression.

I nodded breathlessly when he remained speechless. "Yeah, I came back, and it was too fucking late, okay?"

Jax knew, but Madoc and I hadn't been speaking, and from the looks of it, Jax hadn't told him.

I could still feel everything as if it was yesterday.

I stand at my old bedroom window, stunned and angry. Frozen and hard.

I vaguely recognize the guy. Gavin something. He was from one of her study groups at Northwestern; I'd met him a year ago. I ball my fists. How long did she wait after I left?

Tate is in her bedroom, her arms wrapped around his neck as he holds her close, slow dancing with her. He kisses her, and my stomach coils into a knot.

His blond hair—matching hers—is cropped short, and she laughs as he hugs her close and swings her around.

Six months. She couldn't even wait six fucking months.

I'd waited. I hadn't screwed anybody. Not a damn thing but my hand—a pathetic loser still pining for her and believing she would wait. Holding out hope that I could get her back.

My chest caves, and I zoom in on them, hating that she laughs, hating that he dances with her, and hating that she's moved on.

I still love her. Nothing has faded for me.

I fall into the window, my hands gripping the frame as I watch him kiss her neck. His hands are all over her, and she's smiling.

Why is she smiling? She can't want him.

He falls on the bed, taking her with him. She straddles his waist, and I lunge back, jutting my leg out and kicking the glass, hearing it shatter but not staying to survey the damage.

Let her move on if that's what she wants.

I will, too, and everything will be done.

Bolting out of the house, I jump in my car and head back to my hotel in Chicago, where my team is racing.

I'll forget her.

I try to forget her.

But I don't.

I didn't know when she started seeing that guy, but I knew one thing. She was back in the game before I was.

"Gavin," Madoc remembered. "She tried to move on after you left. They dated for a couple of months, but then she broke things off." He looked me dead in the eyes, but I didn't want details.

"I don't care," I maintained. I didn't want his name or the name of anyone else she'd been seeing.

But Madoc pushed on. "She's been single for over a year, Jared," he pointed out. "She wasn't over you, so she cut things off with him when she realized she'd tried to jump back in too fast. It took her a long time to heal, but she needed to try to move on with her life." He looked at Jax and then back at me. "She only recently started dating someone again," he said quietly.

I cast an angry glance at him but kept my voice low.

"Who?"

"She started seeing Ben Jamison over spring break."

Jesus. Ben Jamison?

"As far as I know, though," Madoc continued, "they're taking it slow. It's not serious yet."

I noticed Pasha staring, unblinking, at the spectacle before her. "What are you staring at?" I growled.

She popped a gummy candy in her mouth. "This is better than TV."

I crossed my arms over my chest, forcing my breathing to calm down as I dipped my head. "If she wants him," I told Madoc and Jax in a calm tone, "then let her be with him."

Madoc let out a bitter laugh. "Take off your pants."

I popped my head up. "Why?"

"Because I want to see what a man with a pussy looks like."

Mother . . . I moved right into Madoc's space, standing chest to chest and glaring down at him.

He fell back a step but stood strong, looking like he wanted to drive a hole through my head with his eyes.

Jax cut between us, pushing me back as I held Madoc's stare.

"Pasha?" Jax stood in front of me, arms crossed over his chest and looking into my eyes as he spoke to my assistant. "Does my brother drive with a charm hanging on his rearview mirror?" he asked. "It has a thumbprint on it."

I dropped my glare to Jax.

"Yeah," she answered. "And it's around his neck when he's on his bike."

Jax continued, his smug smirk pissing me off. "Does he avoid blondes like a preacher in a pink shirt?"

I swallowed, hearing Pasha's snort. "Can't stand 'em, actually," she answered.

Jax continued, holding my eyes, "Does he have an almost unhealthy obsession with Seether? Specifically, the songs 'Remedy' and 'Broken'?"

"I'm to make sure they're on every playlist," she shot back, repeating my directions to her.

Goddamn it.

Jax dipped his chin, eyeing me defiantly. "Now, we can spend weeks going back and forth. You want her. You hate her. You can't live without her one day. You can't stand her the next. And we'll all be ready to strangle ourselves as you two go back and forth, but let me ask you this." He raised his eyebrows expectantly. "What would you do if Tate was in her room right now, curled up in bed and wearing only a sheet? Where would you want to be?"

My face fell, but my body flooded with heat at the idea of her warm body curled up between the sheets.

He inhaled a deep breath, knowing he had my number. "We want everything the way it was," he said firmly. "And so do you."

I shook my head and turned around, away from their eyes.

Yeah, I was still attached to her. So what?

I was happy with my life.

Pretty happy, anyway.

I was the man I had set out to be for her when I left. With a job I loved, I was able to invest in my future and start my own business. The freedom to make decisions—to spend my days doing work I loved—gave me not only security but peace as well. I had the kids at the track, the work at the shop, and the time and resources to explore my ideas and passion. I was proud of how I spent my days and of the man I'd become.

But my brother was right.

She was and would always be the last image in my head when I fell asleep at night.

I turned around and dug my cell out of my pocket, deciding that he was right. No more fucking around.

"Call my accountant." I tossed the phone to Pasha. "Buy the house."

"Jared!" She scrambled off the grass, shock flaring in her eyes. "This house is going to cost everything you have!"

I did no more than raise an eyebrow at her. She held up her hands and looked away, shaking her head. She was pissed off, but she knew the argument was over.

I knew why she was worried, and she had every right to be. She'd put in a lot of work building me, my name, and my business up, and even though it wasn't her money, she cared about my security. I really liked her for that.

I ignored the slight grins Madoc and Jax flashed to each other and started back toward the car, calling over my shoulder. "And call the guys," I shouted to Pasha. "I want my car here."

Tate was right. The game had changed.

She had no idea.

CHAPTER 5

TATE

I slink through a glob of people, carrying my red Solo cup into the kitchen to refill.

Madoc's house is a mess.

Fallon is having fun—alternating between picking up used cups and chatting with our friends, while her husband is downstairs with Jax, playing pool with some guys. Juliet and I mingle around the party, which is overrun with guests.

Everyone had come home for the weekend, and I'd brought Gavin, as well, trying to get my father used to a new guy in my life.

"Hey," he whispers in my ear, coming up from behind. "I'm thinking it's time to get out of here."

I smile, taking Gavin's hand off my stomach and spinning around.

"I don't know if we can," I state. "We've both been drinking."

Keeping hold of his hand, I lead him to the counter, hearing "This Is the Time" *by Nothing More traveling up through the open basement door.*

"Madoc will let us use a room. We can just crash here tonight."

My heartbeat throbs in my ears, but I don't say anything. Use a room?

Gavin and I have been seeing each other for about two months, and there is no doubt that we get along. We are both pre-med, in the same academic fraternity, and he gets along with Madoc, although they're not close.

Jax, on the other hand, will still have nothing to do with him.

My father has also had trouble warming to him, and I know why. His relationship with Jared is close, and it's hard to move on. I understand that.

But I'm trying to move forward. Gavin is fun and smart, and when I'm with him, I don't think about Jared.

It's the only time I don't think about him.

I'm trying to find some semblance of happiness again, but instead of getting easier, it's getting harder.

Every day it's more and more apparent that I don't love him, and it's bothering me.

Lots of people have sex without love, but I've realized one thing. It's different. It's not as good.

"I'm sure we could find a room to sleep," I say quietly, giving him a small smile.

He looks at me. "Don't you have a room here?" he asks. "I thought I heard Madoc mention it once."

I stall, trying to figure out how to answer as I dump out my drink and fill my cup with water.

"I do." I nod. "But—"

Then I jerk, seeing some guys crash into the kitchen, coming from downstairs and yelling as they filter down the hallway.

"But?" he presses.

I look back at him, distracted by the noise.

"Hey!" someone shouts. "Check out this video of Trent!"

I blink, dropping my cup in the sink.

Ignoring Gavin, I round the corner and go to where the guys are sitting in the living room crowded around an iPad. Peering over someone's shoulder, I watch footage of Jared—uploaded today, by the looks of it—speeding around a track filled with sharp twists and turns, and even though I can't see his face behind his helmet, I know it's him. I'd know his body anywhere.

I lose my breath watching him as I allow myself a small smile.

God, he's beautiful. The way he leans and steers the bike, in perfect control.

And he's doing it.

He's doing what he wants to do and living how he wants to live. I watch, and no matter how much I still hurt, I'm so proud of him.

I feel Gavin at my back, but I don't look. The footage on the YouTube video switches to a commentator, and my stomach knots, seeing Jared in the background.

He's signing autographs for some kids as a few race girls—the ones who work the crowd in their sexy outfits—climb onto the bus behind him. Another teammate clutches Jared's shoulders behind him and whispers into his ear before they both start smiling as if sharing a private joke.

The guy then pushes Jared toward the same bus as the girls and follows him up the steps, the door closing.

"Man, that's the life," a guy off to my right comments.

I back away and try to keep an even-keeled expression, even though my heart feels like it's splintering.

Gavin follows me upstairs, and I don't know why, but I take him straight to Jared's and my room.

I need to do this. I don't want Jared anymore. I don't want the pain. I don't want to take a chance that I'll ever be his and go through this again.

Months of heartache, months of trying to move on, and it still feels like he's everywhere.

I've made love to Gavin, and now I can make love to him in Jared's and my bed, and I will have crossed a boundary from which there's no return. It will kill everything inside of me.

Gavin starts kissing my neck, and a tear falls down my face. My skin feels like it's covered in mud, feeling dirtier the more he touches. I don't want this.

I shouldn't do this.

But I close my eyes and lean my head to the side, inviting him in anyway.

His hands cup my breasts, rubbing them in circles over my shirt as he takes my mouth.

He dips a hand inside my jeans, and I suck in a breath. I clench my thighs to keep him at bay, but I don't know what I want.

Gavin makes Jared go away. Gavin always makes me forget. I can do this.

But I still shake my head.

Every second of this makes me feel worse, and I don't want to use Gavin. To make what we're doing dirty, just so I can feel better.

Jared's voice pours into my head. "You've been turning my world upside down for eight years. I can't get enough of you."

I gasp, choking on tears as I push Gavin away and cover my face with my hands.

"Tate, what's wrong?" He sounds worried.

I shake my head and collapse against the wall next to the bathroom, sliding down to the floor. "You have to go," I cry softly. "I'm so sorry, but you have to sleep somewhere else tonight."

He approaches. "Baby, we can sleep somewhere else. What did I do?"

I shake my head again. "Please just leave."

This is Jared's and my room. No one else's. "Please leave," I cry louder.

"Tate," he presses.

"Now!" I shout. "Just leave me alone."

I put my head down on my knees and cry. I don't know why I feel guilty. I'd only ever had sex with Jared until Gavin came along. I don't sleep around, and Jared drowned his sadness and pain in plenty of girls before me.

Why couldn't it make me feel better, too?

I cry for a long time, still hearing the music going strong downstairs and not knowing if Gavin left, went back to the party, or found another room.

A hand touches mine, and I shoot my head up, seeing Madoc kneeling down on one knee.

My face cracks, and I can't hold it back. "Why can't I forget him?" I sob.

He closes his eyes, running a weary hand through his hair, looking about ready to cry himself.

Instead he pulls me in and hugs me, letting me release it all.

"When Fallon was sent away," he starts, choking on his own tears, "I tried to get lost in so many other women." I heard him swallow hard. "But it never helped for longer than a day, and I always felt worse later."

I look up at Madoc. "It's been months. Jared's probably moved on, but I don't want anyone else." I'm sobbing, wiping away my tears only to feel more come to take their place. "It hurts. Everything hurts. I almost cut down our tree last fall, Madoc. What's wrong with me? Why can't I get over it?"

He lifts my chin, tears pooling in his blue eyes. "Do you want to get over it?" he asks.

I narrow my eyes. "Of course I do."

He cocks his head. "I think you still love him, Tate, and I think you know deep down, he's going to be back for you."

I sniffle, dropping my eyes. "I can't trust him. Too much has happened." The tears spill over my lips. "Gavin's a good guy. I need to try to move on."

He nudges my chin, urging my eyes back up to his. "You're forcing it," he insists. "Do you remember senior year? You were stronger when you stood on your own, Tate."

Madoc was right.

The next day, I broke off my brief relationship with Gavin and joined my dad and Jax in working on my car, and that spring, I started racing.

It wasn't until recently—more than a year after that talk with Madoc—that I started seeing Ben, taking it slow but testing out the waters for the first time in a long time.

I sat in my G8, the cool black interior and tinted windows encasing me in my own private world as Limp Bizkit's "My Way" droned through the speakers. The crowds milled around outside, already tipping their drinks as they stumbled around the track, and I held back my little grin, not for once feeling bad that I never joined in. Ben wanted me to. He craved the happy girlfriend who could ease in and out of social situations without complication.

After all, if I was determined to race, why not enjoy the atmosphere and the hype?

But Ben was far too late to make an impression on my personality. I learned back in high school that I was who I was, and I slept a lot better at night when I didn't make apologies for that.

I didn't need them, and I didn't even need the win.

I just need this, I thought as I gripped the wheel and the stick. The blood in my arms felt like it was dancing under my skin, and I was ready.

Yes, Madoc was right.

I was stronger when I stood on my own. And when Jax encouraged me to take up some racing at the Loop, I'd found there was one thing that I did by myself—one thing I owned—that put strength in my veins.

There was no guilt, no pressure—just silence. And I would keep that going when Jared showed up tonight.

Which he would.

I hated to admit it, but he'd put a nice little rush in my blood today. And it wasn't just because of how good he'd looked. Beautiful ink covered more of his arms than it had two years ago, but he still had the same smooth, toned chest that now looked even more incredible, tanned by the West Coast sun.

And of course, all it took was a look for him to get under my skin.

At ten years old, Jared was my friend. At fourteen, my enemy; at eighteen, my lover; and at twenty, my heartbreak. I'd known him more than half my life, and although the roles had changed, his impact was always all consuming.

Always.

I leaned over, digging my mom's *Leaves of Grass* out of my backpack. Tossing the pack into the backseat, out of the way, I opened the paperback, pressing my thumb over the edges of the pages as I fanned them, the soft breeze of the flutter wafting across my face.

Finding page sixty-four, I headed straight for the lines my mother had underlined on verse twenty of Walt Whitman's "Song of Myself."

I whispered, holding the book close to me. "I exist as I am, that is enough."

There were many lines underlined and many poems dog-eared in this old paperback, but I always came back to the ones my mother did herself. Maybe she marked them for herself, or maybe she knew I would need them, but they were always right there being the voice for me she couldn't be anymore. Even though she died of cancer more than ten years ago, I never stopped needing her. So I carried the book everywhere.

Leaning in, I pressed my nose into the crease and inhaled the scent of old paper as my eyes fell closed.

"Dude," I heard Madoc's voice. "Kinky."

I opened my eyes, letting out an aggravated sigh at his big head sticking through my driver's side window.

You would think Madoc was my boyfriend, as much as he hovered, but it was useless to try to get away from it. He'd texted three times to make sure I was showing up tonight. I'd never missed a race, but I knew exactly why he thought I might duck out. The moron thought I had no self-respect.

"I don't want to talk about it," I warned, tossing the book into the glove compartment—which I always did for good luck—and then climbing out of the car.

"Okay." He nodded, stuffing his hands into his gray cargo shorts. "But if I see you sleeping with your books, I'm staging an intervention." He jerked his chin to the backseat, littered with all of my texts for school.

I shot him a look and walked around the back of my car to attach the GoPro Jax had given me. "I got behind on my summer reading because of my shifts at the hospital," I explained, bending down to affix the camera, "and I want to get through these footnotes by the time school starts."

"You're reading the books in the footnotes?" He looked at me like I was wearing head-to-toe orange.

I stood up, placing my hands on my hips. "Considering you're studying to be a lawyer, it might be a good idea for you to dive deeper into your reading lists as well."

He went wide-eyed. "We have reading lists?"

My eyes rounded, but then he laughed, clearly joking. At least I hoped he was joking. "Well, you're not going into surgery tomorrow," he argued. "So take a breath already."

"I can't." I brushed him off, walking back to my door. "I'm just—"

"Worried you'll start thinking about him?" he finished, and I halted.

I let out a sigh, gritting my teeth. "Not now, okay? Don't you have better things to do? Like your mission to start a soccer team in the Caruthers household as soon as college ended?"

But he ignored me. Before I knew what was happening, Madoc darted into my backseat and started gathering my books and backpack.

"Madoc," I scolded, trying to grab my shit. "Give me my books."

He jerked away from me. "I've got them."

"Now!" I whisper-yelled.

"Not tonight." He smiled, shaking his head.

"Why not tonight?" I inquired as if I didn't know where this was going.

But then a husky voice roared over the loudspeaker, and Madoc and I looked up.

"Tate!" My name echoed across the track. "Are you here?"

I grinned and cocked a mischievous eyebrow at Madoc. "Excuse me for a moment," I said sweetly.

"Oh, of course," he cooed, bowing his head in reverence with laughter in his eyes.

I rounded the front of my car, hopped on the hood, and stood tall. "Here!" I shouted, feeling the weight of a hundred pairs of eyes fall on me from the surrounding crowds.

Cheers rang out in the night air as people—men and women—howled and clapped, whistled and chanted my name, and I caught sight of Fallon and Juliet over by the bleachers holding up their drinks and screaming their support.

Zack Hager, the announcer, stood up in the viewing stand with Jax, clearly figuring out the evening's schedule. They only took attendance when someone had canceled. Seeing as how we all had set times before the day of the race, they needed to figure out who was here, so they could push up racers in the line-up.

I jumped back down and eyed Madoc, finishing our conversation. "All of you knew he was coming home and no one told me," I pointed out. "I'm not mad, but I'm not indulging whatever scheme you've worked out. I'm a grownup."

He pinched his eyebrows together and dropped my backpack. "Puh-lease," he grumbled.

And the next thing I knew he grabbed me, hooked an arm

round my neck—putting me in a headlock—and scrubbed my scalp hard with his knuckles.

"Madoc!" I screamed, planting one hand against his back and one against his bicep as I tried to pull my head out of his hold. "You are not giving me a noogie!"

"Noogie?" he argued. "No, grownups don't give noogies. And we're grownups, right?" He carried on, his assault burning my scalp.

"Madoc!" I growled, my voice deep and labored with the short breaths. "Let me go!" I stomped my foot, finally twisting out of his hold.

He backed off, and I straightened, trying to catch my breath as he laughed.

"You're a jerk!" I pushed hair out of my face that had been tugged free of my ponytail.

"Yes." Fallon joined in, walking up with Juliet. "You're just now learning that?" she teased, winking at her husband.

I huffed, yanking my rubber band out of my hair, because it was a lost cause now.

"Ah, that's better." Madoc smiled his approval at my hair hanging loose. I just scowled.

But then something else caught our attention as the crowd around us grew louder, and we all turned toward the track to see what the commotion was.

People moved to the side to clear a path, and I caught sight of Jared as onlookers cheered and screamed.

He was riding his motorcycle from high school—the same one Jax kept in his garage now that Jared had better bikes for racing—and he veered off to the side and backed up into a parking space. It took no time at all before he was swarmed with people: old friends, fangirls, and even fanboys.

I watched as he slipped off his helmet and swung his leg off the bike, flashing a smile to his old friend Zack, and my stomach

tightened when I saw a young woman climb off the motorcycle behind him.

I didn't recognize her, and I ignored the pang of jealousy that
she might be someone he brought with him from California.

Everyone was trying to get his attention, and once again, he
was the center of everything.

Madoc snapped his fingers in front of my face, reeling me back
in. "Are you pissed off?" he asked.

I pursed my lips. "No."

"Well, you should be," he shot back. "That's not his crowd. It's
yours," he continued. "You're the one they came to see."

I inhaled a sharp breath. "I don't care—"

"Now, some of them have long memories," he cut me off, "and
maybe they're interested in seeing what crowbars will fly with you
two in the same space, but nevertheless, he doesn't get to steal the
spotlight in your show tonight."

I got in his face. "I couldn't care less about the—"

But he grabbed my arms, and I was stunned silent when he
shook me.

"What do you care about?" he growled, and I felt Juliet and Fallon still beside me.

I sucked in air, shocked at his roughness. I barely blinked as he
grabbed the hem of my loose black tank top and ripped a slit up the
side.

I gritted my teeth together. "Madoc, what the hell are you doing?" I asked calmly.

He grabbed the two pieces and tied a knot halfway up my stomach. "You're the queen," he reminded me and then plucked the
backpack off the ground. "You own this track and every driver on
it. He's ignorant of that fact, so educate him."

I took a deep breath, not wanting him to see the smile I was trying to hide. Yes, this was mine. The track, the Friday nights, and

the wins. I didn't need to engage Jared. But I was going to keep what was mine.

Turning around, Madoc barked one last order before walking off. "Juliet, get her some fucking lipstick, too."

My eyebrows did a nosedive.

Asshole.

Juliet dug in her bag as I watched Madoc toss my backpack into his car, clearly making sure I didn't have an excuse to be antisocial even after the races.

I looked down at my shirt.

Such a jerk. Even if I undid the tie, my shirt was still ripped.

"Your husband is—"

"A handful?" Fallon finished, her green eyes smiling. "Yes, he is."

I jerked as Juliet tried to get some red lipstick on me.

"Stay still," she chided. "Jax hates gloss, so I found this lipstick that doesn't get him all sparkly when I kiss him. He loves it, but if it smears on your face, it'll take more than a little spit to get it off your skin, okay?"

I let her put the damn lipstick on because—I didn't know why. Maybe it was added armor. Maybe I wanted to be pretty for Ben.

Or maybe I saw Jared take a seat, leaning back on the bleachers, while a girl—a different one than the one I'd seen him arrive with—draped a hand on his knee, interest flaring in every one of her mannerisms.

Maybe I wanted to show him that I didn't need him to make an impression of my own.

The friend he'd arrived with sat on his other side, looking bored and disinterested. Purple streaks flowed through her jet black hair, and glancing up and down her body, I took in her alternative appearance and wondered at how Jared's taste had changed.

I had always been edgy but on the socially acceptable side. This girl was beautiful but a lot busier in her hair, makeup, and piercings than I thought Jared would have liked. He'd always said he appreciated my less-is-more attitude.

I guessed that was a lie.

She wore skinny jeans tucked into combat boots and a black sleeveless blouse that draped flatteringly down her body past her hips. Her wrists were adorned with dozens of metal and jelly bracelets while her ears sported metal from the lobe all the way around to the tragus. Her face had a few holes as well.

She seemed like Fallon, only louder.

Seeing Ben approach him—probably to break the ice sooner rather than later—I headed over with Fallon and Juliet, catching Jared's eyes almost immediately.

Madoc leaned into Jared, speaking close, but Jared's gaze stayed on me as Ben grabbed my hand when I came up. I blinked, smiling up at him and hoping he couldn't feel the sweat on my palms.

"Tate." Jared nodded.

I breathed in and out steadily through my nose, keeping my pulse in check. "Jared."

"Your career really took off, man," Ben said admiringly, speaking to Jared. "Congratulations."

"Thanks," Jared replied without meeting Ben's eyes.

"Clear the track!" I heard Zack holler in the distance as the round-one drivers took position.

"So you two finally got together?" Jared inquired, his words sounding more like a statement than a question.

I arched a brow, turning back to the track and ignoring him.

Ben joined me, taking my lead that I had no intention of indulging a conversation with Jared. Zack announced the next race, and we all watched as he and Jax set up the drivers and sent them off.

The heavy engines shot off, pounding over the screams of the crowd, and I smiled as the cars roared past, the wind sending my hair flying over my shoulder.

Juliet and Fallon chatted, and Madoc hung back, staying quiet. Jared stayed behind me on the bleachers, the heat of his eyes covering my back.

I'd missed that feeling.

"Well." Jared's smooth voice floated behind me. "Our little pond certainly has come a long way, hasn't it? My brother looks like he's outdone himself with the Loop. Some amazing races, hot new drivers . . ."

I slipped my fingers into the pockets of my tight jeans and lifted my chin up, the corner of my mouth tilting in a grin.

"But it's still a small pond," he finished, his hard voice dripping with disdain.

When he tore me down in high school it was to feel better about himself. But now it was to get me to react.

I turned around, meeting his eyes but never giving him what he wanted. He could gloat and wear his self-satisfied smirk, but I didn't play this game anymore.

But much to my surprise, Jared wasn't smiling. He wasn't smirking. He wasn't teasing. His expression was dead cold, and his eyes bored a hole right through me.

There was no anger, no amusement, no threatening tone to his voice . . .

What was he thinking?

"This is Pasha, my assistant." Jared introduced the goth-looking girl he'd driven in with. He turned to her. "Pasha, this is Tate and Ben."

Assistant? Yeah, right. Men and women who were attractive and unattached generally weren't friends. Unless one of them was gay.

"Tate?" Pasha repeated as if she recognized my name, and I saw her shoot a look to me and then back to Jared. "As in . . . ?" she asked him, trailing off as if they shared a hidden understanding.

I narrowed my eyes, noticing that he stayed silent, with his eyes focused out on the race.

And her interested expression turned judgmental as an eyebrow shot up.

She knew something.

I turned back around, just in time to see the racers cross the finish line, and I wondered if Jared had talked about me with her. It would've been unlike him. He rarely confided in anyone, so why her?

"Round two!" Zack shouted over the loudspeaker, making me jump.

I looked over the track, my game face lost, and . . .

And now my blood wasn't dancing under my skin. It was shaking.

Shit.

"On the track!" Zack shouted, and Ben hooked my elbow, pulling me away.

"Shake it off," he told me, cupping my face. "His being here doesn't matter."

I brought his hands down gently, giving him a half smile. I was grateful for what he was trying to do, but I could take care of myself.

I let Ben kiss me on the lips before I turned away and walked to my car, hearing whistles from the guys in the crowd. Even more so this week with Madoc's little impromptu wardrobe alteration on my shirt catching everyone's attention. Sometimes I dressed to kill, simply because it was fun to change it up, but I wanted to be noticed for my driving, not shaking my ass.

Climbing in, I pulled my car up to the starting line and sat next to Jaeger, with Chestwick and Kelley behind us. It was another four-car race, which made it interesting, with the narrow track.

I climbed out of the car to go hear instructions.

All three guys, surrounded by their girlfriends and our friends, crowded around the front of the cars as Jax stood up in the tower doing his techie thing and Zack administered the rules.

I steeled my body, determined that in one minute, I'd be in my car, with my music, and everything else forgotten.

"All right, everyone," Zack rallied us, his bald head shining in the stadium lighting. "It's a four-loop race. The top finishers from last week get the two front spaces this week. No rubbing, and no shenanigans." He pointed around to all of us. "You don't race clean, you won't be invited back."

Rules we already knew and rules that were hard not to break. The track was wider than it had been in high school but not wide enough for four cars. Not rubbing was nearly impossible.

Zack eyed all of us for compliance, and the crowd started chanting names.

"I'm ready," I said, nodding.

Zack peeked over our heads, toward the bleachers.

"Mr. Trent!" He called for Jared, feigning formality. "How about a turn for old time's sake, Mr. Big Shot?" he joked.

He held out his hands, trying to make a big show and get the crowd riled up as they started cheering.

"Sorry, man," I heard Jared say in the distance behind me. "There's only one race I'll take, but I'm not sure she's ready to give me what I want."

"Ohhhh," the crowd nearly panted, and before I let his words sink in, I did an about-face and got into my car without giving him a look.

Everyone cleared the road, and I glanced into my rearview mirror as the engines roared to life. He leaned back on his elbows, looking my way, and I averted my eyes, rolling up my windows and turning up Shinedown's "Adrenaline."

Nothing. I closed my eyes, letting the music sink in. *Nothing was weighing me down.*

Med school was a done deal. The house wasn't important. Ben was no pressure. Jared was nothing but a temptation that couldn't be trusted.

I was on top of the world.

My car door opened, and I snapped my eyes over to see Jared's "assistant" climbing into the car.

"What are you doing?" I barked, watching her settle back and fasten the seat belt.

"Coming with," she answered, pushing her black-frame glasses up the bridge of her nose.

I stared at her, befuddled, because I wasn't entirely sure if she was trying to be friendly or piss me off.

I cleared my throat and looked at her. "You're sleeping with my ex-boyfriend," I pointed out. "Get out."

She reached over, turning down the volume on my stereo.

"I'm not sleeping with Jared," she corrected. "I have never slept with Jared, nor do I ever want to."

I narrowed my eyes, studying her.

She nodded, allowing, "Although we are close, even though he likes to pretend we're not. I saw him almost cry once, and it kind of made me like him more despite the fact that he maintains it never happened," she explained. "But he's not my type, and I promise you of that."

She looked at me firm and serious, and I kind of believed her.

And then I wondered why I cared.

I turned the volume back up. "Out," I ordered, but then she turned it back down.

"I'm bored," she argued. "And I'd like to experience my boss's humble beginnings. If you're lucky, I may start to like you."

I rolled my eyes.

I saw Zack get up on the podium with his megaphone, and I checked to make sure I was in first gear.

"You're a distraction," I blurted out, wishing she'd get out of my car. I was tempted to get someone to haul her out, but it would waste my time.

"I'd say you were already distracted," she retorted, and I snapped my eyes up at her, catching her insinuation.

"Ready!"

I jerked my gaze back out the windshield, not feeling ready.

"Set!" I heard him call, and I blasted the music, shooting her a warning look.

Why was she in my car? Why did she think I was distracted?

And shit, how many laps was I doing again?

Uh . . . four. Four laps. I nodded to myself. *Yeah, four.*

"Go!" he shouted, and I sucked in a breath, gassing the damn car with all of my might.

I yanked the stick down into second and up into third, smoothing into my gears like always. My car was a part of me, and I checked my rearview mirror, seeing two of the cars still behind me and Jaeger at my side.

Coming up on the first turn, I let Jaeger go ahead, and I drifted behind him around the turn. I skidded, going to the outside, but not having to slow nearly as much.

"Whoa!" Pasha shouted as we raced, and I shot down into fourth as I slammed my foot down on the gas and sped ahead, now in front of everyone.

I'd love to say it was merely skill, but the car was a huge part, as well. The size and maneuverability were strong factors.

I shot up into fifth and down into sixth, hearing Pasha's excited breaths next to me. "I thought hanging out in the racing world, you'd be used to this," I challenged, seeing her holding the handle above the door as I tried to keep my mind off Jared, who was no doubt watching my every move out here.

Pasha breathed hard. "I drive for fun, and I watch races, but I'm hardly ever the passenger." She shook her head, smiling. "It's different."

I almost smiled back. Yeah, she was right. Riding with Jared had been a huge rush. No control—you just rode and put your life in someone else's hands.

It was an entirely different experience but still as exciting.

I rounded the next turn and the next, slowly starting to relax.

I finally turned down the music. "You don't know me, okay?" I told her, setting the record straight. "Whatever Jared told you . . ."

I felt her eyes on me, and even though I wanted to know what she knew, I wasn't opening this up for discussion.

No one—especially people I didn't know—made me feel bad about myself. And her look at me earlier had made me shrink.

"The guy you're dating?" she started softly. "Ben? He's a lifeline to you. Something to hold on to so you don't sink, right?"

I peered over at her, confused and shocked at the same time. *Lifeline?*

"You know how I know?" she asked. "Because you're a strong woman, and he's too weak for you. You can't possibly respect him."

"That's ridiculous," I snapped. "You don't know us. You just met us. He's a good guy, and I like him a lot."

"I'm sure you do," she shot back, sounding amused. "As a friend."

I squeezed the wheel, racing past the finish line and continuing for the first turn again.

"He does what you tell him to do," she went on. "He doesn't argue, and he doesn't run away. He's easy to handle, right?"

When I said nothing, she continued, "Jared kept trying to get under your skin earlier, and Ben should've reacted," she mused. "As the guy you're dating, he should've taken offense—at least a little bit—but he was too much of a coward."

I chewed the inside of my lip, fire burning down my leg as I floored the gas.

"You're strong," Pasha gauged. "Someone who likes to be in control. But wouldn't it be exhausting—not to mention boring—always being the one in the lead? Never being challenged?"

I turned up the music again and shook my head.

Ben wasn't boring.

He might not get me hot, but he also wasn't rude, aggressive, and complicated. And I didn't need to explain myself to—

"Jared, though?" she chirped over the music, cutting off my train of thought. "I can imagine that relationship threw you on the ground and fucked the daylights out of you, huh?"

I turned my wide eyes on her, barely noticing Jaeger's car zooming past me.

"Metaphorically speaking, of course," she added.

I breathed out a nervous laugh, stunned into silence. I had to hand it to her. She was bold.

I charged ahead, powering around the turn and missing Jaeger's car by a hair. I sped on, taking the lead again as I tightened every muscle in my body and raced hard, jerking the wheel wildly and making her laugh as I skidded around the corners.

Flying across the finish line two more times, I barely bothered to downshift as I turned, feeling the weight of the car pulling and our bodies trying to go with it.

She started laughing, nervously glancing behind her.

"Go, go, go!" she shouted, smiling from ear to ear.

"You're very weird, you know that?" I commented.

"I consider that a compliment." She beamed.

Jaeger's orange Camaro pulled up on my side, and I swerved into his lane to cut him off, knowing that we'd bump on the next turn if he was too close. Backing off, he pulled behind me, honking his horn furiously.

I raced ahead, feeling the energy down to my bones the way I always did here.

But it was more than that, too. It didn't feel like it was going to be over when the race ended as it usually did.

Tearing across the finish line, I let out a happy laugh, pounding my steering wheel with the adrenaline built up inside of me.

"Woo-hoo!" Pasha screamed, rolling down the window and howling.

I sucked in air, breathing hard as I spoke to her. "So was that boring?"

She acted like it was no big deal. "It didn't suck."

The crowd descended, pounding the roof, and I moved to get out of the car so I could smack one of them, because who the hell thought it was okay to pound on my car?

But Pasha grabbed my arm, and I stopped to look back at her.

"You should ask Jared about the one time I *almost* saw him cry," she said, her happy face turning serious. "I'm sure you'd find it very interesting."

CHAPTER 6

JARED

Jax stood up in the announcer's stand, peering down at me with a grin on his face that said I was way out of my depth. Yeah, I was kind of getting that.

Tate was different.

I shook my head and turned my gaze back to the track, seeing her hop out of her car and talk with the other drivers. So confident. So strong.

But the way I wanted her was still the same.

Jax was right. I could go around about it for days or weeks or another two years, but I'd still come to the same conclusion as he did this afternoon. I loved Tate, and I would always love her.

I'd never planned on letting her go. Not really. Seeing her with someone else a year and a half ago threw me for a loop, and I thought that maybe I still wasn't good enough, maybe I couldn't live up to him, maybe she was finally happy after all the pain I caused, and maybe I could think of her happiness and leave her the fuck alone for once in my life. Maybe, just maybe, we weren't meant to be together.

But there were no maybes now. I wanted her back.

For good.

"Girl," one of the racers drawled, wrapping an arm around Tate's neck as she made her way through the crowd. "I could've won that race. You know I backed off out of pity."

One corner of her lips tilted in a smile as she made her way back over to where Ben stood a few feet away from me.

"We've raced three times," she pointed out, eyeing him. "Why keep racing me if you're purposely going to lose every time?"

I laughed under my breath. "Well, if he beats a girl," I mumbled, pretending to fiddle on my phone, "what has he really won?"

I heard Madoc's snort from a few feet off, and I swallowed, immediately regretting the words.

Awesome. What the hell was wrong with me? No matter how much I liked to think that I had grown up, being around Tate brought out the bully all over again.

I could practically feel Pasha's eye roll next to me, and silence fell on Tate's conversation telling me they'd all heard the insult.

"You don't believe that." Tate's flat voice sounded so sure, and I knew she was talking to me.

I looked up, stuffing my phone into my back pocket as I stood.

"You're a lot of things," she continued, folding her arms across her chest, "but you're not sexist."

"Look who knows me so well," I taunted, acting like her boyfriend wasn't even there.

And he wasn't. He didn't matter.

Tate cocked an eyebrow. "You're not hard to figure out, Jared."

"No, I'm not," I agreed. "I'm just bored."

"Hmmm," she nodded, shooting me with her fake, sympathetic gaze. "That's right. This is all beneath you now, isn't it? We're simply the amateurs entertaining you with our mediocrity." And then she raised her voice, stepping closer as she spoke to those around us.

"He can take stories of us back to his hot shot friends, laughing about his 'roots' . . ." she stopped to add air quotes, much to the enjoyment of everyone listening. "And how far he's come while we're all still muddling along in this no-name town."

I rolled my eyes, knowing how wrong she was. I loved the Loop and my home, and I never let any success I gained go to my head. Anything I said or did to give that impression was simply to get under her skin.

I heard a throat clearing behind me and looked over my shoulder to see Fallon and Juliet smiling in support of their girl. I was kind of alone. Jax was up in the announcer's stand and Madoc was off to the side, clearly not picking a team and just enjoying the show as his eyes shot between Tate and me.

"But if I remember correctly," Tate spoke up again as conversations around us halted and people started listening, "Jared did say he wanted to race, didn't he?" she asked the crowd, looking around and egging them on.

They cheered and laughed, clearly liking where she was going with this.

"Tate?" I gritted out, warning her, but she ignored me.

"Yes, yes, he did say that, didn't he?" she shouted, now having everyone's attention. "He said he wanted a race, and I think Zack and Jax would be more than happy to adjust the schedule for such a prestigious Loop alumnus."

I shot a hard look up to the stand, seeing my brother leaning down on the railing grinning his ass off.

I took a deep breath, crossing my arms over my chest. "I said I wanted one race," I clarified to Tate. "One race with one driver in particular."

She knew what I wanted. What was she doing?

She turned around, looking into the crowd. "Derek! Derek Roman, where are you?"

"What?" I heard his deep voice from off to my right.

Cocking my head, I saw Roman coming through the crowd, using a shop cloth to clean off his fingers. He must've been under the hood of a car.

After all this time, he hadn't changed much. Still looked like a fifties greaser reject with his slicked black hair and plain T-shirts. We used to run into each other a lot at the Loop when I was in high school, and I knew he worked the Loop with Jax now, helping out and such, but I hadn't talked to him. We didn't get along, and Tate knew that.

"You and Jared have unfinished business," Tate reminded him, and I immediately felt the irritation pool under my skin when I realized what she was doing.

"Your last race together was a tie, wasn't it?" Tate knew the answer. She was merely reminding everyone.

"No." Roman shook his head. "I won that race."

"Like hell you did," I blurted out, feeling my rival's challenge like a hot poker in my side.

He laughed, sounding condescending, and I looked over to see Tate's lips curl in mischief as she held my eyes.

"Derek," she said softly. "How about a rematch? Your Trans Am against Jared's bike?"

"That's a dumb race," Roman shot back.

"I agree." I hooded my eyes in boredom. "He has no chance."

"Fuck you," he growled.

"Fuck you," I mumbled, barely meeting his eyes.

"Tensions are hot, everyone." Tate looked to the crowd, holding up her hands. "What do you say?"

I shifted in irritation as the noise became deafening. Shouts, howls, and cheers rang out in the hot night air, and I really wanted to shut her up. Like really shut her up.

"I'm not taking this race!" I heard Roman shout. "A sport bike against my car? That's not fair!"

"Exactly." I nodded, inching toward Tate and ignoring Ben's rigid stance beside her. "And I have nothing to prove, so why would I do this?" I asked her.

"Because if you win," she replied, "you can race me." And then she looked to Ben. "You okay with that?"

He cocked an eyebrow, his hard stare turning amused. She didn't need his permission to race, but she was asking him out of respect. Racing her ex-boyfriend—or engaging in any activity with an ex-boyfriend—was crossing a line.

"I'm not worried," Ben replied, meeting my stare head to head as he spoke to her. "He'll choke on your dust, babe."

*Ohh*s filled the air, and I inhaled a deep breath, just about done tolerating him.

"Well, what about me?" Roman whined. "What do I get?"

Tate walked past me, and I watched as she leaned in close, covering her lips with her hands as she whispered something to him. His eyebrows dug deep and then shot up in surprise, and I immediately knew she had sold him.

I could race him and win, getting what I wanted from her—a little more interaction—but what the hell did she promise him?

He smiled and shrugged. "Okay," he called out. "Clear the track, everyone!" And he raced off to get his car, I would assume.

Cheers rang out as everyone scurried off the track and huddled to the sides, making room for his car and my bike.

And I just stood there, wondering what the hell had just happened. I ate guys like Roman for breakfast. This wasn't a race. The maneuverability of my bike alone was an unfair advantage against him.

"What did you promise him?" I asked as Tate walked by.

"I promised him he would win," she called over her shoulder, following Ben off the track.

I followed. "On no planet would he ever win against a sport bike. Or me." I added.

She reached over, grabbing my helmet off my bike handle and tossing it to me. "Get it on, get on the starting line, and prove it."

She stood there, seeming so sure about herself. So calm and unaffected, and I didn't like this. Any of it.

I missed my Tate. The wildcat who fought back and smiled because she was happy, not because she was planning something to make me squirm. This new cool and calculated woman was a little scary, and I couldn't keep up.

She walked away, and I swung my leg over my bike, starting it and revving the engine, the high-pitched whir loud enough to drown out any other noise here tonight. I pulled onto the track and lined myself up next to Roman's 2002 Pontiac Trans Am.

I loved to race, and even though this didn't compare to my usual venues, my heart still pounded like a two ton hammer.

Jax came over, affixing two Go Pros to my handlebars, one facing the track and another facing me. "She's changed," I commented to him, slipping on my black helmet.

He nodded, keeping his eyes focused on his task. "She's definitely harder to impress now, so step up your game."

I didn't want to step up my game. I didn't want to play any game period. I just wanted to take her somewhere. Cry, fight, even let her hit me, but at the end of it all, she'd be in my arms, her storm blue eyes looking up at me and desperate for only what I could give her. That was my Tate.

I jerked, feeling a hand squeeze my shoulder, and I looked behind me to see Tate climbing on the bike in back of me.

What the . . . ?

"What are you doing?" I barked, noticing her clasp Fallon's half-helmet to her head.

"Riding," she chirped. "It's part of the deal."

"Oh, hell no!" I growled, twisting my head farther around to scowl at her. "It's too dangerous. Get off!"

"If I don't go with you, then you don't get your prize if you win," she explained, her voice calm and even. "And if you back out of the race now, everyone will think you're scared." She shrugged. "Or too stuck-up to indulge us."

"I don't—"

"Oh, look," she interrupted, jerking her chin in a cheery voice. "Here we go."

I darted my gaze to Zack coming off the announcer's stand and back at her as she adjusted herself on the rear seat.

I breathed in and out, not knowing what to do. *Shit!*

"Derek Roman," Zack boomed through the megaphone, "and Jared Trent last raced five years ago this fall! It was one of the most memorable nights we had here . . ."

"Get off!" I whispered over my shoulder to Tate.

"Not happening," she shot back. "Can't make this too easy for you, can we?"

My eyes nearly bugged out as realization hit. *Fuck.* I twisted around to say more, but Zack spoke up again.

"Because it was also the first time we ever saw Tatum Brandt race!" he continued. "To solve the tie between Jared and Derek, we had their girlfriends race. However, the score never really felt settled, and now, five years later, we can give everyone a chance to see who the real winner is!"

Cheers and excited laughter rang out, and I looked over my shoulder, growling low at Tate.

"Get off now," I ordered. "I can't race with you hanging on to me!"

I heard her snort as she wrapped her arms around my waist and leaned down into my back. "It's just a little pond, Jared," she taunted, throwing my words back at me.

I shook my head, gritting my teeth.

She wasn't going to let me race without her on the bike. I

couldn't race like I normally would for fear of hurting her. And backing out now wasn't a choice because . . .

"Are you ready gentlemen?" Zack called, and I groaned.

"No," I answered under my breath. And then I called behind me, "You better hold on." I revved my engine as Derek's Trans Am rumbled next to me.

Tate tightened her arms around me, and I wondered what Ben thought of all this. He was no doubt watching. Had Tate warned him before climbing on behind me?

"I'm going to get you back for this, you know," I threatened her.

She nuzzled in close, her breath tickling my ear. "You can try."

A smile tugged at my lips that I wouldn't let loose.

"Ready!" Zack called, and I faced forward, tensing every muscle in my arms.

"Set!" Tate went rigid against my body.

"Go!"

Liquid heat flooded my body, and screams filled the air as we shot off, our tires spinning, kicking up smoke and the smell of hot rubber as we launched down the track.

My rear end wobbled with the extra weight I wasn't used to, and I gripped the handle bars tighter, trying to stay straight. Derek shot off ahead of me, but I picked up speed immediately, accelerating ahead of him as Tate let out an excited laugh. Her scared arms tightened, and I loved feeling her warmth at my back. I always loved her on my bike.

But as we rounded the first turn, I immediately slammed on the brakes.

"Shit!" I growled, feeling the full measure of the extra weight behind me carrying me to one side and messing up my balance. I couldn't round corners the way I was used to in races—speeding ahead and bending low to the ground—because I wasn't on my racing bike, and I wasn't alone.

Tate gasped, her body settling on my back, since she was seated higher up and leaning down.

I brought my foot down, grazing the ground as I rounded the corner and feeling her wobble at my back. Derek honked his horn, skidding behind me, and I slammed on the gas, charging ahead right after him.

I felt Tate's chest shake against my back, and I knew she was laughing. I hardened my jaw.

At least she was quiet about her gloating.

I picked up speed, able to go much faster than Roman, but the turns killed me. It was no use.

He was able to make corners faster, because he didn't have to slow down as much—or worry about the safety of another person in his car—and I couldn't concentrate, because Tate was on my body and in my head, and she knew what she was doing. I couldn't race like this.

My balance was off, and she knew I was worried about hurting her. In a car, she was somewhat shielded, but out here . . . I was scared shitless, and I wouldn't take the chance. She shifted, we wobbled, and there was no way I could protect her if something happened.

By the time we rounded the fourth turn, Derek was already nearing the finish line, and I felt my stomach roll as I cruised past, pulling to a slow stop past the announcer's stand and feeling the heat of embarrassment cover my skin.

Dammit.

Roman was crowded with spectators, and he climbed out of his car, smiling ear to ear.

I pulled off my helmet, having never felt so fucking humiliated.

I'd just lost a bike race to an old rival I could barely stand in front of a hundred people I went to high school with.

I'm not going to kill her. I won't hurt her.

But I was going to do things to her. I slammed my helmet down on the handle bar. *Lots of fun things.*

I hung my head, breathing in and out steadily as Tate climbed off the bike and stepped up to my side, removing her helmet.

"You know," she started, looking off toward Roman, "You made him pretty damn happy. Derek doesn't really have that much going on in his life," she told me, looking thoughtful. "He has some friends and the Loop, but that's it. He'll never be one to rise high or have the world at his feet. This will probably keep him high for a month."

Her mouth tilted in a little smile, and I looked over to see him laughing with his friends, enjoying the praise and admiration. The win clearly made him feel good, and it probably made him look good. I looked at Tate, realizing what she was doing for him.

I shook my head and gave a half smile. "What did you promise him if he won?"

"Nothing," she replied. "I just guaranteed him he would win."

"You were that sure," I said, knowing she must've told him her plan to ride with me.

She nodded. "He likes me and trusts me. More than he does you."

"Great," I bit out.

She jerked her chin. "Look at him, though." She smiled. "This is probably the best he's felt in a long time." And then she looked back at me. "He doesn't need a reward. He just needed the win."

I looked over at Roman, realizing she was right. He wasn't a threat to me anymore, and I had a lot to be happy about. No harm done.

She let out a hard sigh. "But this really sucks for you, though," she teased, fake sympathy written all over her face. "Jared Trent, up and coming motor bike racer for CD One Racing losing to an amateur on this small pond?" She laughed. "Yikes."

And I watched her walk away, my face hardening as she went up to Ben and wrapped her arms around him.

I climbed off my bike, staring after her.

It was definitely time to step up my game.

It wasn't a turn-on a year and a half ago, so why the hell was I turned on now?

I shifted slightly in my seat, the swirl of heat shooting from my stomach to my groin, and I watched, wanting him to touch her.

I actually wanted it.

I dared him to slide his fucking hand higher up her thigh, so I could feel more of what I'd missed feeling the past two years.

Only Tate did this to my head. Only she twisted my body up like this.

Nothing had changed.

"Jared, what are you doing?" I hear Pasha's breathless voice as she shoves the hotel room door open.

I tip back the rocks glass and down the rest of the whiskey, the thick burn tearing up my throat before it warms my stomach. Dropping the glass to the floor, I fall back onto the bed—one of many beds on which I'd slept alone, completely faithful to Tate—and I feel the tears wet the corners of my eyes. But I tighten my jaw, refusing to let them fall.

I just want everyone to leave me alone.

I breathe in through my nose, defiant, willing myself to either forget or accept what I'd seen tonight through Tate's bedroom window.

She had a boyfriend.

The ceiling spins above me, and I bring my hands up to my head, digging my palms into my closed eyes.

Six months ago, Tate loved me, and now I was nothing. The last time I was nothing to her—the last time she talked tough and tried to convince me that I didn't matter—I'd stolen our first kiss.

And I knew she had lied.

But now . . . she'd shown me that she was forgetting me.

I feel like I did in high school. Before she was mine.

I can't stop the first tear from falling. "Tate," I breathe out, wiping my face quickly.

"Who's Tate?" Pasha sounds worried, and I know she doesn't understand any of this. "Jared, are you crying?"

"Just get out," I growl.

I gave her my extra key, so she could get in to get anything I might forget for tomorrow's race, but unfortunately, she must've heard my commotion when I kicked over the portable bar and broke a bottle earlier.

"You have a race at ten a.m.!" she shouts. "You have to be at the track by seven, and you're drunk off your ass!"

I shoot up into a sitting position. "Out!" I bellow. "Get the fuck out!"

"What the hell's going on?" I hear a male voice and instantly know it's Craig Danbury, the team's manager.

"Oh, my God," he swears under his breath, probably taking in the sight of my drunken disarray.

I don't look up from my hands, but I see his shoes near the door.

"What the hell is wrong with him?"

"I don't know," Pasha says. "And I don't know if he's going to be okay tomorrow."

I press my head between both hands, unable to concentrate on anything except her. She didn't wait for me. Why didn't she wait?

Anger charges through my body, and I want a fight. I want to hit someone.

"He better be okay," Craig snaps. "I don't care what you have to do. Get him a girl or a pill . . . just get him back to one hundred percent by morning."

I hear him leave, and I shake my head. I'm losing control, and I hate this feeling. I never wanted to feel this again.

Pasha's hands land on my forearms as she kneels in front of me.

"Jared," she pleads, "tell me what the hell happened."

I close my eyes, feeling like my body is swaying. "I lost Tate," I whisper, my eyes burning.

"Who's Tate?" she questions. "Is he a friend of yours?"

I let out a bitter laugh, kind of liking the sound of that. I wish our new neighbors ten years ago had had a boy instead of a girl. I wish Tate was a guy I'd gone to school with instead of the girl I liked, bullied, and then fell in love with.

I wish my world had never revolved around her. Maybe we both would've been happier.

"Drink this," Pasha orders, handing me a bottle of water.

I grab it lazily and unscrew the cap, downing the bottle. When I finish, she pushes another one at me.

I shake my head. "Enough. Just leave me alone."

"No," *she pushes.* "You have a race tomorrow. A responsibility to me and your team. Drink this and then go get in the shower, while I go rustle up some aspirin and food. We need to get the alcohol out of you."

She leaves, and I suck in air, trying to ignore the knots in my stomach that I know aren't from the liquor. Gulping down the second bottle of water, I rise on shaky legs and tear off my jeans and boxers as I make my way to the bathroom.

I don't want a life without Tate. I don't want anything without her.

Stepping into the shower, I stumble as I turn on the water. I jerk when the heat hits my body, and even though I should be under a cold spray to sober me up, the hot rush eases my nerves.

I drop my head forward, letting the cascade run down my neck and back, and I suddenly feel the first drop of peace I've felt all night.

Tate's been everything to me for so long, and somehow I thought she always would be. I never doubted it.

In fact, I'd gone to great lengths to stay in her life, be it for good or bad.

And that's when I realize it. I had given her too much power over me.

My first instinct tonight when I saw her with another man was to hit someone, yell at her, confront them both, but something inside held me back.

I'd always crowded her, pushed her and fought with her, and I didn't want to be that guy anymore. I left in the first place so I could grow up.

I hear the bathroom door shut, and I pull back the curtain just an inch to see a young woman leaning against it.

She watches me, and I smooth my hair over the top of my head, trying to place her. She looks vaguely familiar.

"Who are you?" I ask, thinking she might be a groupie or someone's assistant, but I hadn't paid any attention to other women in a long time, so I wasn't sure.

Her big brown eyes look shy. "Pasha thought you might need a back-rub," she replies, her voice sounding so innocent.

I narrow my eyes and watch as she slowly starts to take off her clothes, holding my gaze the whole time, as her meaning becomes clear.

I still, slowly releasing the air in my lungs.

Her light brown hair falls over her shoulder, and my heart rate picks up as piece by piece, everything comes off and she stands naked in front of me.

I whisper under my breath, willing myself to tell her to go.

Just tell her to go.

She's quiet, but I catch the hint of playfulness in her eyes as she cocks her head at me, waiting for an invitation.

"Do you want me to leave?" she asks gently, everything in her look telling me she knows I won't.

I let my eyes trail down her body, and I can almost feel how warm she would be if I touched her.

How nice it would be to have someone in my bed.

I want her to leave, but I don't want to be alone.

Tate's smiles float through my mind, and I steel my jaw as the girl approaches, her presence making the hair on my arms stand up.

She looks up at me with a small smile, and I start to grow hard as I think about her open for me on the bed. I can close my eyes and go at her, get lost in the act and let go of my anger and pain and use her like I have so many other women, but . . .

But I never gain anything from it.

Tomorrow, I'll hate myself and the cheap act, because nothing compares to fucking someone you love.

Needles prick the back of my throat, and I swallow the lump. "Yeah," I rasp, looking down at her. "I want you to leave."

Confusion and a hint of hurt flash through her eyes as she shifts her gaze, probably trying to make sense of why I don't want her.

I close the shower curtain and finally hear the door open and close, and a wave of relief hits me. For a moment, Tate fades in my head, and every inch of my body feels the gust of a second wind.

I'd let my need for Tate make me do so many bad things in the past and make so many wrong decisions, and I hadn't realized how much I still lacked control over my own happiness.

She had been everything, and I'd held myself back, acting out and making all the wrong choices, because my head had been so clouded with her—and I'm not doing it anymore.

I get out of the shower, wrap a towel around my waist, and go to bed.

I have a race tomorrow.

A couple of women came and went over the next year and a half, but it was never because I was angry or wanting revenge. I was trying to move on just like Tate had been. I had wanted to go back and fight for her, but not until I was sure I was going to be good for her. And maybe she wouldn't want me anyway, since she'd moved on. So I let it be.

For a year and a half, I warred between what I wanted and what I thought was right. Either take her back and love her forever, or leave her alone, because all I've ever caused her was pain.

But when I came home today and saw her again, that was it. The battle in my head wasn't there anymore.

She belonged to me. I was built for her.

I looked over, across the dance floor, her table full of our friends and their drinks, while Ben had his lazy hand resting low on her thigh, and I steeled my jaw to prevent the smile.

That touch wasn't going to do it for her.

Not for her.

Tate wasn't a slow burn. She liked to be fed on.

Halestorm's "I Get Off" played over the sound system, and some of our old high school friends sang along on the dance floor. I smiled to myself, remembering how that song always reminded me of her and how we grew up with our windows facing each other. She had a lot of fun taunting me with that window when we were together.

My phone buzzed in my hand, and I slid my thumb over the screen to see a text from Jax.

> **What are you planning to do when she leaves with him tonight?**

I locked eyes with my brother across the dance floor as he flashed me a small, all-knowing grin.

Asshole.

My phone buzzed again.

> **You have no idea, do you?**

I dumped my phone on my table and shot him my middle finger. He laughed and looked at Madoc, who shared his amusement.

What was I supposed to do? Drag her to my car by her hair? Yeah, that would win me points.

But he was right. There was no way I could live with her going home with someone else. As much as I'd learned to control my temper, she was a trigger.

Whatever fling she'd had a year and a half ago, I'd been around to witness only a few minutes of it. Now it was a different matter. Ben wasn't a bad guy, and Tate knew him somewhat well. Shit could escalate quickly between them.

The girl next to me leaned into my arm, and I looked down at her, almost wishing that I could take her home. I was overloaded with energy and adrenaline, and I wanted a girl in my bed tonight.

I could pretend I was going to take her with me. I could talk myself into it and let her body get mine worked up to where I'd shut off, dive in, and play for a while, but I'd be forcing it. There was only one girl I wanted and who knew exactly what I liked.

"Asshole!"

I jerked my head to the dance floor to see Pasha shoving a guy away from her.

Great. Annoyance flooded me like a rain shower, and I stood up, letting the girl's hand fall off my thigh.

Pasha had gotten just drunk enough to let a guy dance with her, and now she'd come to her senses, not wanting the attention.

The guy—late twenties from the looks of him—smiled wide and grabbed her hips, pulling her into him.

"Stop!" Pasha shoved his hands away again, and I walked over, knowing exactly what was about to happen.

The dance floor was practically shoulder to shoulder, so their struggling wasn't going unnoticed. Madoc, Fallon, and everyone else at their table were craning their necks to see what the commotion was about.

The guy grabbed her arm.

Shit.

I pushed through the crowd in just enough time to catch Pasha slapping him across the face.

"You bitch!" he yelled, holding his face.

I jumped between them, standing in front of Pasha.

"Back off," I gritted out to the guy, bearing down on him as he tried to advance.

"She hit me!" he snarled.

I inched into his space, keeping my eyes locked on his. "Better her than me," I threatened.

The dude paused, probably weighing his options, before he turned around and walked his ass off the dance floor. I let out a breath, just as aggravated with Pasha as I was with him. She did this a lot. Letting some guy think they had a chance, only to beg off when she realized she didn't want them after all. She needed to stop trying to be someone she wasn't.

I turned around. "Are you okay?" I asked, but she wasn't looking at me. Chewing her bottom lip, she shook her head.

"I'm gay, aren't I?" she murmured, as if just realizing it.

I nodded, snorting. "I know."

Her head shot up, and her eyes narrowed in surprise. She actually thought no one suspected.

"My father hates me," she sulked. "Now he's going to hate me more."

I hooked an arm around her neck and led her off the dance floor. "You know the great thing about family?" I mused. "They weren't your choice, so you're not responsible. The great thing about friends is that you can choose them."

And I slid my foot around the leg of a wooden chair at Madoc's table and yanked it out, guiding Pasha down into it.

"Guys, you remember Pasha, right?" I jerked my chin to my friends, the flush of heat on the right side of my face not going unnoticed as I felt Tate's eyes on me.

"Hey," murmurs sounded around the table.

I stood, holding the back of my assistant's chair, as Fallon got up and grabbed a bottle of beer out of their bucket. She plucked off the cap and set it in front of Pasha.

I gave Fallon a nod of thanks, knowing that my friends were the best thing I could give Pasha right now.

My eyes drifted to Tate, and even though her gaze was defiantly trained on an empty space across the table, I knew I was the only thing she was aware of.

Her loose waves were draped over one shoulder, blanketing her breast, and she sat still and quiet, as if she were expecting me to do or say something.

I dropped my eyes to Ben's hand rubbing the inside of her thigh, and then noticed that she, too, had her hand on his leg.

Steeling my jaw, I turned around to make my way back across the dance floor when Madoc called out. "Dude, just sit here," he prompted. "Come on."

I laughed at all the eyes on me. "I don't think so," I said, and then added, "Tate's uncomfortable."

Her narrowed eyes instantly pinned me. "We share the same friends, Jared. I can handle it."

I cocked my head, amusement warming my skin. "Really?" I challenged. "Your breathing is shallow. Your fists are clenched. You'll hardly look at me," I assessed, raking my eyes down her body. "And you didn't have your hand on him"—I arched a brow at Ben—"until I walked over here."

I smirked, reveling in the silence that greeted me. "You're right," I taunted. "You're not uncomfortable. You're nervous."

I knew I was right. I knew that if I felt her cheeks, they'd be warm, and if I put my hand over her heart, it would be racing.

But as much as I was satisfied that I'd nailed her mood, I couldn't help but wonder why she wasn't bounding out of the chair and hitting me.

Not that Tate was exceedingly violent, but she'd at least be shouting at me.

Instead, a corner of her full pink lips curled into a sinister grin as she stood up and held me entranced with her stormy eyes.

She arched a brow, looking amused. "Nervous?" she repeated. "I'm actually entertained that you think you occupy more than a bare minimum of my memory, Jared. That's how easily forgettable you were." She inched closer to me, stalking nearer with her calm, even steps. "And I'm actually quite entertained when I look back and think about how much I deluded myself about you."

Her condescending tone made me grit my teeth. A fucking memory?

I was *all* of her memories.

"The only way you can win an argument is by throwing a fist," she taunted. "Your antisocial behavior bored me out of my mind, and your lack of conversational skills in public was embarrassing, to say the least."

What the fuck?

My hot gaze zeroed in on her, and I slowly lifted my chin as anger swarmed through my chest.

I closed the distance with a last step and looked down at her, inhaling her soft scent. I bared my teeth, letting my buried temper seep out. "You liked my conversational skills when we were alone well enough," I pointed out, continuing as I enunciated every word. "In the car, on top of the car, in my shower, in your bed"—I got in her face, growling—"on nearly every floor in nearly every room of your house, you loved my conversational skills then."

I registered a snort behind Tate, and her furious wide eyes turned on Juliet.

Her friend looked up, her face falling at Tate's glare. Madoc's and Jax's eyes were focused on the ground, as they wisely bit back their amusement.

Ben appeared at Tate's side, taking her hand and not sparing me a glance. "Let's go," he said firmly.

Tate looked at me with fury warming her face and nodded. "Absolutely."

But as she let Ben lead her away, she stopped and leaned in, whispering for only me to hear. "You were good for some things," she remarked. "Just not for others."

My lungs emptied as I watched them leave together, and all the while the stares of everyone at the table burned a hole into the back of my head.

Fuck me.

She called to every nerve ending on my body, and I wanted nothing more than to have her underneath me. Despite the fact that she'd just insinuated I was good for only one thing.

I smiled.

The next time her claws came out, she would be reminded of every damn thing that I was good for.

CHAPTER 7

TATE

"You know, it's okay if having him around unnerves you," Ben said softly, holding my hand as we walked up the brick path to my house. "You were together for a long time."

I offered a tight smile, squeezing his hand. "Jared doesn't unnerve me," I maintained. "He aggravates me."

We climbed the wide wooden stairs into the soft glow of the porch light, and I flicked my gaze quickly to Jax's house, noticing that all the lights were still out.

I'd opted to come home, since I'd guessed Jared would probably be staying at Madoc's.

Whenever he got home, that is. He'd had Pasha and a date with him, after all.

I stopped halfway up the stairs, turning to look down at Ben, who was one step below. "I'd invite you in," I started, lightly tugging on the front of his polo, "but it's really a mess."

A flash of disappointment crossed his face, but he offered a quick smile, hiding it well.

The mess shouldn't matter, of course. And it didn't matter. My room was clean, after all.

The truth was I was too distracted to invite Ben in. He deserved my complete attention, and right now, my body and head were too restless. Too roused. I couldn't take him home tonight.

He held my gaze, studying my face with an air of calmness. I knew he knew the real reason behind my excuse, but he didn't say anything. He nodded, accepting what I couldn't put into words.

Ben was a good guy. And a smart one. He told me I was pretty, and he supported my choices. Looking into his blue eyes, I almost wanted to get lost. To find out what it would feel like to have his warm skin against mine. To see if he could make me feel as good as . . .

I cleared my throat, pushing the idea out of my head.

I'd be using Ben to make myself feel better—to feel anything— and we both deserved more. So that's why we needed to wait for a better time.

He stepped up, lowering his lips to mine for a chaste kiss. He tasted like cinnamon this time, and I slowly breathed in his cologne. Backing down, he smiled gently before turning away to leave.

But I stopped him.

I grabbed his upper arm and pulled him back in, dipping my head and diving into his lips as his body jerked in surprise. I teased his tongue with my own and cocked my head to the side, going deeper and enjoying his hitched breath. Ben's hand circled the back of my neck, and my cheeks warmed with his closeness.

This was how it was. Enjoyable. Comfortable. He was a good kisser.

But nothing happened unless I pressed it. When he actually tried to get to second base, he'd asked me if it was okay. I felt bad for feeling disappointed. He was only being polite, after all. But it was like he didn't know what he wanted and was perfectly happy following my direction. He'd wait for my say-so, and I wasn't sure if that would ever turn me on.

It's not that I wanted to be controlled. I just wanted to be carried away.

He backed up, smiling a little bigger before finally turning to go to his car.

Unlocking my front door, I stepped into my house, immediately hearing little claws *tap, tap, tap* on the hardwood floors.

I glanced up, smiling as Madman raced down the hall from the kitchen and shot up, supporting himself against my shins. He must've escaped the confines of Jax's backyard and found his way through our doggy door. Jax and Juliet had been watching him while I was staying at Madoc's. I could've taken him with me, but I had been so busy this week, he got more attention with Jax and Juliet.

He was just a little guy—a stray dog—Jared and I had found ten years ago, and although he'd lived with Jared for most of that time, I was happy he'd been mine the past couple of years.

The little dude never failed to make me laugh. Even now, as old as he was getting, his energy hadn't wavered.

I reached down, petting the top of his head and knowing exactly what the little hellion wanted. Food, water, and a belly rub—all at the same time.

I made my way to the kitchen, walking past the mess the painters had made in the dining room this week. White sheets draped over furniture and on the hardwood floors, and I inhaled the familiar scent of paint.

Of new beginnings and a fresh start.

I refreshed Madman's food and water in the kitchen and took in deep breaths, closing my eyes as I walked back through the foyer, savoring the old memories.

Mom painted rooms a lot when I was growing up. She liked change, so the smell of the chemicals actually comforted me. It was home.

And I hated that I was losing it. My father had turned down two good offers, and while I wasn't sure why, I didn't complain.

I understood that selling the house was for the best. Although I would miss being close to my friends, and I couldn't even think about anyone else living here, I knew I needed to get away from Jared. Away from the memories, away from his old room sitting across from mine, away from a future full of him showing up back in town without warning whenever he felt like it.

So yes, change was necessary no matter how uncomfortable.

When I was little, I cried when my mom had made me donate some of my toys before Christmas one year. She'd said I needed to make room for the new things Santa was bringing me, and even though I didn't play with the old stuff, I almost felt like the toys were people. Who would they go to? Would they be taken care of and loved?

But my mom said that everything is hard the first time. The more you embrace change, though, the easier it gets. Which is why she repainted rooms every couple of years.

Change prepared us for loss, and she was right. It did get easier.

I had to embrace the possibility of a relationship with Ben or whoever else came along, and Jared could do whatever he liked. That's the way things needed to be.

And no matter how uncomfortable it was to be around him, I knew Jared was most likely home to see his mother and be present for the birth of his sister. I didn't want to ruin the visit for him.

I picked my phone out of my pocket and walked into my bathroom while typing out a text with shaky fingers.

I swallowed and sent the text to Jared.

Leave me alone, and I'll do the same.

I squeezed the phone for about two seconds before setting it down on the sink and stripping off my clothes.

And to make damn sure I didn't dwell on him or whether he would respond or what he would say when he did, I brushed out my hair, slipped on my thin white pajama shorts and fitted black Seether hoodie, and got into bed.

Turning off the light, I plugged my phone into the charger and curled under the covers. I wasn't going to wait for him to respond. I wasn't going to wait for him to react.

I wasn't going to wait for him.

I rubbed the sleep from my eyes, finally noticing a text on my phone from Jared.

I can't, the text read. And neither can you.

Glancing at the time on the phone, I saw that it was after two in the morning. I'd been asleep for only an hour.

I'd assumed it was my dad texting, since he often forgot about the time difference and texted at weird hours. But remembering my text to Jared, telling him to leave me alone, I studied his response again. Was he insinuating I couldn't control myself?

"Arrogant jerk," I spat out, my mad fingers typing out my only response.

I whispered to myself as I texted. Don't talk to me. Don't come near me.

I slammed the phone back down on the bedside table and ground my face into the pillow, determined to keep him out of my mind.

It didn't work.

I punched the bed. *What an ass!*

"Pompous, over-confident, son of a . . ." I growled into my pillow, hating that there might be a slice of truth to his words.

I remembered very well how much I loved it when he *didn't* leave me alone. Jared's favorite place was anywhere he could get me naked.

My phone buzzed and lit up again, and I blinked, knowing I just needed to ignore him.

But I lifted my head anyway, still scowling as I read the text floating across the top of the screen.

I won't come near you. Yet. I'd rather watch you.

My breath caught. "What?" I whispered to myself, scrunching my eyebrows together.

Watch me? I swallowed and tried to compose myself, not sure if I was reading that correctly. Picking up the phone, I threw off the covers and tiptoed to the end of the bed, where I peeked out my French doors and through the tree of dense foliage.

Where are you? I texted, not seeing a light coming from his old room. How could he watch me unless he could see me? All of a sudden I straightened, a stream of light slipping through my sheer curtains from a lamp in his old room, now illuminated.

I tucked my hair behind my ear as a nervous heat flared up in my chest. I pushed up my sleeves and crossed my arms over my chest, my heart fluttering with quick beats.

Jared appeared at the window, and I backed away, blanketing myself in darkness. "Shit," I whispered, as if I thought he could hear me. *Why is he home and not at Madoc's?*

At least since he was the one with the lights on, I could see him, but he couldn't see me.

He still wore his black pants from before, but his belt and T-shirt were now off, and he just stood there, looking like he knew exactly where I was. Even from here, I could see his playful eyes, and I knew, without a doubt, that if I opened my doors, he would come over. Just like old times.

Knowing that sent a shiver up my arms.

He brought up his phone level with his waist, texting, and I let my eyes linger on his body—the abs, tight and narrow, that I'd traced with my tongue more than once.

I growled low, averting my eyes.

My phone vibrated, and I slid the screen to look at the message.

> **You were beyond beautiful at the track tonight.**

I narrowed my eyes, trying to harden myself against his soft side. He rarely showed it, which gave it more of an impact, and I didn't want him saying nice things to me.

> **Even after all this time, you still kill me. I still want you, Tate.**

"Don't," I whispered to no one, and then, sighing, I lowered myself to the end of the bed, still seeing his dark form out of the corner of my eye.

I missed the way your body used to move with mine, he texted again. I dropped my head forward, reading the texts as they came in.

> **But I never forgot it.**

> **I remember every inch of your skin. Every taste, every sound you'd make . . .**

The moonlight fell on my lap, and I could see my fingers turning white as I squeezed the phone.

He did know every inch of me, and he could play me like an instrument. His demanding hands and mouth were so greedy, and I dropped my head back, feeling a trickle of sweat glide down my spine.

Shit.

My fingers tingled, and I knew what he was trying to do, and I didn't want him to stop.

Seems you're the one with poor conversational skills tonight, he texted.

I rolled my eyes.

You may think you're different, but you're not. I know you still feel me, he wrote, and I gritted my teeth at his arrogance, even as I clenched my thighs at his memory.

So many times I was inside of you, he taunted. *Tell me you remember, or I'll have to remind you.*

I closed my eyes, my pulse pumping through my body like a drum.

Jared.

I ran my hand down my thigh, fucking loving the rush between my legs. It had been so long.

"Damn him," I gasped under my breath.

Do you want me to stop? he asked.

I took in short, fast breaths as I stared at the screen.

Do it. Tell him to stop, I told myself. This is fucked-up, and he can't have you.

But my skin was on fire. And it felt like home.

Like warmth and peace and no matter what changed in my life, the people I met, the things I lost, or where I lived, if I was in his orbit, then I was home.

Even when I was eleven and it had been one year to the day that my mother had died, Jared was my beacon that day. He didn't leave my side, even when I ignored him. He just pushed me on our old tire swing in the backyard for two hours until I finally stopped crying and started talking. He was my friend. We had a strong foundation.

And then, as he became a man, the feelings became stronger. So much stronger.

I sat there and ground my ass in a small circle, giving myself the pleasure of the friction from my shorts and thong against my skin.

He texted again, and I gave in, reading his words.

> I loved the skin on the curve of your thigh, Tate. The
> part where your leg met your hip. It was heaven, and
> even now, I can still taste it.

My eyes fluttered, and I let my body fall back onto the bed as I
grazed the part of my thigh that he loved.

> You used to grip my hair so hard that you were damn
> near riding my face. Your dad never knew how bad
> you really were.

I ran the heel of my palm over my clit through my pajama shorts
and moaned, thinking about his covert morning visits before school.
He'd sneak in, bury his head between my legs, and go so hard he'd
have to put a hand over my mouth so we weren't overheard.

> Sophomore year when you started track . . . your legs
> got so toned. I thought you were trying to drive me
> crazy on purpose.

I slid my middle finger between my folds over my thin shorts,
and I couldn't help it.
I craved his rough hands on me again.
I tensed every muscle in my chest, bringing my breasts higher,
and I imagined his long fingers sliding under my hoodie, because he
could never keep his damn hands off my chest.

> You always fit so perfectly, Tate. The way you'd arch
> your hips back into me when I fucked you from
> behind.

"Fuck," I groaned at the memory, rolling my hips into my hand
and closing my eyes.

That was your favorite position, wasn't it?

I didn't answer, because he already knew. Ever since the kitchen table, I always loved it when he had me on my hands and knees.

You never melted underneath me, either, he continued. Every time I pushed, you pushed back. I'd thrust my cock inside of you, and you'd push your fucking back up off the bed, rubbing your nipples against my lips and begging for my tongue. You always liked it hard.

The ache at my entrance was so hot and sweet. I needed him so bad. No one drove me wild like he did. The rush of need flooded me, and I felt the wetness through my shorts as I rubbed the nub harder.

I closed my eyes, imagining him flipping me onto my stomach and sliding into me. Sweat covered my brow as I remembered, just like it was yesterday, that fucking fantastic pain I always felt when he entered me. It was a small hurt, but I loved it. He'd hit so deep inside, and the stretch and pressure were sweet.

I brought up the phone to see his new message.

Do you remember graduation night? In my car, out by the lake? It was so hot. Your dress was torn and on the floor of the car, and you put on my necktie. It was the only thing you were wearing.

I remembered. I'd straddled him in the backseat with his tie lying between my breasts. He couldn't take it. He'd attacked like a wild dog, nearly eating me alive.

Tate, you don't know what you do to me. You drive me out of my mind. Your words, your laughter, your tears, your eyes . . . everything about you owns me.

"Me, too," I whispered, a tear spilling out of the corner of my eye and dripping down my temple.

I swallowed, rubbing my legs together to get rid of the ache.

I'm a better man, but there's never been a better woman for me. There's never been anyone like you, he texted.

I fisted my hands, needing to come. I gasped, wanting him to make me come, but I crashed my fist to the bed, refusing to give him the satisfaction.

He'd hurt me too much, and no matter the physical attraction that still existed between us, that hadn't changed. I needed to re-member that.

> I want to crush his fucking hands when he touches you.

But honestly . . . , he continued, it's a hell of a turn-on watching an-other man have what I want.

Yeah, just like me seeing him with another woman. I hated it, and it hurt, but it made me feel possessive, too. It made me want to fight.

> In fact, I'm steel-rod straight right now.

My lungs emptied, and I dragged my bottom lip through my teeth, almost smiling, but I stopped myself. Jared—hard and ready—was a sight that never failed to make my mouth water. I pic-tured him holding himself right now, even though I was lying down and I couldn't see him.

It was another minute before he texted again.

> You look hot. You should take off that sweatshirt be-fore you go to bed.

My eyes rounded, and I shot off the bed, gaping out my French doors. He didn't see me, did he? It was dark in here. Light over there. I ran my hand though my hair, shame heating my face.

Peeking to get my line of sight out the doors, I saw Jared still standing in the golden glow of the lamp that he'd turned on before. Even through the tree and the darkness, I could see the self-satisfied look in his eyes before he looked down and texted once more.

I remember everything, Tate, he texted. And I know you do, too.

I let phone drop to the bed, seeing the amusement in his eyes turn to a dark threat as he pulled the drapes closed and disappeared.

Fuck.

CHAPTER 8

TATE

I pounded along the sidewalk, sneakers cushioning the impact as I leaped over the curb and across the street. Three Days Grace's "I Hate Everything About You" blared through my earbuds, and I was covered in sweat from my stomach up to my head.

I was in good shape, and I normally didn't push for speed on my runs, but the fact that I was gulping in air let me know that I'd gone too far and hard. I never got out of breath on my regular morning jogs.

Slowing to a walk as I stepped onto the sidewalk on my side of the street, I pulled up the hem of my black tank top and wiped off my face.

My cropped black stretch pants were damp with my sweat, and the fabric itched my thighs.

They were pissing me off.

My ponytail dragging across my back was pissing me off. My aching feet, and the fact that I hadn't managed to run my unwanted energy out of my body, both pissed me off.

I hadn't been this pissed off in a long time.

I'd woken to the sound of Jared's motorcycle piercing through my sleep like a flood of hot water over my skin, and I lay in bed, flattened to the mattress, suddenly desperate for one of his morning visits. I'd always been in the mood more in the mornings, and having his naked body nestled between my legs, begging for entry, used to be a damn nice way to wake up.

But he'd sped off, and I certainly didn't want what my body might have craved.

I walked into my house, set my keys, along with my iPod and earbuds, on the entryway table, and walked into the kitchen, Madman trailing behind me. Firing up my laptop on the table, I proceeded with making an omelet while I downed two bottles of water and chopped some fruit.

It had been hard to try to eat healthy with the schedule I kept. The hospital always had boxes of Krispy Kremes, cookies, and other treats floating around, and since I was either reading at the library, reading at home, or working on my car when I wasn't working or at school, I had a hard time not grabbing what was convenient in a rush. Thankfully, my weekends were free, so I food prepped by premaking salads and healthy snacks.

Although I did still snatch up a chocolate-glazed doughnut any chance I got.

Sitting down at the table, I dialed my father for our once-a-week video chat.

"Hey, Dad," I greeted him, cutting into a piece of my omelet with spinach, mushrooms, and cheese. "How's beautiful Italy? Staying away from all of the wine, right?" I teased, stuffing the loaded fork into my mouth.

"Actually, wine is good for the heart," he pointed out with laughter in his blue eyes. My eyes.

"Yeah, one glass," I clarified. "Not five, okay?"

He nodded. "Touché."

My dad wasn't big on alcohol, but I knew he'd taken a particular liking to the food in certain countries where he'd been assigned over the years. Italy being one of them.

But a few years ago his lifestyle finally took a toll on his body. He had a hectic schedule, little consistency in his routine, poor eating habits because he was always on the go, and little to no exercise due to the travel. He had two heart attacks while abroad and didn't even tell me. I had been livid when I found out.

Now I stayed in better contact to nag him more. I'd dipped into my savings and sent him a treadmill for Christmas one year, and I even scoped out the grocery stores in whatever area he lived in, so I could push him to their salad bars and organic selections.

Thankfully, he put up with it. He'd been my only parent for about twelve years now, and he finally got a clue and realized I needed him around for a long time to come.

"Are you at the house?" he asked, looking around me. "I thought you were staying with Madoc and Fallon."

I shrugged, concentrating on my food. "It's the weekend. The workers aren't here, and I wanted to get some yard work in. Making it presentable, you know?"

The yards were actually in great shape. Jax had been taking care of everything while my father was away and I was at school. I'd really just wanted to be home, and I knew, no matter how I tried to hide it, my father could read me well.

"Tate, I know this is hard," he said softly. "Selling the house, I mean. I know you're going to miss it there."

I swallowed the lump of food in my throat, making sure I looked indifferent. "It'll be a hard good-bye, but nothing can stay the same forever, right?" I was trying to stay positive. There was nothing that could be done, and I couldn't expect my father to keep paying expenses on a large house we no longer needed.

"Honey, look at me, please."

I stopped cutting food with my fork and looked up.

He stared at me for a moment, but then frowned and looked away. Brushing his nose with his hand, he let out a sigh.

My heart sank, and I wondered what the hell he was trying to say.

"Is everything okay?" I shot out. "Your heart—?"

"I'm fine." He nodded quickly. "I just . . ."

I narrowed my eyes. "Is it the house? Has it been sold?"

His gaze locked on mine, and he hesitated before replying. "No." He shook his head. "Nothing's wrong necessarily."

"Dad, just spit it out."

He ran a hand through his hair and exhaled a hard breath. "Well, I'm seeing someone, actually," he said. "Someone I've grown very close to."

I set my fork down, my back straightening. Seeing someone? I remembered him talking about going on a date here and there a while after my mom died, but he never introduced me to anyone. Was it serious?

My dad watched me, waiting for me to say something, probably.

I finally blinked, clearing my throat. "Dad, that's great," I told him with an honest smile. "I'm happy for you. Is she Italian?"

"No." He fidgeted, looking very uncomfortable. "No, she lives back home, actually."

"Here?"

His cheeks puffed out as he ran his hand though his hair once more. "This is very awkward." He laughed nervously. "Honey, about a year ago, I started seeing one of . . ." He trailed off, looking like he desperately needed different words to tell me what he needed to tell me. "I started seeing one of your old teachers. Elizabeth Penley," he rushed out.

"Miss Penley?"

Miss Penley and my dad?

"It was sporadic," he explained, sounding more like he was

apologizing. "With my schedule and her job and your schedule, not to mention that when you did make it home here and there, I wanted our time together to be just us." He took a deep breath and continued, "It just seemed like there was never a good time to tell you."

I guess I understood.

He probably could've mentioned it at some point, though. *Jesus.*

"I didn't know if it would last, and I didn't want to mention it until I was sure. It's only gotten really serious in the past couple of months," he explained further, as if reading my mind.

Nodding, I tried to absorb the idea of my dad telling me about someone new in his life. He'd never made this big a deal out of anyone.

But the truth was, I had been worried about him. I always worried about him. Especially with me no longer home during his time at home, I couldn't shake the guilt that he was eating alone, watching TV alone, going to sleep alone . . .

Although my mom would always be loved and important, I didn't want my dad by himself forever.

"Well." I sighed. "It's about time. And I love Miss Penley. She's amazing." But then I narrowed my eyes on him, questioning. "But why, if you couldn't find the time to tell me at Christmas or spring break or over video chat before, are you telling me now?"

He offered a timid smile. "Because I'm going to ask her to marry me."

"Tate!"

I jerked my head to the left, seeing Madoc heading my way.

"Great," I whispered, focusing back out on the track.

After the call with my dad, I came out—as so many others did during the day—to take a few practice runs around the track and enjoy the calm I found here without the crowd.

I was struggling, and I didn't know why. I liked Penley, and I wanted my dad to have someone. His proposing was a good thing, and I should've been happy for him.

So why did I feel like it was all suddenly too much?

The house, Stanford, his relationship . . . I felt as if I were at sail without a rudder or an anchor.

So I came out to drive. To clear my head.

To be alone, which Madoc hated.

"Let's go." The bite in his voice was sharp, and I knew he wouldn't take no for an answer. "Now."

I looked at him again, confusion, aggravation, and frustration probably all evident on my face. "Where?"

He jerked his head behind him. "My house. We threw a party together. Fallon said she texted you an hour ago."

"No." I shook my head, knowing exactly whom I'd see there. "No party."

He halted, pushing his suit jacket open and planting his hands on his hips.

"What are you wearing?" I asked, taking in the black suit pants and jacket and the light blue shirt with the royal blue tie. His clothes and hair were sleek and stylish, and I could never get over how he wound up with someone as alternative as Fallon.

He straightened, suddenly looking affronted. Running a hand down his front, he tipped his chin down at me. "Hot or not?" he asked, turning playful as he referred to his clothes. "I had to go in for my internship for a few hours this morning."

I turned my eyes back out to the track, deciding not to encourage him.

"Let's go." His strong voice nagged again, getting back on topic.

I heaved out a sigh and hopped off the hood. "Knock it off. I don't need you interfering."

I went to open my door, but Madoc flattened his palm against the window, stopping me.

"You're going to run into him a lot in your life," he pressed. "Reunions, friends' weddings, and what about when Fallon and I have kids? Or Jax and Juliet?"

My heart pumped wildly as I realized Madoc was right. I'd be running into Jared a lot over the years.

Shit.

Madoc grabbed my shoulders, forcing me to face him. "Get this through your head, okay?" He spoke to me like my father. "You are as important to us as he is. You're not pulling away again. We're not letting you go."

Like a petulant child, I shot my eyes up at him. I hated his persistence.

Although I kind of liked it, too.

He never let me go. Juliet and Fallon were going to be with these guys forever and have children with them. And they'd no doubt settle here.

And they were all my friends as much as Jared's.

I dug my keys out of my pocket. "Fine, but I'll drive my own car."

"Hey," Fallon greeted me, pulling me in for a kiss on the cheek. Unusually chipper, so I guessed she was probably tipsy, although she seemed otherwise alert.

She wore one of her old gray T-shirts—cut, ripped, and tied—turned into a sexy, nearly backless tank top. Her cutoff jean shorts were already making Madoc drool as he came up behind her, groping her ass and burying his face in her neck.

"Get a drink," she ordered, smiling as Madoc wrapped a possessive arm around her waist. And then she pinned me with her laser green stare. "And relax, okay?"

I spotted Ben outside by the pool, so I left my friends to it and trailed out to meet him.

Madoc and Fallon liked having people around, and Madoc especially loved his parties. It wasn't because he wanted to drink or act out. It was because he loved community. He loved his friends, and he liked good times and good conversation. I had absolutely no doubt that Madoc would end up mayor of Shelburne Falls one day, because that's how much he loved his family. And this town was his family.

And the idea of Fallon in a blue—or red—tailored dress with an American flag pinned to her was pretty funny, bless her heart.

I stepped through the sliding glass doors, hearing "She's Crafty" by the Beastie Boys fill the late afternoon air, and it made me smile finally. It wasn't as crowded as many of Madoc's parties, but there were a good thirty people out here. Most of them dressed in swim shorts and bikinis, while I still wore my jeans and shirt from the Loop.

Walking up to Ben, I put my hand on his bare back, but before he even had a chance to turn around, I felt that familiar awareness that always made the hair on my arms stand up when Jared was around.

Ben turned and flashed me a wide smile, but as he leaned in to kiss my cheek, I glanced over his shoulder, unable to not look.

But Jared wasn't here. I flitted my eyes around, scanning the party, but I didn't see him anywhere.

It was some weird sixth sense I had, and although it couldn't be explained, I always knew when he was close. Could've been the way my neck heated up or my skin vibrated under the surface, or maybe it was just because I expected him to be there, but as soon as I felt him, that's all I was aware of.

Couples caroused and swimmers splashed around, but as I continued to look around, I didn't find him.

He had to be here, though. His assistant, Pasha, was pouring a beer from the keg. I had spotted her purple hair.

"Are you okay?" Ben pulled back, one hand holding my waist and the other holding a plate of food.

"Yeah," I rasped, reeling myself back in. "I'm good. I just . . ." I sucked in a slow breath, trying to shake off my nerves as I pointed my thumb behind me. "I'm just going to run down to the storage and get Madoc some more bottles that he asked for, okay? I'll be right back."

Giving Ben a quick peck on the cheek, I turned around and speed walked for the house before he saw the lie in my eyes.

Of course, Madoc hadn't asked for more liquor from his dad's storage, but I needed a minute away. Veering around the few people in the kitchen and the island of food, I swung the basement door open and jogged down the stairs.

The basement was empty, as early in the party everyone usually socialized together before the women allowed their boyfriends—and husbands—to disappear down to Madoc's game room. The pool table, the skate ramp, and the leather couches all sat unused as I steered myself down the hallway and into the finished bathroom across from the storage room.

"God, baby," a man's rough whisper caught my ears just as I was escaping into the bathroom. "I can't keep my hands off you. Why do you do this to me, huh?"

His muffled voice was accompanied by shuffles and loud breathing.

There was giggling, followed by a girl's voice saying, "I don't do anything, Mr. Trent. Promise."

My eyes flared, and my stomach knotted. *Mr. Trent.*

I heard fabric rip, and the woman sucked in a breath.

Clenching my jaw, I dropped my hand from the door handle and inched toward the storage room door, which was ajar.

"Spread your legs for me," he ordered, sounding strained.

I stopped and listened, afraid to hear but afraid not to.

"Come on," he urged, his voice getting firmer. "Wider. Show me how much you want it."

Oh, my God.

That wasn't Jared. It couldn't be. But the voice was raspy, and I couldn't tell for sure.

What the hell?

I put my hand on the door to steady myself.

"Does that hurt?" He sounded amused.

"Yes," she gasped. "I'm spread so wide for you, baby."

"Do you love it?" he taunted, and I heard a zipper.

"Yes," she moaned. "Oh, God. Please. Fuck me!" Her cry carried into the hall, and my heart was racing.

Was that Juliet's voice?

"I love you," he said, and then let out a low growl as she sucked in a breath.

"Oh, Jax!" the girl cried out, and I immediately let out a long breath.

Jax. *Oh, thank God.*

Not Jared. Just Jared's brother. Also a Mr. Trent. Okay. I felt better now.

Although why was Juliet calling her boyfriend "Mr. Trent"?

I shook my head, laughing to myself. *Kinky kids.*

I turned around, taking a step, but I immediately halted. Jared stood right behind me with his arms folded over his chest. He leaned against the opposite wall and seemed completely oblivious to Jax and Juliet. His eyes were on me only.

A rush of hot anger tensed my limbs, and I steeled myself for whatever he had coming.

"How long's it been?" He jerked his chin, referring to what was happening in the storage room. "How long since you lost control like that?"

It was a rhetorical question. Maybe he actually wanted an answer, but I'd never give him one. I stood there, letting him see me strong and calm. His gaze stayed locked with mine before falling slowly down my body, and I suddenly felt very naked.

I was dressed more than most of the people here, but my faded and ripped jeans were skintight, and my flowing black tank top was nearly backless, held only by the fragile spaghetti straps. And since the top flattered my form more without a bra, I wasn't wearing one.

I felt my nipples harden against the fabric, and I knew the moment he noticed it, too.

Jared's eyes heated with hunger, and his biceps stretched the short sleeves of his black T-shirt.

You may never know what Jared was thinking, but you almost always knew what he was feeling. He was as subtle as a bomb when he was turned on.

Desire flared between my legs, and the heat spread like a ripple in a lake through my body. Jared and I had never failed in the bedroom, and it'd been so long since I'd felt as good as he made me feel.

"How about last night?" he continued, taunting. "I think you lost control then."

Ignoring my plans to escape to the bathroom—since I'd only been trying to have a quiet place to rid my head of thoughts of him and now he was here—I walked past him back down the hallway to make my way out the basement door. I wasn't talking to him.

But then I gasped as he caught me from behind and wrapped his arms around my waist.

"What are you doing?" I bit out.

His arms were like a steel band, crushing my body into his. I breathed hard, nearly stumbling with his weight falling into me.

Shit.

"Tate," he whispered in my ear, desperate. "Would it have been better if I had never left? Would you still love me if I kept living a lie?"

I turned my head away, folding my lips between my teeth.

I never wanted him miserable. Why was he trying to break my heart all over again? I'd just wanted him to stay.

I didn't understand why he needed to leave me to feel whole.

Pinpricks tingled my skin, and his breath on my neck felt like it was flowing through my blood. Having him close felt so good.

I closed my eyes, taking in a breath of air. I needed to tell him to get his hands off me, but I couldn't see straight.

But before I knew what was happening, he spun me around and lifted me up, setting me onto the pool table. He wrapped an arm around my thigh, and I whimpered as he jerked me to the end of the table. I started to fall back, but before I could right myself, he leaned down, dipping his lips to the skin of my stomach.

"Ah," I moaned, shocked at what he was doing. My chest rose and fell fast as his lips and tongue, not to mention his teeth, worked my body and left a trail of sensation below my rib cage.

I fell back onto the table, unable to stop, simply trying to keep my eyes from rolling into the back of my head.

Jared.

Oh, my God. His mouth. And his teeth, tugging at my skin as if no time had passed.

I grabbed the back of his neck, arching my body into him. "Jared, get off me," I groaned, my eyelids fluttering closed. "Please."

But then he sank his teeth into the sensitive skin on my side, and I squeezed my eyes shut, the pleasure racing inside me almost too much.

"Jared, stop!" I yelled, urging him off me even as I clutched his neck, holding him to me.

His lips left my skin, and when I opened my eyes, his nearly black stare, dark with desire, had zoned in on my exposed breast.

Oh, shit.

In the struggle, my shirt was a mess. The spaghetti strap on one shoulder had fallen down my arm, and so had the part of the shirt covering my breast.

Jared looked up at me, raising himself higher as I shook my head.

"No," I warned, knowing what he was going to do.

But he let out a low breath and sank his lips onto my skin anyway, covering my entire nipple with his mouth.

I groaned, feeling warm all over.

He swirled his tongue around my hardening flesh, catching my nipple between his teeth and drawing it out, playing with it. He went slow, diving back down to suck almost painfully hard, but I loved it.

"I said I would be back for you. You know there's only me, Tate," he pushed. "No one else can give you this."

My fist squeezed at the back of his hair, and the pool of lust in my gut instantly cemented, turning hard and cold.

I stroked his cheek with my thumb, looking down at his handsome face. "I know you loved me. I never wanted you unhappy." I spoke through my shaky breath. "But I don't trust you. You always desert me."

I pushed him away and jumped off the table, righting my clothes before I had any second thoughts about giving in.

Without looking back, I jetted up the staircase and back out to the pool, suddenly feeling the urge to go home.

Ben was standing with Madoc and Fallon—Madoc now in swim shorts—and they were all laughing as I came up to stand next to Fallon.

"Did you get the bottles?" Ben asked. "You were gone awhile."

I blinked, remembering the bottles I'd told him I was getting.

Catching Madoc's confused sideways glance at me, I just shook my head. "Couldn't find what I was looking for. No biggie. So"—I looked to Madoc, changing the subject—"how's the internship going?"

Madoc stuffed a chip in his mouth. "Good." He nodded. "I kind of hate the stuck-up pricks in my father's office, and the men are even worse, but I'll get through it."

Ben laughed, and I watched Madoc grab another handful of chips out of the bowl.

"Here," Fallon said, grabbing the bowl and shoving it into Madoc's chest. "You know you're going to eat all of them."

He shrugged and kept eating.

Fallon laughed. "You would think he was pregnant." She smiled lovingly at her husband. "He ate the sushi you brought home yesterday, and the leftovers in the fridge, and then he ordered burgers from the Mining Company. He eats constantly."

I let out a sigh, looking to Ben to gauge his reaction.

"Sushi?" he asked. "The sushi I brought you at work yesterday?"

"Tate hates sushi." A voice came from behind us, and Jared walked up to the cooler, grabbing a long neck.

Ben's eyes narrowed at Jared, clearly aggravated that he was here, but I intervened to ease Ben's mind before anything started.

"Don't worry about it," I spoke to Ben. "I thought I mentioned it, but I guess not."

Jared twisted off his cap, tossing it in the trash as he turned to look at me. He didn't break eye contact as he tipped up the bottle and took a drink.

I knew that look. The one that said he was two seconds from hitting Ben or kissing me. And both would cause a fight.

I looked to Ben, ready to get out of here. "Any interest in cutting out of here early?" I asked. "Go back to my place?"

Ben looked relieved. I hated that my issues were keeping us from having a good time, but at least some space from Jared would mean we could just relax.

Ben nodded and took my hand, leading me off.

"Everywhere you kiss her," Jared belted out to us from behind— and I noticed bystanders turning to look—"just remember that my tongue was there first."

I stopped and turned around, glaring at Jared. It wasn't so bad that people were looking, that a few girls were laughing behind their hands, or that Madoc sucked at hiding his snort.

No, what really pissed me off was being embarrassed in front of

Ben. Of Jared talking about me like I was his personal property and trying to deny me a shot at a relationship with someone else.

Just like in high school.

"Does she still like it in the morning?" he taunted. "That's when she has the most energy."

I lost my composure, mortified at what he was doing. *What the hell?*

The bystanders oohed and giggled. Jared's smirk was vile, and I arched an eyebrow, feeling Ben tense next to me as Jared tried to educate him. Telling him all the ways he knew me.

I squeezed my fists and walked up to Jared slowly.

I let my smile show through my eyes as I whispered. "He knows when I like it, Jared."

It was a lie, but Jared didn't know that. His smirk slowly fell, and the rage in his eyes was evident, even though his face appeared calm.

I turned around just in time to see Ben lunge for Jared, and I gasped as Jared reared back and Madoc jumped in to pull Ben away. "You son of a—" Ben was cut off as Madoc spun him around and walked him off, away from the crowd.

Jared pulled me into his arms, Ben forgotten, and wrapped them around my waist. "You want to play?" he charged, biting out every word so only I could hear.

"Challenge accepted, Tatum. This time I don't want you hurt," he continued, his breath falling over me as he got in my face, "and I don't want you small. I just want you. Do you hear me?" He jerked me into his body. "It will be my ring on your finger and my kids in your belly someday."

I twisted, struggling to free myself as rage kicked in, heating up my face and neck.

He bared his teeth. "Tatum Brandt is my fucking food," he growled. "They all knew it in high school, and not a damn thing has changed."

I yanked my body out of his hold and backed away, moving across the patio as he held my eyes. My hands ached to hit him, and I fisted my fingers and steeled my arms, glaring at him.

And he smiled.

"There's my wildcat," he commented, clearly seeing the anger that I couldn't contain. "You want to hit me, don't you? You want to fight and scream and challenge me back, and you know why?"

I ground my teeth together, thinking about how good it would feel to wipe that smirk off his face.

"Because you care," he finished. "You still love me, and nothing has changed."

I shook my head, and before I could give in and be the old Tate who reacted instead of rising above it, proving him right, I left. Slipping through the doors, back through the house, and out the front door.

Why did he still get to me? Why did I still . . .

I couldn't finish the thought. Tears pricked the backs of my eyes as I dug for my keys, not caring that I was leaving Ben. The day was ruined now, anyway, even if he was crazy enough to still want to spend time with me.

I groaned, feeling my cell phone vibrate against my ass. I was tempted to ignore it, but I dug it out anyway.

She said yes!

I narrowed my eyes, studying my father's text. And then closed them, feeling the first tears fall as my chest shook.

Not a damn thing has changed.

Everything changes.

CHAPTER 9

JARED

The clay of the thumbprint charm was as smooth as water as I ground it between my thumb and index finger. The tattered green ribbon had frayed along the edges after years of being handled, twisted, and abused.

But nothing had changed. It was still loved.

The green still held the same vibrant shade as the tree between our windows, and all of the small lines and curves of her tiny fingerprint had survived.

Weathered but still solid. Fragile but unbreakable.

I lifted the beer to my mouth, emptying the bottle and wishing I'd brought another.

Sitting in Madoc's empty and dark theater room, "Breath" by Breaking Benjamin playing throughout the house, I looked straight ahead at the black television screen—or screens, actually—seeing my own reflection staring back at me. And for the first time in two years, hating what I saw.

I was that guy again. The one who made her cry in high school.

The one who broke her heart and stopped being her friend. The one who was a loser.

I was better than this. Why did I get in her face? Why did I always try to back her into a wall?

"Jared." My mother's voice fell behind me, and I blinked, coming out of my thoughts.

I slipped my empty bottle into the cup holder on the recliner and stood up, grabbing my jacket and sliding my arms into it.

"I thought you'd grown up," she said, sounding far from disappointed. She must've witnessed what happened with Tate. And with her stern eyes and tight lips, she was pissed.

I looked away, hardening my armor. "One of the many things I love about you, Mother, is that you're absolutely clueless as to who I am."

Her chin instantly lifted, and hurt flashed in her eyes, even though she tried to hide it.

I looked away, shame heating my skin. She didn't show her anger, but she couldn't hide the pain in her eyes. It's not like my mom was clueless. She knew that she had burned some bridges with me.

And I almost always reminded her.

Her hand went to her stomach, and I looked down and exhaled, seeing her small frame carrying her new start.

"I'm sorry," I said, barely able to meet her eyes.

"So is that going to be a recurring thing?"

"What?" I asked. "Fighting with Tate?"

"Apologizing," she shot back.

Yeah, I did that a lot, too.

"You're not a child anymore," she scolded. "You have to start being the man you want your sons to be."

I shot my eyes up. *Sons.*

She knew how to make a point, didn't she?

"You've always bullied her." She sighed and took a seat. "Always. You might've been nicer about it when you were little, but all you had to do, even when you were eleven"—she smiled—"was hook an arm around her neck and lead her where you wanted her to go. And she always followed."

An image of eleven-year-old Tate riding on my handlebars as I had the bright idea to race up a ramp and try to fly through the air popped into my head. I'd broken a finger, and she'd needed six stitches.

"But you always protected her, too," she pointed out. "You jumped in front of her, shielding her from a fight or from danger."

I slid my hands into my pockets and watched her calm eyes look at me with love.

"But she was a girl then, Jared, and she's a woman now," she stated matter-of-factly, her tone growing harder. "A man who stands in front of a woman does nothing more than block her view. She needs a man standing next to her, so grow up."

I stopped breathing, feeling as if I'd just been slapped in the face. My mom was never motherly. And she certainly had no business giving others advice.

But fuck me, she was sounding kind of . . . smart, actually.

Tate didn't need to be handled. She was already so strong on her own, as she proved time and again. She needed someone to share things with. Someone to make her life better, not worse. Someone she could trust. Like a friend.

I used to be her friend. Whatever happened to that guy?

I shot my mother a look, never giving away that she'd gotten to me, and walked past her, up the stairs of the home theater.

"And Jared?" my mother called, and I stopped and turned my head back toward her.

"Her father is getting married," she announced. "He called tonight to give me a heads-up to keep an eye on her." And then she took a breath and looked at me pointedly. "Not that you're ever aware of anyone else's feelings but your own, but back off, okay? I'm sure she's a little tender right now."

James was getting married?

I turned around slowly as I searched my head for what that meant. He was selling the house. Tate was going to Stanford. He'd have a new wife when she came home for visits.

And where would her home be? What—or who—was the one thing, solid and constant, that she could count on?

I pushed open the fancy black curtains in my old bedroom in my old house—no doubt an upgrade Juliet had made once she and Jax took over the room after I'd moved out. Since they were still at Madoc's party, I had the place to myself, probably all night.

I threw my leather jacket on the chair in the corner and dug my cell phone out of my pocket, gazing through the forest of leaves to her darkened bedroom. No light, no movement, and no sound came from the house, but she had to be there. Her car was in the driveway.

Dialing her phone, I instantly caught sight of a small light—like a flickering star in a black sky—coming through the tree from her room. Her cell phone.

I watched as it flashed on and off with my rings, and then it went to voice mail, unanswered.

I squeezed my own phone, her silence hurting more than I wanted to admit. Tossing the phone onto the bed, I took off my shoes and socks and lifted up my window, slipping out, one arm and one leg at a time. I pressed my weight on the tree limbs, judging their strength.

After the damage done by the attempted cutting, I wasn't sure how weak the tree might be or how much heavier I might have gotten since the last time I'd climbed into her room.

Holding on to a limb above me, the familiar feel of the bark under my fingers comforting me, I stepped across the limb we'd sat on the first time we met each other and the limb she'd scraped her leg on when she was thirteen and she slipped.

Reaching her French doors, I swung them open, stepped on the railing, and leaped onto her floor.

She bolted up in bed, breathing hard, with fresh tears covering her face. She looked confused and shocked as she supported herself with her arms on the bed behind her.

"Jared?" Her voice cracked as she sniffled. "What the hell are you doing?"

I took in the sight of her pained eyes, the tears reaching her chin telling me she'd been crying for a while.

God, she killed me.

Her sadness used to give me power, making me strong. Now it just felt like a pair of pliers pinching my heart.

Her light blue tank top hugged every curve, and from the sliver of pink and thigh where the sheet didn't cover her, I could tell she was in her underwear. Her sunshine hair was parted on the side and fell over her chest in beautiful perfection. Even crying, she was the most perfect creature on the planet.

And just like twelve years ago when we'd sat next to each other in the tree for the first time, and I'd seen her sad about losing her mom recently, I didn't care who stood in my way or what I needed to do.

I just needed to be in her life.

"I heard about your dad," I told her. Every part of my body had relaxed, because this is where I was supposed to be.

She looked away, her defiant little chin lifting. "I'm fine."

I instantly walked toward the bed and leaned down, gently turning her chin back to me and putting my forehead to hers.

"I'm never letting you go again, Tate," I whispered, almost desperate. "I'm your friend forever, and if that's all I get, then that's what I'm taking, because only when you're here"—I took her hand and placed it on my heart—"do I feel like my life is worth a damn."

Her eyes pooled with more tears, and her chest rose and fell faster.

I cupped her face, rubbing circles on her wet cheek with my thumb. "Just let it go, babe. You wanna cry? Then, let it go."

She looked up at me, the tears in her eyes shaking as she searched mine, and I hoped like hell that she could find some trace of the boy who loved her unconditionally.

And then, as if seeing it, she sucked in a breath, closed her eyes, and dropped her head, shaking with her despair and letting it all go.

I sat down and pulled her into my chest, lying down and holding her tight enough to convey that I would hold her forever if she wanted me to.

Her head rested in the crook where my arm met my shoulder, and her hand lay hesitantly on my stomach as she shuddered with the tears. I brought up my legs and just held her, suddenly warm with the realization that nothing had changed. I'd first shared a bed with her about ten years ago—two kids finding an anchor in each other when life had thrown us too many storms—and lying here, with the familiar shadows of the tree's leaves dancing across the ceiling, I felt as if it was yesterday.

She sniffled and wound her hand all the way around my waist. I rubbed circles on her back.

"It's so stupid," she mumbled, the ache making her voice thick. "I should be happy, shouldn't I?"

I just kept rubbing.

She inhaled a short, shaky breath. "I like Miss Penley, and my dad won't be alone," she cried. "Why can't I be happy?"

"Because you love your mom," I said, taking my other hand and lightly brushing the hair away from her face. "And because it's been just you and him for a long time. It's hard when things change."

She tipped her head up and looked at me, her eyes still wet and sad but calmer now.

I caressed her face. "Of course you're happy for your dad, Tate."

"What if he forgets my mom?"

"How could he?" I retorted. "He has you."

She looked at me, her eyes softening, and I pulled her in closer, tucking her head under my chin. Threading my fingers through her soft hair, I grazed her scalp and then dragged my hand down the strands over and over again.

Her body relaxed into mine, slowly melting like it always did.

"You know I turn dumb when you do that," she grumbled, but I noticed the drowsy tease in her tone.

I closed my eyes, loving the feel of her slender leg sliding up over the top of mine.

"I remember," I whispered. "Now go to sleep. Tatum."

I might've heard her say, "Asshole," but I couldn't be sure.

CHAPTER 10

TATE

*C**heesecake.***

    I flopped onto my back, the pillow under my head feeling as soft as a cloud in a Disney sky after sleeping so well, and I was strangely desperate for cheesecake.

Sweet and creamy and heavenly, and I swallowed, suddenly starving to indulge.

What the . . . ?

I glanced over at the other pillow—empty, but the remnants of his body wash had lingered, and I was glad he was gone. The smell that he'd left behind was so succulent that my mouth was watering for chocolate-covered cherries, champagne, cheesecake, and . . .

Him. God, I was hungry.

It had felt so good to be in his arms last night that I'd slept better than I had in months and awoke feeling calm and excited at the same time.

Heading into the bathroom, I brushed my hair and put it up into a ponytail, washing and rinsing my face afterward. Grabbing the mouthwash, I gargled, ridding myself of the leftover bitter taste of the glass of wine I'd had when I came home last night.

I walked back into my bedroom, taking a second glance out the French doors, which were now closed, and noticed that his old bedroom window was still open.

Hesitating only a moment, I jetted down the stairs, ready to ravage the refrigerator and cabinets to make pancakes and eggs and bacon and maybe some fresh bread. And maybe a BLT.

For some reason a BLT sounded really good.

Why was I so hungry?

I jumped the last two steps and immediately straightened, hearing music coming from the dining room.

Taking a left, I rounded the entryway and halted when I spotted Jared.

The tree on his naked back stretched taller as he reached up and rolled paint in a long strip on the wall and then returned to normal as he came back down, the taut muscles in his back and arms flexing and accentuating the fact that he hadn't gotten lazy during his time away.

He was still wearing the same black pants as last night, but with his shirt off now, and I noticed his hands were splattered with drops of the café au lait color the painters were using as he rolled the thick paint onto the linen-colored walls.

"What are you doing?" I blurted.

His head turned to the side, and he glanced at me and then back to the wall, almost dismissive.

"We helped your dad paint this room, like, ten years ago, remember?"

I dug in my eyebrows, weirded out by how calm he seemed. "Yeah, I remember," I said, still confused as I walked over and turned down Seether's "Weak" coming off the iPod. "We're paying people to do it now. They'll be back to finish the job tomorrow," I told him.

He glanced at me again, a playful smile tugging at the corner of his mouth.

And then he turned his attention back to the wall, dismissing me again, to continue painting.

I stood there, wondering what I was supposed to do. Go make a breakfast that I was no longer hungry for or kick him out?

He changed hands, putting the roller in his left as he absently smeared the paint that had dripped on his right hand on his pant leg. I almost laughed. The pants looked expensive, but of course, Jared wouldn't give a shit.

I folded my arms across my chest, trying to restrain my smile.

Jared was painting my dining room. Just like ten years ago. He wasn't grabbing me, fighting with me, or trying to get in my pants, either. Very well behaved.

Also like ten years ago.

Patience and peace radiated off of him, and my heart skipped a beat, finally feeling some semblance of home for the first time in forever. It was a summer day just like any other, and the boy next door was hanging out with me.

I buried the knot of despair I'd been carrying around and walked up behind him, picking up the second roller in the tray. Stepping up to the wall perpendicular to his, I rolled on the paint, hearing his uninterrupted strokes continue behind me.

We worked in silence, and I kept stealing glances at him, nervous about whose move it was to talk or what I would say. But he just bent over, running the roller through the tray and sopping up more paint, looking completely at ease.

We took turns, collecting more paint and spreading it over the walls, and after several minutes, my heartbeat finally slowed to a gentle drumming.

Until he put his hand on my back.

At his closeness, I stiffened, but then he reached around to my other side and grabbed the stepladder to take it back to his area.

Oh.

I continued rolling paint as he stepped up and worked closer to the ceiling, using a regular paintbrush to get areas neither of us could reach with the roller. I tried to ignore his body hovering over me as I worked my paint to the edge underneath him, but I couldn't help how good it felt to have him close. Like the magnets were aligning again.

Like waking up to a summer rain tinkling against my window.

"You can't use the roller to corner," Jared spoke up, knocking me back into the moment.

I blinked, looking up to see his hand pausing midstroke on the wall and that he was staring down at me. I glanced to my roller, seeing that I'd run right into the next wall.

I mock scowled up at him. "It's working, isn't it?"

He exhaled a laugh, like I was so ridiculous, and climbed down, shoving the paintbrush at me.

"Handle that." He gestured to his brush and motioned me up the ladder. "And try not to fuck up the crown molding."

I snatched the brush out of his hand and climbed the ladder, glancing at him as I started to brush on short strokes and making sure not to cross the blue painter's tape.

Jared grinned up at me, shaking his head before resuming my sloppy painting with a smaller brush, moving vertically down the corners in slow strokes.

I took a deep breath and ventured, "So . . ." I glanced down at him. "Are you happy?" I asked. "In California. Racing . . ." I trailed off, not sure if I wanted to hear about his life out there.

He kept his eyes on his task, his voice thoughtful. "I wake up," he started, "and I can't wait to get into the shop to work on the bikes. Or the car . . . ," he added. "I love my job. It happens in a hundred different rooms, cities, and arenas."

I could have guessed that much. From what I'd seen of his career through the media, he had looked in his element. Comfortable, thriving, driven . . .

He hadn't answered the question, though.

"I breathe fresh air all day every day," he went on, leaning down to give Madman a quick pet, and my brushstrokes slowed as I listened to him. "I love racing, Tate. But honestly, it's a means to a bigger end." He looked up at me, giving a half smile. "I started my own business. I want to build custom rides."

My eyes went wide, and I stopped painting.

"Jared, that's . . ." I stammered, trying to get the words out. "That's really amazing," I said, finally smiling. "And it's a relief, too. That you'll be off the track, I mean. I'm always afraid you'll get in an accident when I see you on TV or YouTube."

His eyebrows drew together, and I winced.

Shit.

"You watch?" he asked in an amused tone, looking at me like I'd been caught.

I pursed my lips and redirected my attention back to painting. "Of course I watch," I grumbled.

I heard him laugh under his breath as he started painting again, too.

"It'll still mean some travel," he continued, "but less than what I do now. Plus, I can build the business back here if I want."

Back here?

So he might want to come back home, then? I looked away, liking the idea of him moving back, and I wasn't sure why. It wasn't like I was going to be here anymore, anyway.

He let out a sigh, regarding his work on the wall. "I love the wind out there on the track, Tate. On the highways." He shook his head, looking almost sad. "It's the only time you and I are together."

I looked back down at him, a lump swelling my throat.

I saw his Adam's apple bob as he swallowed. "I never wanted

other women." His thick voice was practically a whisper. "I left so I could be a man for you. So I could come back to you."

I dropped my eyes, slowly stepping down the ladder.

That was what had been so hard to understand. He had to go off and find himself—cutting me out of his life—by breaking up with me under the guise of not wanting to hold me back while he took however many years to get his shit together?

I locked my eyes on his dark ones and looked up at him, seeing a man who was so much the same, and yet, so different.

But maybe it hadn't been a guise after all.

Maybe I was lucky, because I always knew where my direction pointed me, and I had it figured out. Maybe Jared had had too many downward spirals, too many distractions, and too much doubt to know what truly drove him.

Maybe Jared, like most people, needed the space to grow on his own.

Maybe we had just started too young.

"And what about the next time you need to shut me out, Jared?" I asked, licking my parched lips. "It was three years in high school. Two years this time."

He put his hand on my cheek, his thumb grazing the corner of my mouth. "It wasn't two years, babe."

I eyed him. What was he talking about?

He bent down, wetting his paintbrush some more. "I came back at Christmas that same year. You were . . ." He hesitated, rolling the paint onto the wall. "You had moved on."

I averted my eyes, because I knew right away what he was talking about.

"What did you see?" I asked, fiddling with the brush. I shouldn't feel bad. I had every right to move on, after all.

He shrugged. "Only as much as I could handle. Which wasn't a lot." He glanced at me, holding my eyes.

I could tell he was trying to keep his temper in check.

"I showed up one night," he began. "I'd just gotten started on the circuit, racing and making connections. I was feeling good and"—he nodded—"really confident, actually. So I came home."

Six months. Only six months.

"I knew you were mad at me. You wouldn't talk when I called or text back, but I was finally a little proud of myself, but I was never going to be truly happy without you, too." He dropped his voice to nearly a whisper. "I showed up, and you were with someone."

He blinked a few times, and I felt my stomach roll because I'd hurt him. I wanted to throw up.

Is that what Pasha had been talking about? The time she saw him almost cry?

But I shouldn't feel bad about this. Jared had had sex with numerous women before we were together, and I'm sure plenty since we'd been apart.

"It was six months, Jared." I grabbed some paper towels and turned to him, cleaning up the paint on his hands. "I'm sure you had been with someone else by that point."

He stepped closer, reaching up to play with a lock of my hair. "No," he whispered. "I hadn't been with anyone."

My eyes shot up. "But . . ." I winced, my gut clenching. "I saw you. I saw girls everywhere around you. At the tracks, hanging on you in pictures . . ."

I hadn't moved on because I thought he had, but I never thought he was holding back, either. I assumed . . .

He let out a hard sigh, turning back to his painting. "The girls come with the crowd, Tate. Sometimes they want pictures with the drivers. Other times they just hang around like groupies. I never wanted anyone but you. That's not why I left."

A flutter swarmed through my chest, and I knew that my heart still wanted him, too. No one else had even held a candle to him.

"It was so hard living without you, Tate." His voice sounded weary. "I wanted to see you and talk to you, and I'd lived so long with you as the center of everything, I just . . ." He hesitated, his voice turning thick. "I didn't know who I was or what I was going to offer you. I relied on you too much."

I looked down, realizing that he'd been wiser than me. Jared left because he knew he needed me too much. I hadn't realized how much I needed him until he was already gone.

"I relied on you, too." I choked over my words. "I said it in my monologue senior year, Jared. You were something I looked forward to every day. After you left, I constantly felt as if the wind had been knocked out of me."

In our senior year of high school, when I'd finally had enough of my childhood friend bullying me, I stood up in front of the whole class and shared our story. The loss, the heartbreak, the pain . . . They didn't know what they were hearing, but it didn't matter. I was only speaking to Jared anyway.

His timid eyes urged me as he said, "And now?"

I sighed as I absentmindedly dipped the brush in paint. "And now," I led in, "I know I can stand on my own. No matter what happens, I'll be okay."

He looked back to the wall, responding almost sadly. "Of course you will." And then he asked, "So are *you* happy?" He repeated my own question to him back to me, and I wondered why he asked that. I'd just said I'd be okay.

But I guess he knew that didn't exactly mean I was happy, either. *No.*

No, I wasn't happy. He had been a piece of the puzzle, and nothing had filled the space in his absence.

I ignored the question and kept painting.

"Do you have anyone out there now?" I ventured. "Anyone you're seeing?"

I brushed the wall in short, quick strokes, like I was petting Madman, as I watched him warily.

He dipped the brush into the paint. "After I saw that you'd

moved on, I tried to as well," he told me. "I've seen a couple of women since then, but . . ." He stopped and gave me a teasing sideways glance. "No one's waiting for me."

I cocked an eyebrow, digging the brush into the wall. *A couple of women.*

Now I was jealous.

"I'm proud of you for getting into Stanford." He changed the subject, throwing me off. "Are you excited?" he asked.

I nodded, giving him a tight smile. "Yeah, I am. It'll be a lot of work, but I thrive on it, so . . ." I trailed off, swallowing the lump in my throat.

I did want to go to California. And I definitely wanted to go to medical school. But I didn't want to think about how things were changing forever back here. My dad's marriage. The house going on the market. Having Jared close, but not having Jared.

He stopped painting and looked at me pointedly. "What's the problem?"

"There's no problem," I retorted.

He approached me, cocking his head like he knew I was lying. Like he knew I still wasn't happy.

I lifted my shoulders to my ears, denying it. "I said there's no problem!" I laughed and then looked down. "And you're dripping all over my feet!"

I curled in my toes as paint from his brush fell onto my skin.

"Oh, shit," he said in surprise and lifted the brush up, smacking me in the face.

I growled, squeezing my eyes shut.

"Oh, shit!" Jared blurted out again, laughing. "I'm sorry. It honestly was an accident."

"Yeah." I opened my eyes again, squinting through the paint covering my lashes on my left eye. "Accidents happen."

And then I shot out, running my paintbrush down his face and chest, sending him rearing backward.

"No!" he shouted, holding out his hands and still laughing. "Stop!"

I lunged for him again, and he darted out his paint brush, wetting my arm.

I scowled. "Ugh!" I barked. "You're going to pay for that!"

And I raced after him as he dashed into the foyer. Reaching out my arm, I caught him on the back, swiping my brush up and making the tree tattooed there look a little snow covered.

He swung around and grabbed my wrist, pulling my back into his chest.

I squirmed, sending his brush falling to the area rug.

"Let go!" he ordered, tickling my sides. "Drop it now!"

"No!" I laughed, keeping my elbows locked at my sides to shield myself from his attack.

He grabbed my wrist, pulled it up, exposing my underarm, and tickled. I hunched over, crying out in a mix of terror and delight as my own paintbrush fell to the floor.

"Jared! Stop!" I shouted, my stomach tight with laughing so hard.

He let go, wrapping both of his arms around my waist, and we just stood there, breathing hard as we tried to calm down.

It felt so good. Having fun with him again.

I laid my arms on his, my breath catching in my throat but my heart still racing as I soaked in his heat at my back. My tank top was the only fabric separating his skin from mine, and without thinking, I turned my head, nuzzling into him.

His hot breath fell on my ear, and I leaned into it, feeling the clenching of the muscles in my womb and wanting his touch.

It had been so long since I'd been touched like this. The feel of Jared's lips against my hair was more intimate than the most sexual act anyone else could do to me.

I tipped my chin up, teasing him with my lips as they grazed his. A thrill shot through me, sending flutters through my stomach as I felt him grow hard against my ass.

I inhaled his scent. "Jared," I barely whispered. I darted out my tongue and flicked it along his top lip.

He jerked, sucking in a breath, and I felt a shot of pride at still being able to leave him speechless.

Craning one hand around my face to hold my mouth close to his, he teased, "I thought we were going to be friends." And then I gasped as he brought his other hand over my shoulder and slid it down the top of my shirt, claiming my breast in his palm.

I closed my eyes on a moan. "Good friends," I clarified. "Really good friends." And I felt his lips curl into a smile against mine.

"Tate!"

A knock sounded on the door, and I jumped, blinking.

What?

No.

"Tate, you up?" Fallon said, and I looked at Jared, feeling my body suddenly go cold. *Damn it.*

The ache where I needed him made me groan, and I watched him blink long and hard, letting out a frustrated sigh.

"Fuck," he seethed, letting me go.

I could still feel him through his pants, standing strong and hard, and it was for me. *Goddamn it, Fallon!*

She opened the door, and we both straightened, knowing how guilty we looked. I was sure I had a blush all over my body. I could feel the heat of my skin.

"Oh." She stopped short, her forehead scrunching up. "Hey."

I shifted my eyes, smoothing down my clothes. "We were painting."

Jared snorted behind me, but I ignored him.

Fallon nodded. "In your jammies," she said more to herself than to us. "Perfectly normal."

I arched a brow at her as she stood there in her workout shorts and tank. We ran on Sundays, and I was late.

"Jared?" I cleared my throat, unable to hide the amusement from my face as I turned around. "Go home."

He shot me his little know-it-all smirk, and I jerked when he brushed his palm over my ass and then walked past me, out the front door. Leaning down, he gave Fallon a peck on the forehead. "Your timing sucks," he grumbled and walked past her.

CHAPTER 11

TATE

My friends each brought something different into my life.

Juliet believed that love conquered all and everyone deserved a white-picket-fence life. Fallon believed that choices came with confusion, and if we truly knew what we wanted, then there was no choice. Jax believed opportunities shouldn't be wasted, and the bigger the risk, the bigger the reward.

And Madoc was like me. He was the one I listened to when I wanted to hear my own opinion in a deeper voice.

And the best part about him was that I was a separate entity from Jared to him. He cared about my well-being, even if it didn't serve the interest of his friend.

Sorry about your party, I texted him after I got back from my run with Fallon. I'd produced enough drama over the past two years, and I always felt like I wasn't carrying my weight as a friend. Madoc never cared, though.

Madoc: Nothing to be sorry for. You okay?

I grabbed an apple and jogged up the stairs, desperate for a shower, as my clothes were sticking to my skin.

Yes, I typed. I'll be okay. Don't worry.

Madoc: You need to talk to Ben.

I halted, dropping my head back and sighing. *Jesus.* It was like he could read my mind.

I tapped my thumbs on the keys, sending my reply. I don't even know what's happening yet, okay?

Madoc shot back. Yes, you do.

I rolled my eyes, kicking off my shoes and hitting the power on my iPod dock, hearing "The Boys of Summer" by the Ataris spring forth.

My phone beeped again. Okay, screw Jared. Answer me this . . . do you think about Ben?

I plopped my phone down on the sink and stared at myself in the mirror. I wasn't ignoring his question. He just didn't need to hear the answer.

Sure, I thought about Ben. I didn't think about him like I thought about Jared, though, and that's what had me a little ashamed.

Ben and I hadn't committed to seeing only each other, and we hadn't gotten intimate yet. But I knew he wanted that. Hell, he'd wanted it in high school.

But we were dating, and if Fallon hadn't walked in this morning, I would've gone over the edge with Jared, despite any obligation I might have to Ben.

My phone beeped with another text, and I looked down, almost kicking myself that I'd texted Madoc at all this morning.

Do you want him, need him, and live for him? Madoc asked.

I shook my head, smiling at my friend's insight. *Yeah, okay.* So whether or not Jared was a factor, I still wasn't getting carried away and feeling all lovey-dovey about Ben. Point taken.

Does he make you horny? Madoc continued, and I snatched up my phone again.

"Seriously?" I blurted out at his crass vocabulary.

Do you want to crawl all over him in the morning? he went on, and I let out a loud sigh.

Yeah. Shut up now.

I jutted out my thumbs, typing to tell him just that, when another text rolled in before I finished.

What the hell? Did he take lessons in speed texting?

Does he give you a lady boner? he teased. Make your loins quiver and throb? Do you masturbate to him?

"Madoc!" I growled at my phone, squeezing it tight. "What the . . . ?"

Why so quiet? My phone beeped again. Answer my questions, Tate!

Motherf . . . I clenched my teeth. "I'd talk if you'd just shut up, jackass," I fumed.

He texted again, and I just slumped my shoulders, walking back into the bedroom, defeated.

Okay, real quick: Ben or Jared? he inquired.

Huh?

Ben or Jared? he urged again. Don't think. Just say the first name that pops into your head.

My mouth fell open, exhaling a frustrated sigh. "Wha . . ."

Ben or Jared!!! he text-screamed.

My thumbs shook as I tried to type, but my brain felt like little electric wires were zapping every hair follicle on my scalp.

I squeezed the phone, trying to find the letters.

Now! he beeped.

"Ugh!" I plopped down on my bed, crashing back on the mattress and pounding the sides with my fists, giving up.

Jerk.

I pinched the bridge of my nose, trying to remember what the point of the conversation had been.

Madoc was Madoc. He'd drive you crazy with fifteen questions so you'd figure out the answer on your own, rather than take two seconds to give you the answer himself. He felt the journey was more important than the destination.

Just like me.

I slipped my hand into my hair and rubbed my scalp, exhaling a laugh at the irony.

My phone beeped in my palm, and I groaned.

Gosh, you're quiet today.

I shook my head, amused and exhausted at the same time. I brought my phone up above me, typing my response.

Very funny.

His response came immediately. Shall I tell you what to do?
Yes, I replied.

But you already know.

I typed quickly. Tell me anyway.

His text took only a moment. You tell the guy you're dating that your boyfriend's back.

I let my arms drift back down to the bed as I closed my eyes, sighing. *Yeah, that's what I was thinking, too.*

My phone beeped again. And he's gonna be in trouble . . .
What the . . . ?

Hey-la,hey-la, my boyfriend's back, he continued singing, and laughter tickled my throat.

"You're on crack," I whispered to myself.

I bit my lip between my teeth, and the warm sensation of anticipation started filling me for the first time in years. I brought up my phone and typed.

You see him comin', better cut out on the double, I continued the lyrics, smiling.

He texted again as I headed for the bathroom to shower.

Very good, my young Padawan. Very good.

After I'd showered and cleaned up, I put on some old jean shorts and a black T-shirt to work on my car. Despite the lack of rain—my favorite kind of weather—the sky was beautiful, with barely any clouds, and the light breeze blew the fragrant summer scents through all the windows in the house.

I bounced down the stairs—with new energy in my step—and stopped to listen wistfully at the boys' music carrying through the air from next door. I glanced out the window and spotted Madoc, Jax, and Jared all hanging outside around Jax's Mustang and looking under the hood.

Jared had changed into jeans, and he had a white T-shirt hanging out of his back pocket, and oh, my God . . . a light layer of sweat cooled my back as I took in the sight of the smooth, muscular slope of his back from his neck down to his waist.

The sun beat down on his bare skin, good tunes completed the scene, and I didn't want to be anywhere else.

Heading into my garage, I hit the door opener, the wash of sunlight hitting the tires and then the hood and front windshield of my dad's old Chevy Nova.

I grabbed a clean shop cloth off a worktable and slipped it into my back pocket before tying up my hair into a ponytail.

My feet tingled inside my ratty old black Chucks, so before I could chicken out, I walked outside.

I immediately felt Jared's eyes on me as I unlocked my car, reached in the driver's side door, and popped the hood. I was trying not to look across my yard to where he was, but then I realized that was a little childish.

So I looked over as I lifted the hood and saw Fallon heading toward me. Behind her was Jared, with his back to me and looking over his shoulder. Those damn brown eyes weren't on my face, though.

With his eyebrows pinched together, he looked almost angry as his gaze slid up my legs, slowly traveling up my thighs and to my waist. The legion of butterflies you usually get on a roller coaster was now fluttering between my legs, and I breathed out a slow breath to calm myself down.

His hungry gaze met mine, and then he turned around, a model of control.

But that's the thing. If Jared hadn't really changed that much, then the need he was feeling wasn't being forced away.

It was collecting.

And fuck me if I was in his line of sight when it overloaded.

I dove into my garage, assembling the few tools I'd need as Fallon grabbed a stool from the workbench to hang out with me while she watched. "Wish You Hell" by Like a Storm carried over from Jax's yard, and I busied myself, diving under my hood to perform maintenance work.

During the next hour, Juliet arrived after finishing her volunteer tutoring sessions at the high school. She dashed over, gave Jax a seriously long kiss, and then joined Fallon and me as I replaced some spark plugs, cleaned out some connections, and performed the regular weekly stuff like checking my oil and the pressure on my tires.

"Hey."

I looked up from under the hood to see Jared's assistant, Pasha, approach.

"Mind if I hang out?" she asked.

I jerked my chin to another stool. "Of course not. Have a seat."

She hopped up on the stool, lifting her glasses to the top of her head. She was quiet and cute, and I was really relieved that she seemed easy to get along with, despite her attitude.

Even with the jet black hair with purple chunks, and the eyebrow piercings and studded black belt, she still looked incredibly innocent. She wore skinny jeans and a black and gray flannel shirt, rolled up at the sleeves. Her hair was curled into loose waves, and other than the heavy makeup on her eyes, she was fresh faced.

Juliet kicked her flats to the ground and put her feet up on a footrest on the stool. "So Madoc's pressuring you pretty hard?" she asked Fallon, continuing their conversation about Madoc wanting kids.

Fallon nodded, swallowing the drink she'd just taken from her water bottle. "Yeah," she said with a sigh. "I mean, he's not giving me a guilt trip or anything, but damn . . ." She laughed.

I grinned, gazing over under my eyelashes to watch Jared get down on the ground to reach under the car for something. His thick arms, smeared with grease, the sun and sweat on his tight stomach . . .

I looked away.

"Hi," I heard a male voice behind me.

I dipped my head, getting out from under the hood to see Ben.

"Hey," I blurted out, surprised.

He had his hands in his pockets, and he smiled, looking expectant. Or hesitant.

I pulled out my shop cloth and wiped the few smudges from my hands. Fallon and Juliet had stopped talking, Pasha had gotten up to go explore my garage, and Ben and I had an ocean between us.

It wasn't easy like it had been two days ago.

I looked to my friends, trying to appear calm. "Just a minute, you guys," I told them, and I didn't miss the glance they exchanged.

I inched past Ben, giving us some space beyond their ears.

Standing close, it was hard to meet his eyes, but I did. "Ben, I'm really sorry about the past couple of days," I spoke softly. "I know things have been awkward."

My gut twisted, and I didn't want to hurt him. I almost wished he was a jerk so this could be easier.

"I know." He nodded, looking around before meeting my eyes. "But I think I know why."

His eyes flashed to Jax's house, and I followed his gaze, seeing Jared with his back to us, but leaning his hands on the hood and peering over his shoulder, watching.

"He doesn't pull my strings," I explained. "Medical school is looming, and with the house going up for sale, everything is just—"

"So he's not the reason I haven't slept over?" Ben interrupted. "Or barely gotten you alone in two days?"

He wasn't mad. His raised eyebrows and gentle tone told me he already knew the answers. It wasn't that Ben expected sex, but he knew it was the next step between us. I'd been warm, and now I'd gone cold.

I frowned, wishing he wasn't right.

I knew I still wanted Jared. The chemistry hadn't changed, and no matter what we failed at, we were great in the bedroom.

But there was still love there, too. More than ever, actually. I didn't know if I wanted him back, and I wasn't ready to make that decision yet, but I knew I didn't want Ben with the same passion.

And he didn't deserve anything less.

He gave me a sad smile and leaned in. "I'm glad you gave me a shot." He kissed my cheek. "Good luck at Stanford."

And he turned around, walking back to his car.

I watched him go, feeling a little regretful. He'd made it too easy for me. But no matter what happened, it was the right thing to do.

I turned around, refusing to meet Jared's eyes, because I knew he was still watching, and I headed back for my car. Pasha still stood in the garage, looking after Ben's ride as he sped off down the street, while Juliet and Fallon had continued their conversation.

"Well." Fallon rubbed her neck, acting like they hadn't been trying to eavesdrop. "I'm determined to make the most of this time with just the two of us, but you know Madoc . . ." She trailed off, sounding amused. "The more the merrier. He wants five. I said one. We compromised at five."

Juliet busted up laughing, and I realized they were still talking about Madoc's plans to knock up his wife ASAP. Fallon had two years of graduate school at Northwestern, though, so I knew she'd rather wait.

"Is this your mom?" Pasha called out.

I looked up to see her leaning over a workbench, regarding a frame on the wall. I knew the picture that hung there. My mom, dad, and me at Disneyland when I was five.

"Yeah," I answered, fastening the last cap under my hood.

"How did she pass away?" she asked.

I shot my eyes over to her, confused. "How did you know my mom died?"

Her mouth fell open slightly, and she hesitated.

"Um . . . I," she stammered, her eyebrows doing a nosedive as she searched for words. "Well, I . . ."

And then she huffed out a breath, looking at me with an apology in her eyes.

"He kind of has me send flowers to her grave every year on April fourteenth," she admitted, wincing.

I stood frozen, my hand on the cap while I gaped at Pasha. "What?" I whispered, in too much shock.

"Tate." Juliet's mouth hung open, and I saw her eyes tear up.

I darted my eyes over to Jared, seeing him let the hood drop closed and smile at his brother, a joke passing between them.

"Please don't tell him I told you," Pasha grumbled. "He'll bitch, and then I'll have to listen to it."

Flowers. He sent my mother flowers.

How had I not known that?

I guess I still would've been at college every April, but my father should've known. Wouldn't he have told me?

"What are they doing?" Fallon spoke up, and I looked to see her confused expression focusing over at the guys all slipping on their shirts and hopping in the Mustang with Jared in the driver's seat.

"Jax?" Juliet called, standing up.

He stuck his top half out the passenger side window, looking at her over the hood. "We're just taking the car for a test drive!" he shouted over the deep rumble of the engine. "Be right back!"

Jared slipped on his black sunglasses and gripped the wheel, the tight cords of his forearm visible from here. He shot me a quick glance, the hint of a smile on his lips, before jacking up the music and backing out of the driveway.

And, as if the thunder had only been waiting for the lightning, he roared down the street like a tempest that could not be contained.

My heart fluttered, wanting to be a part of the storm.

I smiled at my friends. "Get in the car."

"What?" Juliet's back straightened, and Fallon started rubbing her hands together.

"Aw, yeah," she teased, standing up.

"What are we doing?" Juliet asked, looking nervous as Pasha stepped forward.

I ignored the question and simply waggled my eyebrows, ready for some mischief, as all three of them piled into my G8.

CHAPTER 12

JARED

"So . . ." Madoc rested his arm on the passenger side door, tapping his fingers as I drove. "Two days. You still haven't lost your touch, huh?"

I held the steering wheel with my left hand, my arm steel-rod straight as I pressed my back into the seat. "What do you mean?"

"She just broke up with Ben," he pointed out, talking about Tate. "You know that's what that was about just now."

I pulled down into fourth, picking up speed. "I don't know shit."

"Don't give me that," he retorted. "You're already planning how you're going to get in her bed tonight."

I exhaled a laugh, glancing out the window. *Fuckin' Madoc.*

When I saw Ben show up, I'd immediately tensed, hating how he looked at her. Knowing what he wanted from her. I had no idea if they were really sleeping together, and I didn't care. As far as I was concerned, she was done killing time.

Madoc was wrong. I didn't want in her bed. I mean, I wanted that, but most of all, I just wanted her back.

"I've got an idea," Jax piped up from the backseat.

I met his eyes in the rearview mirror, seeing his fingers locked on top of his head as he slouched down in the seat.

"What's that, little brother?" Madoc inquired.

Jax smirked at me as he spoke to Madoc. "Well, he could just get over it and ask her to marry him already."

I instantly froze, staring out the front windshield.

Marry. My fist tightened around the steering wheel, wondering how my brother thought that either of us was ready for that. Or was he just tossing any crazy idea out there?

I never thought I wouldn't marry Tate. But it still seemed far off.

Madoc was looking at me, and I knew Jax was waiting for a reaction, but this was none of their business. I wanted Tate forever, but first I needed to get her back. Why the hell would she say yes now?

Jax cleared his throat. "You two have loved each other the longest," he said softly. "Doesn't seem right that you'll be the last to get married."

My eyes shot up, locking with his in the mirror. "What?" I blurted out.

"You little shit." Madoc twisted his head, regarding Jax with shock.

The last to get married? Meaning . . .

Jax's eyes dropped to his lap, and I'd never seen him so vulnerable. "I can't sleep without her next to me," he almost whispered about Juliet. "I love coming home and smelling her cooking. Seeing how warm she makes the house." He still wasn't looking at either of us, and my chest felt tight.

"She gives me everything," he continued, looking up at both of us. "I want to give her my name. I'm going to ask her."

"When?" Madoc asked, and I was surprised he could talk, because I was still trying to wrap my head around it.

Jax was going to ask Juliet to marry him.

"After Zack's bachelor party on Friday," he answered. "I'm guessing that after she becomes my fiancée, going to strip clubs will probably be on my list of don'ts."

Shit. The bachelor party. The one I wasn't planning on attending, since I didn't think I'd be in town.

I'd forgotten about that.

Zack, Jax's partner at the Loop, who helped run races, had been engaged for as long as I'd known him. Finally ready to take the leap, he'd sent out a mass e-mail, inviting every guy in town over the age of twenty-one to Wicked, a high-end club about a half hour away.

I was surprised Fallon and Juliet were letting them go at all. Well, not Fallon, actually. She never struck me as the jealous type.

I gave a casual glance behind me, trying to hide the doubt I was feeling. Not that my brother wouldn't make a good husband or Juliet a good wife, but he was still only twenty-one.

"Jax," I started. "Are you sure—"

"Hey," Madoc cut in. "What the hell?" He peered out through my open driver's side window.

I followed his gaze, my eyebrows instantly drawing together. *What the . . . ?*

Tate pulled up on my side in her G8, with Fallon riding shotgun, and Juliet and Pasha in the back.

She sat in her seat, looking comfortable and casual, and I shook my head at her, because she was in the oncoming lane.

"You're in the wrong lane!" I shouted to Fallon's closed window.

She stuck her hand behind her ear, mouthing, *What?* and then turned to Tate, both of them smiling.

"What the hell are they doing?" Jax sat up, resting his arms over the front seat.

I glanced ahead, noticing the stop sign, and shot out my foot, coming to a screeching halt.

Shit.

Tate stopped, too, and she and Fallon bounced forward with the sudden movement.

I darted my head out. "Roll down your window!" I shouted, shifting my gaze past the stop sign to watch for oncoming cars.

Was she trying to get them all hurt?

Tate's mouth curled in amusement, but Fallon was full-on smiling as she rolled down the window.

"Where are you guys going?" Madoc shouted before I had a chance.

"Doesn't matter." Fallon shrugged. "We'll be going too fast for you to follow."

My eyes widened, while Madoc and Jax laughed, feigning insult. "Ohhhh."

Madoc nudged my arm. "They're talking shit, Jared," he egged me on, and I bit back the smile as I felt the rush in my muscles.

Stepping out of the car—since the street was dead anyway—I walked to Tate's car and leaned down to Fallon's window.

"Is that a challenge?" I asked Tate.

She shook her head, trying to brush me off. "I wouldn't waste my time," she taunted. "I've already beaten you once."

I smiled, arching an eyebrow. "Have you?" I jabbed back, insinuating that I'd let her win our one and only race four years ago.

Her face fell, turning stern with pursed lips, as she focused back on the road, revving the engine.

I walked back to my car, laughing under my breath. "Put on your seat belts," I ordered Madoc and Jax as I climbed in and buckled up myself.

Madoc quickly grabbed for his seat belt, his breath shaky with amusement. I revved the engine, seeing Tate eye me as she did the same. I loved the look of mischief on her face.

"Guys," Jax inched out. "The cops look the other way for like five minutes on Saturday nights when my crew does this, but—"

"You have your seat belt on?" Madoc interrupted, yelling through my window to Fallon. "Get it on!" he ordered his wife.

"You, too." I heard Jax shout and turned to see Juliet saluting him. "Shit," he cursed behind me, and I knew he hated what was about to happen.

Madoc tuned the iPod to Mötley Crüe's "Girls, Girls, Girls," and I looked at him.

He shrugged, looking innocent. "Don't look at me. It's on your iPod, man."

I rolled my eyes, not willing to explain that I wasn't the one loading music onto it. Pasha liked to mess with me. Every once in a while, a Britney Spears or Lady Gaga song wound up tucked between a Slipknot and a Korn song.

Regardless, I jacked up the volume and turned down the air-conditioning. The heat outside kept me irritable and alert. A lesson I'd learned over the past two years.

I heard "Blow Me Away" by Breaking Benjamin spilling out of Tate's speakers, and I looked over, shaking my head and unable to hide the smile.

"You ready?" I shouted.

"You sure?" she shot back.

Little . . . Did she forget that I did this for a living?

"Right on Main, go through two stop lights," I dared her, "and the first one back to the houses wins," I told her.

Without hesitation, she nodded.

"Ready!" Madoc shouted, and Tate and I both revved our engines again and again, looking at each other, my foot getting heavier by the second.

"Set!" Madoc called again, and Fallon's excitement overcame her as her arm smacked the outside of her door over and over again.

Tate met my eyes, and then we both turned back to the road, ready.

"Go!" Madoc roared, and all hell broke loose.

"Shit!" I hissed.

Tate and I shot off, but she must've been sitting in second gear, because she didn't hesitate to pick up speed as she shot forward and then cut right in front of me, just in time to miss the pickup truck that sat at the stop sign ahead of us.

"I told you she was good," Jax said matter-of-factly, but I ignored him.

Slamming down into second and then up into third, I punched the gas, swerving to the left, now that she'd taken my lane, and sped up beside her.

Madoc held on to the handle above the door, glancing over at them anxiously. I shifted down into fourth, inching ahead and thankful for the deserted street.

"Jared, get over in the other lane," Jax advised.

"What do you think I'm trying to do?" I barked, pushing the gas until I'd gotten up to sixth.

Looking ahead, I spotted a white sedan headed our way, and my heart lodged in my throat, seeing it in my line of driving.

My neck craned to see Tate, a flash of fire in her eyes, and she shook her head at me, telling me not to even try it.

"Jared," Jax warned as Madoc held on.

I floored it, staying head to head with Tate.

"Jared!" Jax yelled, and I heard the white sedan honking frantically.

Tate's scared eyes flashed to mine, and I smiled. Twisting the wheel, the muscles aching in my arms, I put the front and back driver's side tires on the curb, feeling the car bottom out before I got the angle I needed.

"Goddamn it!" Jax cursed, and Madoc laughed.

The white car zoomed between Tate's and my rides, still honking. I looked over, seeing Tate turning her head nervously to look behind her, so I took my shot.

Powering ahead, I picked up ten more miles per hour and jerked the wheel to the right, into her lane with just enough space to cut her off.

"Whoo!" Madoc roared, and I caught sight of Jax in my rearview mirror with his head back, hands over his eyes.

I shook my head and tipped my chin down, focusing in on the road ahead. Luckily, this street didn't allow curb parking, so there was plenty of room and no vehicles hiding pedestrians.

Coming up on Main, I braked, spinning the wheel to the right and shifting down to reduce the car's speed.

"Go, go!" Madoc shouted as I heard Tate's tires screech behind me.

I glanced in my rearview mirror and noticed that she spun out, but she recovered almost as quickly.

"Everyone keep your eyes open," I gritted out. "There's going to be a shitload of people up here."

While Sundays were sleepy in the neighborhoods—until afternoon, anyway—the center of town was always bustling. People shopped, lunched, took in a movie, or just enjoyed the square.

I sped ahead, while Tate weaved back and forth behind me, trying to get a look at what was ahead. I could also see the excited movements of the other three girls.

"Oh, shit!" Jax yelled, and I jerked my eyes back to the road.

I slammed on the brakes—seeing a company van backing out of a driveway and into the street—while Tate swerved around me, taking the oncoming lane to go around and zoom ahead of me.

"Fuck!" I growled, jerking the wheel and following behind her.

"Why didn't you just go around?" Jax shouted, taking off his seat belt and moving closer to the front.

"Piss off," I barked and then looked ahead at her significant gain. "God, she's good."

I heard Jax swallow. "Yeah, she's got great reflexes. Better than you, apparently."

Shifting into fifth, I picked up speed and then punched into sixth, starting to see the first stoplight ahead.

"Come on," Madoc urged, and I pushed my back hard into the seat, squeezing the wheel.

Juliet and Pasha kept turning around, checking us out through the back window. Pedestrians on the sidewalk started taking notice, and I spotted them in my rearview mirror spinning around to watch the two speeding assholes—as they were probably calling us right now—barrel down their street. Some guys went wide-eyed, pointing as both our cars raced by, and I heard a cheer through the open windows.

The light ahead turned red, and Tate slammed on her brakes, the high-pitched screeching bringing everyone's attention outside straight to us.

I punched the brakes with everything I had, skidding to a halt right next to her.

"Oh, shit!" someone outside shouted. "It's Jared and Tate!"

But my eyes were on her.

She watched the stoplight, glancing anxiously at me and biting away the smile from her bottom lip. I could tell her leg was bouncing up and down, because her shoulders and head looked like they were vibrating.

"Jax," I said, breathing hard. "You still in good with the cops?"

"Yeah," he answered in a hesitant tone. "Why?"

"Because." And I looked up at the traffic cam perched on top of the stoplight, and glancing left to right and seeing no immediate cars, slammed my back into the seat and gassed it, speeding through the red light.

"Motherfu—!" I heard Tate's curse, but her voice trailed off as I sped away.

Madoc tipped his head back, busting up with laughter, while Jax snorted close to my ear.

People outside cheered, howling and laughing. I glanced in my rearview mirror to see Tate, inching through the stoplight, following my lead, and then taking off when she realized it was safe.

I shifted into fourth and then fifth—the hot summer sun was nothing compared to the lava raging under my skin.

God, I fucking loved her.

Even being on the track—which I loved—wasn't as good as the high I felt when she was near me.

"Jared," Jax warned. "Slow down."

I looked ahead, a smile teasing my jaw.

"Jared," he said again, his voice harder.

I ignored him, shifting my eyes from left to right, looking for danger as I approached the next stoplight.

"Jared!" Madoc shouted, and I punched into sixth, my heart racing and my breathing hitching painfully in my chest.

"Oh, shit!" Jax howled, and we all held our breaths as the light just turned to green, and I flew through the intersection without slowing down.

And then I let out a breath, safely getting to the other side.

"Oh, thank God," Madoc gasped and then looked at me. "You're such an asshole."

I sucked in air. "What?" I acted innocent. "It was green."

Tate gained on my ass, but then I saw her skid into a left turn behind me.

"What?" I said more to myself than to the guys, watching her in my rearview mirror.

"She's cutting through the school," Jax guessed, looking out the window behind him.

"Shit," I hissed, remembering the gates were open for Sunday track practices. She could drive into the front parking lot, go around the side of the school, and out the back gate with almost no traffic or interruption.

"You didn't say what path to take home," Madoc pointed out.

Yeah, I know. Why didn't I think of that?

I rounded the square, cutting into a side street and racing through the less busy area where smaller businesses were closed on Sundays.

I kept up on the gas, my nerves firing with the need to go. I didn't care about winning.

Winners usually don't.

I wanted this, right here, right now, with her. I needed to see her. It was frustrating not knowing where she was.

Rounding two more corners and inching through a stop sign, I sped around the corner to Fall Away Lane just as she was rounding the corner from the other end.

"Go!" Madoc shouted, and I was about ready to punch him. What did he think I was doing?

Full speed ahead on the empty street, we both raced forward, and I screeched to a halt at the curb, followed by Tate not half a second later, the loud scream of our tires filling the whole neighborhood.

"Yes!" Madoc shouted, howling out the window. "Woo-hoo!"

I let my head fall back, my chest expelling every ounce of breath I'd been holding. Jax patted me on the shoulder, squeezing tight once, and climbed out of the car after Madoc.

Tate and the rest of the girls climbed out of the G8, smiling and laughing as Madoc and Jax wrapped their arms around them for a kiss.

Rubbing my hand down my face, feeling the thin layer of sweat, I climbed out of Jax's car and looked over at Tate, her arms crossed as she leaned on the hood and peered over at me.

Her chest rose and fell—she was still catching her breath—and the heat in her eyes was . . .

Jesus.

I took in a deep breath, knowing what she wanted. Knowing everything she still held hostage in her brain and heart that she wouldn't let past her lips. She was still that innocent and timid girl who let me put my hands on her in the chem lab four years ago, but with the armor of a woman who still didn't want to trust. Not that she trusted me completely four years ago, either.

I gave her a half smile, telling her everything with my eyes that she already knew.

Nothing had changed. Especially not our foreplay.

"Do you need anything?" I asked my mom, holding the phone between my ear and shoulder as I fastened my belt. I'd just gotten out of the shower, while Jax, Juliet, Madoc, and Fallon took Pasha and joined some friends at Mario's for dinner.

Tate stayed home to work through her reading list, and I had e-mails, budgets, and a ton of little shit that Pasha had left me to look over, which I'd finished just before I jumped in the shower and my mom called to check in.

"Well, since you ask . . . ," she hinted, sounding cheerful. "Jason has to miss my checkup tomorrow at the doctor. Would you like to go with me?"

I stilled. *She wanted me to do what?*

"To the gynecologist?" I cringed, grabbing my watch to put it back on.

I heard her snort. "He's an ob-gyn. Don't make it weird."

Taking the phone in hand, I dug out one of Jax's black T-shirts, since I still hadn't gone to claim my stuff left at Madoc's. "Um, well . . . I'd really rather not, but if you need me . . ."

I heard her quiet laugh on the other end. "You're precious."

I rolled my eyes, taking the phone away from my ear to slip on the shirt. "What time should I pick you up?"

"Noon," she shot back. "And thank you."

I nodded, even though she couldn't see me. I was trying to be nicer. I thought she'd earned it. But it was damn hard trying to change our relationship when we'd been the same way for so long.

How do you go from not liking and not respecting someone to doing both?

It wasn't going to happen overnight. Not even close. And it felt like there would always be bad blood between us.

But Quinn Caruthers—my soon-to-be little sister—was going to have it all. No one would stand in her way, least of all me.

I'd bury any lingering resentment from my own childhood for her.

I walked to the window, zoning in on Tate sitting cross-legged on her bed with an array of books spread out before her.

Her tanned arms were half covered by her long hair spilling around her, and when she got up to do something with her iPod, I grunted under my breath, feeling my dick tighten and then swell.

"I gotta go," I told my mom. "See you tomorrow." And I hung up.

Gripping my phone at my side, I watched her for all of two seconds—fresh and beautiful and sweet and driving me fucking nuts—before I jogged down the stairs, texting as I went.

Come outside.

I grabbed my leather jacket and keys, dashing into the garage, hitting the opener.

I added **Please** just for good measure, and climbed on the motorcycle.

Turning the ignition, I backed out of the driveway and eased down in front of her house, unlatching the helmet secured to the side.

I knew she might resist, but much to my relief, the front door opened.

She stepped out, folding her arms over her chest, which I knew she did for modesty's sake. She was in her pajamas—shorts and a T-shirt—so she wasn't wearing a bra.

Looking confused, she walked down the brick walkway and cocked her head. "What are you doing?"

I held up the helmet, hopeful. "Nighttime ride?" I suggested. "Your favorite thing in the summertime."

Okay, not her absolute favorite thing, but close.

She looked at me like I was crazy. "I'm in my pajamas, Jared."

"And you'll stay in them," I shot back. "I promise."

She hooded her eyes, unamused by my joke, and I fought to hold back the grin.

Her red plaid pajama shorts were short and awesome, and the idea of her thighs, looking just as smooth and supple as ever, wrapped around my waist was a thrill I'd definitely let myself have right now. Any way I could get it.

She regarded me, the wheels in her head turning, but I didn't miss the flicker of temptation she sucked at hiding.

"Just a minute," she sighed, giving in and spinning around.

She dove inside the house, grabbing a hoodie located just inside the door and her black Chucks. She slipped on the hoodie, sweeping her hair out from underneath, and then sat down on the top steps to slip her shoes on, leaving them untied.

And the amount of sexual rage running through my goddamn body as she jogged down the steps, her long hair dancing in the light breeze and her smile shutting down my heart, made me real damn glad she wasn't sitting in front of me.

Instead, she climbed on behind me, and I handed her the helmet.

Her bare thighs rubbed against the outside of mine, and when she wrapped her arms around my waist, I closed my eyes, savoring the frustration.

"You ready?" I nearly choked on my words.

She snuggled in tight, grazing my ear with something—maybe her nose? "You smell good," she whispered, and I squeezed the handlebars.

Son of a . . .

She was doing this on purpose.

"I'm taking that as a yes," I said, slipping on my helmet.

"You usually take what you want," she retorted. "Don't you?"

I shook my head as her chin lay to rest on my shoulder, determined not to walk into that one. We took off, flying down the street as her front leaned forward into my back and her arms tightened even more.

Taking a few turns, I steered us toward the long city streets where we could drive at a decent speed but not too fast. Cruising easily down the calm stretches of road, I felt her relax and lean into me more, her body moving in sync with mine when I weaved to change lanes or turn.

She felt beautiful. Just like always. My body was squeezed between her tight thighs, and she stayed close. Her head—or chin or cheek—never left my back, and we drove the deserted back roads and neighborhood streets just like we used to. Back when we realized how awful it was to be apart and how much we wanted to be together, no matter what we were doing. We simply had to be touching.

And after about a half hour, she remembered, too.

Her hands drifted underneath my jacket and skimmed my waist, her fingers slowly splaying out across my stomach.

I breathed harder as she rubbed my abs, dragging her fingernails across my skin, where every one of my muscles was on alert, thanks to her.

One of her hands moved down the inside of my thigh, and I felt a flutter in my chest.

She grazed my ear with her moist lips and breathed out my name. "Jared."

I held my hands stiff on the handlebars, almost afraid I'd lose control.

I reached back, taking her thigh in my hand. That soft skin just above the knee teased me. Urging her closer, I strained for control, feeling the heat between her legs hug my back, and I took us back home before I gave in to temptation and pulled over in an alley.

In front of my house, I took off my helmet and sat there, because her fucking hands hadn't stopped, and it felt too damn good.

"I missed riding with you." The warmth of her whisper coated my ear. "Not like at the race Friday night, but cruising like this. It's like dancing, the way I move with your body."

I turned my head, leaning into her mouth as she grazed my ear. "It is. The kind of dancing I'm good at."

And I hissed when she reached around and took my cock in her hand, massaging it and making it painfully hard. It was trying to punch through my jeans.

"Fuck."

I squeezed her thigh and then gave in. Twisting my body, I slid one arm under her arms and gripped her thigh with the other, hauling her into the front to straddle me.

She didn't hesitate. Grabbing the back of my neck, she pulled me into her lips, and I fucking took her mouth with just as much force.

Jesus Christ.

Tate's kisses were like a game. She came in, moving quick as she licked and bit and massaged, then releasing me just early enough to jack me up and leave me hanging. She always teased, letting me taste her tongue as it licked mine, and then took everything away, and I was a damn junkie needing another fix.

And her body. Her tight stomach and perfect legs moving against me and on me were nothing compared to how she looked naked and moving the same way.

Gripping her ass in both hands, I jerked her into my cock, grinding her so she'd feel me even deep inside.

Then I leaned forward, pushing her back on the bike, desperate to slide my hand up her sweatshirt.

But I just sat there, pressing my forehead to hers as we both breathed hard. I knew she wanted it. I knew I fucking wanted it.

Except I was suddenly hit by where this would put us in the morning. We'd fuck, probably all night, and love every second of it. I knew she wouldn't say no if I took her inside right now, but . . .

"Do you want to come in?" she gasped, taking my face in her hands. "Jared, please."

I squeezed my eyes shut, my dick feeling like it was going to combust if it didn't get to her, but . . . damn . . .

I didn't want to just screw.

I wanted her to love me again. I wanted her to say she was mine. And I didn't want to have to bully her about it, either.

Taking a deep breath, I sat up and shook my head. "No."

Her eyes went wide. "Excuse me?"

I heaved out a sigh, feeling like I'd rather chew tin foil than say no to her again.

I took her hands and pulled her up. "Come on," I urged, climbing off the bike. "I'll walk you to the door."

She looked absolutely stunned as she slid off the bike and tucked her hair behind her ear. "Are you serious?"

I almost laughed. She'd always been the one in control in the past, and this was certainly new for both of us.

I put my arm around her shoulder, walking up her walkway. "Take the week," I told her. "Go to your job. Read your books. Take a great big swim in Lake You," I teased, walking up her porch stairs. "And if, at the end of the week, you're ready to give me this," I turned her around and placed my hand on her heart, "then I'll take this." And I slid my hand between her legs, holding her pussy.

She jerked, her eyes rounding again as she stilled.

I leaned in, kissing her lips softly, and then made my way back over to Jax's house before I had a chance to rethink my stupid decision.

Tate and I would fuck.

Hopefully tomorrow, when she was ready to admit that she wanted me back, but until then . . .

I wasn't wasting days, weeks, or even months going round and round. I'd have her heart first.

Walking into the house, I noticed Jax, Juliet, Pasha, and Fallon curled up on the couch and carpet watching a movie, so I went into the kitchen to find Madoc, sitting at the table, making a sandwich.

I slowly lowered myself into a chair and leaned back, needing sleep and my best friend's perspective.

"Are you okay?" he asked, loading his bread with mustard.

I shook my head. "No."

I glanced at him, ready to do something I'd never done before, and confide in him. I wanted him to tell me she was okay. That I was good for her, and that I was everything she needed.

But his scared blue eyes were focused downward, and he inched back.

"Yeah, well," he said warily, "your dick is hard, dude, and it's kind of freaking me out. We'll talk later."

And he abruptly grabbed his plate and can of soda, getting up and leaving the kitchen.

I looked down to see, indeed, I was still completely jacked up from the episode outside.

My chest shook with laughter. "You don't like it?" I called after him. "Freud said everyone was bisexual, right?"

"Yeah, fuck you," he shot back.

I let my head fall back, laughing my ass off.

CHAPTER 13

TATE

A week.

   He'd asked me to take the week, probably figuring I'd take a day, but in the end, he was right.

Go figure.

I needed the time, and I couldn't believe he was the one telling me we needed to slow down.

The next day I'd felt terrible about Ben. About trying to force something that I wanted but wasn't feeling.

After all, Ben was stable, predictable, and calm. Everything Jared wasn't.

And I was tired of being a cliché.

Terminal good girl wants bad boy every time, right?

So I had tried changing my stripes, only to learn that it wasn't a question of bad boy versus good man. It was Jared versus every other guy on the planet, and having him near again reminded me of how awful life had been without him.

Plain and simple, I still loved him.

I realized this about the time I arrived at work on Monday

morning. Then I spent the evening shopping with Juliet, and when I got home, he didn't call or knock on my door.

I definitely expected him to crawl through my window again that night, but when I woke on Tuesday morning, he wasn't there.

So I decided there was no need to rush things. Part of me still didn't trust him. He'd deserted me twice, and although I saw the proof that he'd grown up, there was no need to dive in headfirst every time.

I'd take the week, do my job and my reading, get my car ready for the weekend, and see what happened. I knew the ball was in my court, but also that I liked it when he pursued me. I always had.

But other than a few sideways glances, he'd left me alone.

When I got home yesterday, I saw him and Jax standing in the driveway with a couple of other guys and Jared's Ford Mustang Boss 302. The same car he'd had in high school, and the same one I'd spent countless hours in and done countless things with him in.

I didn't know if they were his friends or coworkers of some sort, but they'd clearly brought his car to him. There was another car in the driveway as well, but this morning when I left for work, it was gone. I figured whoever brought the car must've left.

So Jared had wanted his Boss here. I wondered why.

I sat up, grabbing the water bottle and spraying my face, little specks tickling my skin. Juliet was lying on the lawn chair next to me, on her stomach, with her face buried in her phone, while Fallon had gone inside to grab waters.

It was after seven on Friday night, and even though the sun was beyond the horizon, we were still lying out in my backyard, enjoying the remnants of heat and the drone of summer sounds. Lawn mowers, insects in the trees, air-conditioning units . . . and the buzz on my skin, attuned to every little sound of him next door. His music, his car engine . . .

"What are you doing?" I heard Fallon ask, and I turned to see her looking at Juliet, confused as she set the water bottles down on the little round table.

"What?" Juliet looked up at her.

Fallon sat back in the lawn chair, her emerald green bikini bringing out the color in her eyes.

"That's Jax's phone," she pointed out, catching Juliet red-handed.

I grinned, eyeing Juliet suspiciously just as much as Fallon.

Juliet thinned out her lips, thoughtful. "I heard there's this app where you track each other's phones. I'm trying to put it on his."

"Oh, my God." Fallon reached out and grabbed the phone out of Juliet's hands. "Jax has corrupted you. Are you really that worried?"

Juliet got up on all fours and turned around, sitting down. "You're telling me you're not the least bit concerned that our boyfriends"—and then she pointed to Fallon—"and your husband are going to a strip club tonight?"

"No," Fallon shot back. "You know why? Because I know Madoc." She plucked her sunglasses off the top of her head and slid them over her eyes, continuing, "As soon as he gets to the club, he's going to take a selfie or some shit and send it to me to brag." The casual grin on her lips spread wider. "Twenty minutes after that he's going to text, telling me he wishes I was up onstage dancing for him. And about an hour later, he's going to barge through our door, horny as a teenage boy, and wanting who?" She placed a palm on her chest. "Me. And I won't be home, because we're going out, and he'll be frantic, wondering where the hell I am."

I snorted, covering up my own concern. Jared wasn't my boy-friend. Yet, while I wasn't as worried as Juliet was, I wasn't as calm as Fallon, either.

I cleared my throat, adjusting the tie of my black bikini at the back of my neck. "Juliet, you know better," I soothed. "It's Zack's bachelor party, so cut the guys some slack. Jax won't look twice at those girls, much less do anything with them."

Her lips pursed, and I looked above her, seeing Jax appear at the window, drying his hair with a towel.

He couldn't keep his eyes off her. Especially in her red suit.

"All that will happen," I continued, seeing him smirk and walk away, "is he'll get worked up thinking about the hot mischief he's going to get up to with you when he gets home. You won't get any sleep tonight."

"And Jared?" she retorted, changing the subject.

"What about him?"

"He's the only one unattached," she pointed out. "When the strippers get him all worked up—which they will, because he's only human—who's he going to come home to?"

I shot her a pointed look, wondering why she was baiting me. I was about to shoot the spray bottle in her face, but Fallon saved me the trouble. She threw a rolled-up towel at Juliet's head, at which Juliet threw one back, and they both started laughing.

After another hour, we'd cleaned up the backyard and made some dinner—since the guys were getting food with Zack before heading to the club—and then we parked ourselves outside on the front porch to eat. Juliet still wore her red bikini with a cutoff jean skirt. Fallon had on a pair of white shorts, and I had slipped on a sheer white cover-up.

"Oh, my God."

I looked up, seeing that Juliet had dropped her fork and was staring across the porch, into the distance. She darted her gaze down, glancing to where the fork had dropped by her feet, but then forgot it, shooting her eyes back up.

I followed her line of sight, and my jaw tightened with a smile.

Jax had stepped out of the house, looking a lot different, and Juliet was breathless.

He wore black suit pants and a black jacket with a white dress shirt, open at the collar. His height, due to his long legs, made his appearance all the more forbidding and—I had to admit—pretty damn hot. His black hair, close to the scalp on the sides and longer on top, was styled in sporadic wisps that were pushed to the front. With his shoes, his shiny watch, his gleaming belt buckle—Jax looked sleek and powerful.

I looked over at his girlfriend, rolling my eyes at the sight of her slightly open mouth as she gaped.

"He's not a piece of meat," I teased.

She blinked, coming back to her senses and then slowly rose, walking to the railing.

"Oh, my God."

I turned, hearing Fallon's voice this time.

Just like Juliet, she was staring at Madoc—who'd just exited the house, as well—like she was actually in pain.

"He's such a yuppie." She gave him a wistful look. "But he's so damn cute."

I barked out a laugh.

Madoc was also dressed in black suit pants and a black jacket, but he wore a gray shirt with a silver necktie. Madoc looked great in ties. They fit his style and his broad chest, and the fact that he took care with his clothing choices, always making sure that everything he wore was a perfect fit, only amplified the fact that Madoc being preppy did nothing to quell how hot he got his alternative-styled wife.

Fallon stuck her fingers in her mouth and whistled. "Yeah, baby!"

Juliet joined in, whistling at her man as they both leaned over the railing.

"You guys are idiots," I teased again, standing up to pick up the fork.

They both started laughing, and both men shook their heads, smiling as they headed over.

I crossed my arms over my chest and leaned against the house, watching the girls swing their legs over the railing and sit.

But then my face fell. My stomach dropped, and my breath cut off, and *holy shit*.

Jared had walked out of the house, locking the door behind him, and I looked away, but I couldn't resist.

Glancing back up for another look, I watched him out of the corner of my eye, staring off out to the street as he fastened a cuff link.

A cuff link?

He was wearing cuff links. I finally blinked, my heart beginning to jackhammer with increasing speed.

Jared in a suit made my mouth water. I loved him in his jeans or casual black pants and T-shirts, but when he cleaned up?

Oh, my God.

His black pants draped down his legs, falling just casually enough to look like he didn't care, but his pressed shirt and jacket—both a deep, rich black—didn't hide his body at all. I caught sight of a sliver of his collarbone, since his top button was undone, and then he slipped a casual hand into his pocket and looked over, locking eyes with me.

I turned away.

"What are you ladies going to do tonight?" Madoc picked Fallon off the railing and held her close to his chest.

"Hang out," she chirped. "Make some popcorn."

"Right," Jax shot back, coming to stand between Juliet's thighs as she sat on the railing.

Jared made his way over, pulling out his car keys.

Madoc was kissing and whispering to Fallon. Jax was looking up at Juliet, trying to sweeten her up as she shied away from him, playing jealous.

And Jared stood aloof, ignoring me. I didn't know if he was

looking at me, and I didn't know if he was mad that I hadn't reached out, but I still felt his presence on every inch of my body.

He tugged at me like a magnet.

Jax pulled Juliet down, kissing her nose and then her lips. "I love you," he said, and my gaze flashed to Jared, locking eyes with his.

"I'll be home by midnight," I heard Jax say, but Jared continued to hold me. The heat was unmistakable. But what scared me was how I also saw the coldness.

A wave of déjà vu hit me, and it was like I was back in high school for a moment.

"If you're one second late," Juliet scolded Jax, "I'll have a tantrum."

"I love your tantrums," he flirted, pulling her hips into his.

"I mean it," she emphasized, trying to sound tough, but I knew it was just a game they played. "I will make you bleed if you're late."

"Promise?" he taunted, diving in for another kiss.

I shook my head, keeping my gaze off Jared.

"Jax, let's go." Madoc pulled Jax by the neck, leading him away from his girlfriend.

All three guys walked to Jared's car, every inch of their well-dressed, manicured looks emphasizing that they were men now. It was still hard to wrap my head around it at times, since I'd grown up with Jared and met Madoc and Jax as teens. I'd seen them all—more often than not—in jeans and T-shirts. I'd seen them do the dumbest things and even joined in a few times.

But those boys were gone.

"Jared!" Fallon shouted as Jared opened his driver's side door. "Get them home safe!"

He arched a brow, giving her a condescending look. "They'll be home before I will," he said, looking over at me. "I don't have a curfew."

My eyes stung with sudden anger as I watched him climb into his car without another word.

He started the car and backed out of the driveway, not sparing a glance back.

Asshole.

Oh, sure. *Go have fun. No one's waiting at home for you. If you don't have me, you'll just go play with a random girl, because why not, right?*

I clenched my fists and let my head fall back.

Shit. I was being ridiculous.

Madoc and Jax were going to have fun with their friends. To celebrate. They'd come home just as much in love with Fallon and Juliet as ever.

And Jared was manipulating me. Just like he always did, and I fell for it. He was a grown man who still found it quite appetizing to take a great big bite out of my peace of mind. He expected me to give in and call or text to tell him how much I loved him. Or he expected me to come pick a fight tomorrow about something silly just so I could get a rise out of him. He wanted me mad, because he wanted to draw me out.

As the sound of Jared's engine left the neighborhood, I let the small smile spread across my lips.

He was so used to toying with me. It was like second nature. So why not react and give him what he wanted?

"Wicked is a dual strip club, right?" I asked the girls, already knowing the answer. "Female dancers downstairs and male dancers upstairs?"

Juliet glanced at Fallon, and then both of them looked at me.

As realization hit, Juliet gasped and Fallon threw her head back, laughing.

And then we all shrieked, scrambling for my front door to get ready.

"Hi," I greeted the stocky bouncer with the military buzz cut.

"Hello, ladies." He looked us up and down, and I stopped,

which caused Fallon to bump into me as she veered around into the club with Juliet.

"You let women sit downstairs, right?" I inquired. "If we decided to watch the female dancers later on, I mean."

He raised his eyebrows, amused. "We love our female customers," he played. "No matter what turns them on."

I straightened. *Yeah, I didn't mean that really, but okay.*

Entering the club, I inhaled, not sure what to expect. Cigarettes and maybe the stench of stale liquor, but that wasn't what hit me as soon as I entered.

The scent of golden peaches and rich berries and lilies drifted through my nostrils, filling my lungs with their hint of vanilla and musk. The black and burgundy interior of the entryway was accented with gold fixtures and would probably seem gaudy elsewhere, but here, the less-is-more idea prevailed. It wasn't overwhelmingly busy. The carpets were lush, the walls were a warm but dark violet, and the décor possessed singular objects on which to focus your attention instead of too much to distract you.

We stepped through a doorframe without a door on it and immediately stopped, seeing the low ceiling give way, and the room before us damn near took my breath away.

"No wonder they dressed up," I said under my breath. "This place . . ."

I'd only heard about Wicked. It was halfway between Shelburne Falls and Chicago and was a popular stopping point for men—and women—on their way home from work to the suburbs. It was reported to have great music, the best-looking dancers—which it would, since there were about four universities within an hour of here that had a lot of hardworking students needing good-paying jobs—and it also had a five-star chef.

The guys had to be paying a thousand dollars per table to throw this bachelor party.

A hostess in a tight black dress—much like my own—approached us with menus.

"Hello." Her long, brown hair, bronze complexion, and dark eyes glimmered in the surrounding candlelight. "The ladies' show upstairs doesn't start again for another hour, but we can get you seated."

I barely heard her, looking around for the guys. It was after ten, and while they held only two performances with the male dancers on Friday and Saturday nights, the female dancers performed around the clock.

"Actually," Fallon spoke up, "can we sit down here and have a drink first?"

What?

"Of course." She smiled and nodded. "Follow me."

I let out a sigh and followed, Juliet at my side, with her gaze darting everywhere, probably looking for Jax.

While my curiosity was all for getting a glimpse of the guys tonight, I didn't want this to be about them. Madoc and Jax expected Fallon and Juliet to handle themselves with patience and understanding—which they did—but it would be a hell of a riot to see how they handled themselves when they found out their women were upstairs getting a show, too.

That was the point of coming here, after all.

"Ugh," Fallon groaned as she halted and looked at the stage. "Look at her tits."

I twisted my head, looking up onstage, and immediately I could feel my face falling.

Shit.

A beautiful blonde with lowlights in her hair wore a gold bikini that pushed up her breasts, making them stand out against her flat stomach and perfect skin. And as she held the pole with one hand and leaned back, rolling her hips and bringing the back of her hand up to flip her hair, my gut twisted.

I didn't want Jared to see her. She looked like me, only better.

"I thought you weren't worried," Juliet said to Fallon.

Fallon shook her head, still watching the dancer. "Don't serve me that shit now. You have great boobs."

Juliet grinned, following the hostess. "Madoc likes yours," she reassured Fallon. "Come on."

The hostess sat us down in a semicircle booth of burgundy velvet with a black table and drapery tied back on both sides. A dim lamp hung from overhead, flickering to look like a candle.

"There's no table fee?" I asked, sliding into the booth.

"Not for you three." She winked, handing out drink menus. "Lap dances are fifty bucks, though. Enjoy."

I snorted. Yeah, because we definitely wanted lap dances.

"How do we even know they're here yet?" Juliet asked, looking at both of us.

"They're here." Fallon smirked, flashing her phone and showing the selfie Madoc must have taken just outside the club. "He sent this twenty minutes ago."

One by one, we all let our eyes drift to the sea of customers out and about in the club, looking for the bachelor party, when I knew we shouldn't. The guys should be left alone. Until later, when we let it slip via text or social media that we were upstairs getting our own eyeful.

It took me about two seconds to locate them.

Jared and a team of other guys sat right in front of the stage, off to the right. Zack, Madoc, Jax, their high school friend Sam, with about half a dozen other guys I barely knew, were surrounded by about three smaller tables as they sat back in cushioned chairs with drinks in hand. Jax took a bottle and poured a few shots, handing one to Jared and Madoc, at which Jared tipped his head back, downing the shot. I inhaled an excited breath.

Burying my face in the menu, I mumbled to the girls, "Around the stage. With the girl dressed like a Native American giving Zack a lap dance."

They dove back behind the curtain, and Juliet huddled close to Fallon as they both spied on the guys.

I laughed under my breath.

"Good evening," a server greeted us, stopping at our table. "Would all of you like something to drink?" she asked, setting down napkins.

"Three shots of Jim Beam," Fallon ordered. "Devil's Cut."

"I don't want whiskey," Juliet retorted.

"Good, because they're all for me," Fallon shot back, and I was amused at her nerves. She was always so confident and tough, but my girl did not like her man in a strip club after all.

I set the menu down, pushing all three of them toward the server. "Pineapple and Parrot Bay for her," I ordered, pointing to Juliet, "her three shots and a Newcastle"—I pointed to Fallon—"and I'll have a Red Stripe."

The server nodded without writing anything down and left, and everyone looked back out to the guys. Aside from sporadic glances to the stage to watch the dancers, they mostly just sat back and joked around. Jared sat facing the stage, but his head was turned to the side, and I could tell he was laughing from time to time by how his shoulders shook. A server brought appetizers, and while some of the guys dug in, others continued to just drink.

The show had a main performance—a dancer on center stage—but there were smaller stages spread out with a couple of pole dancers.

Juliet sat back, looking calmer. "They're behaving." She gave a sad smile. "Now I feel bad. We should just go upstairs."

I shrugged. "I didn't want to be down here anyway."

Fallon shot her eyes over to me. "Really? You're not jealous? At all?"

I looked away, running a nervous hand through my straightened hair and bringing it over the front of my shoulder. "Jared is none of my business," I maintained.

"Are you sure about that?" Juliet asked timidly as she stared out to the stage, her body gone eerily still.

"Yes," I retorted. "Let him have his fun."

"Okay." She nodded, sounding forlorn. "Because he seems to like what he's seeing up onstage." And then she pinned me, looking serious.

My eyebrows dropped, and I immediately looked out to where Jared sat. He was still sitting back in his chair, but his full attention was onstage, and when I followed his gaze, I nearly choked on a breath.

My neck heated, and my head was screaming.

Piper.

Jared's ex. The girl he was sleeping with before we got together in high school.

My tight black dress constricted my body more, and I felt sick.

I hadn't seen her in four years. Why was he looking at her?

She had made and distributed a sex video of Jared and me in school, and he was sitting there, giving her his attention like he was actually turned on.

I stayed still, paralyzed not by her, but by him. He should've turned away. He should've left.

After what she did to us . . .

She stood on a smaller side stage with the pole at her back as she bent down at the waist and then flipped her hair back, giving Jared a close and personal view of her tits.

She then rose, put one hand behind her neck and the other behind her back and tugged smoothly at the strings of her top, letting it fall away from her body to expose her tanned and perfect breasts to him.

I looked down, grinding my teeth.

No.

My face ached as tears sprang to my eyes, and I looked away, so Fallon and Juliet wouldn't see.

Fuck him.

By the way he was watching her—making no move to ignore her—and by the way she singled him out, they could have each other.

I dragged in a deep breath and cleared my throat.

Digging in my clutch purse, I pulled out a bill just as the server brought us our drinks.

I tipped my chin up, blinking away the tears in my eyes. "I want to buy a lap dance," I told her, holding out the money. "Not for me, though."

She tucked the tray under her arm and took the money. "Sure. What do you need?"

I leaned on the table, noticing that Jared had finally looked away, before I started speaking to the server again. "Do you see that guy with the brown hair over there dressed all in black? He's lifting a glass to his lips right now." I pointed in his direction, and the server turned to see who I was referring to.

She nodded.

"Can you send him that dancer that's onstage in front of his table when she's done?" I asked and felt Juliet stiffen next to me.

The server smiled. "Of course."

She left, and I closed up my purse, setting it on my seat next to my lap as I ignored Fallon and Juliet, who I knew were staring at me.

"Tate, what are you doing?" Juliet's concerned voice was void of her usual pep.

"Tate, stop her," Fallon urged, referring to the server. "Don't do this. You're setting him up."

I didn't know if Madoc had told Fallon anything about the episode with Piper in high school, but regardless, she knew buying Jared a lap dance was a bad move.

Kind of evil, actually.

I stared ahead, fisting the cold brown bottle in front of me.

I didn't know why I did it. It felt like those times when you want to ask questions or feel you should, but in the end, you don't really want the answers.

I didn't want Jared with other women. I loved him.

But I wanted a reason not to. I wanted one thing to push me off the fence. One thing that would make me never trust him again.

"You want him to fail you." Fallon's quiet voice was raspy, and I looked up to see her eyes pooling behind her glasses.

Then I glanced at Juliet looking at me like she didn't even know me.

"No," I whispered more to myself, shame warming my face. "I want it to hurt."

I knew I always forgot the pain he caused too easily. Not anymore.

Juliet narrowed her confused eyes on me, not understanding. Not understanding that the pain made me stronger. That anger felt good, and if Jared hurt me, then I could feed off it to feel superior.

I could win and not be the one left crying or waiting or trying to live and put up a front when the hole he left wouldn't fill.

"Son of a bitch."

I heard Fallon's curse and looked up, evening out my expression.

Piper had strolled out of the back area behind the stage and was walking through the tables, catching the glances of interested men as she passed by.

She was still beautiful. Complete with the perfect posture of confidence that hadn't dulled, even though her reputation had been ruined after the video.

Her deep brown hair, longer than I remembered, spilled in waves to the middle of her back, and her body shone like the sun on water.

She wore a white jeweled bikini top with a thong, but she did have a gold fishnet wrap around her ass, tied at her hips. However, her behind was almost completely visible through the array of squares in the netting, which made the wrap for show only.

Her eyes were on Jared as she sauntered over, a coy look on her face. For all she knew, he was still angry about the video, but that didn't seem to dull her confidence.

Standing over him, she slowly leaned down, placing her hands on his armrests, and I saw him look up at her and grow still.

She was talking to him, and he was letting her.

My mouth went dry.

Her back arched as she spoke, her leg bent up, and I could tell she was doing her best to get him to notice her breasts as she inched closer to his face.

I couldn't see Madoc or Jax. I couldn't see Fallon or Juliet anymore.

I could only see him drop his eyes, looking like he was struggling with what to do.

Maybe he really wanted it.

They were together once, after all. He'd enjoyed sex with her enough to go back for more. Four years had passed, he had returned to Shelburne Falls, and I still hadn't given him my heart. Maybe he was considering it.

I would never find out, right?

Do it.

The backs of my eyes burned, and my heart raced, and I wanted him to touch her. Piper would be an unforgiveable betrayal after what she'd done to me, and the pain would be extreme. My heart would get hard, just like after he'd left, and I'd be steel again.

But his angry jaw flexed like he was pissed or something, and for a moment I thought he wouldn't, but . . .

"Oh, my God." Fallon looked away.

Juliet looked down.

And I breathed like the room was running out of oxygen.

We all watched as he stood up and she took his hand, leading him through a back doorway to the private VIP rooms.

I slowly shook my head, watching him disappear with her. He

could get a lap dance out here. Why was she taking him somewhere private?

Taking a slow sip of my beer, I straightened my back, refusing to let them see how I felt like someone had torn out my heart and stuck a knife in it.

I wanted to go home.

I wanted to go to bed and get up and read in the morning and get ready for my race and walk away from him as if he'd never mattered.

But instead I crumbled.

I gasped, dropping my head and shaking as I started crying. The tears spilled down, and I couldn't breathe.

Oh, God, why couldn't I breathe?

I pushed on my chest over my heart, willing it to stop trying to beat through my skin.

"Tate," Juliet cried, grabbing me and wrapping her arms around me. "Tate, don't."

She buried her head in my neck, gripping me tight, and I couldn't stand it. The cries suddenly lodged in my throat, and I needed air.

I shrugged her off and scooted out of the other side of the booth. "Just give me a minute." And I ran for the bathrooms, through the same doorway where Jared and Piper had disappeared.

But as soon as I entered the darkened hallway, a hand clamped over my mouth, and I tried to scream. I twisted and struggled as an arm wrapped around my waist and hauled me up, carrying me through another door.

No!

My heels dropped off my feet as my legs thrashed above the ground, and I heard the door slam shut as I tried to bite and struggle away, but he had me too tight.

The hard body at my back swung us around and walked me into the closed door, his breath at my ear.

"You kill me," he said, and the shaky breath sounded like he was almost crying.

Jared.

I stilled, sucking in short breaths through his fingers as he set me down.

His threatening whisper was filled with pain. "You really do kill me, Tate."

He wasn't with Piper. I had barely seen the dimly lit room when he'd walked me in here, but I had noticed seating and a table.

But no Piper.

He'd been expecting me. He'd known I was here.

He tightened his arm around my waist, and I didn't move except for my hands shaking. I was afraid of him. He felt enraged, and I hadn't seen him like this since the night I shut down one of his parties senior year by turning off his electricity.

"I knew the minute you walked into the club," he growled in my ear. "I was amused. I actually thought you were jealous."

His mouth went to my hair as he inhaled shallow breaths, clearly angry and about to lose control.

"I loved you watching me," he said. "But then you had to pull this shit." His voice grew hard. "She comes over saying someone bought me a lap dance, and I knew right away it was you. You really think I'm nothing, don't you? You thought I'd want her?"

I shook my head. "I didn't think that—"

"Then why test me?!" he yelled, cutting me off and slamming his fist into the door ahead of me, making me jump.

He let me go, and I spun around, seeing his chest rise and fall hard—and the whole time he looked at me like I'd betrayed him.

Guilt dug at my insides, and I couldn't even look at him. I was low, and I'd assumed the worst about him, and he was beyond hurt.

Before I'd always felt either on an even keel with Jared or that I was above him. Better in some way than the guy who had bullied me for so long.

But right now, he was too good for me.

I didn't know where Piper was, but he wasn't with her, and that was all that mattered.

When he looked down on me, the disdain and disappointment in his eyes closed in on me like a grave.

Veering around, he grabbed the door handle, and I shot out, wrapping my arms around his chest and burying my face in his back.

"Jared, please don't go." My voice shook, and his body froze. "Please?" I begged. "I didn't think you'd do anything with her," I whispered, keeping my forehead on his back. "I wanted you to, though. I wanted it to hurt."

He stayed still, listening to me in the quiet room.

"It's easier to be angry and pass judgment than it is to take a chance. It feels stronger."

I felt his chest inflate with a breath. "Yeah, I know that feeling."

I laid the side of my face on his back, hugging him close. "Nothing feels right without you. Not school or home," I cried. "Everything is just giving me enough air to get to the next day without you. I never stopped being yours."

He dropped his head back, letting out a sigh.

I swallowed, taking my chance. "I love you, Jared. I've always loved you, and I will always love you."

There was no one but him, and even when he wasn't around, he was. I would never be free of him—because I didn't want to be.

CHAPTER 14

JARED

lowered my head, the stress that had built up in my nerves slowly
ebbing away. I couldn't believe she'd finally just said it.

All the nights. All the time and the phone calls and texts I'd
sent . . . Every day, it had seemed as if she was moving farther away
from me, and the memories of her were only dreams that had never
been real.

Tatum Brandt loved me, and I was never letting her go again.

"I know what I want," she said, her voice thick with unshed
tears. "I know where I'm going. I know what I stand for, and I don't
do things that I don't want to do." She turned me around, her eyes
holding me still. "And even so, without you in my life, I'm not
happy. For better or worse, you've been my other half since I was
ten years old, and I can't imagine a future I'd want without you in it.
You're the love of my life."

Looking down at her, seeing the stormy expression in her eyes
fill with expectation and nervousness—what would I do or say?—
there was only one way to carry on. One way to move on.

There were no more words. Nothing to discuss and nothing to

resolve. Every inch of me was hers, and I was sick of living without her for another second.

"Do you still love me?" she prompted quietly when I didn't say anything.

I looked away, licking my dry lips as I knelt down, picking up her heels off the floor. Sitting up on one knee, I wrapped my hand around her slender ankle and helped her foot into her shoe, one following the other.

"Jared, say something," she begged, the worry making her voice grow thick.

But I didn't.

Let her sweat a bit. I was so sick of talking.

I just wanted my girl.

Standing up, I took her hand and pulled her through the door, heading back out into the club. She missed a step but caught herself, and picked up her pace to keep up with me.

The music danced around us, and I glanced at Tate's booth, seeing that Madoc had found Fallon and was hugging her back with his lips on her neck. Juliet was near the stage, sitting on Jax's lap, watching a dancer as he kissed her shoulder.

Good. They had rides home, then.

"Where are we going?" Tate sounded worried. "Are you still mad or something?"

I smiled to myself, leading her out of the club. Digging out my keys, I hit the button to unlock the car as soon as we hit the parking lot and moved swiftly, opening up the door for her.

"Get in," I told her. She blinked, looking confused, but got in the car, swinging her legs in so I could close the door.

Moving around the rear, I opened my door and immediately sat down and turned my head to look at her.

"Jared." She shook her head. "Why won't you talk to me?"

I reached over, lifting her underneath her arms, and slid her body over to sit sideways on my lap, her legs lying over the console.

Her back rested against my door, and her face, inches from mine, turned wide-eyed to me.

I reached up, cupping the side of her face. "Can we just skip to the end?" I asked softly. "I'm tired of missing you, Tate."

And that was it. No more talking, no more arguing, no more denying what couldn't be changed . . . I only lived in her orbit, and I would die there, too. There was no choice to be made.

I brought my hand up, threading my fingers through her hair and holding the back of her head as I hovered my lips over hers.

"I love you," I whispered and pulled her in, my mouth sinking into hers as her shocked whimper vibrated across my tongue.

Her sweet smell filled my nostrils as I sucked her tongue into my mouth and barely let her up for air.

I loved playing with her. I held her tight, so I could do whatever the hell I wanted. For three years in high school, I'd denied myself what I wanted, and for the last two years, she'd kept me from reclaiming what I wanted, and my peace of mind was fried.

By the time I was satisfied, she wouldn't be able to walk.

I moved over her mouth, sinking my teeth into her bottom lip and dragging it out and then diving back in again to play with her tongue.

She whimpered again but didn't even try to resist me as I controlled the kiss. My lips hummed with the feel of her, but before I could slide my hands anywhere I wasn't going to want to let go of, I pulled away, sucking in a breath.

Her chest rose and fell hard, but she opened her mouth again, coming at me for more.

I pulled back, shaking my head, and she searched my eyes, looking pained.

Before she could protest, I started the car, sliding my hand under her arched knees to shift.

Although it was hard to drive, I wasn't moving her. I doubted I'd let her away from me for a very long time.

Pulling out of the parking lot, I jumped onto the highway, feeling her settle into my lap and turn her tears into an excited little breath as I sped down the road. I still had my left hand behind her back and in her hair, so I was shifting and steering with my right.

And the whole time I was trying to keep my lead foot light on the gas, because I was dying to get home and inside of her. My cock was painfully restricted as it tried to grow but couldn't. It was already swelling as if it knew the feel of her thighs less than an inch away, and her wet tongue licking her lips right now.

She nuzzled her nose into my neck and held my head with her hand as she sucked in a breath. And then I let out a groan, damn near shutting my eyes as she nibbled under my ear.

"Tate," I breathed out, reaching down to adjust my swelling dick. *Fuck.*

Damn, she knew what she was doing. Her tongue darted out, so softly, licking and then kissing my neck and then trailing kisses across my cheek, and eating me up like I was a damn dessert.

I breathed in and out, punching the shifter down into sixth as the trees loomed on both sides of the dark night. We were in the middle of nowhere and wouldn't be home for another half hour.

"Jared," she whispered in my ear. "Please."

And before I knew it she'd reached behind her neck and unclasped the neck tie, letting the top of her little black dress fall to her waist, exposing her breasts.

My eyes flared, fucking hating her for a split second as I darted my gaze to her breasts, and I couldn't touch her, because my damn hand was driving the damn car.

I jerked the steering wheel right, and then seeing that I veered, I let out a frustrated growl. "Baby, please," I begged.

She dove into my neck again, teasing, "You always liked my tits," she taunted.

The blood in my dick raced, and I winced as it tried to stretch under my pants.

"I can feel you," she said, nudging my hard-on with her ass. "And you feel you so good."

Jesus, Tate. Stop. Please stop. I wanted her in a bed.

Her nose rubbed against my cheek, and she looked up at me. "I don't think I can wait until we get home." Her eyes looked desperate. "Please," she begged again.

I shook my head, letting out a sigh as I looked her in the eyes. "Two years, and you're going to make me fuck you in a car, aren't you?" I damn near pouted.

She smiled, and I shifted down, skidding into a right-hand turn onto a country road, because there was no way I was going to win.

Hell, I didn't even want to anymore.

I barreled down the gravel road, still going nearly eighty miles an hour and not giving a shit that the rocks were kicking up under my tires and probably chipping the paint.

Tate was devouring my neck, and my goddamn hands could barely stay steady on the road.

"Baby, damn," I gasped, taking her lips and kissing the shit out of her as I tried to drive.

Veering to the right again, I flew onto Tanner Path, which was nothing but a small road—barely big enough for one car—that lined one of the little inlet ponds that served as runoff from the river. Sinking far enough into the darkness, where no car would venture this time of night, I slowed to a halt, the grind of the gravel music to my ears.

Setting the parking brake, I shot the seat back for legroom while she kicked off her shoes and swung a leg over my thighs, straddling me.

Her eyes spilled fire, looking like a starving animal before she grabbed my shirt between the buttons, ripping it open.

"Damn," I growled through my teeth, reaching behind her back and ripping her dress in two as well, tearing the scraps away from her body.

Grabbing her hair at the back of her head, I pulled her neck back and took a handful of her ass in my other hand before taking her nipple in my mouth.

She gasped, her body shaking with shock, and I felt high as she slowly melted. She grinded on me, in nothing but her black lace G-string, and I couldn't believe how painfully turned on I was. My dick was fucking begging for her warmth.

I bit and sucked, trailing my hands all over her, squeezing and yanking her hips.

"Now," she whimpered, squirming against my cock and digging her nails into my bare chest. "Jared, now."

I opened the driver's side door, giving myself more room as I set my leg outside and reclined the seat back just an inch.

"You still on the pill?" I breathed hard, unfastening my belt.

She nodded frantically, leaning down to kiss and nibble my chest.

I freed my cock, grabbing her ass and pushing her up over it. She sucked in a shaky breath, and I took the delicate fabric of her G-string in my fist and leaned into her forehead. "Your pussy will feel my tongue tonight," I growled, "but for now . . ." I yanked, tearing the material away from her body, the pathetic threads disappearing in the black interior of the car.

She wrapped her smooth fingers around my dick, which stood as stiff as a flagpole, and positioned it underneath her, working me into her tight body. My jaw dropped open with my gasp as I crowned her.

Looking into her eyes, her full, beautiful breasts begging for my attention, I punched my hips up and sheathed my cock so deep inside her that she screamed, hitting the roof with her hand as she moaned and took in breath after quick breath.

"Jared!"

I held her hips, my body tense and tight as I closed my eyes and sank in to the hilt.

My cock throbbed inside her, and slivers of pleasure shot from my stomach and thighs, all leading inward to my groin.

Fuck, she was tight.

I took her ass in my hands and rocked her into me, my lips layered with hers. "Fuck me, Tate," I breathed out, begging against her mouth. "Fuck me like you hate me."

She pulled her hips back, and then slammed into me again, throwing her head back with a moan.

"Yes," I growled.

Her back was pressed against the steering wheel, and I dived down, sucking a nipple into my mouth as she fucked me.

Her hips rolled into me, grinding her wet heat into my body so I felt every tight inch of her. She moved up and down my cock, faster and faster, back and forth, her hips rolling forward and backward, forward and then backward again, and I held her sweet body, already glistening with sweat as she rode me like I was her fucking toy.

She leaned back, flashing me a grin before she ripped my shirt and jacket wide, bringing them both down my arms.

"Get it off," she ordered.

I whipped the jacket and shirt away, my fucking dick throbbing a mile a minute inside her as I tossed my shit I don't know where. She reached down, reclining the seat all the way and hooking her thigh over mine, hanging it out the open door.

And she rode me hard. Her hand fisted the seat belt strap on the side of the door, while her other hand gripped my chest, and I held her hips, watching her look so beautiful it almost hurt.

"Oh, Christ," I groaned, gripping one of her tits so hard I was probably bruising it. "Baby, your hips are like a fucking machine."

Her head had fallen back, and I tensed every muscle in my chest and abs as I arched my head back, too. She was relentless, not breaking pace for a second.

"You don't like it?" she asked, and I opened my eyes to see her face tilted up to the roof.

She gasped. "I'm sorry, baby," she said breathlessly, smiling, "but love you or hate you, this is how I fuck you."

And then she rose, coming down even harder on me, no longer rolling her hips but bouncing.

I squeezed my eyes shut, taking her attack. *Shit.*

Blood flooded my cock, but I didn't want to come yet.

"Everything else may change, but never the way I love you," I whispered, more to myself than to her.

Resuming old habits, when she wanted to come one way, and I wanted to have her another way, I found myself taking control to bring her over the edge. Arching my hips up, I thrust between her thighs, holding her hips tight and bringing her down, impaling her just as hard as she was sheathing me.

"Oh, God," she moaned, and I leaned up closer to her, sucking on the flesh of her breast as I fucked her from the bottom. "I love when you do that."

I smiled against her skin and lay back down, taking control, thrusting and grinding, fucking her deep, and rubbing my thumb over her clit.

"Come on," I urged, feeling her hair and her sweat graze my fingers on her back. "I want you spread for me on the hood, so I can taste how wet you are."

"Yeah," she breathed. "God, I love you, Jared."

And she rode me faster, grinding more and more when my dick found the perfect spot, massaging her until her whole body tightened up and she started moaning.

"Jared," she cried. "Oh . . ." Her hips fucked again and again and again, and she dug her nails into my chest, throwing her head back and coming all over me.

Her muscles tightened and squeezed around my cock as her orgasm moved through her, and I gripped her breast, every muscle in my body on fire from trying not to come.

Her hips stilled, and her breathing slowed as she dipped her forehead under my chin. "Again," she begged. "Please."

I took her mouth, kissing her hard. I ate up the taste of sweetness and sweat and wanted to promise her a thousand things I knew, without a doubt, I'd give her. No matter what I had to do, she was worth everything. Nothing and no one was ever as perfect as us together.

I sat up, holding her by the waist in order to lift her out of the car and around the door. She wrapped her legs limply around me and held on as I placed her on the hood, my cock sliding out of her.

She lay back, bringing her knees up and closing her legs.

But I shot out, grabbing her knees and spreading her thighs wide. "You just screwed me like an animal that couldn't get enough," I teased, loving the sight of her plump breasts ready and waiting. "Don't get modest now."

My pants hung loose at my waist, and I palmed my cock, not that I needed much help staying hard.

Leaning down, I pressed my tongue onto her wet clit and moved in quick circles, massaging her, because I knew exactly what she liked but was afraid to ask for.

Tate liked my tongue. She didn't want fingers as much as that, and even though I was doing this to her—licking and flicking and fucking her with my mouth—I was doing this for me.

It was such a simple act, but nothing we ever did together was simple. It was a moment in an ocean of moments that kept us alive from one minute to the next, and it was heaven.

I had spent my life living and feeding off pain. The neglect brought on by my mother's alcoholism, the blood spilled by my father, and the loss and loneliness I caused myself by denying what was as simple and necessary to me as breathing.

I ignored truth and reason, because it was easier to believe that my power defined me rather than admitting I needed anyone. Rather than admitting the reality.

That I loved Tate.

That she loved me.

And that together we were invincible.

It had taken me years to learn, but I'd spend the rest of my life making up for it.

I trailed my tongue up the sides of her body and then came down, sucking her into my mouth. She cried out and grabbed my hair, pulling me back as she sat up.

"Now." She yanked my hips in, wrapping her legs around me.

Taking her underneath her thighs, I slid her to the edge of the hood and thrust back inside of her, her moans traveling down my throat as we kissed.

She wrapped her arms around my neck, and I leaned my hand down on the hood as we stayed chest to chest.

I pumped hard and fast, two years' worth of desire to unleash as we made love on the hood of my car. Her head fell back as her cries filled the night air, and I thrust deep, eating up her lips and neck as she struggled for breath.

"Tate," I groaned, feeling the fire inside ready to explode. "I love you, baby."

And I unleashed, pushing so deep and hard that she bit my lip. I came, spilling inside of her, her body holding me hot and perfect.

I gasped, sweat trickling down my temples as I breathed against her shoulder. I released my fingers, realizing I'd been squeezing her hips, probably to the point of pain.

I heard her swallow. "Again," she demanded, and I let out a tired laugh.

It felt good that she was so needy. I couldn't get enough of her, either.

"At home." I leaned up and kissed her cheek and then her forehead. "I want a bed."

"Whose home?"

I kissed her nose. "Ours."

CHAPTER 15

TATE

Jared took my keys, unlocking the front door of my house—or his house, now that I knew he had put in an offer—and I was so thankful that it was dark outside.

My dress and underwear were in pieces somewhere in his car, and I wore only his suit coat, while he trailed into the house behind me in his black pants with his shirt hanging open, since I'd ripped off the buttons.

"I can't believe you bought the house," I said, folding my arms over my chest to keep the coat closed. The only time I wasn't modest was during sex.

"You didn't have to do that," I continued, keeping my voice gentle, even though I kept having to blink back the tears as I looked around my home.

"Don't start looking for something new to worry about." He closed and locked the door, coming up to wrap his arms around me. "You're going to Stanford," he stated, "and who the hell knows where we'll settle, but I just couldn't let the house go yet."

He looked around, a thoughtful expression on his face. I felt the same way. I wasn't ready to say good-bye, either.

"If we sell it later," he appeased me, "then it'll be our decision when we're ready, but—"

I darted forward, cutting him off as I wrapped my arms around him and squeezed him tight. "Thank you," I choked out, tears lodged in my throat. "Thank you so much."

I knew he was worried about what I thought. Did this mean we were settling here after med school? Did this mean I wouldn't be able to entertain the possibility of practicing medicine elsewhere if an opportunity arose?

But I wasn't worried about that. He was just assuring me we didn't have to make any decisions yet. The house was ours to do with when we were ready, and we weren't losing it unless we wanted to.

My dad would get a new place with Miss Penley—Elizabeth—and while I'd get used to it, I knew it would feel strange visiting him in a place I'd never lived in. Holidays might never feel the same way again.

Now—I looked around at the warm walls and shiny wooden floors—I'd always have the house I grew up in to keep my memories alive.

Our first Thanksgiving, when we'd invited Katherine and Jared over, and Jared ate my vegetables for me so long as I took his cranberry sauce, which he hated.

The hot summer day my dad chased us out of the house when Jared and I set out to prove that nothing was really nonflammable.

The mornings in junior high when he'd sneak back through the tree to his own room after having slept over, only to show up a half hour later to walk me to school.

I sighed into his neck, smiling. "I bought something for you, too," I said in a sweet voice.

"You did?" He sounded amused. "Today?"

I shook my head and leaned back, looking up at him. "About a year ago," I clarified. "I saw it and immediately knew I had to have it for you. I've been saving it ever since."

His sexy mouth curled into a smile, a curious look in his eyes. "I'm a hard guy to shop for," he warned.

I backed away. "Come up in five minutes." And I turned around, jogging up the stairs.

As soon as I entered my bedroom, I tossed his jacket on the chair in the corner and went into the bathroom to freshen up.

He'd made a mess of me. My hair was tangled, my body was sore, and I had red marks on my hips from his hands.

But I'd be lying if I said I didn't love it. Jared devoured me like food. No one loved me like he did, and I lived him. And loved him.

Jumping into the shower, I spent maybe fifteen seconds rinsing the sweat and sex off, before jumping back out and brushing through my hair.

Going to the top drawer of my chest, I reached into the back and pulled out the lingerie that I knew he never needed me to wear but would definitely love.

The black lacy top was a cross between a tank top and a corset—however, while traditional corsets laced in the back, this one laced in the front. I stepped into the matching G-string and slipped my arms into the top, lacing the long, black silk ribbon through the loops, so that they crisscrossed in the front, leaving the skin of my stomach exposed through the ribbon as it threaded upward to tie between my breasts.

I'd always been embarrassed to try stuff like this. Jared was low maintenance, and he never gave the impression he wasn't perfectly happy with my pajama shorts and tank tops. And I had been intimate with Gavin so rarely that I never got around to experimenting with lingerie.

But Juliet inspired me. She and I had trailed into a shop one day, and then the very next day we had to go back, because Jax had destroyed the nightie she bought and gave her his credit card with instructions to replace the negligee and to buy some more as well.

I was jealous at the time. Her giddiness and happiness made me long to feel that again.

I glanced up, seeing a light fall across my floor, and I stepped over to the window, peeking through my sheer curtains to the house next door. Jax pulled down Juliet's dress to expose her naked back, and then he reached behind her to pull the curtains closed.

I smiled to myself, remembering the day almost two years ago that I'd had to tell them, "Hey, I can see everything. Would you mind . . . ?"

Since then, they'd been careful about making sure the window was closed—because they were loud, too—and the curtains drawn.

I was glad Juliet had her happily ever after, but I also knew it was past time for my own. Spinning around, I walked for the bedroom door, not wanting to waste another second of the five minutes I'd told him to wait.

"Tate, baby," a sleepy voice whispered against my hair. "Your phone."

Jared's arm tightened around my back and jostled me gently awake. I blinked my eyes open, realizing that my phone was ringing on the nightstand. I lifted my head off his chest and looked down at him, my dreamy cloud not lifting from my brain as I smiled at him.

His head lay to the side, facing the French doors, and his eyes were closed as he breathed peacefully.

Reluctantly turning away, I held the sheet up to cover my chest as I reached over to grab my phone.

"Hey, what's up?" I answered, seeing Juliet's name on the screen. Glancing at the clock, I saw it was only six thirty in the morning. Jared and I had been asleep for only a couple of hours.

"Sorry," she shot out. "I saw Jared's car over there, so I'm sure you're . . ." She hesitated just long enough to make an innuendo. "Busy," she finished.

A grin tugged at my jaw. "Nooooo," I drawled out. "I was sleeping. What do you want?"

She cleared her throat. "I know you wanted to work out today, but I need to cancel. I'm drained this morning, okay?"

"No problem," I sighed, twisting my head at the sound of thunder rolling outside. "I'm not going anywhere, either. Would you text Fallon to let her know?"

"Yeah, sure." She yawned.

If it was going to rain, then it would be a bad day for an outdoor workout anyway.

"Are you okay?" I prompted, noticing that she sounded unusually tired for a morning person.

"Yeah," she reassured me. "Just up too late. See you in a while."

"All right, see you later," I told her, shivers lighting up my skin as Jared's hand trailed up the inside of my thigh.

"Bye." And she hung up.

I put the phone down and looked over, seeing Jared still half asleep, his wandering hand creeping farther up my leg.

Nuzzling back into his arms, I traced the lines of his jaw and lips with my eyes. Trailing my hand down his chest and farther to his abs, I took in the script tattoo on the side of his torso that he'd gotten when I was in France five years ago—*Yesterday Lasts Forever, Tomorrow Comes Never*—and the *Until You* he'd had Aura, his tattoo artist, add more than a year later when we finally got together senior year.

He'd added more tattoos since we'd been apart.

There were two feathers on the other side of his torso, one inscribed with *Trent* and the other inscribed with *Brothers*.

And looking up on his left pec, I raised myself up, struggling for shallow breaths as I read the script.

I exist as I am, that is enough.

Right there, my quote inscribed over his heart. Happy tears sprang to my eyes. I couldn't believe it. He'd remembered the poem.

Lowering my head, I rested over his chest, promising myself that I'd never let him go.

His hand came up and started caressing my hair as he began to stir, and I felt him brush against my leg, his arousal growing harder.

I leaned over the side of the bed, picking up my now useless lingerie, which had two hooks ripped off because he got impatient fiddling with the ribbons in his mad rush.

"I liked that stuff," he mumbled, making me drop the lace. "Who knew I'd like you in clothes more than I liked you naked?"

I leaned up over him, shooting him an insulted look.

He barked out a laugh. "I didn't mean that exactly," he backtracked. "But it definitely enhanced your points of interest."

I rolled my eyes and swung my leg over his body, straddling him as the thunder cracked through the sky.

I leaned down, whispering over his mouth. "Let me see what I can do to enhance your point of interest."

And I snaked my way down his body, hearing him suck in a breath and grab my hair as I took him in my mouth.

Jared stood at the kitchen sink, looking even sexier doing dishes than he did when he worked on his car.

I'd made breakfast, and afterward he started cleaning up, just like he always did. As a kid Jared grew self-sufficient, and he was good about cleaning up, even when we had lived together for a couple of years in college. Thank goodness that hadn't changed.

I joined him at the island and placed my dishes in the sink.

"Jax borrowed my cooler last month," I told him, holding his hips from behind and kissing his back softly. "I'll be right back, okay?"

We were off with a group of other drivers today for a nice cruise up to Chestnut Mountain for lunch. Even with the light drizzle outside, nothing was stopping me from making the trip. Jared with me in a car. And a long drive with music. In the rain.

A perfect day.

He twisted his head, kissing me. "My duffel is in my old room," he muttered between kisses. "See if he can grab me a change of clothes, would you?"

I nodded, sinking into his mouth again before pulling away to leave through the back door.

My clothes got sprinkled as soon as I stepped off the back porch, but I didn't speed up into a run. I never ran in the rain. My bootcut jeans covered my legs, but my toes were bare in my black flip-flops, and while my fitted black polo shirt wouldn't go see-through with getting wet, my arms—bare in their short sleeves—already glistened with the light drizzle.

Stepping through the gate, I traipsed across Jax and Juliet's re-vamped backyard, complete with a finished deck and a landscaping scene. Fallon had used her engineering and designing expertise to experiment with their space, making it even more beautiful and inviting.

I opened the back door and called out, "Jax!" I stepped in, clos-ing the door behind me. "Juliet!"

"In here," I heard her voice from the bathroom off the side of the kitchen.

Thunder rippled outside, and I bit back my smile as I damn near bounced to the bathroom.

But I stopped short, seeing Juliet leaning over the toilet, coughing.

"Whoa, are you okay?" I rushed to hold her up.

"Oh, I'm fine," she grumbled, flushing the toilet and leaning back up and wiping her mouth with a hand towel. "One drink. One damn drink last night," she complained, "and I wake up feeling like crap. Why am I such a lightweight?"

"You are." I laughed, drawing her a glass of water. "I remember high school."

She arched a brow, glaring at me. "I don't want to relive that. You looked hot, and I was trying to be nice."

"By throwing a beer on me?" I shot back, handing her the glass. "To cool me off, you said?"

She snorted and shook her head at the memory of how tipsy even a little liquor got her before taking some water. She'd never been a big drinker, which was probably good, because neither was Jax.

"I need to grab my cooler," I told her over my shoulder as she followed me out of the bathroom. "I assume it's in the garage?"

She nodded, setting down the glass and righting her dainty red peasant blouse, loosely tucking the hem into her jean shorts.

"And I need to get a change of clothes for Jared. Is Jax in the bedroom?" I inquired, not wanting to walk in on him.

"He's in his office." She jerked her chin to the stairs. "You may as well grab Jared's whole bag. He probably won't be spending any more nights here," she teased.

Yeah, probably not.

I turned to leave, but she caught my hand.

"I'm happy for you," she said, her tone even and serious. "You and Jared . . . I didn't always think he was good enough for you, Tate," she admitted. "But there was a time when I didn't think I was, either."

I stood there, happy that she'd surprised herself.

She squeezed my hand. "He's a good man."

I smiled and kissed her on the cheek. "Thanks."

Running up the stairs, I stepped into Jax and Juliet's bedroom and spotted Jared's black duffel in the corner by the window.

Quickly stuffing the spilled clothes inside, I lifted the bag by the straps and flung it over my shoulder, thankful that his time in ROTC had at least taught him how to pack light.

I made my way for the door but stopped, spotting a circular black leather box on the dresser.

My jaw tingled with excited energy as I picked it up. I knew I shouldn't open it, but I had a feeling that Jax was going to ask Juliet soon. And if the ring was just sitting out, then he must've already asked her. I wanted to see it.

But then if he did, why hadn't she told me?

I glanced at the door, seeing no one in the sliver of hallway visible, and looked back down, cracking open the box.

My heart pitter-pattered in my chest, and I felt a rush of excitement in my limbs.

The ring was on a platinum band encrusted with small diamonds, while the centerpiece was a princess cut surrounded by smaller chips. I didn't know about carats, but the stone had to be nearly as wide as her finger.

"Wow." I brought my hand to my mouth, covering my whisper. "Holy—"

"Shit?" I heard Jax finish and looked up to see him stepping into the room.

I smiled at him through the happy tears in my eyes. "Are you asking her to marry you?" I inquired. "Or have you already asked her?"

I was so excited for Juliet.

He looked away, the words caught in his throat. "Yes, actually," he stammered. "But that's not the ring I'm using."

At my confused look, he shut the door behind him and spoke low.

"That's Jared's," he told me. "He left it here when he came home a year and a half ago."

Jared's . . . ? What?

"He left it here when he came home to propose to you," he finished, the solemn look on his face clearly waiting for my reaction.

My lungs emptied, and I just stood there. I couldn't move.

Jared came home more than a year ago to propose to me?

I dropped the bag, leaning against the dresser, and closed my eyes, walking myself through what he must've felt when he saw me with someone else. Buying a ring, coming home still as in love with me as when he left, and seeing . . .

Jax grabbed my face, turning me to look at him. "Look at me, Tate." Our eyes locked. "Stop, okay? You did nothing wrong. As with everything, it was bad timing." His hands cupped my face firmly, and I breathed in and out, trying to move past the ache of regret. I'd never wanted to hurt Jared. But he'd hurt me when he left, and I'd had to push him away.

"You are the love of his life," Jax continued, "and there was never any question that he was going to make his way back to you and fight for you sooner or later. What's important is that you both move on. You've got a life to live, memories to make with each other, and babies to have." He shook my face with his last words, bringing me back. "Don't waste another minute."

He was right. He was always right.

I could spend hours or days feeling bad about Jared wanting to marry me long ago, but I hadn't meant to break his heart. I was simply trying to protect mine.

Now he was here. He loved me, and I loved him. And we were happy. Case closed, and no looking back.

"Jax!" Juliet yelled from downstairs.

He dropped his hands, running into the hallway.

"What's wrong?" He peered over the railing.

"Check your phone! Madoc just texted," she said, sounding worried. "Katherine just went into labor. She's having the baby now!"

CHAPTER 16

JARED

We dove into the elevator, Jax and I with the girls at our sides, and my phone about to crack under the pressure of my fist.

After Madoc's text, Tate had come through the backdoor carrying my duffel, and I had her go start the car while I slipped on some clothes. Jax and Juliet had sped off right away, while I swung by Madoc's house and picked up Pasha. She'd been keeping pretty busy, hanging out with Jax at the Loop and hiking with Madoc, Fallon, and Lucas—their little brother from the Big Brothers Big Sisters program—this past week, but for some reason, I didn't want to leave her out of things.

So I took a small detour, picked her up, and hit the road.

And of all the fucking inconveniences, my mother was in Chicago for the weekend with Jason, since her city friends had convinced her to go to some baby exposition bullshit when she should've been resting.

We sped the entire drive and caught up with Jax.

Once inside the hospital, I sent Pasha to the gift shop to buy flowers. I considered making sure my mom and sister were all right more important than personally picking out her floral arrangement. So while she did that, the rest of us raced up to the third floor.

My muscles tightened in anticipation, and I could feel a trickle of sweat trail down my back. I didn't know why I was so nervous.

It wasn't worry or discomfort. It was definitely nervousness. I rubbed my mouth over my T-shirt on my shoulder, wiping away the thin layer of sweat.

What was I supposed to do with a baby? It was doubtful there would be any connection. Our differences in age would most likely prevent us from bonding.

And it was a girl. What was I supposed to do with a girl?

Luckily, she was little, and it would be a long time before she really interacted with anyone.

But part of me was also depressed by that fact, too.

Madoc, and even Jax, would no doubt catch on very quickly how to play with her and talk to her, but entertaining, much less tolerating, people was never my strong suit.

But I did want her to be close to me. I just had no idea what the hell to do to make that happen.

Madoc had texted that my mom was in suite seven, and since it took us nearly an hour to get to Chicago, navigate traffic to the hospital, and park, the baby was already here and so were Madoc and Fallon, since they'd left before us.

I didn't knock. Barging into the room, though, I slowed, seeing Madoc standing by my mom's bed with the baby already in his arms.

"I got her first," he teased. "Sorry."

He wasn't at all sorry, judging by the shitty-ass grin on his face, but it was okay. I stared at the tightly wrapped pink bundle in Madoc's big arms, looking like nothing more than a little loaf of bread, and I tried to wrap my brain around the fact that that was my sister.

I couldn't even see her, she was so buried in blankets.

Tate stayed at my side, and I could feel my mom watching me as Jax veered around to go to Madoc's side.

"Hey, Quinn Caruthers," he sang, putting a gentle hand on her head.

Madoc looked at her with awe, already in love, while Jax loomed at his side, and I could tell he was itching to get her into his arms.

I didn't know why I felt like a third wheel. I glanced at my mom, who was watching me with patience.

"All of her brothers." She reminded me, urging me with her eyes to go get a closer look at the baby.

I inhaled a deep breath and walked over, flanking Madoc's other side as I dropped my eyes and took in the little bit. The little bit of nothing who was already succeeding in making my knees buckle.

"Isn't she perfect?" Madoc said holding her up on his forearms in front of his body, so we all could see.

And everything inside of me gave way.

My chest splintered in a hundred different cracks, my hands tingled, and what I felt was almost a craving to hold her.

Her glistening eyelids covered her eyes in sleep, so I couldn't tell their color, but the rest of her had a reddish tint that made her look like she'd been through the ringer today.

Her plump new cheeks looked soft and fragile, her nose was no bigger than my pinky nail, and the little triangle gap between her lips as she breathed—every little thing—felt like it was digging its way into my heart. I reached out, unable to resist slipping my finger into her fist.

How could anything be so little?

The tiny fingers—as frail as matchsticks—wrapped around my finger, and my throat swelled, and I tried to swallow against the painful ache, but it was too much.

"We're your brothers, little girl," Jax cooed.

"Yeah." Madoc laughed. "You're so screwed."

Everyone laughed, high off the rush of a new baby, but I was falling. The blanket shifted, and I looked down to see her little feet nudge their way out.

"Jesus, she's little," I breathed out, amazed. I looked up. "Mom, I . . ."

But my mom was crying, tears streaming down her face, and I immediately felt like shit that I hadn't gone to her first.

"Are you okay?" I asked, trying to slip away from Quinn's little fist, but it was no use.

She shook her head clear, smiling. "I'm on top of the world," she assured me. "The picture I'm looking at right now couldn't be more perfect." And she started crying again, looking at Madoc, Jax, and me. Jason brought her head into his chest, looking completely disheveled himself.

"She's going to be a blonde," he pointed out, referring to his new daughter.

"How do you know?" Jax asked, curious.

"Because she's practically bald. Just like Madoc was."

Madoc snorted and shot his dad an annoyed look.

I put my hand on top of her head, amazed at how it fit in my palm. I felt Tate watching me and looked up to see a smile in her eyes.

"You want to hold her, Jared?" my mom spoke up.

I shook my head. "I don't think—"

But Madoc was already on me, handing her off. I brought my arms up, feeling them shake under the weight of her weightlessness.

"Oh, shit." I breathed hard.

"Language." I heard my mom's faint mumble.

Madoc took his arms away, slowly lowering her head into the crook of my arm, and even though she weighed nothing, I was afraid I wouldn't be able to hang on to her.

Different from any other feeling I'd ever had.

I pinched my eyebrows together, studying every little inch of her sweet face.

"She's so small," I said more to myself than to the others.

"She'll grow," Jax commented, peering over my shoulder.

I shook my head, not believing that I was once that little. "So helpless . . ."

Tate finally appeared at my side and kissed her forehead. "A girl with you three as her brothers will be anything but helpless." She laughed.

My chest suddenly shook, watching as her mouth opened in a little oval as she yawned, and—*holy shit*—I was going to die. Could she get any cuter?

I laughed so I wouldn't cry. "I feel like my heart is breaking, and I don't know why. What the hell?"

"It's love," I heard my mother say. "Your heart isn't breaking. It's growing."

Tate wrapped her arm around my waist and leaned her head on my arm, both of us watching Quinn.

I leaned down, brushing a kiss on her cheek and inhaling her baby scent.

Jesus, I was pathetic.

"My turn," Jax shot out, nudging in.

Reluctantly, I handed her off, careful to support her head. I was unnerved by how much I didn't want to give her up.

Hell, I even hated the thought of ever having to leave Shelburne Falls again.

"Oh, God!"

We all turned, stunned out of our baby trance as Juliet dove for the wastebasket and vomited, turning away from us to hide her display.

"Juliet!" Jax shouted, handing the baby off to our mom as he and Tate rushed over to help.

"Baby, are you okay?" he asked as Tate pulled back her hair.

"Oh, my God," she groaned, dry heaving over the garbage. "I'm so sorry. I don't want to make the baby sick if I caught something."

"Here." Jax handed her some Kleenex to wipe her mouth and supported her body with his arm.

She pushed him away, lurching again and emptying just about everything else she had in her stomach.

"Oh, no." A nurse walked in, shoving the water pitcher at me as she rushed to Juliet's side.

"I'm sorry," Juliet mumbled, holding her hand over her mouth, a pink blush settling on her skin.

I put the pitcher down on my mom's little dinner table and poured some water for both her and Juliet.

"No harm done," the nurse soothed. "Come with me." And she placed a hand on her back, guiding her out.

Jax and Tate made a move to follow, but Juliet stopped them. "No, you stay. Both of you," she ordered. "I'll be fine. Stay with Quinn. I'll see you in the waiting room."

"You're not fine," Jax shot out.

"Stay," she commanded. "Please, I'll feel bad. I'm just going to the bathroom, anyway. I'll see you in a minute."

Jax stood at the doorway, watching her go, and the rest of us took seats on the couch, laughing at Madoc taking selfies with Quinn.

"Looks like the cruise is shot," I commented, noticing that the time on my phone already read after four in the afternoon.

By the time we'd gotten to the hospital and visited with my mom, Jason, and Quinn, it was nearly time to head home for Tate's race tonight.

Thankfully, the weather had cleared up, so Jax was expecting a full crowd.

"It's okay." Tate nuzzled in under my arm, wrapping her arm around my waist. "This was a much better day anyway."

She looked over at Jax on her other side and then up at me. "Your sister is a very lucky girl. You both know that, right?"

Jax and I shared a look, laughing to ourselves.

"What?" Tate looked back and forth between us.

I shook my head, knowing what she meant, but . . .

"Well," I started, "my first thought was that she needs other kids to grow up with. She'll be lonely."

"Yeah," Jax chimed in, lifting his water bottle to his lips and agreeing with me.

"Well," Tate argued, "you may be surprised at how much you'll all make sure she's *not* lonely."

"Good point," I added. And she was probably right. My mother was spot on about our roles with our sister.

As soon as I held her fragile, helpless body, I'd known that I would run into the middle of a stampede for her.

"Hey." Jax approached the nurse's station. "My girlfriend was sick. A nurse took her somewhere, but I haven't seen her or heard anything."

"Juliet Carter?" she said right away. "Yeah, she's in room two."

"They put her in a room?" he asked, confused, and Tate shot me a worried look.

The nurse nodded and gestured to the left with her hand.

I dug in my eyebrows, a little worried.

Even though I'd grown pretty fond of Juliet, she was still normally off my radar. Her interests, hobbies, and well-being weren't high on my list of priorities, so I'd never paid her much mind. But I had to admit she was head over heels for my brother, as well as loyal and nurturing. And she worked hard, never expecting things to be handed to her.

She deserved him, and he deserved her.

Jax barreled for room two, pushing open the door, while Tate and I quickly followed.

"Jesus," Jax cursed as soon as he entered the room. "Is she okay?"

We rushed in, seeing her asleep on top of the covers, looking peaceful and still wearing the same clothes as before.

He rushed to her side, looking her up and down. "What the hell?" he whispered, turning to the nurse who had trailed in behind us.

She stopped, a stunned look on her face. "I'm sorry, sir?"

"What's wrong with her?" I said softly, careful not to wake Juliet.

Tate had stepped up next to Jax, looking down at her friend.

"I just came on duty," she explained. "As far as I know, though, she's fine. They just wanted her to rest and get hydrated." She looked around to all of us. "She'll be fine to leave in a bit. No worries."

"Well, is something wrong? She's my girlfriend." Jax's worried eyes were trying to connect the dots just like the rest of us. But with no luck.

"Not at all." Her voice sounded light. "It's very common to have a hard time holding anything down in the first trimester. She'll be fine. Just make sure she drinks as much water as possible."

Jax's eyes nearly bugged out of his goddamn head, and I almost choked on my breath.

"Tri-what?" I forced out.

"Jax," Tate gasped, looking between us, smiling with her hand over her mouth.

"I'm sorry." Jax shook his head, zoning in on the poor young nurse. "What the hell did you just say?"

Realization dawned, and she straightened. "Oh," she said, looking caught. "I'm sorry. I thought a doctor spoke to you." She inched up to the bed, embarrassment warming her face.

"She's pregnant?" Jax blurted.

The nurse nodded, checking the water pitcher on the table. "Yes, about five weeks. From what the other nurse said before she left, it doesn't sound like your girlfriend was aware, either." She turned to leave and then faced Jax again. "And I am sorry again. I thought you were informed."

She left the room, and Jax leaned down on the bed, staring at Juliet. Tate squeezed my hand, and I felt a sudden need to get her alone. It had been a crazy day.

Jax brought up his hand, caressing Juliet's face, and then placed it on her stomach, looking like he was trying to wrap his head around the news.

"Let's go," I whispered to Tate. My brother needed to be alone with his girl right now.

Keeping hold of Tate's hand, I led her out of the room and walked down the hall, finding the single-person restroom. With all the chaos today, not to mention that we still had her race tonight, I needed to steal a few minutes with her.

Pulling her inside, I backed her up to the door and took her by the neck, crashing my mouth down on hers.

She moaned, surprised as she slipped her hands under my T-shirt to hold on to my back. Her mouth was so warm, and I nibbled her lips, too damn hungry to get my mouth on the rest of her body.

"So," she tried speaking between kisses, "a kid for Quinn to grow up with. Just like you wanted."

I unbuttoned her jeans and slid them down over her ass and grabbed her naked flesh in my hands as I continued attacking her lips.

"I love you," I whispered. "I want everything with you, Tate."

Then I knelt down, sliding the jeans and underwear off her legs, taking the flip-flops with them.

She threaded her fingers through my hair and dropped her head back, gasping as I swung her leg over my shoulder and ran my tongue over her clit.

"You'll have everything with me." She sucked in mouthfuls of air. "I'm yours, Jared."

"Damn right you are," I growled, licking the smooth skin of her delicate heat. I snatched her up between my lips and sucked.

"Oh," she moaned, looking down to watch me.

"I saw the ring in Jax's room," she admitted, her voice shaking. "I know about when you came home. I feel terrible, and I don't know that I should, but . . ."

The tip of my tongue prodded her entrance while she spoke, and she squirmed against my lips, wanting more.

I pulled away, rubbing circles over the nub of her clit with my thumb. "I was shattered when I had to leave you," I explained. "I hated myself, but I had to go. I had to do it. Just like you had to try to move on and live in a world I didn't try to dominate all the time."

I gripped her sexy-as-hell ass and brought her in again, eating and taking her hard.

"Jared," she whimpered. Then: "Why did you want to marry me?"

Huh?

I leaned back, seeing her desperate eyes, on fire with love but rippled with need.

Standing up, I wrapped my arms around her and held her body close. "How could I not?"

How could she not know that she was it for me?

"Twelve years," I continued, "and I have never stopped wanting you, Tate. Not for a single day have I been free of you." I put us forehead to forehead, nose to nose. "I want everything. I want you to finish school. I want the wedding with our friends and family. I want the house, and I want our kids, Tate."

I pressed my lips to hers until I could feel my teeth digging into the inside of my lips.

"And if you don't want some of that or any of that," I pointed out, "then I'll bend, because above anything else"—I looked her in the eye—"I want you."

Her beautiful blue storms pooled like the rainy days she lived for, and I pulled back, unbuttoning my jeans, never satisfied that I'd have enough of her.

Lifting her by the backs of her thighs, I slid her down my cock, kissing her to drown out her sudden cry.

Thrusting inside of her, I whispered against her mouth. "Forever."

She closed her eyes, a blush crossing her cheeks. "Forever," she complied. "After we settle an old score, of course."

And I shot my eyes up, seeing her lips curl with an idea.

"An old score?"

"Mmm-hmm," she confirmed, keeping her eyes closed. "You and I have unfinished business, Jared Trent."

Shit.

CHAPTER 17

TATE

"I don't get the point of this." Jared pulled on his black hoodie. The rain had cooled everything down considerably.

"Simple," I explained. "We've had two races, and I haven't won one yet. I want one more chance before we start a new slate."

"What are you talking about?" he shot back, running his hand through his brown hair and making it stick up in perfect messiness. "You won the first one we had four years ago," he pointed out.

"Did I?"

His face fell, and he looked annoyed as he arched a brow at me.

I smirked, reaching through my open back window and grabbing my own hoodie.

"Tate." He came up, placing his hands on my waist. "You and I don't need to race."

"We do." I put my foot down. "This is my last race, Jared."

He fell silent, and I turned around, looking up at him studying me. Taking his hand, I leaned back into the car and pulled him close, wanting privacy from the Loop crowd a few feet away.

"We'll always share our love of cars," I started, keeping my voice even. "And we'll have a lot of fun driving and pulling our own little stunts in the years to come, but . . ." I took a deep breath, trying to find the right words to make him understand.

"Growing up, I always thought I'd share this with you," I admitted. "From the first time you mentioned the Loop when we were ten, it was going to be Jared and me at the race. Jared and me in our car. Jared and me a team." I swallowed down the dream that really never came to fruition.

I cleared my throat. "When you left, it was like what you were talking about when you were on your bike on the track . . . about how it was the only time we were together. Remember?"

He stayed still, studying me warily. I could tell he was concerned that I'd be giving up something I loved for the wrong reasons.

"Well"—I nodded—"that's what the Loop has been like for me ever since you left. A way to be close to you when I fooled myself into thinking it helped me survive without you." I shook my head, dropping my eyes. "It didn't," I confessed. "I have no glory to seek here, and I have no interest in pursuing anything more advanced. Medicine is where my ambitions lie, and although I love driving, the only way I want on this track from now on"—I met his gaze—"is if we're in the same car."

I liked driving, but it wasn't love for me like it was for Jared. And I didn't want to enjoy it without him anymore.

I tightened my arms around his waist. "I know your heart is on the track, but I don't need this, and I don't want it unless I'm sitting next to you. It's time my energies went elsewhere."

He grazed his fingers down both sides of my face, sending shivers down my arms. "But you love this," he maintained, looking at me with concern.

"I *like* this," I corrected him. "I *love* it with you."

He tipped my chin up, kissing me, and in less than a moment, my body heated. I loved the way he tasted.

"So . . ." I pulled back, blinking away the haze he'd created. "It's my last race, and the last time you and I will be opponents—or enemies, for that matter—and I want it to be you. No one else."

The corner of his mouth lifted. "And what makes you think I won't just let you win?"

"Because it's also a bet," I retorted, the mischief thick in my voice. "If I win, I get to propose to you in front of all of these people."

He rolled his eyes, walking away from me.

"And it'll make you feel really feminine in front of the huge crowd and their phone cameras," I went on, talking to his back. "And it'll be a superinteresting story—if not a little unmanly—to tell our children someday. And my father will probably lose all respect for you, but when I get down on one knee, baby," I teased, "you're just going to melt and swoon."

"Good God," he whined, turning around and looking like he ate something bad. "I think I lost a testicle listening to this." And then he turned back around, ordering over his shoulder, "You're not proposing."

"But, sweetheart," I yelled, catching the others' attention. "You love it when I'm alpha."

Bystanders laughed, and I smiled as Jared shook his head as he walked away from me, probably seeking escape by going to find Jax and Madoc.

I locked my car and slipped on my hoodie as I walked over to Juliet sitting in a quad chair next to Jax's car.

"How are you feeling?" I asked, seeing a fleece blanket and two bottles of water lying next to the chair on the ground.

"Shaky," she admitted. "But I'm okay. Jax wanted us to stay home, but when I heard you and Jared were racing I insisted we come."

I picked up the blanket and folded it, setting it on Jax's car.

"How did he take the news?" I asked, looking over at him and seeing Madoc giving him shit.

"A lot better than me." She sighed. "He has a case of water in the trunk and actually put a blanket on me, as if it's not summertime," she complained, sounding cute. "He already YouTubed how to deliver a baby in an emergency, so I think he warmed up to the idea pretty fast," she joked, laughing.

"And you?"

She shrugged, letting out a breath. "I'm on the pill. Or was," she added. "We were never careless, even after two years of being together. I definitely wasn't prepared for this." She stared off, and I followed her gaze to see her watching her boyfriend. A slight smile graced her face. "But he keeps touching my stomach, like he'll be able to feel it move already." She laughed. "I would never have tried to have a baby right now, but I just look at him, and all of a sudden I can't wait. We're actually having a baby together."

I leaned down, giving her a big hug. It was nice to know Jax was planning on proposing before they knew about the baby. Seeing her still bare finger, I guessed he was going to make an occasion out of it.

And thanks to the impromptu news today, it would probably be sooner rather than later.

"Everyone is here for you, you know that, right?" I told her. "And Fallon will be pregnant soon, so you won't be alone."

She looked at me, confused. "How do you know that?"

I sighed. "It happens in threes. Katherine, you, and it won't be me, so . . ."

We laughed, knowing it very well could be me, but with Jax having a baby, I was sure Madoc would play it up and get Fallon to fold.

"Tatum Brandt!" someone bellowed. "Get your ass over here!"

I shot up, staring wide-eyed into the crowd. *What . . . ?*

I glanced at Juliet, and she just smiled, recognizing Jared's voice, too.

Staying frozen in place—because I didn't answer to that name, and he damn well knew it—I finally saw him rise above the crowd as he stood on . . . what I could only assume was his car's hood.

His head cocked to the side, and the spectators looked between him and me. The music cut off, and I watched his easy, self-satisfied body language as he spoke.

"You want to race me or what?" he challenged, the same defiant and cocky attitude in his expression that I hated and loved in high school.

My heart picked up pace, and I crossed my arms over my chest, inching toward the crowd.

"You know I do," I replied with sass. "Why are you acting like you have better things to do all of a sudden?"

"With you?" he shot back. "We definitely have better things to do."

The crowd buzzed with laughter at Jared's clear innuendo, but I smiled, unembarrassed. I'd learned to fight back a long time ago.

I looked around at the crowd. "I think he's afraid I'll win, don't you?" I asked my rhetorical question and heard the amused crowd turn to him for his reaction.

He jumped down from his car, and we walked toward each other through the parting crowd.

He jeered, "You win? I've raced here twice as much as you have. I think I can handle seeing you in my rearview mirror, Tatum," he joked, getting my heart pumping faster with his mock insults, which gave me déjà vu. Which, I guessed, was why he was egging me on.

To get me pumped up.

I put my hand on my heart, feigning sympathy. "Oh, but sweetheart? Didn't anyone tell you?" I approached him, smiling. "This is a chicken race," I informed him. "I won't be behind you. I won't be next to you." I leaned in to whisper. "I'll be coming at you, baby."

The smirk on his face slowly fell to his feet, and I bit back the urge to laugh.

Priceless. Damn, I'm good.

Jared's heated eyes turned fierce, and he looked around for his brother.

I snorted as Jax stepped up, rolling his eyes. "Thanks, Tate," he said sarcastically. "I hadn't told him yet."

"What is she talking about?" Jared's hard voice sounded tense, and I tried not to grin. It wasn't often I could surprise him.

"Uh, yeah," Jax inched out, sounding apologetic. "It's a new feature here, brother. You both take off from the starting line but in opposite directions," he explained, glancing at me. "You have the whole track to work with until you pass each other, which you'll do in your own lanes," Jax gritted out, telling me specifically, since I'd never done this before either, and he wanted to make sure I understood.

I raised my eyebrows, eyeing Jared. "But at the finish line . . . ," I hinted.

"At the finish line," Jax took my cue, "on the last turn, you have to cruise in between the barriers to make the finish count."

He pointed to the waist-high plastic barriers, sometimes used in road construction, that were being positioned behind him to make a single lane on the track.

"That makes a lane only wide enough for one car," Jax observed.

I couldn't control the bounce in my feet. "Exactly," I remarked.

"Whoever makes it first . . ." Jax nodded. "Well, you get the idea."

I swung around, heading for my car as Jax blew a whistle, clearing the track.

"Tate!" Jared shouted, his voice being drowned out in the crowd. "I'm not doing this!"

"If you don't," I called over my shoulder, "someone else will, and I won't be as safe with them as I will be with you, right?"

I opened my car and climbed inside.

"You're a brat!" I saw him growl in the middle of the crowd.

I cocked my head, sticking it out the window. "I love you," I shot back, teasing.

And thank goodness he didn't put up more of a fight. Hesitating only a moment, he shook his head, looking defeated, before turning around and walking for his own ride, which already sat on the track.

Jared's car was a piece of art, and everyone had been all over it since we'd gotten here.

Turning the ignition, I revved the engine and brought my hands up, squeezing the steering wheel against the hot rush in my blood.

The crowd had dissipated, either going farther off to the sidelines or to the bleachers, and I released the clutch, pulling myself up onto the track. Swinging around, I pulled up next to Jared, both of us facing opposite directions and our driver's sides sitting next to each other.

"You've never gone easy on me," I told him, my tone serious. "Don't hold back now."

He stared out the front windshield, clearly hating what I wanted from him.

Reaching over, I cranked up the music and then gathered up my hair, tying it up into a ponytail.

He finally looked over at me, and a smile crept out as, he too, reached over and turned up his music.

"Welcome, everyone!" We heard Zack's voice come over the loudspeaker.

I looked over to see Madoc and Fallon sitting on the bleachers, while Jax and Juliet crossed the track in front of my car, heading over there as well.

The crowd, a mix of high school students as well as friends from way back, took out phones to start videotaping. Many of them were well aware of Jared's and my history, so they had a vested interest in seeing this little showdown.

Jared's mouth curled into a grin, and I couldn't help my foot tapping as anticipation sent shivers up my spine.

He knew I liked the way he looked at me, and he was trying to throw me off. Okay, maybe not on purpose, but whatever.

"These two," Zack started, booming over the speaker, "need no introduction. It's a matchup that rivals any we've ever had here, and they never fail to bring a few fireworks to the Loop."

The crowd cheered, and I checked the shifter to make sure I was in first.

"Jared and Tate?" Zack continued. "Best of luck."

The spectators cheered, and I let out a hard sigh as Jared rolled up the window.

I did the same, lowering the music for a moment.

"Ready!" Zack boomed, since from the position I was in, I couldn't see the signal lights.

"Set!" I heard, swallowing through the dryness in my mouth.

Jared and I both pressed the gas, too excited to contain it.

"Go!" The roar raged through my ears, and Jared and I tore away from each other, the screech of our tires sending the crowd cheering louder.

I shot down into second and then up into third, gaining speed quickly and smoothly. Jared and I pulled farther and farther away from each other, and glancing in my rearview mirror, I was surprised that I didn't really like seeing his distance away from me increase. I could almost feel it on my skin.

Just like magnets.

His brake lights flashed, and I tightened my grip on the steering wheel, seeing him skid around the next corner.

Shit.

Hitting the gas, I shifted straight into fifth, skipping fourth altogether and spinning around the turn. The rotten thing about my car was that it was about three hundred pounds heavier than his, so he could maneuver quicker and easier.

Shooting back into third, I hit the gas, charged ahead, and shot back up to fifth and then sixth. Jared's muscle car looked like a rocket blowing up rainwater on the track as it raced ahead toward the next turn.

I tensed my thigh muscles, feeling a thrill creep up my insides. *Damn, he was hot.* I couldn't see him through his blacked-out windows, but he was still managing to turn me the hell on.

Surfing around the next turn, I charged ahead, staying on my right as Jared plowed toward me, and I let out a laugh as he passed.

I loved racing him. I always felt the rush, and no matter whom else I'd raced, nothing felt as good.

A chill spread over my skin, despite the hoodie, and I didn't hesitate to barrel around the next turn, charging ahead.

I didn't want to win or need to win, but I wanted to have this with him.

My music cut off, and my phone started ringing on the touch screen. I pressed Accept Call.

"Yes?" I answered.

"What happens if I win?" Jared asked, and his velvet voice caressed my skin.

I hesitated, not sure how to answer. "Then . . ." I searched for words. "Then I guess I trust that you'll always give me your best."

He was quiet, and I could hear the crowd ahead.

"And if I lose?" he asked, sounding unusually sad. "Will you still trust that I gave you my best?"

A lump rose in my throat, and I blinked away the sudden tears.

"Jared." I folded my lips between my teeth, trying not to cry. He wanted to know if I trusted him.

"I can't promise I'll wake up every day operating at a hundred percent, Tate," he admitted. "No one can."

I heard his voice change as he struggled to round the last turn, and I shifted down, doing the same, the steering wheel trying to pull against me as I skidded.

"But"—he breathed hard from the exertion—"I can promise I'll always put you first."

"Then, prove it," I urged in a thoughtful voice. "Meet my match."

I shot down into fifth and then up into sixth, seeing his lights ahead.

This was it. One of us was going between the barriers, and the other would be forced to take the lane to the outside, and he was fucking with my head right now, and I just wanted him to race.

"Tate . . . ," he said in a hesitant voice.

"Jared, just go," I pressed. "It's you. It's only you. You're the only one who challenges me, so challenge me! Don't hold back. I trust you."

I squeezed the wheel, my eyebrows pinching together as I pressed myself back into the seat.

Go, go, go . . .

Shooting for the starting line, I pushed the gas to the floor, seeing him charge ahead, both of us in the path marked by the barriers.

"Tate!" he barked.

"Go!" I yelled.

Jax had lines marked on the track, giving drivers notice for their last chance to exit, but judging my space, I knew I was going to make it.

I was going to make it, and I didn't want Jared to ease up. *Give me everything!*

I held the wheel, my arm like a steel bar, and sucked in breaths as my heart beat like a jackhammer.

"Fuck!" Jared cursed, barreling straight for me. "Tate, stop!"

His car, my car, one lane, right for each other, the barriers in three . . . two . . . one . . . and . . .

No!

I screamed, twisting the wheel right, every muscle in my body in a nightmare of pain as I swerved out of his way and passed the barriers, nearly whimpering out of fear as I winced.

Oh, God!

I let breath after breath pour out of me as I took quick glances behind me several times to see that he was on the other side of the barriers, too.

He'd tapped out. Just like me.

Shit. I dropped my head back, terrified by what had almost happened, as I slowed to halt.

Shaking my head, horrified and relieved at the same time, I realized the irony.

He'd put me first. Just like he'd promised.

The crowd descended, and I climbed out of my car, feeling shaky and weak.

"You're absolutely crazy!" I heard him yell as he made his way through the crowd. "Does Stanford know how reckless you are?" he attacked.

I straightened but averted my eyes, feeling a little contrite. He had every right to be pissed. I'd messed with his head, telling him to give me his very best, which would also put both of us in danger. Which choice had I expected him to make? But before I had a chance to apologize, he threw a small box at me. "Here."

I shot up my hands to catch it.

"Open that," he ordered.

I studied the cylindrical black leather box and immediately knew what it was.

He stayed a few feet back, but the crowd surrounded us, and I saw our friends push to the front of the audience.

I did as he said and opened it, revealing the platinum band, the princess-cut diamond that had been meant for me. Gasps exploded in the crowd and even some squeals, probably from the high school girls who thought his rudeness was cute.

I twisted my lips to the side, taking in his angry arched eyebrow.

"So this is how you propose?" I asked sternly. "Because I kind of have a problem with a ring being thrown in my face and you not kneeling like my father would expect."

I looked at Jax and a laughing Madoc and continued, "Not that I expected Jared to kneel—I know he's not the type—but I damn well expect a gesture, and—"

I looked down, seeing Jared in front of me on one knee.

"Oh," I whispered, shutting up.

Snorts could be heard in the crowd, and I let him take my hand as he smiled up at me.

My heart pounded, and butterflies swarmed in my stomach.

"Tate." He spoke slowly, looking into my eyes in a way that was still so much like the boy I grew up with but more like the man I'd grown to love.

"You're written all over my body," he spoke low, just for us. "The tattoos can never be erased. You hold my heart, and you can never be replaced."

I pressed my lips together, trying to stay composed.

He continued, "I only live when I'm with you, and I'm asking for your heart, your love, and your future." He smiled. "Will you please be my wife?"

My chin trembled, and my chest shook, and I couldn't help it. I covered my smile with my hand and let the tears fall.

The crowd around us started cheering, and I caressed his face as he stood up and lifted me up off the ground.

"Now, that's how you propose," I joked through my shakes.

"You going to answer me, then?"

I laughed. "Yes." I nodded frantically. "Yes, I would love to marry you."

After the Loop, we escaped.

Just the two of us to Mario's for a late dinner and then home. I couldn't stop the flutter in my chest.

I think it was the happiest day I'd ever had.

Jared had slipped the ring on my finger and held me close, tucked under his chin as we called my father on Skype with his phone.

Apparently, he'd asked my dad a year and a half ago, and true to fashion, my father didn't share business that wasn't his to share or interfere in situations he knew needed to play out. We also found out that was why he'd never accepted other offers on the house. He knew Jared would come home eventually.

I looked up at Jared, resting my head on his arm behind me. "I'm sorry about the tree," I said, feeling bad as we sat in the middle of it, me between his legs and lying back against his chest.

"I know." His voice was gentle. "It'll heal. Everything does with time."

Looking down, I studied the ring, feeling its happy weight on my finger. There were still lots of things to work out—living arrangements while I went to school, his career—but it was small potatoes considering what we'd survived to be together. Two assurances I had come to realize about life: Almost nothing turns out exactly the way you plan, but I'd be happy only if he was by my side. There was no choice.

"If you don't like it, we can exchange it," he spoke up, seeing me admire the ring.

"No, I love it," I assured him. "It's perfect." And then I smiled. "My new lifeline."

Jared snorted, remembering my lifelines from high school. The things I always made sure to have on me when I went out, just in case I needed to escape him.

He leaned in, kissing my hair. "I don't want to wait to marry you," he whispered, and I nuzzled into him, loving him so much.

I didn't want to wait, either.

CHAPTER 18

JARED

Three Months Later

"Knock it off." I jerked away from Madoc's hands as he fiddled with my tie.

"But it's crooked," he argued, yanking me back. "And it looks like shit."

I gave in, standing still and trying not to feel creeped out as another guy straightened my necktie.

My entire suit was black, of course, but I'd added a vest for extra effect.

Madoc leaned in, his mouth inches from mine. "Mmmm, you smell good," he purred.

I jerked back, wincing. "Get off me," I grumbled, shoving him away, and he hunched over, his face turning red from laughing so hard.

Jax hurried over to my side, smiling. "She's here."

I grinned but then hid it right away. Grabbing the back of my neck, I put my head down and tried to get my pulse under control. Hell, get my temperature under control, for that matter. I felt sweat on my back, even though it was late September and the weather had started cooling off already.

I looked around the pond—our fishpond—and focused on the small man-made waterfall display with little rapids cascading down the rocks, and I remembered her here when we were little.

This was where I'd thought I lost her when I was fourteen, so as a measure to make sure that no bad memory ever controlled us again, we both agreed that this was where we'd be married.

This was the start of new memories and new adventures.

Jason and Ciaran, Fallon's father who had employed my brother for a time and become part of the family in a way, stood off to the side, chatting casually—which was surprising, considering they worked on opposite sides of the law. My mom—glowing and with newfound energy—sat on a ledge, holding Quinn in her arms, while Pasha stood next to the pond's edge dressed in a tight silver and black dress, standing out like a sore thumb.

Lucas, Madoc's "little brother," played on his phone, while Lucas's mom and Miss Penley—or Lizzy, as we were allowed to call her now, but I refused, because it was weird—cooed over my new little sister.

James, Tate's dad, and his new fiancée had bought a house between Chicago and Shelburne Falls, an easy commute that wouldn't disrupt either of their jobs. They were planning a summer ceremony next year.

Juliet, Fallon, and James were all with Tate, I assumed, and Madoc and Jax were standing up for me.

"You know, you didn't have to do this," Madoc spoke up, straightening his own tie. "Jax is your brother. It would make sense that he'd stand up for you at your wedding."

I saw the officiant approach and pointed out to Madoc, "You're my brother, too. I can't choose between either of you any more than Tate could choose between Fallon and Juliet."

When we'd had to tell the officiant the names of my best man and her maid—or matron—of honor, we didn't second-guess ourselves. Fallon and Juliet for her, Jax and Madoc for me.

"You know we could've just had this at my house," he suggested. "There's plenty of room on the grounds, and you wouldn't have had to limit the guest list."

"We limited it out of preference," I corrected him, "not necessity. Tate and I wanted small and private," I told him, knowing he preferred big and flashy. "And we wanted it here," I added.

"Okay." He dropped the subject, accepting my reasoning. And I knew he understood.

Although Madoc had had an impromptu wedding at a bar, I don't think he regretted it for a second. He loved Fallon, and they had just wanted to get married. The rest didn't matter.

Tate and I waited a little longer than he and Fallon did, but not by much.

We'd spent the rest of the summer between Shelburne Falls—relaxing with our friends and enjoying our family—and California, looking for an apartment near Stanford and spending time at my shop.

Once school started, Tate got settled in as I commuted home to her as much as possible. The wedding date and details here were already set, so all we had to do was fly in and then fly out.

For Christmas, we were spending a week here with family and then a week locked in a cabin in Colorado for a delayed honeymoon. Tate had it in her head that we'd ski.

Yeah, no.

Just the thought of her walking around a cozy cabin dressed in nothing but a long sweater that showed off her beautiful legs in the firelight . . .

I might ski. If she was really nice.

After the ceremony today, we were having a small, private dinner and then going home to our house; we were already having fun planning what to renovate whenever we were able to make it home in the future.

"You didn't invite a shitload of people to your house for a party tonight, did you?" I shot Madoc a knowing look. He loved parties and looked for any excuse to have one.

But he looked insulted. "Of course not," he answered and then jerked his chin, standing up straight. "Here we go, dude."

I turned my head, hearing the music start, and suddenly my pulse starting raging—pumping like a machine gun under my skin—and I focused on the path next to the rocks. Where I knew she was coming from.

Four cello players sat above us on a rock landing, playing Apoca-lyptica's rendition of "Nothing Else Matters," and everything hurt as I looked around. In a good way, I guess. I just wanted to see her so badly.

Juliet came first, dressed in a light pink, knee-length dress, her hair spilling around her, and I heard my brother's sharp intake of breath. Her small baby bump was visible under her high-waisted dress, but she looked great, having gotten over the morning sickness.

Fallon trailed behind her in a gray dress similar to Juliet's, her hair in long curls, and I caught her wink at Madoc before coming to stand next to Juliet on the other side of the officiant.

I darted my eyes over to the rocks again, keeping them glued there. I hadn't seen Tate in more than twenty-four hours because our friends had decided that keeping us separate would make the wedding day more special. But I couldn't wait anymore.

I'd waited for years.

She appeared, arm in arm with her dad, and I smiled, locking eyes with her.

"She's beautiful," I heard Madoc say.

I blew out a slow breath, feeling my eyes burn as my throat tightened.

I blinked away the tears and clenched my jaw, trying every-thing to keep myself steady.

"Just look at her, okay?" Jax whispered. "Hold her eyes, and you'll be fine."

I swallowed the needles in my throat and looked up at her again, seeing the joy and peace all over her face.

Why did I feel like I was in pain?

She'd never looked more beautiful.

Her strapless dress had a sweetheart neckline—don't ask how I knew that shit now—that featured glimmering jewels on the bodice that brought out the glow in the smooth skin of her neck and arms. The bottom of the antique white dress was tulle that held layer upon layer all the way to the ground, and even though the dress was beautiful, I didn't care about every little feature. All I knew was that she broke my heart looking like a dream that was all mine.

Her hair hung perfect in loose curls, and she wore light makeup enhancing every bit of her. Looking down, I saw white Chucks peek out of the dress as she walked, and I couldn't help but laugh to myself.

She stepped up, not taking her eyes off of me as her dad kissed her cheek and handed her over.

I knew it wasn't a politically correct practice anymore—fathers handing responsibility for a daughter's care over to a man—but it meant something to me.

And I never doubted that she'd take care of me just as much as I did her.

I clasped her hand in mine and felt James's hand grip my arm reassuringly before he stepped aside.

I looked up at the officiant, nodding at him to get going.

"Can you hurry up?" I urged, hearing Madoc and Jax laugh at my side.

I didn't mean to be rude, but Tate was like a meal I was being forced to stare at as I starved.

The dude smiled and opened his folder to begin.

I looked down at Tate, barely hearing his words. "I love you," I whispered.

I love you, too, she mouthed, smiling.

The people around us listened to the officiant's short speech about love and communication, trust and tolerance, but I didn't take my eyes off Tate for a single second.

It's not that we didn't need to listen. We knew we didn't know everything, and we knew we were going to fight. We'd learned too many lessons the hard way to take for granted how far we'd come.

But I couldn't not look at her. It was too perfect a day.

The officiant passed it off to me as Jax handed him the rings, and he handed me Tate's.

I put it on her finger, sliding it only halfway as I spoke only to her.

"As my friend, I liked you," I whispered. "As my enemy, I craved you. As a fighter, I loved you, and as my wife"—I slid the ring the rest of the way on—"I keep you." I squeezed her hand. "Forever," I promised.

Silent tears spilled down her cheeks, and she smiled, even though her chest shook. Taking my ring from the man's hand, she slipped it on my finger.

"When you left me the first time, I was devastated," she said, speaking of when we were fourteen. "And when you left me the second time, I was defiant. But both times I regret," she admitted, keeping her voice low. "I always fought with you instead of fighting for you, and if I commit to doing one thing differently for the rest of our lives, Jared"—she inhaled a deep breath, steadying her voice—"it would be to make sure you always know that I will fight for you." She blinked, sending more tears down her cheeks. "Forever."

I knew it without needing to hear her say it, but it still felt good to hear. Being a kid was hard. Being a kid with no one to count on changed my life. And hers. She knew how much I needed her.

I saved the officiant the trouble and took the back of her neck in my hand before pulling her in for a kiss.

Wrapping an arm around her waist, I pressed her body into

mine and kissed my wife for almost longer than necessary, getting lost in her taste and scent, before pulling back slightly to lean my forehead into hers.

Laughter and snickers erupted around us, but I didn't care. I'd waited long enough, in my opinion.

After the ceremony, Madoc slapped me on the shoulder as we all trailed toward the cars. "I'll lead," he instructed, meaning what, I didn't know.

We had a lot of cars between us all, but I saw no reason to make a parade.

But whatever.

Climbing in the black limo behind Tate, I closed the door and instructed the driver to follow the GTO. He then closed the privacy glass, and I wasted no time hauling Tate into my lap.

I bunched up the dress to allow her legs to straddle me, and the poor girl sank into a cloud like it was a patch of quicksand. I saw just her face.

"I really love this dress"—I slid my hands up her silky thighs—"but it's a pain in the ass."

I took her hips in my hands and pulled her in for a kiss, not caring that she was messing up my hair, which my mother had made me style to perfection today.

The limo took off, following the GTO and trailed by everyone else.

"Our wedding turned me on," I admitted, slipping my hand inside her underwear. "Will you let me get to third base right now?" I teased.

She nuzzled into my neck, kissing and playing, and—I closed my eyes, groaning—*fuck dinner*. We needed a room.

But horns sounded outside, and Tate sat up, peering out the window.

"What the hell?" she breathed out, sliding off my lap.

I winced, my cock stretching painfully against my pants.

Looking out the window, I immediately rolled it down, seeing the city street littered with all of our friends. All of them not invited to the ceremony, because it was family only.

What? Horns honked, people whistled, and I even noticed a few of Tate's old track teammates clapping.

Although it was a surprise, it was kind of touching to see the people we'd grown up with sharing this.

"Oh, he did not . . . ," Tate seethed, thinking the exact same thing I was.

Madoc.

He'd told everybody.

And speak of the devil. I leaned out the window, seeing that Madoc had done a U-turn and cruised past us, grinning from ear to ear.

"I lied," he admitted, all too proud of himself. "Huge fucking party at my house." And he sped off laughing.

Tate's wide eyes met mine, and she shook her head, amazed.

All of these people were going to be there, apparently.

I rolled up the window, and Tate slid back onto my lap, sighing.

"He's got rooms," she taunted over my mouth, looking at the bright side. "Lots of rooms for us to get lost in."

And I leaned up, grabbing her lips with mine as I shucked off my jacket. "Who needs a room?"

CHAPTER 19

TATE

One Year Later

"You need to relax," Pasha scolded, standing next to me. "It's his last race, so stop fussing."

I craned my neck while fidgeting with my hands, seeing Jared weave around all the twists and turns, and I really hated how his bike always looked like it was about to tip over when he leaned into a curve.

"I can't," I choked out, sticking my thumbnail in my mouth. "I hate it when he's out there."

All of us stood off to the side—Pasha, Madoc, Jax, Juliet, Fallon, and me—lucky enough in not having to stay in the bleachers with the crowd, but unfortunately, we didn't have as great a view, either. Jared's mom and stepdad were up there, and Addie, Madoc's housekeeper, was back at the hotel with Quinn and Hawke, Jax and Juliet's infant son. The speedway in Anaheim was packed with fans wanting to see Jared's last race, and although he was going to miss racing, we decided he needed to focus his full attention on the business, JT Racing.

He'd made good connections during his time here, and while I finished medical school—when I finished—he had every confidence that we'd be able to take the business back home and his clients with us.

"And it could be a bad one if he has to worry about you worrying," Pasha complained. "Let him enjoy it."

I tried to, but racing on the bikes always put me on edge. At least the car offered some sort of protection. Like armor. Biking wasn't like that, and racers fell into two groups: those who had been in accidents and those who would be in accidents.

It was only a matter of time. Which is why I was ecstatic that Jared was retiring.

"I'm fine," I lied. "I just feel sick."

Fallon came over and wrapped an arm around my shoulder, trying to soothe me.

"Beer, please!" Pasha shouted into the stands, and I looked to see her going over to one of the guys selling in the bleachers. "Want one?" she asked, looking back at us.

"Water," I shot back. "Thank you."

She brought back the drinks, and the motorcycles whipped past us, the high-pitched whir buzzing in my ears as my hair went flying.

I couldn't look.

"And you know"—I continued talking to Pasha—"as well as I do that he'll jump in for a sporadic race here and there. He's still so young. He'll want to do this again."

"You both are coming home next week, right?" Jax asked, looking away from the race at me.

"Yeah." I nodded. "We're driving. We should be in by Thursday."

It was summer break, and although I had lots to do to get ahead for my classes, we were excited to head home and relax with our family and friends.

"Good." He looked back at the race but kept talking. "I signed Jared up for some off-roading stuff at the Loop next weekend, so don't plan too much, okay?"

I twisted up my lips. "You know Jared hates off-roading," I reminded him. "If it's not fast—"

"I just want him to learn the lay of the land," he shot out, appeasing me. "Juliet and I will be off to Costa Rica in a few months, and I trust him to look in on things better than I trust anyone else."

That's right. I'd almost forgotten.

Jax and Juliet weren't letting a baby slow them down. Their son would be coming on their adventures with them. Juliet had a yearlong teaching contract—which she'd delayed when she got pregnant—while Jax had secured a job with Outward Bound down there and also continued to perform computer work on the side. Legal computer work.

Jared would be keeping an eye on the Loop operations in his place when we were in town.

"I'm bringing Lucas," Madoc told Jax. "If Jared is willing, he can take him with him off-roading. The more mentors the kid has, the better."

I smiled, thinking of how great Lucas had it. Madoc and Fallon treated their "little brother" like one of their own, and I had no doubt the kid had a promising future ahead of him with the support system he'd gained. He had a good mom and great friends.

"Come on!" Everyone started screaming, seeing Jared in his superflashy red-and-white racing suit, which he was forced to wear.

He tore across the finish line, and it felt like those tires were driving over my heart.

"Yes!" Jax and Madoc roared, shooting their arms into the air and then doing double high fives.

I put one hand over my heart and another over my stomach, aching from the worry.

The crowd cheered as the race ended, and I smiled, seeing Jared ignore everyone who tried to talk to him as he ran up to me, dumping his helmet on the ground.

"You see?" He lifted me in the air. "I'm always safe."

And then he brought me down, crashing his lips to mine in a way that sent me reeling. I almost cringed, hearing cameras go off as we kissed, but I looked at it as a step up that I wasn't in a towel this time.

He set me down, wrapping his arms around me.

"Eh"—I shrugged my shoulders—"I'm not so worried about your safety anymore," I lied.

He raised his eyebrows. "No?"

"No." I shook my head. "Just that you win."

I leaned in, threading my fingers through the back of his hair and inhaling the scent of his body wash.

"And I wanted you in a good mood," I told him. "I can't give you happy news on an unhappy day."

He cocked his head, looking at me, confused.

"And the prize money will help," I continued, "since you're the only working member in the household, and I'm about to cost you a lot of money," I teased.

He shot me a cocky grin. "And why's that?"

And when I leaned in to tell him why I needed him safe, why no obstacle could keep me from being happy right now, I felt his breath give way and his chest cave.

And tears immediately sprang to my eyes when he knelt down in front of everyone—cameras flashing in the background and gasps from our friends going off around us—and kissed my stomach, saying hello to his child.

TATE

Seven Years Later

Fanning myself with the copy of *Newsweek*, I grunted as I bent down to pick up Dylan's shoes off the carpet.

The July heat had me so aggravated that I was tempted to staple her shoelaces to the floor if she kept dumping her belongings everywhere.

Jared was next to no help when it came to building our daughter's sense of responsibility. Yeah, she was only six years old, but we didn't want her spoiled, did we? I constantly had to remind him that she'd be a teenager someday, and then he'd be sorry.

But Dylan Trent was a daddy's girl, and heaven help him when she started wanting boyfriends and late curfews instead of candy and toys.

"Why's it so cold in here?" I heard Madoc bellow from down the hall.

I shook my head and tossed my daughter's shoes on top of the hamper in our private bathroom, shutting off the light as I left. "It's hot as hell," I grumbled under my breath so he couldn't hear.

I took a long look around the room, finally satisfied that it was clean and the laundry was put away. I knew Madoc and Fallon didn't care about messes, but I did when I was staying in someone else's house.

I pulled Jared's long-sleeved blue-and-white pinstripe dress shirt away from my chest and continued fanning cool air down through the opening at the neck as I sat down on the edge of our bed. His mom had bought him a bunch of stylish Brooks Brothers dress shirts for his business trips, but he'd wear only the black or white ones. The blue- and pink-striped ones were mine, and they, along with my cotton pajama shorts, were my uniform these days.

Madoc pulled up outside my bedroom door, scowling at me with his hands on his hips.

"It's cold in here," he accused, eyeing me as the culprit, since I was the one burning up these days and keeping his house at subzero temperatures.

I let out a fake sympathetic sigh as I continued fanning myself. "Don't make your problems my problems, man," I replied sarcastically.

He'd just gotten back from his office in Chicago and was still dressed in his black pinstripe suit pants and white dress shirt with the sleeves rolled up. His silver tie hung loose around his neck, which always looked like it had been yanked to near death by the time he got home every day.

Madoc loved his job, but it was also hard on him. Going against the grain, he'd decided to work in the public sector, putting away the criminals his father worked to keep free. You would think it would be hard on their relationship, but actually, both Caruthers men thrived on the "game," as they called it. I think going head-to-head in the courtroom or conference room brought them closer together.

He rolled his eyes at me and then shot me a snarky little look as his eyes raked up and down my body. "Does Jared tell you how hot you are even though you're overweight?"

I straightened. "I'm not overweight. I'm pregnant."

"Nice try." He sneered. "But you only have one kid in there."

I flung the magazine at him just as he ducked back into the hall. Splaying my hand across my stomach, I huffed a breath. *Jerk.*

Being a doctor, I knew what an acceptable weight gain was during pregnancy, and I was in fantastic shape, thank you very much.

Madoc shot his head around the corner again. "Jared's on video chat, by the way," he chirped. And then he was gone.

I smiled, loving the sound of those words. I put my arm behind me to push myself up off the bed.

Being nearly nine months pregnant with my second child, I agreed with Jared that I shouldn't be at our house—the house I grew up in—alone with Dylan. Since Fallon was taking a year off from her work at an architectural firm in the city to nurture some independent projects she wanted to explore, she was the perfect babysitter if I "decided" to go into labor ahead of schedule. With Jared away for several days, he didn't want to take any chances.

I waddled down the stairs, the weight in my stomach making my legs and back ache. I once again vowed to myself that this was the last time I was going to be pregnant.

I'd made the same promise to myself after Dylan, but Jared and I knew how lonely being an only child could be, so we decided to have another. Of course, he'd had his brother, Jax, but that wasn't until later.

I heard growling somewhere in the house and footfalls above, and I looked up, knowing who it was. I was going to have to go up to the third floor after the call with Jared and get the kids under control. Madoc's twin sons, Hunter and Kade, had Dylan bouncing off the walls these days. Fallon and Addie had run out for groceries, and I was hoping Madoc was upstairs trying to reel the kids in.

With Quinn here, too, the house was a den of madness and noise today.

Pulling out the chair at the kitchen table, I sat down in front of the laptop.

Jared smiled at me. "Hey, babe."

My stomach fluttered. "Hi." I smiled back, loving his wrinkled white dress shirt, messy hair, and loose necktie. "God, you look good," I teased, ready to eat him with a side of fries.

Someone in the background gave him a clipboard to sign, and he glared at me as he took it. "Don't start with me," he warned. "I've been craving you like crazy. I'm tired, hungry, and horny, and I can't wait to get on that plane tonight."

"Shhhh . . ." I laughed, looking around for Madoc and the kids. "This house is full of people. You can talk dirty to me later," I told him.

Jared was in California, and from the view of the background with large crates and forklifts, he was in his warehouse. He had an office there, which Pasha normally ran, but he had to make visits every few months for meetings and quality-control checks for JT Racing—JT standing for Jared and Tate, as I later discovered.

He stood at a table with the bustle of the warehouse behind him, and I couldn't get enough. Even at thirty, my husband was hot.

Hotter, actually. Why did men age so well?

"So how's my son?" Jared handed the clipboard back to the guy at his side and looked at me with his full attention.

"Sitting defiantly on my bladder," I joked, patting my belly. "Other than that, he's doing well."

"And you're in the clear?" he asked. "The hospital has all of your appointments covered?"

"Yes." I nodded. "My full attention is on my family for the next few months."

I'd only recently gone on maternity leave, since the hospital was shorthanded. But as we were getting down to the wire now, I was glad when they finally took on extra staff. Now I could take my time off without worry.

Screeching hit my ears, and I winced as I twisted around, seeing Kade and Hunter chasing Dylan with a—I squinted my eyes—was that a plunger?

Dylan swerved around the island, her soft brown hair bouncing over her shoulders as she hurried away from their advance.

She crashed into my side, clearly seeking cover, and I put an arm around her.

The boys—both six—ran up and pulled to a halt, glowering down at her.

"Leave me alone!" she shouted, kicking out her right foot to keep them at bay.

Kade held up the plunger, and I shot my hand out as Dylan screamed. "Oh, no you don't. Put it down," I ordered him.

Just then, Madoc ran in, breathing hard and looking pissed.

"Madoc!" Jared barked, jutting out his pointer finger. "You keep your sons away from my kid. I mean it."

Madoc's eyes rounded. "Keep *them* away?" he said, surprised. "Your little . . . ," he gritted through his teeth but then stopped.

Stepping up to cover Dylan's ears, he whispered to Jared, "I love her. I absolutely do, but she's a viper, dude," he growled low. "She filled her water gun with toilet water and was shooting them with it!"

Jared snorted and twisted away to laugh.

I rolled my eyes and jerked my head, telling Madoc to take his madmen elsewhere.

This was a classic example of how Jared and Madoc parented. Neither one would ever admit that their kid could do any wrong. Madoc took as much pride in his sons as Jared did in Dylan.

And I'd warned Jared about not laughing at her antics in front of her. It only encouraged the behavior.

No matter how funny it was. Or how much the twins probably deserved it.

I pulled Dylan up onto my lap, her little yellow Chucks rubbing against my shins. "Hi, Daddy," she chirped. "I miss you."

I smiled at her sweet little voice, loving her rosy cheeks and big smile.

AFLAME

"Hey, Blue Eyes," he greeted her back. "I've got some surprises for you."

"Jared," I groaned, my ass starting to shoot daggers up my spine from the hard chair. "Honey, her room is full of your surprises. Less is more, okay?"

He shot me his cocky little grin like I should know better.

He always incurred extra fees for overweight baggage on his return trips. Always due to the presents he brought her. T-shirts, snow globes, stuffed animals, autographed pictures from drivers he worked with . . . the list went on. She was outgrowing her room.

My old room.

"Madoc!" I heard a shout and turned to see Lucas coming through the sliding glass doors from the pool with a Gatorade in hand and Quinn with her arms wrapped around his waist.

Dylan and her daddy chatted as I watched Madoc walk back into the kitchen.

But Lucas shot off his mouth before he could say anything. "Dude, get your sister off me, please."

Quinn tightened her arms around Lucas, and I smiled at how much grief she'd been giving him lately. At twenty, Lucas had no patience for an eight-year-old with a crush.

"I love Lucas," she said, giggling. "I'm going to marry him."

"The hell you are!" He looked down at her with intolerance . . . and maybe a little fear, too. "Dude, seriously," he urged Madoc. "It's creepy."

"Come on." Madoc leaned down and pulled his sister off Lucas's body. "You're going to make Lucas run back to college." He nudged her toward us. "Your mommy and daddy will be here soon. Go say hi to Jared."

Quinn—with her mother's chocolate eyes and her father's blond hair—came over and saluted Jared and then grabbed Dylan's hand, both of them running back outside.

Her relationship with Jared was one of few words. I think

Quinn was closest to Madoc. She saw him more. And she had a lot of fun with Jax.

But I think she was a little nervous around Jared. She looked for his approval and respect, even though her worry was unnecessary.

Jared was in awe of her.

He may not have been as easygoing as Madoc, but he loved teaching her things, and he made sure we were at every one of her recitals and birthday parties.

"Did Jax say when he and Juliet would be home this summer?" I asked, finally alone with Jared.

"Baby, I lose track of what country they're in." He sighed. "Bhutan or Bangladesh or—"

"Brazil," I heard Madoc chime in from the refrigerator, where his head was buried.

I snapped my fingers. "Brazil. You were close," I teased Jared. "It was something with a B."

"I wish he'd just stay home." Jared looked aggravated. "I'd like to know my nephew more than by just pictures."

"Soon," I appeased him, looking over to the wall in the kitchen with family photos. Jax was sitting in front of a waterfall, his head facing toward the camera, with Juliet hugging his back, both of them dirty and sweaty and smiling.

And sitting, hugging Juliet's back, was their son, Hawke, now seven.

"I'll call him today," I told Jared. "The house needs to be prepared."

Jax and Juliet had finally decided to settle back down in Shelburne Falls in Jared's old house next door to ours. It had been almost nonstop travel and work for them with nonprofit organizations setting up schools all over the world for the past several years. Hawke didn't slow them down, either. When he was one, they carried him in their backpacks. Now he sped ahead, carving out the trail before them.

However, they'd become more and more homesick and were determined for us all to raise our children together. Hawke loved his cousin Dylan and wanted to get to know Madoc's boys more.

So they were coming home, and Fallon, Addie, and I were taking it upon ourselves to get the house ready, since it hadn't been cleaned in forever and needed to get stocked with food. All I worried about now was keeping a good eye on Dylan trying to make use of the tree to go hang out with her cousin.

I wiped the sweat off my forehead and puffed out my shirt, trying to get air in.

"I can't wait until he's born." I groaned, talking about our son. "I'm dying to get back on your bike. I miss the wind."

Jared leaned down on his elbows, his eyes smirking at me. "Me, too," he whispered. "We need a date night. And soon."

I fanned myself harder, thinking about our last date night. Jared and I jumped each other any chance we got, but once in a while we made time for just the two of us to get out for the night away from the house. It usually ended with us in the backseat of his car.

Some things never changed.

The sliding glass door opened behind me again, and I heard Dylan. "Kade, do you want to go swimming?"

I turned around to see Madoc's son walk off away from her. "Leave me alone," he snarled. "I don't hang with girls."

Her eyes fell, and my heart broke a little. I was about to go to her, but Hunter—Madoc's other son—came up behind her. "I'll go swimming with you," he offered.

She paused and then offered a little smile with a nod, taking one last look toward the hallway where Kade had disappeared before following Hunter back outside.

I knew Lucas was out there with them, so I didn't worry.

I shook my head at Jared and breathed out a laugh. "You do realize that Hawke, Kade, Hunter, Dylan, and Quinn will all be in high school at the same time, right?" I said, foreseeing a very tu-

multuous future ahead of us. "For at least two years out of the four?"
I reminded him.

Quinn was the oldest at eight. Hawke was a year behind her,
and Dylan, Kade, and Hunter were only a year behind him.

"Relax." He grabbed his jacket and slipped it on. "I don't think
anyone can get in as much trouble as we did."

Looking at him, I mused about all the years of ups and downs
and how much crap we'd both put each other through.

We got into so much trouble.

High school would've been more fun for me if I'd met Jared's
challenge sooner, but who knows? Maybe we wouldn't be here otherwise. I wouldn't trade any of it, because no matter what happened
before or what would come next, I would always choose him.

Jared was my home.

My throat ached as I swallowed. "I'll love you forever, Jared
Trent," I whispered, my eyes pooling with tears.

He reached out and ran a finger down the computer screen, and
I knew he was tracing my face.

"And I've loved you forever, Tatum Trent."

THE END

Dear Reader,

Jared, Tate, Madoc, Fallon, Jaxon, and Juliet represent a piece of who I am. I put so much of my heart into creating them, and they are not imaginary to me. It's a difficult good-bye, but then I guess most good-byes are.

The characters of the Fall Away series all represent a confused time in our lives when making fast choices is easier than living with them. Now, as adults, we understand that even though adolescence is hard, making mistakes is necessary.

Parents, teachers, and mentors try to keep us on the right track and steer us away from poor decisions, but without those hard lessons, we don't grow. The Fall Away couples were meant to remind us of that.

My only hope is that you've come out of this series knowing that everyone has a story, mistakes are inevitable, and life goes on.

Embrace your imperfections. Their lessons make you better.

None of us are unique in our suffering. But we are unique in our survival.

I am forever grateful that you've given me a forum in which to share some of my own life lessons, which I had to learn the hard way, and I cannot tell you how much your words of encouragement have meant to me.

While the journeys of Jared, Tate, Madoc, Fallon, Jax, and Juliet will now continue off the written page, you may have noticed that I left a finger in the book, so that it doesn't close completely. I may explore their children's stories someday. There are no plans to do this, but I'm interested in leaving the possibility open.

For now, though, other stories are wanting a life of their own, and I hope you continue to read my work long into the future. The adventures are just beginning.

Thank you for reading these books. Thank you for giving me a chance to be in your lives. And thank you for joining me on this journey.

Love,
Penelope

ACKNOWLEDGMENTS

To my husband and daughter, both of whom sacrificed to see these characters live. Now we can go to Disneyland!

To my support system at New American Library, all of whom put up with my endless questions and work hard to protect my vision for the Fall Away Series. Thank you, Kerry, Isabel, Jessica, and Courtney for your trust, advice, and help.

To Jane Dystel at Dystel & Goderich Literary Management, who found me, and thank goodness for that! You're always working, and I always feel important. Thanks to you, Miriam, and Mike for staying on top of everything and taking care of me.

To my street team, the House of PenDragon, who are a wonderful group of women—and one guy—who hold one another up and create a community of friendship and fun times. Thank you for helping me on this book!

To Eden Butler, Lisa Pantano Kane, Ing Cruz, Jessica Sotelo, and Marilyn Medina, who are all available at the drop of a hat to look at a scene or provide quick emergency feedback. Thank you for walking with me through this process and being honest.

To Vibeke Courtney. Plain and simple, this is all you. If I had never met you, I might never have tried writing a book. And without you, it would never have been successful. My writing was nearly all narration before you got your hands on it, and you helped create my voice. Thank you, thank you, thank you.

To the readers and reviewers, thank you for keeping my work

alive and showing your love and support! I need your words more than you know, and I thank you for taking the time to give me your feedback, thoughts, and ideas. I hope I can continue to give you characters you want to reread over and over again!

Next to Never

To Johanna and Debbie
who said I couldn't sit with them at lunch . . .
waves

PLAYLIST

"Breaking the Habit"	by Linkin Park
"Comedown"	by Bush
"If You Could Only See"	by Tonic
"It's Been Awhile"	by Staind
"Like a Prayer"	by Madonna
"Lips of an Angel"	by Hinder
"Remedy"	by Seether
"Sober"	by P!nk
"Cradle of Love"	by Billy Idol
"Stronger"	by Through Fire

CHAPTER 1

"Move it, Quinn!" I hear Jax bellow, clapping his hands. "Come on!"

I race between two other players, shuffling the soccer ball between my feet and feeling my black and orange jersey sticking to my back.

I love soccer. I love soccer. I love soccer.

No, I don't. I hate soccer. I'm thrilled it's the end of my senior year, and this is my last game.

"Over here!" I spot Maya Velasquez out of the corner of my eye, calling to me.

I swing back my right foot and shoot the ball over to her just as I see someone dive into my space.

"Suck dirt, Caruthers." And then all I see is a green jersey crashing into me and shoving me to the ground.

"Ugh," I growl, wincing.

Damn it! A silvery ache shoots through my ass and my back as I peer up, squinting against the sunlight. Simone Feldman, from the Weston team, smirks down at me with a gloating expression in her green eyes.

But then, much to my enjoyment, someone knocks into her, making her stumble. She falters, but she doesn't fall, and I laugh, seeing her knocked off her high pedestal. *Thank you, Dylan.*

I glance to the left and see exactly who I expected to see. Dylan, my brother Jared's daughter, who's only two years younger and on the same team as me, runs backward, toward the goal, grinning at me.

Simone and everyone else move on, leaving me behind, too.

"Get up, Quinn!"

I hood my eyes and groan, recognizing the voice behind me. Standing up, I spin around to see Madoc as he tosses his black suit jacket on a bleacher and loosens his light blue tie. He must've rushed here after work to see the game.

"Shake it off!" he orders, clapping his hands like Jax. "Let's go!"

I roll my eyes and turn back around, powering on. There are a million other things I'd rather be doing—journaling, cooking, swimming . . . homework, laundry, getting a cavity filled—but Madoc, Jax, and my dad, for that matter, love having their kids in sports. For my brothers, it's exercise and good, clean fun. For my father, it's trophies on a wall and another extracurricular for my college resumes.

Not that I need soccer anymore, anyway. My admission to Notre Dame next fall is secure.

"So." Madoc comes up after our win, hooks an arm around my neck, and plants a kiss on the top of my head. "I had this great idea where you could maybe intern with my campaign over the summer."

"You mean you had this great idea where you could get free, easy labor."

I hear him *tsk* like that's sooooo not what he was thinking, but I know Madoc. He's my most fun-loving brother, he's easy to talk to, and I always feel most at ease around him, but he's also used to getting anything and everything he wants.

And while I'm sure he wouldn't mind paying someone to work

with his campaign, he can bend me and boss me around a lot easier than someone he barely knows.

"Come on," he says, trying to work me already. "You're polite, well-spoken, and you follow directions. Plus you're family. I won't get accused of getting kinky with an intern."

I snort, despite myself. He can always make me laugh.

But I tell him, "I have other plans. Ones that are far more fun than sitting in a cubicle all summer and cold-calling voters, begging them to make you mayor."

"Plans? Like what?"

I shrug and pull out my ponytail and elastic headband. "I thought of traveling."

I don't look at him, but it takes him a moment to respond.

"Why haven't I heard about this until now?" he asks.

Because I haven't made definite plans. Because I haven't told anyone. Because I have no idea where I want to go or what I want to see.

Because Dad will never let me go.

"Have you talked to Dad about it?" he asks.

I stuff my towel and hair ties back into my backpack, ignoring him.

"Quinn, as much as I'd love to see you spread your wings, there's no way he's going to allow it." He hands me my water bottle. "You know you need months to prepare him for something like that, and he would never let you go alone." And then he adds, his tone turning clipped, "And if he did, I wouldn't. Besides, I thought you both decided you'd take the summer and get ahead with some courses at Clarke before going off to Notre Dame in the fall."

Jesus.

I keep my expression impassive, trying not to look annoyed. In a few months, I really will be gone, and then I'll miss Madoc—and everyone else—so I'm trying not to act like a brat.

I swing the backpack strap over my shoulder. "Yeah, I know. Forget I said it. It's just something I was tossing around." I roll my eyes at him, turning it into a joke with a smirk. "I guess I'll try to wait until after college to start living my life."

"'Atta girl." He gives me a light punch on the arm, grinning. "Besides, you know Jared has events lined up all summer, and with Pasha busy setting up the production line in Toronto, who's going to handle his scheduling? And then Jax and Juliet will need your special touch up at the summer camp for the planning of the fireworks show on the Fourth, and—"

"And yada yada yada . . . I know!" I grumble. "I can't be replaced. No one else can do what I do, right?!"

"Of course not, Quinn-for-the-Win. We need you."

I shake my head and walk around him, heading for the locker room.

God, I love him. I love all of my family. But each one of them knows how to manipulate me.

None of them would tell me to go. No one will say "Just do it!" or "What do *you* want to do for your summer, Quinn?"

Jax and Jared assume I'm fine. Madoc wants all of his family around him all of the time. My nieces and nephews are too caught up in their own lives to care what I'm doing, and my parents . . . well, they want me happy. But they don't want me to make any mistakes, either. Hell, a two-day sex talk preceded my very first date.

But I'm their baby. Their second chance.

Not that there was anything wrong with my brothers. They turned out well. But I gather my parents didn't have much to do with that, either.

No one knows what I want. No one looks closely enough.

No one except Lucas.

After my shower, I quickly dress in some jean short cut-offs and a gray V-neck and dry my hair. I unclasp the strap of my backpack and slide off Lucas's baseball cap that he gave me before he left town three years ago. I always carry it with me.

Three whole years, and I haven't seen or talked to him. After grad school, he moved to New York for a job, but his architectural firm had him assigned to a project in Dubai. He's been living in the Middle East, for the most part, since he left Shelburne Falls. It doesn't feel like he is ever coming back.

I know he isn't technically part of our family, but Madoc had mentored him since he was eight, and he's been a part of my life since I was born.

After he left, I sat down a few times to write him—letters, e-mails, Facebook messages—but something always held me back from sending them. Like maybe I was afraid he wouldn't write back.

Maybe, just maybe, he tolerated annoying little Quinn Caruthers and all of her stupid questions while he was stuck here, but now he doesn't have to anymore. Why should he even bother, right? I don't fit into his life anymore. He's twenty-nine now. Important, busy, sophisticated . . .

And he hasn't written me, either, so . . .

Pulling the light blue Cubs cap down over my eyes to shield the sun, I start the walk to the bike rack in front of the school.

"You know, I still can't believe that you don't have a car!" someone shouts behind me as I unlock my bike. "It's like a *thing* in our family, Quinn!"

I laugh to myself, recognizing Dylan's tone. Yes, car-love definitely runs in our family. So much so that one of my brothers—her father—owns a company that designs and engineers performance automotive parts, while another brother runs the town's racetrack.

Looking over my shoulder, I see her pull up in her dad's old Mustang Boss 302—which he gave her when he bought his brand new Shelby.

She grins at me through the open driver's side window.

"Outdoor air pollution is one of the top ten killers on Earth," I tell her, unwinding the lock from the bars. "Thousands of people in this country die every year due to air pollution, and the best way to decrease it is by walking or riding a bicycle." I smile, trying to look smug, and stuff the lock into my backpack. "I'm just doing my part."

"Can you do mine, too?" Kade, my nephew, strolls up and throws his duffel bag into the bed of his truck, chuckling to himself.

"And mine," his twin, Hunter, says, doing the same. They both must've just gotten done with their workouts in the school's weight room. Bulking up for the junior year football season in the fall.

I twist my lips to the side, disgusted at the gas-guzzling penis-enhancer Madoc bought his sons that won't make their manly areas any bigger despite what teenage boys like to think. He purchased the big black truck for them in hopes they'd learn to share—and be forced to go places together since they fought a lot.

The pollutants from it are probably strong enough to kill cockroaches . . . underground . . . in Antarctica.

Actually, I'm not *that* concerned with pollution. I just enjoy riding a bike, because it's something where I don't fall in line with the rest of my family, and it gives me an excuse to take longer to get home. More me-time and all that.

Dylan smiles at me, a gentle look in her blue eyes. "I'll see you tonight, okay?"

I nod and slip my backpack on my back. Pulling out my bike, I hear Kade and Hunter's truck fire up behind me, and they, along with Dylan, charge out of the school parking lot, mostly empty now since school ended two hours ago.

Climbing on my bike, I push off and pedal out of the parking lot, inhaling the fresh scent of lilacs that carries on the light wind around the school.

I love this time of day, right before parents get off work but after school lets out. The streets are quiet, and the sun is falling to the west. It's warm, but it's not beating down on my shoulders and neck like it does during midday. Glimmers of yellow peek through the cluster of leaves overhead, and I speed down streets lined with cars, hearing kids in their Rollerblades playing hockey in a driveway.

Since it's Friday night, I don't have to worry about rushing home to do my schoolwork or study. It's nearly the end of the year, after all. Final papers and projects have already been turned in, final exams are scheduled, and graduation practice is in full swing. I'm in the homestretch.

It's also Dylan's big night. In addition to just getting her license and her father's old car a few months ago, she'll be making her debut at the track tonight. I have to be there.

But first . . . I cruise around a corner and keep pedaling into the center of town. My hair blows behind me, and I love the feel of the wind in my clothes. I smile to myself, thinking about how the boys keep begging to get me a car, but wouldn't they just flip their lids if they knew I might actually be interested in a motorbike instead?

As I race up to High Street, I turn right and ease on the brake as I pull up next to the curb in front of a shop on the corner of Sutton and park my bike.

Standing and gazing through the old wooden French doors with chipped red paint, I see everything looks the same as it was yesterday when I came here. Cobwebs block my view, but I can make out the broken-down counter of the old café, the stools with cracked vinyl, the empty, dusty shelves, and a chair overturned on the floor with random bits of debris scattered around.

Stepping to the left of the door, I peer through the display window, its shelves also coated with a thick layer of dust.

I would take those shelves out. Potential customers want to see the inside of a store before they enter, so yeah . . . take out the shelves, so they can see what kind of place it is.

I chew my bottom lip, the excitement sending off a wave of butterflies in my stomach.

I'd also paint the outside brick a cream color, like a pastry, and then I'd paint the doors turquoise, my favorite color. It would make it bright, like summer. Inviting, happy, quaint . . .

Perfect for a summer business.

I'd also add a few tables with umbrellas out front, a menu with not only pastries and baked goods, but also an assortment of refreshers and maybe some ice cream.

And I'd leave the doors open all day, so the neighborhood can smell the breads and sweets all the way down the street.

"Hey," I hear someone call to me.

I turn my head and see a guy come around from behind me. He's wearing jeans, a white T-shirt with writing on it, and he's young, probably about my age, but I've never seen him at my school.

"What's your name?" he asks, and I spot a group of guys standing down the sidewalk from where he came, talking and laughing.

I turn away, looking back at the old bakery. The FOR LEASE sign in the window has a phone number with it. I'm not trying to be rude to him, but he doesn't get personal information about me simply because he thinks he's cute. Especially if I don't know him.

"You go to Falls High, right?"

I ignore him again, turning for my bike to go home.

But my cap is plucked off my head. I whip around, seeing him hold it high and away from me, grinning.

He waves the hat back and forth. "What do I have to do to get you to talk to me?"

"Asshole," I say. "There. I talked. Now give me the hat back."

But he just laughs.

I dart out my hand, trying to snatch it back. "Give it to me!"

That hat hasn't left my possession in four years. If I'm not wearing it, I'm carrying it on my backpack. Lucas will come home someday, and he'll want it back. My stomach starts to churn, thinking about how I can't lose it.

"It's kind of old and ratty, isn't it?" the guy, whose name I don't care to find out, comments. "I can take you to a Cubs game and get you a new one."

I shoot forward again, grabbing for the hat, but I just miss it as he pulls it away.

"You still didn't tell me your name," he chides, smiling like he just loves this little game of his.

I bare my teeth, breathing hard. Moving forward, I slam my palm into his chest, pushing him backward and making him stumble. Taking my chance, I reach out and grab the hat out of his hand.

He shakes with laughter and grins at me as I squeeze the cap in my fist.

But then his face falls and his eyes focus over my head. "Can I help you?" he asks, an annoyed tone to his voice.

A shadow falls over me, and I feel someone at my back. Twisting my head, I see Jared, my oldest brother, hovering over me and looking at Asswipe like he's just dying for the kid to give him a reason.

"Oh, no," I hear someone say. I look behind the guy and see another kid heading up to us. He swings an arm around the shoulder of the guy talking to us and pulls him back. "I'm sorry, Jared. He's new in town." He pulls the guy back until they both turn around and head away, the scared one mumbling something in the new kid's ear.

And then they're gone.

I sigh and twist around, facing Jared. "I handled it," I tell him. "You're really embarrassing sometimes."

He cocks an eyebrow. "The sister of the head of JT Racing driving a bicycle is embarrassing."

I growl under my breath and pull the hat down on my head again. *I'm not having this conversation.* Jared, Madoc, and Jax had just been waiting for me to turn sixteen, get my license, and pick out a car. They couldn't wait to work on it, make modifications, whatever . . .

They're still frothing at the mouth for me to change my mind.

"Do you want a ride home?" he asks. "I was heading there, anyway."

I glance at his pickup, parked at the curb, with his eight-year-old son, James, and Madoc's daughter, A.J., sitting in the backseat.

But I turn away. "I'm cool. Heading for the biker bar first," I say nonchalantly, climbing on my bike. "Maybe do some cocaine. Have unprotected sex."

"Wait!" he calls.

He heads for his truck, still idling. "This was sent to our house accidentally." He reaches through the passenger side window and pulls out a yellow package.

Stepping up, he tosses me the bubble mailer, and I catch it, instantly feeling something solid inside. Turning it over, I see that it's addressed to me, but the top left-hand corner is empty.

"There's no return address." I glance up, holding out the package to him. "You don't want to check it for anthrax first?"

He rolls his eyes at me and walks for the driver's side of his car, Seether's "Remedy" blasting from inside.

But I can see a hint of a smile under his scowl. "I'll see you tonight," he says. And then he jerks his eyes over to the sidewalk where the group of guys is loitering. "And you!" He points to the jerk that was hassling me. "There's two more of me in this town. Don't forget it!"

The guy instantly tenses and turns away, trying to act like Jared's not talking to him. I laugh to myself and stuff the package in my backpack.

Sometimes I hate how my brothers hover. And sometimes I love it.

After getting home and parking my bike in the garage, I head straight for the kitchen.

My dad is probably still in the city, and my mom is usually out running errands night and day now. Since Madoc is running for mayor, she'd enlisted herself as his event coordinator and is constantly meeting with venues, caterers, musicians . . .

This is the time of day I like best. No one is home, there's no pressure, and, for a little while, I'm relaxed.

Dropping my backpack on the kitchen counter, I grab a Fresca out of the refrigerator and jog upstairs to my bedroom. I want to get in the pool before someone shows up to distract me.

Slipping on my white bikini and grabbing a towel from the bathroom, I take my backpack off the counter downstairs along with my drink and carry everything through the doors leading onto the back patio.

The rush of the waterfall spilling over rocks as it cascades down into the pool immediately relaxes me, and a smile pulls at my lips. When my parents moved us back to Shelburne Falls from Chicago and decided to put in a pool, the waterfall was one of the things on my wish list. It reminded me of the trip to Yosemite our family took when I was eleven. Nearly everyone opted to stay at camp and swim or fish, but Jax, Lucas, and I hiked the Mist Trail, past two waterfalls.

I can still feel the cool spray hitting my arms and legs as we hiked the steps. I can still hear the thunder of the water and feel the force of it rushing past us. And the smell . . .

Evergreens, water, and earth. Like sunrise in a cave.

My dad knew how much I loved the trip and had the waterfall put in, even though I only mentioned it once. He does so much to try to make me happy. And even though we still keep an apartment in Chicago, since my parents have to be there so much and it's easier than living out of a suitcase in a hotel room, I've rarely been back since moving here before freshman year. I'm not a city person.

Taking another sip of soda, I set my stuff down on one of the patio tables, feeling the late afternoon sun warm my shoulders. I dig in my backpack for my iPad, but then pause on the envelope Jared gave me.

I'd nearly forgotten. Pulling it out, I survey the front of the package again, seeing that it's addressed to me, but it was sent to Jared and Tate's. That's weird. I'd never used their address. And there's no return address, but the postmark reads Toronto. I eye it curiously. I don't know anyone in Canada.

As soon as I tear away the top of the package and peek inside, I'm hurrying to reach in and pull out the book the envelope contains.

A used book.

It's a hardcover with a tattered paper jacket, the edges slightly torn and curling. Peeking back inside the envelope, I see that there's nothing else. No note. No business card. Nothing.

Setting the envelope down in confusion, I'm wondering who would send me an old book.

In search of clues, I fan the pages so that the scent of aged paper wafts into my nostrils. The book is in decent shape, but the edges of the pages are slightly tattered, and the spine is broken in.

Closing the book, I read the front cover. *Next to Never*. There's no author. That's strange.

Turning the book over, I scan the back cover, reading the synopsis.

And quickly stop, rolling my eyes. I toss the book back down onto the table.

Romance. While I'm intrigued by who would send me a random book, I don't care to waste my time.

Instead I walk to the edge of the pool, step in, slowly descending up to my calves, and then my thighs and waist. Pushing off, I dive beneath the surface, completely submerging myself as the cool rush of water soothes my body and caresses my scalp. I pop up through the surface, pushing my hair back, and then return to the edge of the pool, reaching up to grab the envelope again.

Toronto.

Pasha's in Toronto, I guess. But I'm not close with her, and I don't get the impression sappy chick novels are her thing. And I don't know anyone else there, so . . .

In fact, the only other person I know that lives outside of this state is Lucas. I highly doubt, though, he'd send me a romance novel. Especially when he hasn't kept in touch.

Tossing the envelope down, I reach up and grab my iPad, tapping my finger on the search bar and watching the cursor start blinking. My hands shake for a moment as I hesitate, but then I just start tapping away.

Lucas Evan Morrow.

The blue circle starts spinning, and my heart flips in my chest as my stomach starts to cave. I don't want to see search results, and the other part of me just wants them to pop up really quickly to get this over with.

I still have time. I can turn off the iPad right now, because the only thing better than knowing is wondering, right? I'm a curious girl, but what if I don't like what I find? I'd gone all this time without Googling him. I'm happier that way. What if he's gotten married? Is serious with someone? Has he turned into a jerk with male-pattern baldness and a beer belly? He's almost thirty now, so what's the point of obsessing—

And then . . . a flutter hits my belly as image after image starts to load onto the screen.

Oh, God.

I lick my lips, all of my questions fading away as I'm suddenly lost.

There he is.

There are images upon images. Him at meetings, grand openings, parties . . . some of them are official—Lucas shaking hands with other businessmen and foreign sheiks—and then, in some, it doesn't look like he even knows he's being photographed. Head bent down and that look of stern concentration in his brow that I remember so well.

He's beautiful. A sudden sob lodges in my throat but I catch it just in time.

I've missed him. I didn't realize how much until now, except now I understand why I've refrained from looking him up. It hurts too much.

I grew up with him, talked to him and saw him regularly, and, in all this time, he hasn't written or called or come home. He forgot about all of us, just like I'd told him he would.

No. I don't want to see his life that I'm not a part of.

But as I gaze into his eyes, like the blue of the Pacific ten minutes after sundown, I also realize it's something else, too. As my heart pounds, tears that I hold back stinging my eyes and every muscle in my chest tightening at the sight of him, I realize as I look at his gorgeous face that it's more than missing him.

It's longing.

His clothes have changed. He is almost always in a suit in nearly every picture, looking taller and older, with his tie tightened, and a flexed jaw like he's in a constant state of preparing for a confrontation.

Where's the guy with greasy hands who helped my brothers in the garage and taught me how to play in the dirt?

"Hey."

I pop my head up, hearing a call behind me. Hawke comes through the doors from the kitchen, and I turn the iPad over, hiding the screen.

He throws a towel onto a lounge chair and walks up to the pool, pulling his shirt over his head.

"Turn around," he warns.

I roll my eyes and do what he asks, knowing why. Behind me, I hear the shuffle of clothes as he strips off his shorts and shoes, getting naked, and pulls on swimming trunks, no doubt. Hawke is my nephew but we're not related by blood. A fact he uses to test the lines in our family. We would never hook up, but he likes to remind me that we *can* if we want to. You know . . . "for practice."

As soon as I hear the splash of water, I turn around and see his dark form gliding under the water toward me. He pops up, flipping back his hair, longer on the top, shaved on the sides, and his lip and eyebrow rings glimmer in the sunlight.

"Hi," I say. "You weren't at school today."

"Had some stuff to do."

He floats backward, and I can tell I'm not going to get any more information. Hawke skips school rarely, but lately, it's getting more frequent.

But although I'm curious, I'm not really worried, either. He keeps his grades up and doesn't seem to be getting into trouble. Hawke knows how to take care of himself. I just hope his mom doesn't find out. She pushes education. A lot.

Growing up, it wasn't "if we go to college," it was "when we go to college."

"Are you off-roading tonight?"

He stands back up, shaking his head as he walks toward me. "No, but I can if you want to come with me," he teases. "I'll let you drive."

"I don't know how to drive."

He stalks closer, a playful look in his eyes. "It's time you learned." He puts his hands on the edge of the pool at my sides. "Enough fucking around. If you can't practice on me, who can you practice on?"

I nearly laugh. "You mean practice *with* you?"

He shrugs. "Either or." And then he grabs my iPad from behind me, flipping it over. "What are you looking at?"

"Nothing," I burst out, suddenly on alert as I dart out to grab it.

But his eyebrows shoot up when he no doubt sees what's still on the screen. His eyes fix on me, and a drop of water falls from his hair down the side of his face.

"Still?" he inquires.

My shoulders tense, my guard going up, and I snatch the iPad back, turning it off again.

"They would never let it happen," he states.

His words loom around me like a cage, and I don't need him to clarify. I know what he's talking about.

My wonderment with Lucas at eight had turned into a crush by the time I was fourteen. And now, at seventeen, it still sits there, this small, constant flame in the back of my heart. Despite the distance, the loss of contact, him being twenty-nine years old and a full-grown man . . .

Oh, Jesus. Hawke is right.

Madoc *might* come to terms with it, as well as Tate and Juliet. But Jared, Jax, and my father?

They only see in black and white.

I force down the tightness in my throat and put the iPad away, turning around to Hawke.

"So . . . ," I broach, changing the subject. "This 'stuff' you're doing . . . is it illegal?"

He hoods his eyes. "That's insulting."

"But still . . . is it illegal?"

He splashes some water on me. "Forget it. I'm not telling you shit."

"Why not?"

"Because one look from my dad and you crack."

I laugh and splash him back. That's probably true.

"What are you reading?" he inquires, reaching over me. I see him take the hardcover book off the table.

"Be careful!" I wince. "Your hands are wet."

"'What if you met your soul mate too late?'" He reads the back cover. "'Would you let them go or would you hurt the ones you loved and risk everything to be together?'" He stops, wrinkling his eyebrows to look down at me with mischief in his eyes. "Lucas is only like thirty. It's not too late."

"Shut up," I bite out, trying to grab for the book.

But he holds it up, pushing my hands away as he continues to read.

"'On a cold winter night, Jase sees a young girl in an empty parking lot, and he doesn't know what to do first: get her name or get her into his bed.'" Hawke busts out laughing, shaking as he turns his eyes back on me. "What the hell is this crap?"

"Just . . ." I snatch the book and throw it back up on the table. "Stop being an asshole for five seconds. It's none of your business."

"Women are totally into porn. I knew it."

His gloating smirk is pissing me off. "It's not porn," I tell him. "I don't think it is, anyway. Someone sent it to me in the mail."

"You don't know who?"

"No." I shake my head and lean back against the edge of the pool. "And there was no note, either."

"Mysterious," he mumbles and then looks over at me again, waggling his eyebrows. "Are you going to read it? See if he gets her into his bed?"

This is why he's my least favorite relative. He's constantly trying to bait me.

But he's also the one I'm closest to. Hawke always thinks of himself last, and I admire that about him.

"You do know what happens when you get into a man's bed, right?" he asks.

"More than what happens when a girl gets into your bed, I hear."

He chuckles. "Don't test me, Quinn. Remember that we're not actually related."

I look over at him again, seeing his cocky smile, while his hands dance back and forth underneath the water.

"Oh, and what are you going to do?" I retort. "Convulse on top of me for fifteen seconds and then fall asleep?"

He lunges for me, and I squeal as he wraps his arms around me and picks me up off my feet.

"No!" I scream, but my stomach flips, and I'm laughing anyway.

He tosses me a couple feet, and then I'm free-falling.

My laugh follows me under the water.

Yep, definitely my least favorite relative.

CHAPTER 2

With a few hours left until Dylan's race after I've showered and dressed, I figure I can kill some time, trying out the new strawberry tart recipe I found online yesterday. My parents will be home late and probably hungry.

"Dude," I hear as I open the door. "Have you started reading this?"

I pop my head up to see Dylan lying on my bed with the hardcover I got in the mail today.

I laugh to myself. "No. Romance isn't my thing."

"Not your thing? Who doesn't like love stories?"

I toss my towel down and gaze over at her. She's so different than me. Snarky, fun-loving, up for anything . . .

"If you want to read it, go ahead."

There's silence as I stand at my dresser and dig in my makeup bag, starting to pick out what I need.

"Happiness is a direction, not a place."

What?

I spin around. "What did you say?"

She raises her eyes. "You told me I could read it."

Yeah, not out loud. But that line . . . I know that line.

"That's a sentence in the book?" I go over to her to take a look.

Sure enough, it's the first sentence. Weird. That same quote is inscribed on a gold compass my mom gave me when I was twelve.

A compass I gave Lucas the last time I saw him, in exchange for his hat. I thought it would ensure he'd come back to return it. It hasn't.

And I don't think it's mere coincidence that a mysterious book from a mysterious sender containing a quote I'm familiar with has found me.

"Do you want me to read more?" Dylan asks.

No, not really. But I can't help but feel a little curious now.

I shrug and walk to my dresser again. "Just a little more, sure."

JASE . . .

Happiness is a direction, not a place. Or so they said.

I fucking hated that saying. Like I wouldn't be happier anywhere else but here right now.

I ran my fingers through my short blond hair, smoothing away the mess the wind had made, and skirted around a couple at a high round table as I made my way to my father's nook in the back. It was dark, secluded, and quiet, but it allowed him an excellent view of the action. And my father liked to see everything.

"The one thing I can count on about you"—he smiled like he'd swallowed something bad—"is that you can't be counted on."

"Where you're concerned?" I replied lazily as I unbuttoned my jacket and slid into the semicircle booth without looking at him. "Of course not."

I dumped my keys on the table and gestured to the waitress who made eye contact. She knew what I drank. I was here every Friday night at six o'clock sharp for the weekly rundown with my father.

"You're right, Jase," he agreed. "I expect too much from you apparently."

His dry tone reeked of disappointment, but I didn't give a shit. At twenty-six I was already disillusioned enough to feel sorry for my own infant kid. What kind of family did I bring him into?

"I was in court in Chicago," I explained. "What would you have me tell them? That you want weekly reports on my sperm count, so you can have a busload of grandsons in hopes that one of them will make it to the White House someday?"

Sarcasm was something I hadn't grown out of.

"Stop whining." My father swirled his Jameson in his rocks glass. "Tell them that you have an important meeting."

"I hate lying. You know that."

I dug into my breast pocket and pulled out a silver cigarette case, taking a cigarette and lighting it. Tossing my lighter down on the table, I focused straight ahead of me, knowing my father was watching me through the swirls of smoke.

He was weighing his words, deciding if it would be worth his energy to chide me.

I blew out the smoke, biting back the smile tugging at my mouth. The day I graduated from law school last spring was the day I stopped letting him push me around. I had my degree, and I had the upper hand. He needed me more than I needed him, so once I'd secured my future, I put my foot down.

He'd bullied me into taking up the law, which even though I found little enjoyment in, I was actually adept at, and my forced marriage to Maddie was already hanging on by a thread. She was as unhappy as I was, and our son was the glue.

As much as I loved her, it was only a matter of time.

The waitress set down my drink—GlenDronach, neat—and disappeared.

"How's the kid?" my father asked.

I smiled, my son's sweet face flashing in my head. "Perfect," I replied. "He came out of the womb with a smile, and I don't think he's stopped since."

"He's strong." My father nodded, eyeing me. "He needs brothers."

"He needs a father," I shot back, blowing out smoke and hating the dirt taste in my mouth.

"You know I hate smoking."

"I know," I replied. "Is there anything else you wanted to ask me tonight? Other than about my child?"

He sighed, probably annoyed that I wasn't playing along. "And Madeline?" He leaned forward, his midnight blue suit a sharp contrast to the red booth. "How is she?"

"Fine." I nodded, tapping off some ashes in the ashtray. "Probably busy redecorating. She already has the kid in mommy and me swimming and Gymboree."

"She's a good woman." He leaned back, looking at me pointedly.

I fisted my fingers, accidentally snapping the cigarette in half. "You don't have to tell me that. I know my wife better than you."

Maddie was my best friend.

Or rather she used to be.

We grew up in the same circles, were thrown together at social functions growing up, and were even "encouraged" to attend the same university. Lucky for our parents we hit it off and always kept in touch when we were separated. She attended boarding school down south, while I attended military school, but we wrote and talked on the phone. She knew me, and I cared about her.

Unlucky for us was the knowledge that our parents had a plan. Arranged marriages are supposed to be a thing of the past, but they're still very much alive and well, and it's ruined the close relationship Maddie and I once shared.

The stress of forcing myself to make love to someone I didn't think about like that was killing me. She was still trying, but I'd shut down.

And it killed me to hurt her.

I could feel my father's judgmental eyes on me, and I hurriedly tucked my cigarettes and lighter back in my jacket, getting ready to leave. I couldn't do this tonight.

"Son," he started, "I love you—"

I let out a bitter laugh, cutting him off. "Don't even try. Unlike me, you're terrible at lying."

"And I do want you to be happy," he continued, ignoring my insult. "I know you and Maddie are having problems." He lowered his voice. "You're practically separated, sleeping on your office couch half the week or in spare bedrooms in your house."

How did he know that? *Damn it.*

"There are ways for a married man to find satisfaction outside of his home."

I shook my head before throwing back the rest of my drink. "You really are a piece of work, you know that?"

To my father, happiness was power. And taking anything you wanted was powerful. He had no boundaries, and no sense of right or wrong.

But I did.

I may not have been in love with my wife, but I did love her. I may not want to yank up her skirt and fuck like her like I couldn't live without her, but I did care about her. We hadn't had sex in months, and even though I knew things were ending between us, I wanted to protect her and respect her.

I let out a breath and slid out of the booth, standing up and grabbing my phone and keys.

"This marriage cannot fail." My father leaned forward, issuing his order. "You're getting more and more distant by the day, and you need to keep it together. You'd be surprised how easily another woman can—"

"Another woman," I growled, cutting him off, "isn't going to fix what's missing."

"I know what's missing," he retorted, looking me up and down. "You have no lust for anything. Every day is the same. You already feel like you're sixty years old, right?"

I froze, staring at him.

"Life is so dull"—he spoke slowly as if knowing every thought in my head—"even food seems boring, doesn't it?"

My knuckles cracked, and the room felt like it was getting smaller.

He leaned back, eyeing me with his self-satisfied fucking face. "We keep a suite at the Waldorf, Jase. You're not getting a divorce, so I suggest you use the room whenever and however often you need it."

I shook my head and spun around, bolting out of the bar without even stopping to get my coat.

Jesus Christ. What a fucking prick.

The frigid March evening cut into me, but it was a welcome relief from my burning temper.

I powered down the sidewalk, my gaze driving over the concrete, and I couldn't seem to get a handle on myself. I couldn't make myself happy and keep my family intact. Why couldn't I find a balance? Maddie wasn't the problem. I was. Why didn't I want her?

She knew I didn't love her like that when we married, and it was the same for her, but we thought it would grow into something bigger.

I'd see her standing at the refrigerator in the mornings dressed in my white T-shirts, her long, beautiful legs and angelic face equal in their perfection. Any man would desire her. So why couldn't I? Why couldn't I slip my hands inside of her clothes and whisper in her ear how beautiful she was? Or how much I needed to be inside of her right then? Why couldn't I give her the husband she deserved?

I rounded the corner, heading into the rear parking lot, lost in my thoughts, when I heard hushed chatter. I looked up and immediately halted.

My eyes narrowed at the sight of two kids hovering around my car, fiddling with the handle of my BMW.

What the . . . ?

"Hey!" I burst out, charging forward as both of their heads shot up. "Get away from my car!"

"Run!" one of the guys shouted, darting around the car and breaking into a run. "Come on, Kat!"

I raced over, seeing one of the kids shooting down to grab tools off the ground.

"Thomas!" he shouted after the other kid had already run off like a coward and saved himself.

But it was too late for this one.

These fucking kids were out of control, and I hoped like hell he was old enough to taste a night in jail.

"Come here, you little shit." I swooped down and grabbed the kid by his black sweatshirt and yanked him up.

But my face immediately fell.

It wasn't a boy.

Not a boy at all.

It was a young woman.

She breathed hard, both fear and fight blazing in her chocolate eyes as I held her by the collar. I stared into the warmest brown hue I'd ever seen, and a glow of light sweat covered her flushed cheeks.

My mouth went dry.

Her long brown hair was tucked into the collar of her hoodie, but strands blew across her face with the light wind, and I squeezed her sweatshirt tighter.

"Let go of me, asshole!" she shouted, struggling and squirming to get away. I narrowed my eyes, amusement fluttering through my chest.

She twisted, throwing out her pathetic little fists, and I almost laughed.

I jerked her up. "How old are you? Didn't your parents teach you to keep your hands off other people's things?"

"Look, I'm sorry, okay?" she yelled, tears filling her eyes despite her tough act. "I promise we won't do it again. We just needed the money."

"Tell it to the cops," I snapped, even though I had no intention of calling the police.

Her worried eyes darted around her, and I could tell she was struggling not to cry.

"How old are you?" I demanded again. Did she have parents responsible for her?

She shot angry eyes at me but clamped her mouth shut.

I got in her face. "How old?" I yelled.

But the next thing I knew, she'd swung her fist, bringing it down across the side of my face, and I reared back, loosening my grip on her.

Shit!

I grabbed my face, trying to force my stinging eye back open, but all I could make out were legs and ass as she darted away, into the night.

I squinted, rubbing the ache in my cheek, and I swallowed blood from where my teeth had cut the inside of my mouth when she'd hit me.

I composed myself and moved toward my car. But then I zeroed in on something on the ground, and I reached down to pick it up.

A wallet.

It had to be hers. Fake red leather with a coin compartment. Opening it up, I immediately went for her license and picked it out.

"Kat," I said slowly, eyeing her bright smile and dark eyes.

And then I looked at her birthdate, since she'd refused to tell me.

Nineteen.

A smile tugged at the corner of my lips. "Old enough to know better," I said to myself.

The address read "14 Truman Street," and I turned the card around in my fingers, thinking about what to do.

I could have them arrested. Or I could save myself some aggravation, because they were only common street punks, and toss the license into the Dumpster. I had better things to do. Who really cared, anyway?

But then her eyes flashed in my head, and I suddenly knew what I wanted to do. My interest was piqued. The fear and the way her breathing shook. The vulnerable tremble to her bottom lip. The anger and the way she slapped me as she found the courage to fight.

What was her story?

Slipping the card into my pocket, I climbed into my car and sped out of the parking lot. Truman Street was on the other side of town, and I had no clue if she and her little pal even had transportation or they were just counting on taking mine, but I suspected I wouldn't even find her home. If that was her real home, that is.

I sped down the street and took a left on Main, cutting through the downtown and driving until the businesses and pedestrians were behind me. I couldn't see everything as clearly at night, but I could tell that the manicured lawns of emerald green had now turned brown and patchy, and the houses became smaller and older as the neighborhoods changed. The once-white siding of a trailer was tinged yellow under the porch light, and I couldn't help but feel disgust at the garbage lying on some of the lawns.

After a few minutes, I finally pulled up on Truman Street and slowed my car, seeing number fourteen across the street. The house was dark with no lights illuminating the outside.

I gazed around the neighborhood, picturing my son inside one of these trailers or dilapidated houses. There was no way in hell.

"We could've been arrested!" I heard a woman shout.

I followed the voice and saw a girl across from number fourteen, leaving a trailer and carrying a small child. She chased after a man walking away from her.

It was them.

She adjusted the child on her hip, holding the poor kid close, since he didn't have a jacket. It looked as if they were picking him up at someone else's house.

"What would've happened to our kid?" she shouted after the guy, the father, I presumed.

He crossed the street, heading to number fourteen, and she trailed behind, carrying the child. He opened the door and disappeared inside, leaving her out there alone.

What a fucking prick. She was just a kid.

And the kid had a kid. I couldn't have her arrested.

Taking out my cell phone, I dialed a number and held the phone to my ear, waiting for him to answer like he always did.

"Hi. It's Jase," I informed him when he picked up. "I need all the information you can find on the residents of Fourteen Truman Street."

"Okay," Brown answered, and I knew he was probably writing the address down. He was on the company payroll, and an investigator my father's firm used often. "I'll get back to you within forty-eight hours."

"Twelve." And I hung up.

———

Dylan stops reading there, but I can see her eyes move across the page as she silently reads.

"Hey," I complain. *I was listening to that.*

I walk over and throw myself onto the bed, landing on my stomach next to her. Dylan turns to me, cocking an eyebrow.

"She tried to steal his car," I explain, "and now he knows exactly where she lives. You can't just stop there."

We hover close, both of us reading to ourselves.

———

JASE . . .

A week later, I walked into Denton Auto Repair, a piece-of-shit shack probably built in the thirties with chipped white paint and a dank cement floor in the "lobby." The walls were stained yellow, probably from old cigarette smoke, the blue counter was cracked, and the two vinyl couches were ripped. I held back my sneer, trusting in the fact that the place had been in business a long time. It probably had a good reputation.

But under normal circumstances I would never step foot in such a grimy shithole whose mechanics would probably take my car out for a joyride after they talked me into leaving it overnight. I had other business here, though.

I closed the door behind me, the sun setting outside and evening approaching, and pulled out my handkerchief, absently wiping off my hand before stuffing it back into my pocket.

Two men loitered around the lobby, and when I looked to the front counter, I found it empty. This was where she was supposed to work. I'm not sure what she did, though. Clean, maybe?

"Mr. Hutcherson," a female voice called, and I jerked my head to the left.

A young woman strolled behind the counter, coming in through the door leading in from the garage area, and heat immediately warmed my chest. I watched as she stapled paperwork and offered the man who'd stepped up to her counter a smile.

Jesus.

Her dark brown hair shone, tied up in a messy ponytail, and I caught hints of red in the strands around her oval-shaped face that I hadn't noticed last week. Her chocolate eyes were deep and warm, and I swallowed the lump in my throat, staring at her full bottom lip.

I clenched my fists at my sides, and tried to breathe normally, like I didn't want to walk right over there and . . .

She wore jean shorts that weren't too tight but just short enough to see a good amount of thigh, with a white V-neck T-shirt tucked into them that kind of drowned her. Did it belong to her boyfriend?

I walked slowly forward, as if on autopilot, and stepped into line behind the other man, Hutcherson, I would assume, to await my turn. She smiled at him and handed him his keys as he paid the bill. I noticed she had a grease stain on her neck as well as a few black smudges on her shirt and several on her hands. She must've worked on cars, too.

It was dark that night, and I didn't get a good look at her then, but seeing her again, I knew . . . it wasn't the adrenaline that night or the cold weather or the frustrated state I'd been in after fighting with my father.

I didn't want to punish her. Or help her. I'd wanted to see her again, yet I shouldn't have come. But my family was out of town, and I'd told myself it was just curiosity. That's all it was.

You'd be surprised how another woman can . . . Can what, Dad? Can tempt me like this? Can distract me from everything I hate in my life and make me feel alive again? For just a few minutes?

It was a bitter fucking pill to swallow that he might've been right. Everything had become paint-by-numbers in my life, and for the first time in a long time, the lines were blurred. I felt like I could stretch out my arms and not run into a boundary.

And for the first time ever, I felt dangerous to someone. I liked it.

"Can I help you, sir?"

A male voice to my left spoke up, and I turned my head. It was a young guy with red hair and a dark blue mechanic's shirt. His name patch read "Josh."

"Yes. I'd like you to pull my car into the garage." I reached into my pocket and pulled out my keys, handing them over. "I've only been waiting forever."

My tone was curt, but only because I knew it would fluster him and send him on his way. I was dealing with the girl, not him.

"Uh . . . ," he stammered, wide eyed, but I wasn't interested in conversation. I looked away, telling him we were done.

"Sure, absolutely," he finally responded.

He took the keys from me and darted outside, probably knowing he wouldn't have a hard time determining which car belonged to me. Not every person who drove a German car was a dickhead, but every dickhead drove a German car.

Hutcherson moved on, and I stepped up to the counter, staring at the girl as she stapled more papers and tucked them into a plastic sleeve with a set of keys.

"Hi," I said, keeping my voice low and calm even though my heart was jackhammering in my chest.

"Hey," she replied, not looking at me. "Just a minute, please." And then she spun around, pushing a button and speaking into an intercom. "Can someone pull that Honda out? Pickup's here."

And then she slid the plastic sleeve onto a hook on the wall and twisted back around, finally looking up at me.

"Hey, I'm sor—" She froze. Her eyes widened, and I held back my grin, feeling the pulse in my neck throb as I waited for what she'd do now. She recognized me. The thin fabric of her T-shirt moved up and down as her chest rose and fell in heavy breaths, and I simply watched her beautiful skin turn a delightful shade of pink.

She finally blinked, finding her voice. "Hi," she said breathlessly, looking down and fidgeting with something on the counter. "Um, we're actually about to close, sir. I'm sorry. One of the guy's daughters has a birthday party tonight, and the other mechanics are leaving with him. We can schedule you for tomorrow if you like."

I studied her, wondering how she thought she was going to just play this off. We both knew why I was here.

I knew I should take the out she was offering. I should leave and go home to wait for my wife and son.

But that wasn't what I found myself doing.

"What about you?" I tipped my chin at her. "Are you a mechanic?"

But she just shook her head. "No. I'm sorry."

I gave her a knowing smile and looked down at her hands, dark grease caked around her nails.

She followed my gaze and fisted her fingers, hiding them. "Maybe on a Buick or a Toyota," she replied, "but you don't want me messing with your fifty-thousand-dollar engine. Trust me."

I smiled to myself, because she didn't realize that she'd just given herself away. How did she know which car was mine? Had she seen me drive up?

Or rather, did she remember that she'd tried to steal it the other night?

"I just need an oil change."

"Well, like I said . . . we're closing early."

"I'll pay," I insisted. "Double your rate?"

"She'll do it." Someone spoke up behind her, and I looked to see a middle-aged man rolling a tire past her.

"What?" she burst out, spinning her head around to glare at the man. "I have to get home."

"Do it," he ordered, continuing out to the garage, away from any further protest.

Must be her boss.

She turned back to me, a scowl marring her once-sweet face. And I finally saw the same temper I saw the other night when she hit me. I pulled out my wallet from the inside of my suit jacket and doled out three one-hundred-dollar bills onto the counter, not taking my eyes off her.

"Is that enough?"

She stared at the money—the money I knew she needed—as she no doubt weighed the risk of what was happening here. She didn't know what I wanted—neither did I—but she knew I hadn't called the cops yet, so there was a chance to get out of this. She also knew that if she sent me away, she lost control of the situation. Or whatever control she now had.

Her eyes finally rose to meet mine, and I saw a hint of mischief cross her pretty young face.

She leaned forward, nearly whispering. "How bad do you want it?"

My fingers tightened around the wallet, and my stomach dropped a little, catching the taunting edge to her words.

Was she playing with me?

And I watched in awe as she reached over, smoothly swiped the three hundreds off the counter, and then plucked another hundred out of my hand, making it four. Stuffing them in her back pocket, she left me there and headed into the garage.

I didn't even try to hide my smile. She had my complete attention. Just for a while. Just for tonight.

I stood outside the garage, half-in and half-out, smoking a cigarette as the darkness shrouded the road and the surrounding woods, and watching her out of the corner of my eye. She raised my BMW up on the hydraulics and tucked a couple of tools into her back pocket as she walked underneath the car and bent her head back, loosening the plug to the oil above her.

A tune played on the radio, and it was hard to keep my eyes off her. Especially when she kept swaying ever so slightly to the music, probably without realizing it.

I was impressed, though. I half expected her to call for help. She and I were alone here now, after all. Maybe that loser guy she was with would bring some friends over to send me on my way with a few threats? But no . . . as far as I could see, she hadn't called anyone. She just got to work on my car.

Smart kid.

I nodded to the bulletin board, which had a five-by-seven portrait of a brown-eyed boy—about six months old—pinned to it. "Is that your son?"

She jerked her head back down at me, as if just noticing I was there. Her expression turned guarded, but she glanced at the picture before quickly turning back to her job under the car. "That obvious?"

I watched her, thinking about how hard it must be to raise a child at her age. I couldn't imagine whoever the father was being much help. Especially if it was that piece of shit from the other night.

"He has your eyes," I said.

"And my ex's temper," she stated in a clipped tone. "I can tell already."

Ex. "You're too young to have exes." I blew out a stream of smoke and dropped the butt, grinding it out with my shoe.

But she just ignored me.

I stepped into the garage, my suit coat open, and my hands in my pockets. "Do you go to college?"

She glared at me. "Customers aren't supposed to be in the garage."

But I ignored her and keep pressing. "You don't want to work here for the rest of your life, do you?"

"I have to work, College Boy," she bit out. "With a kid to support, I don't have time for school."

I wanted to laugh at her spunk, but I held it back.

She came out from under the car, tossed down some tools, and pressed the hydraulics button, lowering the car again and looking impatient.

"My son is about the same age," I told her.

"At home with the wife?"

And I held her gaze, all humor gone from my mood. She was smart, I'd give her that. Strolling slowly over to her, I pulled my hand out of my pocket, taking her license with it, and tossed it on top of the toolbox in front of her.

"Talking to a woman who isn't my wife isn't a crime," I said, stating it like a threat. "Trying to steal my property is."

She stood there, staring at the license with her name and address on it, her chest rising and falling in quick, shallow breaths. *Now you're scared, aren't you?*

"What do you want?" she asked.

"What do you think I want?"

Her breath shook for a moment, but then she turned her face to me, clenching her teeth so hard, I could see her jaw flex.

"An apology, of course," I said, as if what else could I possibly want from her?

"I want you to leave."

"Then you need to finish my car," I shot back, my eyes falling to that little black smudge on her slender neck.

Her eyes turned angry, and she hesitated. But she popped the hood and got back to work. I turned and headed for the other side of the car, leaning against the toolboxes and crossing my arms over my chest.

I knew I should just leave. She was scared, and she already had it rough enough.

Just get in your car, go home, and leave the kid alone.

"What are you going to do?" She leaned over the car, upending an oil container into the engine and letting it empty. "Why are you here?"

"How long have you been married?" I asked, ignoring her question.

I saw her swallow and then answer quietly. "A little over a year. But I'd barely call it a marriage anymore. I'm trying to get a divorce."

"Trying?"

"It's none of your business."

No, it wasn't. But I was making her my business.

"And you thought what you were doing was healthy?" I charged. "Letting him get you caught up in criminal activity, so he can get money to get high?"

She shot me a scowl while leaning over the car and pouring in another bottle. "And you're any better?" she replied, her tone getting harder. "Don't think I don't know what you want. You would've called the police already if justice was what you were after." She stood up, grabbing a cloth to wipe off her hands. "No, you think I'm vulnerable and you can take advantage."

No. That wasn't what I wanted. I wasn't trying to prey on her.

So why the hell was I here then?

"Isn't that it?" she taunted, walking slowly toward me with a look in her eyes. "Does it turn you on—the dirty trailer park girl? You think I'll be wild, don't you?" She stepped up to me, her breasts brushing against my crossed arms. Leaning in, she dropped her voice low and sexy, and I could feel the heat of her body. "That's what you've been thinking about, isn't it? At church on Sunday, giving your clean wife a clean kiss on the cheek"—she offered a small smile—"you were thinking about my ass and how dirty and good and naughty I'm gonna feel . . ."

My breathing sped up, and I stared at her full bottom lip, feeling like I'd suddenly gotten myself into trouble.

Licking her lips, she leaned in further, whispering, "Pathetic fucking college boy. You wouldn't know what to do with this ass."

And then she rolled her hips, barely brushing mine in a little tease, and I groaned, my breath shaking. The contact sent my body reeling, and I was fully hard and hot with need.

She pulled away slowly, a smirk on her face, because she knew what she was doing to me. She might be a tough little scrapper most of the time, but the girl could be sexy as fuck.

And she'd just issued a challenge.

I watched as she took the oil can out, replaced the dipstick, and closed the hood of the car.

"Keys are in it." She turned to me, the gloating look in her eyes still there.

Keeping my gaze on her, I reached into my jacket and pulled out my billfold again, taking out a business card. Not breaking eye contact, I placed it on the toolbox.

"Whenever you're ready to give me that apology," I told her.

Please don't lose it.

And please don't use it.

CHAPTER 3

"Oh, wow." Dylan lays down the book on the bed and turns her wide eyes on me. "That was hot. What do you think is going to happen when he sees her again?"

She giggles and turns the page, but I grab the book out of her hand.

"You can't be serious. He's a jerk."

"He is not," she argues and tries to take the book back. "He's awesome."

"Whatever." I laugh, rolling onto my back and holding the book away from her. "He's trying to pay her for sex."

"No, he's not."

"All those hundreds?" I remind her. "Then what's the money for?"

She shrugs, reaching over me to try to grab the book back. "He knows she needs it. I don't care. I want to know what happens next!"

I hug the book to my body, laughing when she tries to pry it away.

"Oh, come on." She pouts and gives up, lying at my side on her back. "Think about if it were Lucas, and you were . . . changing his oil."

I roll my eyes and mumble, "Shut up."

Of course she doesn't.

Propping herself up on her side, she rests her head on her hand and looks down at me, her voice turning sultry and playful. "Alone in the shop at night," she taunts. "An older man in a hot suit who knows what he's doing . . ."

My stomach flips, and I can't stop the image that springs into my mind. Lucas . . . seeing me for the first time in so many years . . . and everything's changed.

"Think about him looking at you that way. Like how Jase looked at Kat," Dylan says. "Like you're a woman and he wants what a man wants from a woman, because his body's on fire and he needs his hands on you."

Lucas's eyes fall down my body, like all of a sudden he can't stop himself, and my breath escapes me, my lungs emptying at the thought of his gaze turning dark and possessive like Jase's did with Kat.

An electric buzz runs under my skin, but I shake my head, clearing it.

Jase and Kat. My parents, Jason and Katherine, could easily have gone by those nicknames in another life.

But I've barely ever heard anyone call my dad Jason, let alone something as informal as Jase. It's "Dad" to Madoc and me. "Jason" to my mom only. And "Mr. Caruthers" to everyone else.

"Yeah, well," I say, pushing the fantasy of Lucas away, "I'm not like her."

"Like what?"

"Hot." I let out a sigh. "I'm not hot. I'm just sweet and kind and boring."

Dylan falls back again, and we both stare up at the ceiling.

"Yeah, me, too," she breathes out. "I wear a tank top, and my dad tells me to go put some clothes on."

We both laugh, because with a dad like Jared, she has it just as tough as me. Jared doesn't parent his kids based on what's right or wrong. Quite simply, if it makes him uncomfortable, he isn't having it and that's that.

But Dylan is better at sneaking around her father's hang-ups and getting away with more. I'm not used to pushing the boundaries with my parents.

I want to be, though. I want to be like what Jase said. *Dangerous to someone.*

I gaze straight above me and slip my hand behind my head, whispering slowly, "Pathetic . . . fucking . . . college boy." And then Dylan's voice joins mine as we both say at once, "You wouldn't know what to do with this ass."

Heat pools in my belly, and Dylan and I both start to laugh.

"I kind of feel hotter now," she tells me.

"Yeah, me, too."

"Okay, then." She takes the book from my arms and flips onto her stomach, opening it up. "Let's keep reading. Learn some more dirty talk."

JASE . . .

I shouldn't have left her my card. What the hell was I thinking?

I'd met the girl twice, and in that time, there were already a dozen moments when I should've done something differently, like walked away.

I knew what I should do. I knew what I shouldn't do. I knew the difference between right and wrong, but if, by some miracle, I saw her again, what I knew wouldn't matter in the face of what I wanted.

And that couldn't happen.

It had been a week since I'd left her my card in the garage, and thankfully, she hadn't called. I wouldn't seek her out, so as long as she didn't call me—which she wouldn't, since she probably thought I was a piece of shit, anyway—then everything would be fine.

I had the strength to stay away from temptation.

And then the fucking money. Throwing my weight around like I could buy anything I wanted. I hadn't really been trying to buy her. Just a few minutes with her.

Walking into my house, I heard the clock chime nine as I closed the door behind me and made my way across the dark foyer. Maddie was still at her parents' with our son, so the house was deathly quiet. The baby was only a few months old, but he already loved music, so I was used to walking into the house on any given day with a wide range of tunes playing loudly: classical, oldies, eighties rock . . .

Now, nothing. I was missing him, and Madeline had called earlier today to say she'd be staying an extra week on top of the time she'd already been away.

She was avoiding me. And as much as I missed my kid, I was kind of glad she was gone. In her absence I didn't have to put up a front while I was at home.

Until she returned, anyway, and I was forced to deal with the stalemate we were in. Would she want to keep the house? Would I stay in the city permanently, so far away from my son every day? Our family's firm handled everything for her father. What would happen to those accounts now? The thing about our marriage was it wasn't just us. There were a lot of people who'd be affected.

I set my briefcase down and unbuttoned my jacket, walking upstairs to change. I threw on some jeans and a T-shirt and came back downstairs to rummage through the refrigerator. Finding a large bowl of chicken salad Maddie had left, I fixed myself a sandwich and took it into my office so I could get right back to work. I wanted my own firm in the next five years, so if I worked hard enough, built up my clientele and my reputation, I'd be able to be my own boss and set my own pace by the time my son was in school and started to remember what kind of father I was. I'd failed Maddie, but I'd make sure that kid was never sad.

I spent the next hour researching a couple of cases as well as answering a few e-mails and finishing my opening remarks for the GM lawsuit. The proceedings would start next week, so I'd be home even less than I was now. I was half tempted to just get an apartment in the city. The commute was starting to take too much of my time.

Rummaging through the papers on my desk, I stopped. Where in the hell was that fax? I'd grabbed it before I'd left work.

"Briefcase," I mumbled, standing up. I headed back into the foyer and popped open my case, sifting through file folders for the white piece of paper I needed. But then I noticed a flashing red light from inside the dark case. I picked out my cell phone and turned it on, seeing a missed call from twenty minutes ago. It could've been any number of people—a client, Maddie, my father . . .

But my heart suddenly skipped a beat. I didn't recognize the number, and I couldn't stop myself. I redialed.

"Denton Auto Repair," an out-of-breath voice answered.

And I closed my eyes, fighting the heat drifting over my body. Shit.

"Hello?" Kat said when I didn't say anything. She sounded stressed.

I cleared my throat. "You called me?" I forced myself to say, knowing I should hang up.

She was silent for a moment, and I could hear her labored breathing. My guard went up. Was something wrong? It was after ten. The shop closed two hours ago. Why was she still there?

"Look, I'm sorry," she blurted out. "I shouldn't have called. Forget it."

"What's wrong?" I barked before she could hang up.

"Nothing. I'll be okay—"

"What happened?!"

I heard her suck in a breath, and I immediately picked up my keys and grabbed my wallet out of my briefcase, not even thinking.

"Are you close?" she asked, her voice sounding hesitant. "I'm at the garage. My ride never showed, there's no one else I can call, and there's a weird car sitting outside. I just—"

"I can be there in ten minutes," I said, already walking out the door and not even caring why she'd called me of all people. "Don't go outside."

"Thank you." I heard the relief in her voice.

I hung up and hurried into my car without any hesitation. That repair shop was off a secluded country road. No way in hell was she walking home.

I sped the entire way there, punching the stick shift into fourth and then fifth, my headlights falling against the blacktop highway and no other cars in sight. I wondered who her ride was that didn't show. Probably the ex. Right now, I wouldn't mind running into him again.

Finally, I spotted the lights of the repair shop ahead and slowed the car.

I swung into the parking lot and immediately noticed Kat, ripping her arm away from a man who'd grabbed it, another man standing beside him. I slammed on the brakes and yanked up the parking brake, jumping out of the car.

"I don't have your money!" Kat yelled, trying to walk around them. Why the hell had she come outside?

"Then maybe we'll have you work it off for him," one of the guys snarled. "Huh, honey? Now tell us where he is, because one way or another we get paid!"

"Go to hell!" she barked, and I raced up, putting myself in front of her and shoving one of the guys back.

"What do you want?" I demanded, my shoulders squared and rage pouring out of every goddamn pore on my body.

Both guys were dressed like street thugs, ratty clothes and greasy hair, once of them sporting a huge tattoo on his neck.

"Fuck off, man," the dark-haired one growled. "She owes us money. Our business is with her. Not you."

"I don't owe you anyth—"

"How much?" I asked the guy, cutting Kat off.

He stared at me, narrowing his eyes and looking like he was debating whether or not to deal with me.

"Four hundred," he finally answered, his voice growing calmer.

I held his gaze and reached into my pocket, pulling out my wallet.

"What?" Kat cried behind me. "No!"

But I took out four bills and handed them over to the punk. "You don't come near her again. You understand?"

But he just took the money and smiled lazily, like all was right with the world now. "Thanks," he replied and then looked around me to Kat. "Nice doin' business, Kat."

And they both turned and headed back to their car. I stayed in front of her, feeling the heat of her anger on my back.

But I had my own fury swirling like a tornado under my skin. What the fuck was the matter with her? Why would she come outside the shop if she'd noticed a car lurking around? And what the hell would she have done if I hadn't shown up?

What would they have done to her?

She came around me, her face twisted in anger. "I don't need your help."

"Then why the hell did you call me?" I barked.

"I forget!" she yelled back, spinning around. "Screw off, College Boy."

I widened my eyes and ran my hand through my hair, fisting it. Jesus Christ! What did I do wrong? She called me.

I watched her walk back to the garage, her tight blue jeans ripped to hell, grease stains up her forearms, and her dark gray T-shirt falling off her shoulder, exposing her skin, and I didn't know if I was angry or turned on or both. Every single one of my muscles was hot and as hard as a rock. Every. Single. One.

Charging after her, I grabbed hold of her arm, twisted her around, and threw her over my shoulder, hearing her yelp as I stood there, wrapping my arms around the backs of her thighs.

"What are you doing?" she screeched, and I saw her black baseball cap fall to the ground and the ends of her dark hair sway around my waist.

"I don't know, but it's fun," I told her. "I can hold you like this all night. I'm kind of enjoying it, actually."

"Let me down!"

"Not likely."

"Jase!" she protested again. I actually don't think I ever introduced myself. But then I remember having written my nickname with my cell number on the back of my business cards.

I stood there like I was waiting for the fucking bus until she calmed down and stopped acting like a child.

"Actually, you are getting kind of heavy." I grunted and shifted her on my shoulder. "Maybe if I stripped you down, it'd be a lighter load? You game, Trailer Park Princess?"

"Don't call me that."

"Then stop calling me College Boy."

She tried to twist out of my hold, throwing my balance off. "Please!" she cried.

And when I didn't budge, her breathing slowed, and she finally lowered her voice. "Jase?" she said, and my fingers tightened on her, loving the sound of my name on her lips. "I'll let you take me home, okay?"

Okay. But I didn't put her down.

Instead, I carried her all the way to the car, hearing her angry little growl behind me, because she knew I didn't trust her to not run away.

She dragged my ass all the way out here and put me in the middle of her drama. I was taking her home safely.

I put her feet on the ground and opened up the car door, letting her climb in. More like she just plopped down in the seat, pouting, but she was in the car, nonetheless. Walking around to the driver's side, I climbed in, fastened my seat belt, and started the car.

"Who were those guys?" I asked her, turning on my headlights and pulling onto the dark road.

"It doesn't matter."

I arched a brow, turning to look at her. "I asked you a question."

I'd forked over four hundred dollars to get her out of trouble— what she did with the other four hundred I'd left last week, I had no idea—so she could damn well give me some answers.

"Dealers," she finally answered. "My ex owes them money, so they were shaking me down, trying to find him."

"Do you know where he is?"

"He's never far."

I shook my head, turning my eyes back out to the road.

Dealers. She said it as if it's all so normal.

What would they have done if I hadn't been there? What if they'd shown up at her goddamn house with her son there? Is that what she wanted him growing up around? Fucking losers and trash and drama . . .

I tightened my fists around the steering wheel, hearing the leather grind in my fist. "You're a mess," I bit out in low voice. "How the hell can anyone live like that?"

I saw her turn to me out of the corner of my eye. "You don't know me. Don't forget that."

And then I saw her put her baseball cap back on, folding her arms over her chest.

We sat in silence, and I stared ahead, the white lines in the middle of the road racing past my car as I considered what the hell I thought

I was doing. She had a point. I had no right to judge her. Her reality was far different from mine. I had money, an education, experiences that constantly reminded me how big the world was. She was a teenager who would probably struggle for everything for the rest of her life.

But . . . despite our very different lives, we were both here, weren't we? She, coming to me, because even though she would never admit it, and given how little she knew about me, she did know I would come through for her. And me, racing to her in the middle of the night, because all the money, education, or experiences in the world couldn't buy what she made me feel.

"I do know you," I admitted. "Because I'm just as much of a mess as you are."

I could feel her eyes on me, and I wondered what she thought of me. Was I the asshole rich guy trying to prey on her? Was I some idiot she thought she could hustle to feed her kid?

Or could she feel me as much as I felt her on every inch of my skin? Had I been in her head at all over the past week? Because she was constantly in mine.

I saw her pick something out of the console and glanced over to see her open my wallet.

"You're right," she said, pulling out a picture of my son. "He's about the same age as mine." And then she put the snapshot back and set my wallet back down. "Someday . . . they'll be all grown up, with their own problems, and all of this will be over." She leaned her head back, musing. "Sometimes I just pray for time to go quicker, ya know? Like I just want to fast-forward to forty, and hopefully the hard part will be done."

I nodded. "Like this is all just a shit preamble to something better."

"Yeah." Her voice was gentle and soft. "We'll have it together, we won't be confused anymore, we'll be excited about tomorrow . . ."

I kept driving, letting her words linger in the air.

She knew. She knew exactly what I was feeling, because we weren't so different.

I turned into town, heading for her house, and she didn't seem to notice that it was odd I knew where she lived without her telling me. Sprinkles of rain started hitting the windshield, and I turned on the wipers, slowing my speed.

"Why did you marry him?" I asked her.

I heard her take in a deep breath, but she didn't seem angry I'd asked.

"I thought he would change," she answered. "In his rare, genuine moments, he convinced me he loved me. But if I were listening more closely, I would've realized that he just wanted to bleed me dry. Cooking, cleaning, my paychecks from the garage, sex . . ." She drifted off and then continued. "He barely even remembers I exist anymore, except when he needs money. He hasn't touched me since I was five months pregnant. He didn't like the way my body looked anymore."

I couldn't help myself. I looked over at her, gazing at the smoothness and glow of her bare skin where the shirt fell off her shoulder, and the rise and fall of her breasts as she breathed. She had a beautiful figure, and he was a fucking idiot.

"Why did you marry her?" she asked me in return.

I turned my eyes back out to the road as I wound my way through her neighborhood.

Because I didn't see you first.

"Because I love her." I told her the truth. "I grew up with her, she comes from a good family, my father thought it would be—"

"Yeah, I get it," she cut me off.

But I wasn't sure she did get it. I loved my son's mother, but my love for Maddie was like everything else that never changed in my life. It was constant and routine. It never challenged me or hurt me.

Or excited me.

I was never hungry or wild for it. I never longed to feel her.

It was just there. Like my house, my job, my car . . .

I pulled up to the front of her house, a small light shining through the living room window, but the rest of the street was dark. Rain poured down heavily now, blanketing my windshield in sheets of water.

We sat there silent for a moment, and I turned to look at her, knowing she wanted to say something.

She stared out the window, making no move to get out. "What do you want with me?" she asked quietly.

I almost laughed. Not because I found the question amusing, but because I found it far too tempting. What did I want? Nothing. Everything.

"When I know, so will you," I told her.

She smiled to herself and looked over at me, holding my eyes.

"What?" I asked.

But she just shook her head. "It's weird. For a single moment . . . I didn't want to fast-forward."

And my stomach flipped as she held my eyes, everything in them telling me she felt what I was feeling.

I could touch her. I could reach over and take her, and guide her into my lap and touch her if I wanted to.

"You'd better get out of this car," I warned.

She tried to hide her smile, but I still saw it. And I watched her finally climb out of the car and into the pouring rain.

I didn't want to fast-forward, either. In fact, I wanted time to slow as much as possible.

She rounded the front of the car, her hair turning black as it got wet, and came to stand at my window. I watched as the rain drenched her clothes, the shirt molding to her breasts and running down the olive-toned skin of her chest. I tightened my fist around the steering wheel again.

And then slowly, she leaned down and placed her lips against my window, closing her eyes and kissing it.

I watched as she backed away, holding my eyes, and then spun around and ran to her house, disappearing into the warm glow.

Now I knew.

I put the car in first gear and drove off, knowing exactly what I wanted from her.

CHAPTER 4

"Damn." Dylan glances at me, and I know we're both thinking the same thing.

"Don't worry," I tease. "Someone is going to want you like that, so badly Jared will go crazy. Be careful what you wish for."

She scoffs and turns the page to the next chapter. Dylan really has no clue.

All she sees is what's right in front of her. Guys are drawn to her, because of her spirit and smiles. She's a happy person, and she makes people feel good when they're around her.

I'm not like that. I'm just kind of there. Like empty space.

And my mind circles back to Dylan's question. What if Jase was Lucas? Would he see me as anything other than his friends' kid sister? Would he feel that kind of physical pull to me?

I doubt it.

Lucas knew me when I needed to get pushed on the swings and all I wanted to watch on TV was the Disney Channel. I'd been kissed, I'd been touched, but I'd never felt compelled to experience more.

What did Jase want with Kat? What did he want to do to her? She was only slightly older than me, so what did he see in her that men didn't see in me?

But I guess that's not true. There were boys who had been interested in me.

I was still curious, though . . . what did desire feel like for someone when one woman could give him what he needed but not another?

———

JASE . . .

Stepping through the front door, I walked into my home and immediately saw Maddie sweeping into the foyer. Our son sat on her hip as she swung his diaper bag on her other shoulder. "You're home early." She forced a small smile, her voice light.

"Where are you going?" I asked, setting my briefcase down.

I reached out a hand and rubbed Madoc's bald head.

"We have a doctor's appointment," she said, wiping some drool from the corner of his mouth. "Just a checkup, and then we're going to the library before I drop him off with my mother, so I can meet with the caterers for my sister's wedding."

"Well, here then." I held out my hands, ready to take him. "Just leave him with me, and you can do what you need to do."

Just because we were practically roommates these days didn't mean I wasn't still my son's father.

"Oh, Jase." She laughed like it was a joke. "Have you ever changed his diaper? You'd be calling me in ten minutes, breaking down."

"I think I can handle it." I reached out for him again. "I went to Harvard."

But she just shook her head and walked around me. "I don't have time to show you where the formula is, how to make it, the toys he likes to play with . . . trust me," she said, kind of sounding like she was talking to a child. "Use the peace and quiet to get some work done. I'll be home in a few hours. We have dinner with your parents later, so I laid out a suit for you. Just don't forget to shower," she instructed. "You kind of smell like that cologne your mom bought you last Christmas that I threw away. Did she buy you another bottle?"

"Maddie?" I argued, seeing her open the door. "I want him—"

"It'll just stress me out," she fought. "Making me come all the way back here when you need help . . ." And then she kissed the air between us. "Love you. Bye."

And she pulled the door closed.

For a few minutes I stood there, trying to figure out why she thought I couldn't take care of my son. Why she seemed in such a hurry to leave.

It was me, no doubt. I'd cut her off for so long and put him in her care so much, she didn't know how to let me help her with him.

Or maybe she didn't want to be around me any more than I wanted to be with her.

My phone rang in my briefcase, and I opened it up to retrieve it. Hitting the green Call button, I brought it my ear.

"Yes?"

"This is Rhodes BMW, sir."

"Yes?"

"Sir, the car you wanted delivered today was sent back."

Sent back? What?

I tore the phone away from my ear and ended the call. *Sent back?*

Digging under some files, I pulled my wallet out, stuck it in my breast pocket, and headed for the door.

I'd purchased a car for Kat, not expecting anything, and I could understand her being compelled to not accept such a large gift, but hell . . . She could've been attacked the other night. She was nearly attacked, actually. You would think a young woman with a child to worry about would choose sense over pride and take a vehicle that would improve the chances of keeping her and her kid safe.

It wasn't like it was a new car, either. If she thought the gift meant I was intending to keep her as a mistress, I'd damn well put her in a brand new Bimmer, or better yet, let her pick the car and color herself.

Climbing into my car, I shifted it into gear and sped off. The daylight spilled through the trees, and I was grateful it was finally warm. I worried about Kat. I hated where she lived, I hated the environment her son was faced with every day, and even though he was too young to notice now, he eventually would. Coming home at night, I wondered about her and him. Were they warm? Were they safe? Was he properly fed?

I wanted her to have everything and to not worry about anything.

Passing through the denser neighborhoods, I drove by the high school, when it occurred to me that Kat probably graduated from there only last year. We were only seven years apart in age, but worlds apart in education and experience.

It should've unnerved me. But instead, it excited me. I liked how she was different from other women I'd known.

Young, impulsive, angry . . . and completely unrefined. She felt so forbidden to me, and I wanted her.

I also liked how she seemed to need me, just a little.

Finally giving in and pulling in front of her house, I turned off the car, hesitating a moment. I wasn't sure if that son of a bitch was home, but I was completely prepared to do what I had to do.

Leaving my car, I made sure to lock it, and I walked up to her house, passing through the creaking gate of the chain-link fence and up the steps.

"Hello?" I called, knocking on the wooden screen door.

"Yes?" someone called out, and I spotted a shadow approaching through the screen.

The door whined as she pushed it open, and I saw a woman, not much older than Kat, with short blond hair and a baby bottle in her hand.

"Is Kat here?" I asked.

Her eyes fell down my form, looking hesitant, and I immediately got the impression that people in suits in this neighborhood meant bad news.

"I'm a friend," I explained.

Her eyes narrowed. "Oh, are you Mr. Slater? She babysits for you and your wife, right?"

She babysits, too? In addition to working at the garage?

"Sure," I answered, not knowing who this woman was and deciding to protect Kat. "That's me."

This woman could be a friend of her husband's. No use telling the truth, just in case he decided to take it out on her. Not that I'd gotten any information saying he'd been abusive with her, but I had my suspicions. He was the type.

She jerked her head. "Yeah, she's in the backyard. I'll walk you."

She stepped out the front door, and I backed away to let her through as she jogged down the porch steps and around to the side of the house. I quickly followed, but as soon as we neared the rear of the home, I started to slow.

Kat lay on her stomach on the grass, perched up on her elbows, as a small child with her brown hair squealed while catching water from their sprinkler in his little green cup.

She wore a short white sundress with blue flowers and thin straps over her shoulders that carried to her back, and all I could do was gaze down at her beautiful, smooth skin.

The dress was completely plastered to her body. Oh, my God.

The sprinkler, which I assumed to be homemade since it was just a two-liter bottle taped to a hose with water shooting out of the two dozen or so holes, was hitting her as she lay on the grass, drenching her back, arms, legs, and dress.

I could see the olive tones of her skin through the wet material.

"Kat?" her friend—or maybe it was her sister—called.

Kat turned her head toward us and locked eyes with me, her smile falling.

I cleared my throat and slid my hand into my pocket. "Did you forget?" I asked, acting casual. "You're babysitting tonight. Remember?"

Her eyebrows nosedived and she started to rise. "Huh?"

Her friend laughed and looked at me. "Yeah, I think she forgot."

"Do you have someone to watch your son?" I asked Kat and then looked to her friend, explaining, "Mine has a cold. We wouldn't want Jared to get sick."

Kat sat up, and I dropped my eyes, taking in the way the fabric fell over her body. While the front of her dress wasn't as drenched as the back, it was wet in certain areas and her chest dripped with water.

I struggled to breathe, and heat pooled in my groin.

Her friend finally sighed. "I can do it, I guess."

I smiled, my veins running hot with the prospect of being alone with her. "Thank you."

Her friend walked over and picked up Jared, whose name I'd learned from the investigator's information, while Kat just sat there, looking a little lost.

"I'm Deena, by the way," her friend said as she passed by me, carrying Jared. "I take care of all the kids in the neighborhood."

I reached out to take the hand she offered. "Jase."

She nodded and walked past me, probably into the house to get Jared out of his wet clothes.

"What the hell are you doing?" I heard Kat ask in an accusing tone.

I turned my gaze back to her to see that she'd stood up. The dress stuck to her body, and her thighs glistened with water.

"You refused the car," I pointed out.

She approached me with a challenge in her eyes, keeping her voice low. "You can't buy me. I don't know what you want—"

"I want you to have reliable transportation for your safety," I said, cutting her off. "You're telling me you can't use a vehicle when you have a child? What if he needed a trip to the ER?"

"You want me to owe you," she corrected. "You're married, and I'm not a whore."

She brushed past me and ran up the steps to the house in her bare feet. It only took a moment before I spun around and charged after her.

Swinging open the screen door, I stepped into the kitchen and caught her arm, pulling her back to me.

"I don't want you to owe me," I said in a low voice, staring down at her while we stood chest to chest. "I just . . . I think about you, and I want . . ."

She stood there, her chest rising and falling, like she was too afraid to move and too afraid to run.

A girl like this was used to disappointment—used to being used—but I wasn't going to hurt her. I wasn't going to steal from her or hit her, and I wasn't going to make her do things that put her in danger.

And when I looked at her, I didn't see just a piece of ass. I saw something to look forward to.

I took a step, walking into her and slowly backing her toward the wall. "My marriage is on paper only, and it's over. I already know that. I don't want to hurt her, but I've never thought about her the way I think about you. I see the way you look at me, kid. This is not one-sided on my part." I called her out. "Is it?"

She remained still, her breathing trembling like she couldn't fight, but she was too afraid to give in, as well. She didn't want to fight me.

"Now we can keep this clean, if you want. I can make good on that lie and let you babysit my son," I suggested. "Would you prefer that?"

I kept walking her backward, invading her space.

This was what I was good at. Threats and intimidation. I knew I shouldn't, but I loved the way she retreated. I never felt powerful outside work, faced with my failures at home, and I was completely turned on.

"I'd pay you well," I told her. "And at the end of the night, when I drove you home, I'd try not to pull off the road." I reached down and grazed the inside of her thigh, still dripping with water from the sprinkler, making her gasp. "And I'd try not to get you into the backseat of my car." And then I leaned down, whispering against her lips. "Because I have very good control . . . until I don't."

She ran into the wall and let out a whimper, and I let my eyes fall

335 NEXT TO NEVER

to her breasts, seeing the shape of them perfectly outlined through the wet fabric. I clenched my jaw, already feeling her in my mouth.

I placed my finger under her chin and raised it, tipping her eyes up at me. "Is that what you want?" I asked. "To be something for me to play with?"

Her hips grazed mine, and she bit her bottom lip, turning her head away.

The heat of her thighs was so close and I couldn't hold back anymore. Reaching down, I grabbed the back of her thigh in one hand, cupped her face with the other and pressed the full length of my body against hers, our lips an inch away from each other.

"I don't want that, Kat," I whisper. "You know what I want? I want you to think about me. Do you think about me?" She stood frozen, her eyes squeezed shut, but her body started making little movements, grinding on mine and getting me hot.

"Yeah," I gloated. "You do, don't you?"

And I reached under her dress, grabbed hold of her soaked panties, and ripped them clean off her body, the tearing fabric like a shot of fucking heroin to my veins.

She let out a small cry and wrapped her arms around my neck.

"You think about wrapping these legs around me and opening that shirt for me, so I can touch you," I recited as I lifted her up and guided her thighs around my waist. "You think about a dark room with a big bed and laying out on twenty-four-hundred-dollar sheets with nothing but me between your legs."

"Yes," she breathed out.

I inched my mouth closer to hers, layering our lips so that we were both just inhaling and exhaling, tasting each other.

I reached down between us and slid my fingers along the smooth skin of her heat, feeling how wet she was.

Fuck, I couldn't wait.

Holding her with one hand, I worked at my belt, unfastening it, and then scrambled for the button and zipper of my pants.

"Okay, I've got everything!" a voice called.

But I barely fucking cared. I took her mouth in mine, sinking my lips and tongue into her and claiming her. The taste of water hit my mouth, and a rush of warmth washed over me as I gripped her wet thigh in my hand.

"Call when you're done later!"

Kat pulled away from the kiss. "Thanks, Deena!" she shouted, out of breath. "I'll pick him up later."

And then her lips were on mine again as she slipped her tongue into my mouth and bit down on my bottom lip. It was so good, an electric shock coursed down my spine.

"Goddamn it." I slammed one hand into the wall by her head, losing my cool.

But I went back for more, covering her lips with mine and feeling my hands hum every single place I touched and held her.

I didn't know where the bedroom or living room was, and even though it would only take a moment to find out, we didn't have that much time. I needed her.

"What are you waiting for?" she taunted in my ear. "Or does College Boy need his twenty-four-hundred-dollar sheets to fuck me like a man?"

I growled and spun her around, taking both of us to the ground. What a mouthy little brat.

On my knees, I whipped off my jacket, tie, and ripped open my shirt, throwing it off to the side.

Coming back down on her, I kissed her hard, while pulling the cold strap of her dress down and grinding between her legs.

I dove down, cupping her breast and covering the nipple with my mouth. "Jesus, you're perfect."

She moaned, squirming as I kissed and teased her, tugging at her with my teeth.

"Condom?" I was embarrassed to have to ask, but I hadn't needed them in a while, nor was I planning on this.

She nodded and reached for her purse on the kitchen chair. I watched as she pulled one out and handed it to me.

I unwrapped the condom and reached down, rolling it on. "He's not allowed to touch you at all anymore."

Positioning myself at her entrance, I stared down at her and suddenly felt her tense.

"I'm a little scared," she said.

I wasn't sure what she meant, though. Clearly she'd been with at least one man before.

But then it hit me. The whole reason she refused the car. She was worried about where this all led, and I didn't have the answers any more than she did.

I could only tell her what I could promise. "I've got you."

She drew in a breath and pulled me back down, eating me up and clawing at my back as I pushed myself inside her.

"Ah," she panted, throwing her head back.

"Oh, God," I groaned, sinking deeper and shuddering at the wet heat. Fuck, she was tight.

Pulling slowly out, I thrust back in and felt everything in my body come alive. The hairs on my arms stood up, a buzz coursed under my skin, and I'd never wanted to kiss someone so hard she'd break.

Her husband could walk in the front door, and I wouldn't stop.

"Jase," she whimpered, lifting her head up and her whole body going tense. "Oh, God."

"You coming already?" I snatched up her lips, teasing her.

"Yes." She slipped her hands inside my pants, grabbing hold of my ass to pull me deeper inside of her, and then bit my jaw, whispering against my skin. "More. Harder."

I pushed myself up on one arm, sliding my other hand under her ass, and watched in fucking awe as her body moved underneath me and her face tensed up in pleasure as I rode her harder and harder.

Sweat glided down my back and glistened on her top lip. I felt her body clench up around me, and then she let out a scream as she moaned and took everything I had to give.

Her body shook and her neck arched back, opening for my mouth.

"You're so beautiful," I whispered against her neck, biting it. "Even hotter when you're getting fucked."

I thrust a few more times, harder and deeper, riding her like I couldn't get enough. She spread her legs wider, and I sucked her nipple into my mouth again, groaning as my orgasm crested, and I finally spilled, sinking as deeply as I could and trying to feel every inch of her.

Her warmth surrounded me, and I couldn't move anymore, savoring the feel of her body under mine.

"So what's with the tattoo?"

I pulled my head up to see her calm, amused eyes as if we hadn't just rutted like animals on her kitchen floor.

I glanced at my left arm, high up, just below the shoulder joint, seeing the tattoo.

"You don't look like the type," she mused.

I gave a weak laugh. "I'm not. It was a misspent weekend in Hong Kong when I was twenty-two," I explained. "I'd just graduated from college, was headed off to law school, and my buddies and I did a lot of things we shouldn't have."

I felt her shake with a laugh. "But why a circle?"

I shrugged, not sure how to explain. It had made sense at the time.

The tattoo was a circle designed to look like it was painted with a paintbrush. However, there was a flaw. The brushstroke stopped just before it met the beginning of the circle again.

"It's a perfect circle," I told her. "The same diameter any way you measure it. Even, clean, perfect." And then I dropped my forehead to hers, closing my eyes. "But it's incomplete."

I'd loved its one flaw. I'd loved the artistry and skill that it took to tattoo this perfect circle without a stencil, and I loved how it was left open and unfinished.

There was so much right about it, but still, it was incomplete. Still missing something.

I pulled out of her and stood, disposing of the condom and cleaning up. Pulling my pants up, I zipped them and fastened my belt before leaning back down to help her stand.

Taking her in my arms, I kissed her, her breast still exposed and her damp dress hanging off her body.

"Things are going to change," I told her. "I want you out of here and away from him."

But she just fixed her dress and shook her head. "I don't want money from you."

"Do you want things for Jared?"

She darted her eyes to me, a small scowl on her face. "Stop using him against me."

I let out a sigh, exhausted after the sex, and took her chin, tipping it back up so that her eyes met mine.

"A house in a better neighborhood—with trees and a front yard and friends?" I asked. "A car, so you can get him to school or the doctor or the grocery store."

But she took my hand away and looked at me defiantly. "No," she argued. "I liked this. I don't want it to change. I don't want to be your pussy-at-the-ready. I want to be surprised and carried away again. Nothing else between us. Just this, okay?"

I kissed her forehead, letting her have her way, because I was too tired to fight right now. I was happy she didn't regret today, and I was even happier that she wanted more.

Things would change, though. I knew what I wanted, and I always got what I wanted.

One way or another.

————

The book shakes in my hand, and Dylan and I just stare at the page.

"Jared?" she says, sounding confused.

"Madoc?" I follow suit, remembering the names mentioned in the text.

Caruthers?

And then it seems to hit both of us all at once, and she scurries to sit up. "Grandma?"

"Mom?" I whimper.

Oh, my God.

Oh, my God! I bury my face in my pillow and scream, every muscle in my body tightening with shock and distaste. "Oh, my God, no!"

She snatches the book away and turns the page, a devilish little grin of excitement on her face.

"Give that to me, you perv!" I grab for the book and throw it across the room, where it slams against the wall and lands on the floor. "I can't believe we just read that!"

She busts up laughing, keeling over so that her forehead crashes into the comforter. "That was epic!" she screams, punching the bed with her fists.

"Ugh!" I groan and shiver at the same time, trying to rub the cooties off me. "We're not reading any more."

"Why?" She pops her head up and looks at me like a kid who wants candy.

"Because it's your grandparents, and it's my parents, and gross!"

"It's not my grandparents," she argues, trying to reason. "It has to be just a coincidence. I want to read more."

Her eyes are still lit up like a kid going to see Santa. She crawls off the bed and makes a mad dash for the book, but I scurry after her. Both of us fall on the floor, trying to get the book away from each other, but we just end up laughing.

"It wasn't graphic," she protests. "You should see what's on my Kindle. This is nothing."

"No!" I bellow and yank the book free of her grasp.

I stand up and hold it behind my back, glancing at the clock. "Oh, look, the time. You need to get ready for your race."

She twists her lips up in a pout and darts her eyes to the clock, too. It's after six. In all honesty, we should get going, and she knows it.

"I'm going to pick up James at his friend's house and grab something to eat," she says, walking for the door. "I'll be back to pick you up in a bit, so be ready. And bring the book!"

She opens the door, walks out, and then quickly spins around. "And let me know if you get to the twenty-four-hundred-dollar-sheets part with his mouth—"

I reach up to cover my ears, but she's already slammed the door closed.

CHAPTER 5

KAT . . .

Running my hand down the countertop, I felt the cool, clean surface, no peeling or knife marks from years of using it as a cutting board. I slipped off my sandals to savor the smooth hardwood floors and the way they shone with the sun coming through the kitchen window.

The house was beautiful.

A white two-story with black shutters and a full front- and back-yard and garage. *Damn you, Jase Caruthers.*

He bought me a house.

The grass was a green like I'd only seen in magazines, rich and lush, and when I looked out the window, the view was even more stunning. Just more houses with more of the same, but it was a completely different world to me.

He'd chosen well. He knew what a parent would want for their child.

But I couldn't take it. He could come in, make demands anytime he wanted, and I could be as trapped by him as I was by Thomas.

So what should I do then? Stay in my crappy house in my crappy neighborhood with Thomas? He didn't care about me or his son, and tomorrow would be more of the same.

And in a year, still nothing would be different. Fighting to stay afloat while Jared grew up with no more opportunities than I had, and eventually I'd be on to child number three from another failed relationship, simply eating and breathing to exist with no plans and no future, watching my kids repeat the same mistakes.

I looked over at Jared, seeing him crawl across the floor. There was still time. Still time to make his life better before he became old enough to remember all of the bad.

I ran my hands up and down the thighs of my jeans, remembering the pile of overdue bills on the counter at home, the empty refrigerator, the rent we were two months late on, how I was scrounging for everything . . .

That could end right now. And the icing on the cake came when I looked at the deed sent to me in the mail today.

I was the owner, not Jase. He gave me this house with no strings attached. I could kick him out and keep him out. If I wanted.

I shouldn't take the house.

And upon arriving, I was surprised with the same car I'd refused last week, sitting in the driveway. The keys and a cell phone sat on the kitchen table with no note and only one number in the phone. I'd never had a cell phone, and everything, all at once, felt like dream.

I walked into the living room, already thinking about what it would look like with furniture. Jase had made sure to bring in the necessities. There was a couch, a kitchen table, a few chairs, a bed and a crib, a radio that was currently playing "Cradle of Love," but he'd left everything else to me.

"What do you see out there?" I smiled wide at Jared, walking over to where he'd pulled himself up to the window.

He couldn't walk yet, but it wouldn't be long. I peeled back the curtain, seeing the house next door, and a large maple, full of green leaves, standing between the two houses.

"Pretty cool, huh?" I peered down at him, and he just gazed back up at me with so much curiosity in his eyes. He never made a lot of baby talk, but those eyes always said it all.

And I loved that look of wonder in his face. I wanted to see him climb that tree and have a dog to play with in the yard, and I wanted to see him ride his bike down this street.

And—I hated to admit—I wanted to see Jase walking around this house. Not in his boring, tight-ass suits but in a T-shirt and jeans, coming up behind me and kissing my neck as I made our dinner at the kitchen counter.

I walked to the table and picked up the cell phone he'd left, not knowing what the hell to say to him. He hadn't called since the night in the kitchen or to see if I got the deed to the house. And judging by the cell phone he left, he was leaving the ball in my court. I didn't have to do anything.

So why did I want to hear his voice?

I'm a mess, too. His words came back, and I saw that look on his face all over again. The one that said not much made him happy. *Like all of this is just a shit preamble to something better.*

I dialed the one number in the phone, letting it ring several times as my heart started pounding.

And then I heard his voice.

"Kat?"

A flutter hit my stomach at his quiet and gentle voice, and all of a sudden, I could barely speak. I dropped my head, speaking low. "Hey."

But he just sat there, not saying anything. All I could hear was his breathing, remember the taste of his lips when he held me the other night.

"Aren't you going to say anything?" I asked.

He released a nervous laugh, and I stood frozen, my eyes on Jared but my head consumed with Jase.

"I'm a man who gets paid a lot of money to talk a good talk," he explained. "But you're my kryptonite. I feel like a sixteen-year-old kid who can't form a fucking sentence."

I chewed on my bottom lip, loving that I had any power over him. "I like the house."

"Just 'like'?"

I ran my hand over the bannister as I walked down the hall to the kitchen. "I love the house. Jared loves the yard. I . . ."

I stopped, unable to get over the lump in my throat. I knew what I wanted, and I knew what I should do, and they were complete opposites. The war in my head was in deciding if the consequences were worth it.

He was silent as well, and I didn't know if he was trying not to push me, if he'd reconsidered, or if he honestly didn't know what to say. I had no idea if I'd been his only affair, but I gathered this was new territory for him. He bought me a house and car. I had to be important to him, right?

But then again, he wasn't asking me to divorce Thomas. And he hadn't offered to do the same.

I looked down at the floor, so nervous my stomach was as tight as a knot. "What do you want with me?" I asked again.

"Whatever you want to give me," he answered. "I want a woman who can't get enough of me, Kat. If you can't give me that, then keep the house and the car, and don't call me again."

I closed my eyes as tears pooled. It was too much.

I could enjoy a man and sever the emotions when it was just sex, but . . . I was old enough to know, if you crave someone bad enough, sex turns into something else.

And "something else" can get very complicated and very painful.

"Jared goes to sleep at seven," I nearly whispered, gripping the phone as anticipation swirled in my stomach. "Do you have a key?"

His voice was raspy. "No."

"I'll leave the door open for you then," I told him. "Please hurry."

Thomas would find out where I was. I hadn't seen him in four days, but he'd pop up. I'd heard he was fooling around with someone else, something that I didn't doubt. Let him get her pregnant and hopefully that would be the last I'd see of him.

Of course, I wouldn't wish him on any woman, but whoever she was she would learn her lessons as quickly as I'd learned mine, no doubt.

After feeding and bathing Jared, I settled him into his new crib, brought the radio up, and turned on some faint music and rubbed his back until he fell asleep. I discovered early on he didn't care for my singing, but if I played the radio, the kid fell to sleep pretty quickly. He liked noise.

I'd picked the room that faced the tree between our house and the neighbor's for him, knowing that he would probably like it as he grew up. I'm sure he'd be trying to climb the tree in a few years, but I'd worry about that later. Moving in to my own home was enough of an adjustment for right now.

Traipsing back downstairs, I finished putting away everything I'd managed to salvage in the rush to leave my former place and set up the lamps and pictures on the mantel.

A mantel. I put my hand over my mouth, hiding my smile. I had a mantel.

I walked to the door, making sure it was unlocked, and flipped on the porch light. I should probably go clean myself up. He would be here soon.

I was still wearing the same clothes from earlier today, the baggy blue jeans that fell off my hips and an old Shelburne Falls High Pirates T-shirt with the bottom cut off, exposing my stomach. A souvenir from my cheerleading days.

I unwound the rubber band from my hair, letting it spill down my back, and headed into the kitchen to grab a glass of water before I went to the shower.

"If I knew your ass was worth this much," a deep voice drawled behind me, "I would've pimped you out a long time ago."

I spun around, my breath catching in my throat as the water in my glass spilled on my shirt and stomach.

No.

Thomas stood in the entryway to the kitchen, filling the space and cutting out the light, as he held Jared in his arms. His blond hair was slicked back into a ponytail, and I could smell the cigarette smoke on his jeans and jacket from here. A cry escaped as I darted forward.

"Thomas, give him to me!"

But he reared back, shaking his head at me. "What? I can't see my son now?" He wrapped his fist around Jared's arm and squeezed until the baby started crying. "I bet if I tell the courts you're a high-priced whore, they'll consider me a better parent for him."

"Give him to me!" I screamed, tears welling as I leapt for him. "You're going to hurt him!"

"No, I don't think so." He knocked me back and then released Jared, looking down at him and speaking in a light, childlike tone. "Someone has gotten a little big for her britches and thinks she runs the show now. Mommy's been bad."

And then he looked to me, rocking Jared back and forth on his hip. "But you know the drill, right?" he said. "You want to keep me happy, you know what to do."

I balled up my fists, glaring at him. Storming over to my purse on the counter, I grabbed the wad of bills in my wallet. Forty-two dollars.

I walked over and shoved it in his hand. "That's everything I have. Now get out!"

"That's not everything." He tsked, stuffing the money in his pocket and holding out his hand again. "Car keys."

"It's not my car," I growled.

"All right," he said, looking falsely sympathetic. "Say, 'Bye, Mommy.'"

He turned around, taking Jared with him.

"Thomas, stop!" I cried.

Turning around again, I retrieved the keys from my purse and handed them over.

"Atta girl." And then he looked me up and down. "Now you know what else makes me happy, right? Come on. One last time before I leave."

I shook my head, flashing my eyes quickly to the knife that sat on the counter.

"Now!" he barked, making me jump. "Or I'll do you right here and let him watch."

I shook, tears streaming down my face. If I lunged for him, Jared could get hurt. I'd never overpower him, and he could run off with my kid.

I swallowed the sobs in my throat, staring at him through blurry eyes as I pulled my shirt over my head, leaving me in my bra.

But then I blinked, seeing a dark form behind him, and I sucked in a breath.

Jase.

He crept slowly up the foyer, but Thomas must've sensed him or saw my eyes flash to him, because he twisted around.

Jase lunged for him, wrapping his arm around his neck, yelling, "Kat!"

I rushed forward and caught Jared just as Thomas dropped him.

"Oh, my God," I cried, holding my son in my arms and standing there as Jase slammed Thomas into the wall, my car keys falling out of his hand as his head hit the corner.

He grunted and closed his eyes, still standing but no longer fighting.

"Now I want you to look at me and memorize my face." Jase spun him around, holding him up by the collar. "Because the next time you see me, it will mean the end of you. You know why?" he growled, a mere inch from Thomas's face. "Because I'm smart, I'm rich, and I know people who can make you wish you were dead. I can do whatever the hell I want and no one can stop me. If you ever"—he slammed him into the wall again—"come near her or her son again, I will make sure every shit bag in gen pop thinks you're a rapist, and you know what happens to rapists in prison, right?" He leaned into his ear, but I could hear his whisper. "No one will keep you safe. I will make sure of that, and it won't stop until you're crying like a little girl."

Thomas gasped for air under the pressure Jase was putting on his neck, and I hugged Jared closer, turning him around—away from the two men—and crying.

"You understand?" I heard Jase say. "Good. Now leave, and go far away before I make you go away. I'll find you when it's time to sign your divorce papers."

I waited, finally hearing uneven footsteps trod along the floor before the door opened and closed. I turned around to see Jase come right for me.

Holding on to Jared with one hand, I clutched onto Jase with the other, burying my face in his collar.

"Are you okay?" he breathed out, one arm around my waist and the other on the back of my neck. Jared whimpered between us.

I nodded, kissing the top of Jared's head. "I am now."

He placed his finger under my chin, lifting it and kissing me softly on the lips.

"You were amazing," I whispered against his mouth, feeling his lips curl into a small smile.

"Oh, you liked that, huh?"

I gave a weak laugh, readjusting Jared on my hip. "And I thought you were just a pampered yuppie. Are you like that in court?"

"Oh, no." He kissed my forehead. "People are watching then. But you don't want to see me at a business lunch. That's pretty scary."

"I'm sure."

He walked over to the back door, turning on the porch light and checking the lock. "I'll follow you upstairs." He turned and guided me out of the kitchen. "We'll move Jared's crib into your room until I can get an alarm system set up here."

Jase locked the front door and went upstairs to make sure all the windows were closed and locked before moving the crib from Jared's room to mine. I rocked Jared in my arms until he stopped crying and passed out on my chest, finally fast asleep. I stared down at him, his little eyelids fluttering from time to time like he was having a bad dream. I didn't know if babies had those, but I just wanted to erase the past nine months from this kid's life like none of it had ever happened. He was going to be happy now.

I ran my fingers over his arm, seeing the red mark from where Thomas had hurt him, and tightened my arms around him. *He'll never get to you again.*

Jase came into the room and took off his jacket, laying it on the bed like that's where it always went, and walked over as I stared down at Jared, sleeping in the crib.

"He won't be back."

"I know." I brushed a hand over Jared's hair. "You were a hassle, and he doesn't like hassles. He's off to whatever's next. I'm not worth it."

His hot breath fell against my ear, sounding desperate, as his arm slipped around my bare stomach. "Yes, you are."

I turned around, wrapping my arms around his neck and pressing myself into him as I kissed him hard. I held him so tightly and breathed him in, the sandalwood in his aftershave heating my blood and making my body tingle. So safe.

His mouth moved over mine, the heat of his lips spreading down my neck and into my stomach. I flicked his tongue with mine, gripping his collar as he slipped a hand inside my baggy jeans, taking my ass in his hands. His tongue and lips left a heated trail across my cheek and down my neck, and I moaned.

"Jase."

I'd only ever been with Thomas. I'd never been kissed like this. He tasted me and teased me, and if I closed my eyes, I could imagine that he was mine.

This was our house, I'd wake up next to him in the morning, and all I had to worry about tomorrow was taking Jared to the park and what I'd make us for dinner.

He kissed along my jaw, darting out with his teeth to bite every so often. I pressed my body into his, feeling how hard he was, and my clit began to throb. I groaned, feeling like if I ground into him just a little I would come.

"What are you smiling at?" he asked.

I kept my eyes closed and my head tipped back, giving him full access. "You. I like the way you kiss."

He didn't move for a moment, and then I felt a kiss below my ear. "Like that?"

I smiled wider and tapped the corner of my mouth. "Do here."

He did, and I felt tingles spread down my legs.

"And here." I tapped the corner of my eye.

He placed a small kiss there, and I shivered even more than when he used his tongue.

He pinched my chin between his fingers, and I opened my eyes to see him gazing down at me.

"You're going to turn my world upside down, aren't you, kid?"

I wrapped my arms around him and buried my face in his neck, hiding my smile.

I hoped so. I didn't want to hurt him, and I didn't want him to hurt me. I didn't want to hurt his family or mine.

But I just didn't want to stop feeling this.

Nothing else existed. No one else was between us.

This was our house and our bed. Ours.

Walking into Lockes-on-the-Bluff, a quaint pub-style restaurant up in the hills, I let the door fall closed behind me and immediately inhaled the aroma of steak, wood, and earth. The bar on the lower level was underground, and the scent of water—like in a cave—carried up to the restaurant, giving it a subterranean feel, enhanced by the dim candlelit setting. It was cleaner, closer, and probably better paying than the repair shop, so I thought I'd give it a shot.

"Hi," I said after I'd set down my purse on the bar stool. "I was wondering if you were hiring. I have experience serving and bartending."

Serving, yes. But I'd never actually bartended. It didn't matter. These places never checked work history, anyway.

The bartender capped the bottle he'd been pouring and walked over.

"Well, you can fill out an application, and I'll leave it for the day manager," he suggested. "He usually handles the hiring."

"Thanks."

I sat down and took a pen out of my purse as he handed me an application. Glasses clinked to my left, and I heard laughter coming from the restaurant. Glancing around, I took in the setting, admiring the servers' uniforms. Black slacks with white shirts and burgundy ties.

One of the few places an undereducated nineteen-year-old could make good money off rich patrons and not have to take off her clothes.

But then I turned away, rolling my eyes at myself in my head. Yeah, right. Jase didn't pay me for sex, necessarily, but I was definitely a kept woman.

And I needed to keep making my own money to make sure I didn't accept anything more from him than I already had. I could make excuses for the house and car, justifying that I would do what was necessary for my son, but I couldn't delude myself that it was okay to let Jase pay the bills and buy the food. That was on me and needed to stay that way.

Turning my eyes back to the paper, I stopped, catching sight of a man and a woman at a table. I couldn't help but stare.

Jase was sitting next to a blonde in a white dress, with an older man at the table with them. She was young, a few years older than me maybe, and laughing. A weight hit my chest, making it harder to breathe as I watched Jase smile at her.

Why was he smiling at her?

It was her. His wife. I knew it was her.

And she looked so different than me. Pristine, manicured, stylish . . . her hands and nails as she picked up her champagne glass looked as perfect as a marble statue, and her diamond studs gleamed bright enough that I could see them from here.

Even the diamond on her finger appeared to wink at me as it caught the light.

I looked back to Jase again and froze. He was staring right at me, and he was no longer smiling.

Shit.

I turned my head away and cleared my throat as I picked up the pen and tried to concentrate.

I knew it. He wasn't getting a divorce. He never said he was, and I wasn't surprised.

I wasn't. I knew this would happen.

I blinked, refocusing and bending my head to my task. Name, address, references, work history . . .

I couldn't work at a restaurant where he brought his wife, could I? It would make us both uncomfortable. It had only been a few weeks since I'd moved into the house, and while my divorce was well on its way, we hadn't discussed his marriage at all.

He was married. He wasn't getting a divorce. Wise up, Kat.

"What are you doing here?" a voice demanded at my side. His tone was quiet but with an edge as if I were a child who'd stayed up past my bedtime.

I tensed and glanced up, seeing him stand at the empty bar, several feet away from me. Enough to appear as if he wasn't speaking to me and we didn't know each other.

"I can't be here?" I challenged, starting to print my information on the form.

"Is that an application?"

But before I could answer, the bartender approached. "Can I help you, sir?"

"GlenDronach," he ordered. "Neat."

The bartender walked away, and I continued my work, stealing a glance at the table and seeing his wife still talking to the older man.

"A job?" Jase asked. "Kat, if you need more money—"

"I don't need more money," I shot out under my breath. "Jesus."

"I'm sorry. I didn't mean that."

I calmed my temper and kept my voice low. "I wanted to take classes during the day, so I'm looking for an evening job."

He moved a few inches closer. "You shouldn't get an evening job," he told me. "If you go to school and work, Jared will never see you. And if you work nights, when am I supposed to spend time with you?"

The bartender approached again, and Jase straightened as he accepted his drink.

"I'll have them add it to your dinner bill, Mr. Caruthers," he said, glancing between us as I put my head back down.

"Thank you."

When the bartender was gone, I peeled my tongue off the roof of my mouth, growing bolder.

"Tell her you're taking your son to the park and come over to my house," I replied sarcastically. "Our boys can play while we screw upstairs."

He slammed his drink down, making my pulse quicken. "Knock it off."

"Just go back to your dinner," I bit out under my breath and then looked to the bartender. "Excuse me, may I have a rum and Coke, please?"

"Coming up."

I didn't like Jase making demands on how my life would go. He was getting what he wanted. What did he care?

And for that matter, what did I care?

"I don't want you drinking alone. You're upset."

"I'm not upset."

I was jealous.

I pushed the paper and pen away and grabbed my purse. "I'll be right back," I told the bartender.

I hurried to the other side of the restaurant and down the hallway, toward the restrooms. But before I could escape, Jase caught my arm and spun me around, backing me into a dark corner.

"I'm sorry."

I snickered, stuffing the pen in my purse. "The first of many apologies, I'm sure."

So this was going to be my life. Would it be worth it? Up until a few weeks ago I hated my life, and I struggled, but I liked who I was. Now, everything was the complete opposite.

How does one man make that happen?

"Is this how it's going to be?" he challenged. "We're going to run into each other in public from time to time, Kat. You have to be able to handle this until I get everything sorted out. I will do right by you. I promise."

I tipped my chin up, steeling myself. "She's beautiful."

"Don't."

"I should've known she'd be beautiful," I went on, laughing at myself. "Your car, your suits . . . You like to put on a nice sheen for everyone, don't you? So they don't see how much you like to play in the dirt." And then I cocked my head at him. "Do you have sex with her?"

He stiffened, his eyes like blue fire.

"Can I have sex with someone else then?" I asked, trying to sound innocent. "Someone to keep me entertained when you're not around?"

His jaw flexed as he regarded me. "I wouldn't if I were you."

I stared into his eyes until my own burned, and I couldn't look at him anymore. What was I doing? My life was about me and my son, and now, as the days went on, it was increasingly about him.

Jared had to be in bed, because Jase was coming over. I couldn't date men and bring them to the home another man paid for. Sometimes I waited for hours for him to show up, and sometimes he never did. I couldn't call him at work, and I couldn't call him at night. I couldn't leave messages, and he couldn't take me out in Shelburne Falls.

How was I supposed to be important to him when we weren't growing into anything more than what we were?

"She wasn't real to me before," I said calmly. "She's real now. You take her out, she has your name . . ." I raised my eyes, meeting his. "I didn't want to be this woman. The stupid girl from the wrong side of the tracks, thinking her rich lover was going to save her from the trailer park. I didn't want you, and then when I did, I didn't want strings, and you've bent me every time I tried to resist. Guys like you never leave your wives, and I'm an asshole for wanting you to." A thousand pinpricks hit my throat, and I had to pause so I wouldn't cry.

"No." I nodded. "We fuck, you pay the bills. That's really what our arrangement is, isn't it?"

"That's not how it is," he implored, taking my face in his hands. "I will leave her."

"If that were true, you would've done it already. And how fucking awful am I if I want you to do that to her?"

"It was going to happen with or without you," he said, holding my gaze. "The state of my marriage isn't your fault."

I wanted to believe that. But this was a slippery slope.

There was a thin line between an affair being easy or it being disastrous. If you had two people who wanted sex or companionship, a little variety, per se, and you both had a lot to lose, then you had a mutual understanding of what was expected. But . . . and here's where shit often hit the fan . . . someone inevitably fell in love.

The only man, other than my son, who my life revolved around was Jase. I, on the other hand, wasn't the only woman in his life.

"If I'd met you first, this wouldn't be an issue," Jase told me. "You're the one I want. My father owns the law firm I work in, Kat. If I divorce Maddie, I lose the job and everything I've worked for. We just have bad timing. We'll get through this." He rubbed a circle on my cheek. "When I make partner, I can do whatever I want."

I turned my eyes away, knowing what I should do. Don't they all say that? "Just wait. We'll be together, I promise. Just a little more time."

If only I could just enjoy him and not be feeling what I'm starting to feel. I squeezed my eyes shut, holding the tears back.

"When it's just us," he whispered, his breath on my lips, "alone and warm, and I'm holding you, that's who I am, Kat. That's who I look forward to being when I'm leaving work and I can't get to you quick enough." He kissed me, soft and gentle. "Stay with me. I can't lose you."

I shook my head, trying to not to let his words get to me, but I started crying anyway. I dipped my head into his chest, slipping my hands inside his jacket and hating the way I was starting to bend again.

If I trusted him—just gave him a chance—what did I have to lose?

Someone cleared their throat nearby, and I pulled away, taking in a quick breath. "Excuse me," a male voice said.

Jase stood up straight, breathing nervously and turned around. The man standing behind him was the one who had been seated at the table with Jase and his wife. He was older, and his blue eyes shifted casually between Jase and me.

"Be discreet," he told Jase and then looked at me, tipping his head. "Young lady."

And I caught the shadow of a smile as he disappeared into the men's room.

Jase's body went stiff and he pulled away, adjusting his tie and jacket, not looking at me.

Was that his father?

"Go home, okay?" he asked, his tone curt. "I'll give you what you need. You're not working nights."

And then, without waiting for me to respond, he left me there, making his way back into the restaurant.

Jesus. It was all about him.

His demands, his life, his schedule, his pace . . . Was I happier than I was before?

I brushed my hair away from my face and fixed my dress, knowing the answer without even thinking about it. Yeah, I was happy. When he was around.

But when he wasn't, the lows were lower than they were with Thomas, because of one simple fact . . . I never loved Thomas.

I thought I had, but if what I was starting to feel for Jase was any indication, then he had the potential to hurt me a lot more than my ex.

Walking back out, I stopped at the bar to pay for my drink and quickly downed it, closing my eyes as the warmth of the alcohol coursed through my veins and coated my stomach.

Jase passed behind me, walking his wife out of the restaurant and helping her into her coat without sparing me a glance. But I caught her eye, a fraction of a moment longer than I should have. Had she seen Jase and me talking at the bar? Did she feel the tension on him I could?

They left and I sat down, disobeying orders. How long would I wait for him? A year? Two? Forever?

I wanted to be with him, but I was starting to fear that I was holding back for fear of missing out on his promise to me. What if he left her? I had to try, right?

But there were no answers. Only silence. The alcohol smoothed out the edges, and the tightness in my muscles began to ease. The worrying ache in my head dissipated, and the storm of emotions and questions brewing in my mind started to look like the picture through a telescope. Far, far away.

"Can I have another, please?" I asked the bartender.

While I waited for Jase, I may as well enjoy myself. Hopefully, I wasn't missing out on more than I was waiting for, though.

———

I close the book and let my head fall back against the headboard. I'm glad there wasn't more sex, but I was too curious not to keep reading. So many things no one ever told me.

My mom shouldn't have waited for him. She should've left his ass until he got his shit together. She was right. If he wanted her, then he wouldn't have been able to wait, right?

But then I remember that this is just a book. They're married now, happy, and I don't know for sure that this is about them. Couldn't it be a coincidence about the names, Fall Away Lane where Jared's and Jax's houses are located, Lockes-on-the-Bluff where Madoc takes his mom to dinner every time she's in town . . . ?

If it is real, who could've written it? Who would know all this stuff about my parents?

And who sent it, believing I needed to have it?

Hopefully, I wasn't missing out on more than I was waiting for, though.

I can't help but think that this is true for a lot of us.

"Quinn!" I hear Dylan call from downstairs.

Shit, she must be back already. I hadn't realized how much time had passed.

"Coming!" I shout.

Stuffing the book in my satchel, I check my hair in the mirror and run out of my bedroom.

Passing my parents' room, I stop and think, remembering my mom's box of keepsakes in her closet. I remember being enamored of her journal when I was a kid, but she wouldn't let me read it.

If this book is true, the person who wrote it has to be close to at least one of my parents. They had to get the story somewhere.

Cracking open the door, I creep inside, knowing they're not home yet, but Addie could be lurking around somewhere, too.

I close the door and dash into my mom's closet, walking past the clothes and shoe racks, the handbags and jewelry. I loved playing in here as a kid. Trying on her things and pretending I was as sophisticated and beautiful. I kind of like finding out she didn't always have it together. That she was far from perfect.

Taking down the white box on the shelf, I dig through it until I find her black journal underneath her old yearbook.

Holding it in my hands, the nerves under my skin are firing so hard I almost feel sick. I don't want to read this. It's private, and I love my parents. I don't need to know all their secrets, because it doesn't change how much they mean to each other and me.

But someone sent the book to me for a reason.

I absently fan the pages, not ready to look, but the book automatically falls open in the middle and I widen my eyes in shock.

"Oh, my God."

Sitting between the pages is a small pile of one-hundred-dollar bills and a business card. An old tattered one, yellowed from age, and it has my father's name on it.

I count out the money. Four hundred. The same amount Jase gave Kat for changing the oil in his car.

We sail down the highway, the radio blasting with Madonna's "Like a Prayer," and I have to laugh as I look over at Dylan.

She's bouncing against the back of her seat, singing at full volume.

"This song's like really old, you know?" I shout, teasing her.

She smiles, punching the stick shift into fifth. I grab onto the safety bar, because she freaks me out when she drives.

"It's sexy, though," she taunts, turning down the volume. "Did you know it's about a blow job?"

I shoot my eyes over to her. "It is not!"

She laughs, nodding. "It is! Listen." And she starts singing along with Madonna, "'I'm down on my knees, I want to take you there.'" She eyeballs me. "See!"

I look away, turning it over in my head as my entire childhood shatters. How many times have I danced to this around my house? In front of my parents?!

Squeezing my eyes shut, I bury my face in my hands and practically growl. My mom is right. My dad shelters me, and now my younger relatives are teaching me shit. *Awesome.*

"Just . . . drop me at Jax's," I blurt out, changing the subject. "I need to talk to Juliet."

"Are you sure?"

I unfasten my seat belt as she makes a small detour, turning onto Fall Away Lane. "Yeah, I'll catch a ride with them. Don't worry. I'll be there."

"Okay, see you soon then," she says with a hint of threat in her voice, like I'd better be there or else. I know she's nervous about her first race tonight. Even though she's been on that track and many others her father has taken her to her entire life.

Walking up to Jax and Juliet's house, I slow my steps as I take in the white two-story with black shutters, looking at it with new eyes now.

My father bought this house. I wonder if my brothers knew that. No wonder my mother never took Jax's money for it. It wouldn't have been right. My father gave it to her as a gift, and she passed it on as a gift.

If my dad had never bought the house, Jax and Juliet wouldn't live here now. Jared might never have met Tate, at least not until high school, and Hawke, Dylan, and James might never have been born without all those events that brought everyone together. It's incredible how something that seems so insignificant can alter the lives of so many. How our family started out so unsure, but now, here we are. Practically a clan.

I walk into the house without knocking, which is pretty much standard in our family. There's so much coming and going, everyone knows not to walk around naked.

Making my way toward the kitchen, I stop when I hear Jax's voice, then I notice Hawke at my side. He must've come in behind me.

He's sweating, wearing only black shorts and a backpack with no shirt. "I'm home!" he calls, rounding the bannister. "I'm gonna shower, and I'll meet you at the track, Dad."

"Ok, hurry up," Jax tells him. "It's Dylan's night."

Hawke heads upstairs, and I continue into the kitchen, seeing Jax come toward me.

"Hey. What's up?" He plants a kiss on my forehead.

"I just need to talk to Juliet. Are you riding separate?"

"As usual." He grins. "See you there." And then he walks around me, heading out.

Juliet is at the sink, using the hose to spray water over a plant, and I stand and watch her for a moment.

I admire all of my sisters-in-law: Tate for her strength and the way she stands up for herself, and Fallon for the way she doesn't bend and sticks to her convictions. But Juliet is a little different.

I always looked up to her, because I liked how girly she was. Or is. She flaunts her femininity.

She's beautiful, and despite the fact that she teaches high school English and Literature and writes young adult books on the side, she never gives in to pressure to fit a mold or hide her personality to meet an expectation.

I love how she wears her personality. The big necklaces that are a perfect contradiction to her jean shorts and T-shirt, the heels she wears with skinny jeans, the lip gloss the color of cotton candy . . . all of those things were a very big deal to an eight-year-old who looked at this woman and saw glamour.

But somehow, I've never really stopped idolizing her. Not even a little. I like her style, and as I grew up, I started wanting to be more like her. Someone sexy that drives my man wild. She's carefree and walks with confidence.

Sometimes I come over just to look in her closet and try on the soft, flowing shirts and Jimmy Choos.

"Hi," I finally say, coming to sit down at the kitchen table.

She turns her head, her green eyes sparkling with a smile. "Well, hey. This is a nice surprise. I don't feel like I see you enough."

I take off my bag and set it on the table. "It always smells like cookies in here. No wonder Jax keeps you around."

She snorts, carrying the plant across the kitchen to set on the back porch. "Yeah, he says he keeps me around because I'm hot."

Whatever. Jax likes to joke, but they're perfect together, and he knows it. Just like Jared and Tate and Madoc and Fallon.

"So what's up?" She dusts off her hands on her jean shorts.

"Nothing. Just thought I'd catch a ride with you tonight."

"Sounds good," she says. "I'll be ready in a few."

Jax and Jared usually go early to help set up and organize the spectators, while Tate and Juliet come separately, so they have a car to bring the kids home early and get them in bed.

Juliet only has Hawke, but she and Jax took in lots of foster kids over the years. They didn't have anyone staying with them now, though. A fact that, I think, Hawke enjoys. He's an only child who hardly ever gets to enjoy being an only child.

"So . . ." I feel my heartbeat pick up pace. "Are you writing anything right now?"

I know what I want to ask her, and I feel tempted to spit it out, but I'm not sure I really want to know, either. So I ease myself into it.

If the person who sent the book wanted to be known, they would've included a return address.

But I have to know who sent it.

She finishes wrapping up their leftovers from dinner and puts them in the fridge. "I'm working on something. Another part of the same series," she explains. "It's hard to find time to write, though, and this summer shouldn't allow much more time."

Juliet writes fantasy when she's not teaching—it's a series about teens who live in a postapocalyptic society where ancient warrior regimes have taken over.

However, she and Jax finally got their summer camp open up at Black Hawk Lake, so her time off from teaching wouldn't really be time off. She'll be busy all summer, which will leave little time for writing.

I trace the grain of the wood of the table and ask hesitantly, "Have you ever . . ." I look up at her. "Like, written romance or anything?"

She stops what she's doing and looks at me. I suddenly feel awkward.

But she shakes her head. "No," she replies quietly, looking away again. "Never had much interest. Why do you ask?"

I shrug. "No reason."

But disappointment weighs on me. She's the only writer I know.

I draw in a deep breath and stand up. *Screw it.* It's Dylan's night. I'll finish the book, because I can't not, but it's almost time for some fun.

"Can I check out your closet?"

She shoots me a very happy look. She doesn't have any daughters, so I know she enjoys being able to do girly things with Dylan and me.

"Have at it," she says. "We're about the same size now, so feel free to borrow something." And then whisks past me, whispering, "Something that will piss off your brothers."

I let out a laugh and grab my bag to head upstairs.

Hell yeah.

JASE . . .

I climbed the stairs, hearing my father's coughing break up the silence in the otherwise quiet penthouse. The skyscrapers of Chicago loomed outside the windows behind me, blurred in the rain spilling down the glass, and I passed pictures on the walls of all of our great orchestrated family moments. My parents decided to stay here at their apartment in the city, close to the doctors, when we found out my father was dying.

Go figure. I was the one who smoked, but he got lung cancer.

I pushed open his bedroom door and stepped inside. The home nurse was leaning over his bed, holding up his cup as he struggled to drink, and then she put it down and pulled up his covers.

She walked over to me, carrying a bloodstained hand towel and whispering, "He's close to the end, I'm afraid."

I cast him a glance, taking in his frail hands gripping the sheet, his sunken cheeks and chapped lips, and his withered body, so small and thin. His white pajamas looked like a sheet thrown over a skeleton.

My father has always been larger than life to me. I never felt close to him, but as a kid, he was still a god. *Now look at him.*

He started coughing again, and I nodded at the nurse, brushing past her to head over to his side of the bed.

I reached down and wrapped an arm around his convulsing body, trying to support him as he hunched over and hacked. "Here, let me."

"Stop it!" he barked, slapping at my arms. "Don't act like you wouldn't rather be anywhere else."

Jesus. I released him and stood, running a hand through my hair as I watched his body shake and fight for air. He pulled away the towel, and there was more blood. I clenched my jaw, suddenly unnerved. This wasn't my father.

He fell back on his pillows again, breathing hard, and I turned away, taking off my suit jacket. I tossed it on a chair and loosened my tie, taking a deep breath and trying to face him.

I'd barely been around to visit since he was confined to his bed a few weeks ago. The disease hit him fast and hard, and I didn't know why it was difficult to see him like this. I wasn't sure I would even miss him, after all.

Was it just hard to muster empathy? I didn't really know. I just knew that I was confused.

"Your mother is off shopping," he said, looking up at me and sounding short of breath. "For a trip to Italy she's planning to help herself get over my death."

He started laughing, his voice thick with phlegm, and I saw blood coating the inside of his lips.

Dorian Gray. That's who he reminded me of. All my life, he seemed like a young man, living large, but now . . . the weight of a life's worth of consequences descended at once, his true character showing all over him. Decrepit, ugly, weak . . .

He was dying horribly. And alone. My mother was counting the days, and I couldn't say I blamed her.

"I wanted more, Jason." He looked up at me, his eyes now desperate. "I thought I would be more. The friends, the parties, the meetings, the power and money . . . you think it means something, but look at me," he pleaded, drawing in shallow breaths. "I'm dying alone. Everything will carry on, and you start to realize that, while your name may last awhile, you're replaceable. I'm almost already forgotten."

I leaned down and pulled the cover back up. "That's not true."

But he grabbed my hand, stopping me. His cold fingers curled around my fist, and I stared at our hands. The same size, the same nails, the same wide knuckles . . .

"Do you love me?" he asked quietly.

I raised my eyes hesitantly, staring into a reflection of my own thirty years from now. Will I be asking Madoc that same question? Will I have to?

When I don't answer, my father lets go of my hand and looks away. "No one's here. And when they do show up, it's a lie."

"Do you care?"

He shot his eyes over to me again, the despair evident. "I don't want to die alone," he admitted. "Your mother won't miss me. And all the women over all the years . . . they gave me nothing that lasted. I ruined my marriage. I ruined my family."

I sat down, a ten-ton weight sitting on my shoulders. Burying my head in my hands, I felt his words curl their way through my head.

I wasn't him. Kat was the only woman. I didn't run around town. She was special. Madoc would understand. We won't be here in thirty years, Madoc hating me for never being there for him, choosing whores over our family, and hurting his mother.

I couldn't do this anymore.

My father was dying, and afterward I would finally be free to determine the course of my own life. A life with Kat, and our kids, including Madoc.

"Dad, I'm in love with Kat," I told him. "I can't give her up . . ."

"It doesn't matter," he cut me off. "You'll fail her, too."

I stared at him, his words from over the years still so ingrained in my head. Failure is a choice that easily becomes a habit, he would always say.

And doubt took root. What if I married Kat? What if it failed? What if the whole reason I latched onto her in the first place was because I was simply weak and greedy? Just like him.

Where would Madoc live if Maddie and I divorced? Would he hate me? Would Maddie remarry and give him someone in his life who was worlds better than me?

"All that matters is Madoc," he went on. "Don't disappoint him. Don't hurt him."

My son. A child who was starting to notice his parents and, not only how they love him, but how they love each other. I already knew he loves her more. And why wouldn't he?

"Your son is the true love of your life, Jason. When it's you lying here, you'll want to know that you survive in him. That he'll keep you alive. That he'll mourn you."

I blinked rapidly, turning away, so my father didn't see the tears in my eyes.

"Nothing is more important than him," he whispered, his wheezing growing more labored. "I wish I had been a better father. I wish I could undo everything I've done to make you hate me."

He reached out a hand off the side of the bed, fighting to breathe.

I stared down at it, knowing I should take it. Knowing he needed me. There was no one else, after all.

But this wasn't us. It was never us. He denied me love and affection all my life. When I had the need, he didn't have the will. Now that he had the need, I found that I just wasn't willing to fake affection for him.

His hand fell to the side, limp and empty when I didn't take it. "I wish . . . ," he gasped. "I wish you loved me."

CHAPTER 7

KAT . . .

Pushing open the screen door, I spotted Jared, flying down the street on his bike. Tate stood up on his pegs behind him, holding on to his shoulders. My heart raced every time they did that. I glanced next door, seeing her dad, James, mowing the lawn and at the same time keeping an eye on them as well.

"Jared?" I shouted, slipping on my heel. "Come inside!"

I heard the squeak of his brakes, and Tate broke out in laughter as he swerved side to side, trying to stop.

She and her father had just moved in a few months ago, and I was so happy Jared had a kid right next door to play with. Even if she was a girl—and he pouted about that at first—they were practically insepa-rable now.

"I don't want to come in!" he argued.

But I just shook my head, knowing that was coming. He constantly argued. "I have to leave."

"Then leave."

I closed my eyes, groaning under my breath.

At five, he'd been a handful. At eight, a little bit of a nightmare. And now at ten? He was practically unstoppable.

I charged down the steps and across the yard, seeing Tate jump off the bike, because she, at least, still respected adults. "Stop with the attitude," I bit out. "I have things to do, so I'm going to drop you at Deena's. Get your backpack."

"I don't want to go to her house!" he yelled. "Tate doesn't have to go to a babysitter!"

"Because Tate's dad is home," I argued, and I suddenly noticed the lawn mower had stopped.

Since it was summer, the kids didn't have school, but Jared was still too young to stay home alone.

"Now," I gritted out.

"You're not even working today!"

"He can stay with us, Kat."

I turned to see Tate's dad coming into the street, wiping his hands on his shop cloth.

Well, that would be easy, wouldn't it? And under normal circumstances, I wouldn't have a problem with it. He ate at their house at least once a week already and even spent the night a couple of times.

But no, Jared needed to learn how to follow directions.

"That's okay. Thank you." I evened out my voice, trying to calm down.

But when I turned back to Jared, he and Tate were gone, speeding down the street again.

"Jared!" I yelled again.

I looked at my watch. Damn it. I should've left a half hour ago. I wanted to miss the traffic.

"Honestly, Kat," James spoke up again, "it helps me out. They entertain each other, and I can get some work done. I was going to take Tate out for pizza later. They'll have fun, and he can spend the night."

I looked back to Jared, following him with my eyes and wishing he'd stay away from the corner like I'd told him. What if a car sped around there?

I closed my eyes and let out a breath. My nerves were shot.

"Are you sure you don't mind?" I asked, finally giving in. I couldn't tackle my son today. If he was happier here, let him stay here.

James just smiled, another instance of his easy demeanor. "We'll see you in the morning."

He walked away, and I dropped my head for a moment, feeling defeated. Why couldn't I fall for a nice guy like him? One who was single, an excellent dad who stopped everything for his daughter, and seemed to understand so much without my saying anything.

I was pretty sure he knew my story, and we'd barely talked. It was the look in his eyes sometimes.

He was the type who wouldn't interfere and tell me I was neglecting my kid. He wouldn't tell me that if I hadn't gone out with my friends last night, I wouldn't be tired and hungover today. He wouldn't tell me how to raise my child.

He was simply there, picking up all the slack I left hanging.

Even if I were interested in him, though, I didn't believe he was any more available than Jason. James's wife had passed away last spring, and I got the impression he'd continue wearing his wedding ring for quite some time yet.

I made it into the city around four, and I'd dressed semi-causal, wearing a short black sleeveless dress, layered on the bottom half. I'd also left my hair down, kinky with the natural curl Jase liked, and all pushed to one side, over my left shoulder. The makeup was minimal, but I made sure to wear red lipstick and the perfume he liked. We were supposed to be going to Movie in the Park tonight, and he was taking care of the picnic and blanket.

Over time, we'd gotten into a routine. He knew what time Jared was supposed to be in bed, and he'd call me before he arrived to make sure the coast was clear. Sometimes I met him at his suite at the Waldorf in Chicago, but now he had an apartment there, so we used the suite less. He even let me decorate the apartment. To make it ours.

I could call him at work or at certain times when I knew he'd be alone, and sometimes I saw him a few times a week, and other times I wouldn't see him for a month. It sounded terrible when I put in into words or tried to explain it to Deena, but the strange thing was . . . it had become normal. Somewhere along the way my expectations had shifted. They'd lowered, and my hopes had settled at a more realistic level.

Since his father's death several years ago, his career had taken off, and he was at the top of his game. I took solace in the knowledge that "he needed me." He loved me, right? So we stole our moments where we could, and when it was just us, everything was perfect.

And someday, hopefully soon, Madoc would be old enough to understand the divorce and accept seeing his dad with someone new.

I'd gotten my accounting degree years ago, I held down a decent job, and I had a lot to be grateful for. He'd given me a lot, and I knew I shouldn't feel bad about demanding more from him over the years, but I did. Why did feel like I owed him?

Deena would ask why I stayed. Why I kept running back to him and putting up with it instead of finding a man who wanted only me. Why did I let myself be used in a way that made me so miserable?

And I always had to correct her. I wasn't miserable.

I was deliriously happy.

Because I was irrevocably in love with him. I'd rather be unhappy ninety percent of the time just so I could feel what I felt with him the other ten percent of the time.

I'd rather leave my son with sitters to be available for Jase on a moment's notice, only to drink myself into an oblivion to chase away the guilt after he'd left.

I'd rather be lonely and feel like a piece of shit every day only to have it all wash away as soon as he kissed me.

That was the sickness. My entire life revolved around him, because I was a woman in love in a horrible situation. He was like a drug that I couldn't give up—everything depended on getting my next hit. Unfortunately, though, I needed the hits to come faster, and when they didn't, I soothed myself with alcohol.

My God, how I'd changed. Where was the girl who taunted him in the repair shop that night? The one who spit his intentions back in his face?

Walking into his office building, I took the elevator up to the twenty-sixth floor and texted James, telling him to tell Jared I'd see him in the morning and that I loved him.

Jared.

I closed my eyes, letting out a heavy breath, because I wanted to cry thinking about him. He was so smart. He was starting to catch on to me. How much longer before I'd pushed him to the side so often I wouldn't be able to pick him back up?

Thomas would've been a horrible father, but if I'd stayed in that dump, surviving and fighting, because I had no choice, maybe Jared would've had a better mother than the one he has now.

I stepped off the elevator and walked down the marble corridor to Jase's office. I wasn't sure what he told his assistant when I came by, but she didn't give me curious or judgmental glances, so I guessed he was rather good at lying, in and out of the courtroom. Rounding the corner, I quickly stopped and stepped back, shielding myself behind the wall.

Shit. What was she doing here?

I edged back toward the corner again, trying to figure out what I should do. Jase and Madeline, his wife, stood outside his office, in front of the receptionist's desk, chatting and smiling. A boy was with them, and I knew it was Madoc, even though I'd never met him. He looked exactly like his father.

Jase was blocking his door, not inviting them in, so they were either on their way out or he was trying to get them to leave. He knew I was coming, after all.

"Mom's dragging me into chick shops," Madoc complained. "Help."

But his mom just laughed, lightly knocking him on the arm. "Don't act like you don't like shopping, kid. Besides, you need school clothes. No more uniforms next year."

Jase smiled at both of them, his hands in his pockets and looking a little nervous. Yeah, I'll bet you are.

I'd seen his wife several times over the years, in a restaurant or in the paper for some city project she was helping with. Sometimes on the street or in her car.

She wore a tight, gray sleeveless dress that fell to her knees and hugged every curve. Her heels were a dark pink, and her tan was flawless. Her hair was cut shoulder-length and styled with big curls, and as every time I saw her, she was perfect, right down to the Gucci handbag.

Kind of what I thought I would be like if I ever grew up. I straightened, looking down at my dress that seemed so simple and my childish flats.

I wondered what Jase saw in me. I looked okay, but I didn't carry myself like that.

I guessed they were in town to shop, especially since Jase said Madoc had talked his way out of attending any more Catholic school and would be allowed to attend public next year. He needed regular clothes, probably.

"Can you meet us for dinner?" his wife asked.

But Jase just let out a sigh, looking immediately uncomfortable. "I wish I could, honey, but I'll be buried until morning. You may as well head home without me after you're done shopping. I'll probably just stay here tonight."

I couldn't see her face, but she was silent and I saw her head dip a little. My stomach churned.

"Okay," she replied quietly. "We'll see you when we see you then."

And then she put her hand on Madoc's back, both of them turning and walking my way.

I immediately put my head down, digging in my purse for my

phone. She passed by me as I pretended to dial a number, but I know she turned to look at me.

Placing the phone to my ear, I acted like I was on a call, while she and her son waited for the elevator. But inevitably, the pull got to me. I flashed my eyes over to her and found her staring at me. My heart began beating faster, and I watched as her eyes fell quickly down my body and back up to my face, before turning away.

She knew.

And she just stared ahead, her chin trembling as I watched her and Madoc walk into the elevator.

I'd been wondering what Jase saw in me over her, and she'd probably just wondered the same thing. We were both wondering why we weren't good enough.

I stayed in the hallway long after the number on the elevator had descended to one, and I knew she was gone.

This wasn't working. It never worked, and it would never end. She was miserable, and her son wasn't an idiot. He knew something was wrong.

I was miserable, and my son wasn't an idiot, either. He knew something was wrong.

The only person happy here was Jase, because he got the best of both worlds. And I was only happy when I saw him.

Which was next to never.

And for so long, I'd accepted it. Because I didn't think I deserved something more.

Thomas and my parents wouldn't or couldn't be there for me, my friends had their own problems, and I was trying to raise a kid on my own. I never thought I'd have all the things I have now. I was supposed to be grateful and not selfish, right?

So I let him steer us, and I rarely made demands, believing that his stated concern about wanting to make sure Madoc was old enough to understand a divorce was legitimate.

It wasn't. Deep down I knew it was just a way to hold me off.

Tucking my phone back in my bag, I walked into his office, his assistant waving me through. She must've known I was coming.

With a steady hand, I slowly swung his office door open and stepped in, closing it behind me.

Jase stood across the room, staring out the windows, but turned when he heard me enter. Immediately, his shoulders relaxed and a relieved smile crossed his face, looking like a small weight had lifted. He loosened his tie, drawing attention to his neck, and desire flared up inside me. It was my favorite part of his body. Soft but toned, and kissing him there drove him wild.

"Hi," he greeted softly, walking toward me.

His eyes never left mine, and this was the part where I always lost my resolve—when Jase looked at me, after all this time, like I was still that teenage girl in the garage. Fascination with a hint of lust like I was the only thing that existed in his world.

It was a pretty lie. I pushed the feelings down.

"I thought she didn't come to your office," I said, remaining by the door.

He slowed to a pause and watched me, realization crossing his face. He knew I'd probably passed her in the hall.

Giving me a closed-mouthed, contrite smile, he walked toward me, opening his arms. "You look beautiful."

He leaned in for a kiss, but I quickly turned my head away so that his lips brushed my cheek instead.

He pulled back and stared down at me. "What's wrong?"

I adjusted the bag hanging on my arm, unable to look at him. If I looked at him, I'd start tearing up and then he'd soothe me and we'd be back where we started.

"I came to tell you I'm not going to be at the apartment tonight," I replied. "I'm going home where I belong."

He remained still, his hands frozen on my arms as he gazed at me, probably having no doubt what was happening.

We'd been through this before. So many times.

Sometimes it was him. *"I love you, but the guilt is too much." "I can't do this to you anymore." "My kid will hate me like I hate my father." "How do we build a relationship from where we've started?"*

But within days we were in each other's arms again.

Other times it was me. *"Why are you such a coward?" "I need a life of my own." "I hate who I am with you."*

And within a month and no matter whom I tried to date, I couldn't shake Jase. I never could.

"So you came all the way to Chicago to tell me that?" he charged, his tone turning clipped. "That you're going home? To the home I bought you, you mean?"

I glued my teeth together and froze, thinking that if I didn't say anything I would be safe. For at least a moment.

He leaned his head down further, invading my space and trying to catch my eyes. "Hmmm?"

A knot lodged in my throat, because I was afraid. I could walk out of here, go home, and wake up tomorrow, probably feeling worlds lighter having rid myself of him. But then days would pass, I'd get lonely, he'd start calling or coming by after trying to give me my space, and the emotions, the longing, and the fucking memories of how good we were together in the good times would make me give in and agree to be his again. We always came back to each other.

He breathed out a nasty laugh. "Give me a break," he said, calling my bluff as he walked away. "Get over here. Now."

I fisted my hands and stayed planted to the floor. If he'd been sweeter, maybe I would've gone to him. But now it was a matter of pride, and believe it or not, I still had a little of that left.

His jaw flexed, and his eyes burned when I didn't move.

"I don't fuck my wife anymore," he growled from across his office. "And you know nothing about my responsibilities and obligations. You have no idea what goes on in my head, Kat. Now get over here."

I shook my head, still not leaving but still not budging.

"Now!"

"No!" I lashed out, glaring at him. "It's over! I'm sick of your shit!"

"Oh, Kat's mad again," he mocked, tossing out a lazy smile. "Okay, how much will this cost?" He pulled out his billfold and started throwing money into the air. "Twenty-forty-sixty," he counted and then stopped. "Oh, I'm sorry. You like hundreds, don't you?" And he began tossing more bills out, reminding me of the day at the repair shop when I'd taken an extra hundred out of his wallet.

"You son of a bitch!" I shouted, running for him and throwing out my hands, hitting him in the face a few times.

He caught my arms, holding the wrists so hard they burned.

"It's not over," he ordered, seething in my face as he backed me up. "It doesn't end until I say it does."

And then I fell back on the couch; his body came down on top of me. I let out a cry, but it was muffled by the weight of him on my chest.

"You don't need me here," he said, touching my head and forcing himself between my legs. "And you don't feel me here." He touched my chest over my heart, his breath falling on my lips. "This is where you want me." His hand slipped down between my legs, rubbing me where I was already wet. "I'm going to have it tomorrow, and the next day, in my car, here in my office, at the Waldorf in our room where the men in my family fuck their pretty mistresses, and you're not going to keep me off you, Kat, because you're mine."

I shook and cried as he kissed me, slowly trailing his mouth across my cheek and biting my lips.

"That smart mouth," he whispered, "and that soft skin that doesn't taste like anything but you." He gripped my panties in his hand, and I gasped as he tore them off my body.

I squeezed my eyes shut. *Stop. No.*

But the words never left my lips. They never did, because I loved him. I always wanted him.

He unfastened his belt and pants and pushed inside me, finding me just as wet as I always was. I let out a cry, feeling him fill me.

"You can say whatever you want"—he thrust harder, stretching me and filling me and making my knees bend up to get him deeper—"but you can't give me up any more than I can give you up. It will never be over."

He layered our lips, my bottom one between both of his like he always did, both of us breathing and panting, doing the only thing we knew how to do. The only thing he wanted from me.

I stopped crying, and everything turned numb as he thrust into me and panted, and I moaned as we both came.

This is what we were. It was all we'd ever be. There would never be anything more.

He lay on top of me, his chest rising and falling on mine, and I couldn't hear anything. All around me was like white noise, and as much as I tuned my ears, I couldn't hear or see what was next. I couldn't see tomorrow. I couldn't see Jared or me. There was nothing.

I squeezed my eyes shut, the sobs in my stomach building and tightening until I felt like I was going to scream.

I'd dropped the ball. I'd given him too much power over me.

I barely existed anymore.

My head hung to the side, and I pushed out from underneath him. I sunk to the floor, my torn panties lying beside me.

"I love you," I whispered, staring at nothing ahead of me. "But please stay away from me. Please."

His voice was quiet and strained. "I can't."

I dropped my head, my chest shaking and tears spilling over. Grabbing my purse from where it had fallen, I ran to the door. But before I could open it, he was up and off the couch, and his body was behind mine, caging me in and keeping me from leaving.

I cried, turning around and feeling nothing but despair. "Look at me," I pleaded. "Look what you've done to me."

His eyes were turning red, and I saw tears pooling. He swallowed, finally looking like he had no idea what to say me. "I never wanted to hurt you."

I stared at him, holding his eyes. Could he see how I looked? Did he care that I was suffering?

"Then let me go," I told him. "Please let me go. If you love me at all . . ."

I turned to leave, but he slammed his hand against the door, his breath shaking his chest with each inhalation.

"Kat, please," he begged in a whisper. "Please don't do this."

I pulled the door open anyway, refusing to turn around and look at him. But I turned my head just enough for him to hear me.

"You said you were going to give me everything, and you didn't. You can't," I charged. "I would've eventually gotten away from Thomas, but you?" Tears started falling again as pain filled my chest and my gut. "You've made a mess of me."

CHAPTER 8

KAT . . .

Charging through the school, my heels dug into the floors, their clacking echoing down the hallway as I made my way to the main office. This was the fourth time this year I'd been summoned to Jared's school either to take him home or to meet with the principal about his behavior.

Everything was fine before last summer. Or somewhat fine. I should never have let Thomas take him. Jared had been off the rails ever since, and I knew why, but he refused to let me help, and I was at my wits' end. Thank goodness that bastard was in jail now.

But even so, the damage was done, and my son was different. He was more like his father than ever now.

I barged through the heavy wooden door and entered the office, stopping and immediately scanning for Jared.

Seeing him and another boy sitting in the chairs along the wall, I couldn't help but lash out.

"Bullying?" I burst out. "I'm absolutely disgusted. What were you thinking?"

Jared stared ahead, looking bored and ignoring me.

"It wasn't bullying," someone grumbled, and I looked to the kid a couple of chairs down from him. "Josh Rutgers is such a baby."

I'd never seen the kid before, but I gathered he and Jared were in this together.

"Who are you?" I demanded.

He smiled, holding out a hand. "Madoc Caruthers. You're my brother's mother, huh?"

Brother's mother. Caruthers. "What?"

I took in the blond hair, the demanding blue eyes, the expensive shoes and brown leather jacket, the stylish roll to his jeans . . . *Oh, Christ.*

"Like, how old are you?" he asked, giving me a nice, long once-over that was completely inappropriate. "Were you ten when you had Jared?"

"Caruthers," I repeated, ignoring his flirting as I walked over to the boys. "Is your father Jase Caruthers?"

"Yeah. You know him?"

"No," I snapped and turned away, looking to Jared. "Get up."

He rolled his eyes and stood up, following me to the receptionist's counter.

Shit. They were friends. How did I not know that?

Mrs. Bauer, the principal's assistant, saw us and stopped what she was doing to approach. "The principal had to leave for a meeting," she informed me. "But Jared's suspended for three days. He's responsible for staying caught up on his work while he's gone. You need to sign this."

She pulled out a piece of paper and pushed it in front of me with a pen.

I picked up the pen and started scanning the document. "What happened exactly?"

"A guy was messing with Tatum Brandt," Madoc answered, coming up to the counter to stand next to us. "So Jared and I sent him on his way."

"The boy was merely asking her to the school carnival," Mrs. Bauer clarified. "And these two proceeded to steal his clothes while he was in the shower and hang them on Miss Brandt's locker with a very vulgar message written on the underpants."

She said the last part in a horrified whisper, and I heard Madoc snort next to us, doubling over and laughing as I felt Jared smile next to me.

I turned to him. "Why would you do that to Tate?"

"Because he likes her," Madoc interjected.

"Shut. Up," Jared growled.

Anger filled my chest, and I swallowed it down, because I knew it was exactly what Jared wanted. What was the matter with him? He lived for confrontation these days, and our arguments were a constant occurrence. I had no idea what to do with him.

The bottle of rum I had at home flashed in my mind, and I swallowed again, the dryness in my mouth like sand. I signed the paper quickly without even reading it.

I didn't care. I just wanted to get out of here.

"Madoc," a deep male voice called.

I froze. No, no, no . . .

Madoc turned around at my side. "Hey," he replied in a casual tone. "I swear I didn't do it."

The pen shook in my hand, and I could feel the heat of his eyes on my back.

I hadn't seen him in so long.

"Oh, of course not," the man responded. "It's never your fault."

His voice was getting closer, and I closed my eyes for a moment, not wanting to turn around, but I knew there was no way I'd get out of here without him seeing.

In the five years since we'd ended things, a lot had changed.

But not enough. The anger still festered within me, time having healed nothing.

"Nope, never," Madoc responded. "Everyone should have a kid

like me." And then he turned back around, winking at the middle-aged receptionist across the counter.

She scowled, tsking at him, and pushed another piece of paper—I assumed for Jase to sign—forward. Madoc must be suspended, too.

"Just take them home," she instructed. "Be back on Friday."

I saw Jase's black suit out of the corner of my eye as he stepped up to the counter, Madoc between us. He pulled the paper closer, as if reading it, but then I felt his eyes fall on me.

Damn it. I locked my jaw and steeled my eyes, so he wouldn't see how nervous I was as I glanced over at him.

His eyes narrowed, and he seemed to stop breathing before quickly turning away, picking up the pen to sign the paper.

Yeah, I wasn't expecting this either, College Boy.

We'd done a great job of avoiding each other the past few years. I knew which pubs to stay out of, and he knew to avoid High Street, since that was where I worked.

And even though I was no longer dirt poor and struggling, I made sure not to frequent fancy restaurants or the country club, where I might see him. And since Jase led such a blessed life that he didn't ever have to step foot in a grocery store, pharmacy, or McDonald's, we hadn't crossed paths.

Except for once on the street while watching the Fourth of July parade, and that was two years ago.

He signed the paper and handed it over to Mrs. Bauer, and then I saw him look our way again.

"Jared?" he said, peering around me, surprised.

My son turned his head to look at Madoc's father, and I glanced between them. Jared didn't remember him, did he? We were careful.

Unless Jared had run into him at Madoc's house, since they were friends.

Jase regarded him, though, as if he was seeing him for the first time.

"Yeah?" Jared asked, sounding annoyed.

But Jase simply turned away. "You're both getting suspended together." He handed Mrs. Bauer the pen, talking to Madoc. "How come I've never met your friend before?"

"Probably because he's at our house more than you are," his son shot back.

I smiled, taking too much pleasure in that comeback. Madoc might not be giving Jase the hell Jared gave me, but it was something, and I liked knowing someone in his life was holding him accountable.

A cell phone rang, and Jase pulled his out of his breast pocket, checking the screen. Tapping a button, he slipped it back into his pocket. "May I please have my stepdaughter, Fallon Pierce, as well?" he asked Mrs. Bauer. "Might as well pick her up while I'm here and save Addie the trip."

The receptionist gave him a look, her mouth twisting in annoyance. "Of course," she finally grumbled.

Heat covered my skin, and I wasn't sure if it was Jase or the mention of a stepdaughter. I knew he'd remarried quickly after his divorce from Madoc's mother years ago.

Very quickly, in fact.

Yeah, men like him didn't know how to be without wives to handle their houses and kids and schedule the fucking gardeners and caterers. All so they can have everything and sacrifice nothing.

But it wasn't me. He had his dirty fun with the trailer park girl. He couldn't marry her.

I ground my teeth together and swung my purse over my shoulder.

"I'm going to go wait in the car," I heard Madoc say as he grabbed his father's keys off the counter.

"Yeah, me, too." Jared plucked my set out of my purse.

But I shot out my hand, snatching them back. "Absolutely not," I snapped. "You don't move a muscle without my say-so. You got that? And you will apologize to Tate as soon as she gets home from school."

"I'm not doing shit," he bit back and turned around. "I'll be in the parking lot."

"Jared!"

But all I could do was watch as both boys walked out of the office, leaving Jase and me alone.

"Genetics is amazing, isn't it?" Jase commented at my side. "Jared hasn't seen his father since he was a baby, and yet there's so much of the man in him."

I darted my eyes to Jase, my nostrils probably flaring. "You don't know Jared or anything he's been through, so don't act like you do."

Spinning around, I walked out of the office, trying to get far away from him.

But he was on my heels instantly. "Well, I'm wondering if you even know him."

I clutched my purse strap, fisting my hand around it to keep it from shaking.

"And what do you mean 'what he's been through'?" he asked. "He hasn't seen his father, has he?"

I charged down the hallway, his familiar scent of sandalwood, angelica, and something else I couldn't place washing over me like an ice-cold martini. I licked my dry lips.

"Kat?" he pressed when I didn't answer. "Please tell me you weren't stupid enough to let that man near him."

I refused to answer. Jase was out of my life, and I wasn't sure why he felt the need to act concerned. He might not be a criminal like Thomas, but they were both neglectful fathers. He had no right to judge me.

A young woman, about Jared and Madoc's age, came down the stairs, catching us right before we walked out the door.

"Hey, what's up?" she asked, clutching her backpack straps at her shoulders. Her eyes moved from Jase to me, and then back to Jase.

"I needed to pick up Madoc, so I thought I'd grab you, too," he answered.

Ah, the stepdaughter.

Her green eyes turned annoyed behind her glasses. "Awesome," she bit out. "Moron screws up, and I have to go home, too."

Jase sighed and pushed open the door for her. "Just get in the car."

She strolled outside and he looked to me, gesturing with his arm. I walked through the door and stopped at the top of the steps, watching the kids in the parking lot. Jared's face was buried in his phone, while Madoc made faces like a five-year-old at his stepsister.

"They seem to get along well," I mused, not caring I sounded sarcastic. "I heard you remarried a couple of years ago. Congratulations."

He let out a long breath, descending the stairs with me. "Life moves on, I guess. How about you? Are you seeing anyone?"

I stared at him, with his face like stone and his voice almost bored like he was asking me if I'd tried the new restaurant on High Street yet.

He almost looked calm.

But then I noticed that he wasn't breathing again.

I tilted the corner of my mouth up, letting out a small smile. "Like you said, life moves on."

I held my pen in my hand, sitting curled up in the dark living room in the chair. Music played from the stereo, and I covered my legs with a blanket, staring at the words on the paper, the beautiful oblivion of the rum heating my veins and clouding my brain.

He was never mine. I knew that much all those years ago, so why the hell did I let him in? My chest ached with a sob I wouldn't let out, my eyes burning with tears. I swallowed the lump in my throat and picked up my drink, forcing it all down my throat.

I never learned how to be someone. Who was I without him?

His life had moved forward in our time apart. Jase now ran one of the most successful law firms in the country. Many mornings I woke up faced with him in my newspaper and, as always, he won everything he went after. Nothing had ever distracted him, least of all losing me.

I, on the other hand, remained still. I'd rarely dated, and I hadn't moved forward in a long time. My heart was still broken.

And that was proven after seeing him this afternoon and completely falling apart as soon I'd gotten home. Jared charged for his room, slamming the door, and I made for the freezer, pulling out what was always in there, and chasing the promise of escape. I could forget him every night.

Or remember him. If I drank enough.

I clutched the diary in my hand, holding it against my knees, and dug my pen into the paper.

"I wish I'd never met him."

"Who?" a voice asked. "My father?"

I popped my head up and saw Jared leaning against the door frame between the living room and the foyer, staring at me with his hands in his pockets.

"Yeah, your life would've been better if you'd never met him and I'd never been born, wouldn't it?"

I glanced back down at the words I'd written. Had I said them out loud?

Looking back up, I shook my head. "That's not what I was talking about." I closed the diary, leaving the pen inside when I set it down on the end table.

He continued to watch me, and I heard rain begin to fall against the window as the clock chimed on the mantel. What time was it?

Taking a quick look at the clock, I saw it was after eight. I hadn't made dinner, and he hadn't eaten anything, having been up in his room since one this afternoon.

I combed my hand through my hair, my stomach churning at how disgusting and pathetic I was.

My voice was barely audible. "I'm sorry, baby."

"Don't call me that."

He strolled over to my side and gazed out the window, through the shimmer of rain. The shadows of the leaves outside fluttered across his face, and he seemed much older than his fifteen years.

Jared hadn't had a hard life the way his father or I did. He never wanted for much, and there was always food in the refrigerator and decent clothes on his back. And there were times when I was a good mom. He wasn't always alone.

Unfortunately, though, Jared learned at a very young age that while he could've had it worse, he also could've had it a lot better. Tate's dad was a single father, after all. How come he could be there for his kid, and I couldn't?

His father abandoned him and abused him, and his mother was so busy making up for her lost youth that she neglected him.

His eyes darkened as he stared out the window and narrowed his brow. All I could feel was the distance between us. I couldn't remember the last time he let me hug him.

"You should go over there," I said quietly.

"Where?"

"Tate's."

That was what he was seeing when he stared out the window. Her house sat right next to ours, and she was the only thing that ever made him happy.

"Yeah, you'd like that, wouldn't you?" he ground out. "Get me out of your hair?"

"What?" I leaned up, putting my feet on the ground and staring at him. "Jared, no—"

"Tate can screw off and go to hell," he growled, cutting me off. "I hate her."

I shot out of my chair, but I was too fast. My mind fogged over, and my balance teetered suddenly. I grabbed onto the back of the chair for support.

"Jared, what's the matter? What happened?" I pressed. "You need your friends."

But he just glared ahead. "Not her. She's just like everyone else. Doesn't give a shit about anyone but herself, stupid fucking cow."

And then he spun around and headed out of the room.

"Jared!" I yelled, chasing after him, but my knees wobbled, and I felt like I was falling. "If this is your friend Madoc's influence," I choked out, trying to swallow the acid creeping up my throat, "I don't want you hanging around him anymore!"

"Yeah, good luck with that," he laughed and opened the front door. "Why don't you fucking wake up for a change, huh? He's not the bad influence. I am."

He stepped onto the porch, and I grabbed his arm, pulling him back around.

"Don't touch me!" he bellowed, his eyes dark and his breathing heavy. He yanked his arm away, and I stood there, my blanket falling off my arm and my work clothes wrinkled.

Fear wracked through me, and I was frozen. I couldn't speak.

His eyebrows dug in, and he looked like he was going to hit something. Or someone. For a moment, I almost let out a cry. It was like looking at Thomas all over again.

My stomach shook, and I just wanted to fold. I was afraid of him. I was afraid of my kid.

And it was my fault.

The times he'd been pushed off to his grandparents or friends and my never being there, the neglect, the way I never put him first . . . I'd never been his mother, because I never made the choice to. I grew up with him, not for him.

I could barely speak, my throat swelled with so much pain. "I wish . . . ," I whispered, letting my eyes fall. "I wish I was a better mom, Jared."

He was silent for a moment and then spoke up, his voice low and calm. "And I wish you'd just go away."

I shut my eyes, feeling the tears spill over as I heard his steps travel down the porch and disappear. When I opened my eyes, he was gone, and I couldn't see him through the rain and darkness.

I let the blanket fall completely, and I turned around, my steps faltering as I walked back into the house.

What the hell have I done? Why had I given Jase so much power over my happiness? What if Jared ran off and left me, because it was nothing less than what I deserved?

A ringing pierced the silence, and I jerked my head to the left and right, trying to follow the sound.

My phone.

Jared.

I ran to my purse where it lay on the table by the stairs and pulled out my phone. But before I pressed Send, I caught sight of the number on the screen and my heart skipped a beat.

What?

He hadn't called since . . .

He never called. Not since a few weeks after we ended things, but I never answered. Not the first time he called or the tenth time. After a while, he got the message. He let me go.

A spark of want flared in my veins. So long . . .

Slowly pressing Send, I rested my back against the wall and slid down, bringing the phone to my ears as I bent my knees and fell to the floor.

There was silence, but probably because I was supposed to say something, and I hadn't yet.

I wouldn't.

I heard a breath on the other end, and chills ran over my skin.

"I still think about you," he said, his voice quiet and pained. "Every day. So many times every day." And then he let out a breath. "It was harder than I let on, seeing you today, and I know I shouldn't be calling, but I needed to hear your voice again. I've never stopped missing you."

Tears filled my eyes, and everything in front of me blurred. "It didn't stop you from marrying again."

He was silent for a moment, and all I could feel was despair. I didn't know if it was him, me, or both of us, but the tale had become too twisted to set right anymore. We knew that much.

"I'd hurt you so much," he admitted. "I used you and tore you apart and made you unhappy, and . . . I thought if I stayed away you'd be better off. I thought if I married someone else, I'd forget you and what I did to you and Maddie and my son, and my fucking heart wouldn't hurt so much. I should've come for you, but why would you want me anymore? You had to hate me, right? I could barely stand the sight of myself."

I clenched my lips tightly to keep from crying out loud.

"That's my greatest regret," he went on, his voice cracking with sadness. "I regret cheating on my wife. I regret never being there for Madoc when I should be, but you . . ." He drifted off. "I wish I could go back to that day at the garage and see you again with your messy pony-tail and your warm, beautiful eyes, with that grease stain on your neck that I kept wanting to touch . . . and I wish I would've left when you told me to leave."

I hugged myself, pressing the phone to my ear and letting the tears fall as I listened.

"I wish I could've left you like that and never taken your life from you and never hurt you. Just left, because I'd be happy knowing you were going to be better off for it. That the fire in your eyes would never have died."

My chin trembled, and my chest shook. A sob escaped, and I brought my hand to my mouth, covering it to muffle the noise.

"I wish I could do that," he continued. "But that's the fucking thing, you know? If I went back to that day, saw you in that thin white T-shirt, and your breathing so nervous, because you were afraid of me but still had the courage to fight back . . . No matter how much I'd want to, I'd do nothing differently." His voice grew stronger. "Nothing. I wouldn't be able to stop myself. I'd dive right back in, even knowing how badly everything would end, because you're the only life I've ever had, and I couldn't not have you." His voice shook, thick with tears he wasn't letting out. "I'd crash and burn a thousand times just to have you."

I squeezed my eyes shut and broke down, hanging up the phone and finally letting it all go.

I still loved him, and it was so difficult to figure out why, if we could be so good together, why were we so terrible together, too? How could something be so right and so toxic at the same time?

But as I sat in my dark house, the buzz of the alcohol making my limbs heavy, I realized that maybe I was my own worst enemy. And maybe Jase was his. We weren't toxic together, because even apart we were miserable.

And we weren't a mistake. Maybe it was everything keeping us apart that was a mistake.

Jase Caruthers couldn't fix me, and I couldn't fix him. Plain and simple.

We just weren't right for each other yet.

Maybe in another life . . .

———

"Hey, can I talk to you for a sec?"

"Can it wait until we get to the track?" Jared asks, sounding stressed. And then he raises his eyes from James's shoes, making sure they're double knotted. "Are you riding with me?"

"No, she's with me." Madoc grins. "I'm making her drive."

He and Kade pick up the cooler and plop it down on the porch, heading back in to gather the GoPros and camera bag.

"Dylan!" Jared bellows to her somewhere in the house. "You need to leave! Jax wants you to do more practice runs before you're up!"

"Ugh," she groans, walking in from the dining room. "I've been doing practice runs since I was twelve. I think I got it."

Madoc tosses something to Kade, nearly hitting me in the face, and Tate, Fallon, and Juliet all rush back down the stairs, one of them kissing me on the forehead as they pass.

I close my eyes and ball my fists. "Can you just stop for a minute?" I bark. "I have something I need to show you."

"Well, then, hurry," Jared snaps, finishing James's shoe.

"I found this book," I tell him. "Or it was sent to me, I mean. I'm pretty sure it's about Mom and Dad. It's like their love story or something."

"What?" Tate asks, scrunching up her face in confusion as she puts on her sunglasses and Fallon sprays sunscreen on Madoc's and Kade's necks as they walk by.

"Look." I take out the hardcover and hand it to Jared, opening to the bookmarked page so that I can point to the names that are eerily close to my parents'. "Kat and Jase."

Tate comes over to look at it, but Jared couldn't look less interested. He hands the book back and pats his jeans, probably for his keys and wallet.

"And they have sons, Jared and Madoc," I point out. "They live in a small town in Illinois, she had a baby with some asshole, he's married, their sons are friends, and Jared is in love with the girl next door who he picks on every day at school." I glance at Tate and then back to Jared. "Did you really do that?"

Jared just laughs to himself, pulling his phone off the charger in the nearby living room and sliding it into his back pocket. "Who would write a book about our parents? It doesn't mean anything."

Everyone gathers the rest of their things, pulls on shoes, and heads for the front door.

"Let's go!" Jared yells.

I groan under my breath and grind my teeth. *Damn it!*

I have to spin around and head to the porch, calling after him as everyone drifts across the lawn. "Did you tell Mom that women were high-maintenance bitches that needed to be walked more than once a day?"

Everyone suddenly stops and Jared freezes. I hear a few gasps, and I think there's a snort from Kade.

I see the muscles in Jared's back tighten through his T-shirt, everyone is absolutely silent, and I'm tempted to smile.

Yeaaaaaah. I have your attention now, don't I?

I'd read a few more chapters while I was at Jax's, and things between Jared and our mom only got worse over the next year. He said some really interesting things as the arguments escalated, too.

Slowly, everyone turns around to face me, and Jared stares at me, looking stunned, while Tate gives him a horrified look.

"Jared, you didn't," she says.

But he can do nothing but rush to his own defense. "I was like sixteen!" he bursts out, breathing heavily. "Jesus Christ, I was probably drunk!"

He charges over and takes the book away from me, opening it to a random page and scanning.

I hold out my hand. "Give it back."

"Like hell!" he barks.

"I can tell Tate what you called her behind her back when you were fifteen," I say loudly. "Now give it back."

He shoots his worried eyes over to Tate, who simply cocks her head to the side and puts her hands on her hips, looking a little pissed. He then glances at Dylan, who looks half-amused and half-embarrassed. Knowing the man Jared is now, it's hard to believe he was ever cruel—or ended up winning Tate when he treated her like crap back then—but Dylan rolls with things better than anyone I know. It is kind of entertaining to realize your parents aren't perfect. And hey, even better to have that pointed out in front of everyone.

He scowls and hands the book back. "Quinn," he starts, trying to explain. "I was a huge asshole in high school, okay?"

"Yeah, no duh."

And then Jared twists his head to the side and glares at Juliet. "Did you do this?"

She snorts, and I realize he's thinking the same thing I was.

"Oh, yeah," she says, playing with him. "I totally wrote it. You know you had it coming, right? All the years you guys spent disrespecting women"—she flashes a look at Madoc—"never dreaming that someday you'd have a daughter, a sister, and a niece, whom you adore. It was totally me. Payback is slow but sure. Mwahahahaha!"

Tate and Fallon laugh at her side, and Jared focuses back on me. "Quinn . . ."

But I just roll my eyes and shake my head, walking around him. "Forget it. It's fine."

Nothing has changed in how much I love my brothers, and I know he went through a lot growing up, but damn . . . what a little asshole!

CHAPTER 9

The Shelburne Falls Racetrack takes up several acres in the middle of the countryside, run by Jax and heavily invested in by Jared, Madoc, and Tate. They all raced here years ago, and as the Trents and Carutherses slowly took over management and expansion, it had grown far beyond its original single dirt course circling a dinky little pond.

Back in the day, it was called the Loop, and all you needed was a car. Races were informal, and usually consisted of unsupervised teens hanging out to have a little fun.

Now, instead of the original one loop, there's two. The new one isn't completely square like the original. It features twists and turns, as well as being much longer than the original. The tracks are paved, there are contracts and rules, and there are managers in place to keep everything running smoothly. While some balk at how much the Loop has changed, Jax knows what he's doing. To keep people interested, you have to keep introducing something new. And since attendance has grown to twenty times what it was when it first started, procedures had to be put in place to keep everyone safe.

But still, it's completely free to attend just like it's always been. The track makes its money from sponsors, concessions, and merchandise.

Following the rest of my family, I slip my bag strap over my head, tossing it in the backseat of Fallon's car. I'll most likely get a ride from her on the way home. She and Madoc live so close to me, after all.

As I walk over the grassy area, I notice a couple of guys I went to school with turn and nod a "hi."

I tip my chin back up and resist the urge to chew on my lip. Juliet's leather skinny pants fit like a glove, and the off-the-shoulder white T-shirt I'd borrowed flows down past my ass but left my bare shoulder exposed. She'd slapped some red lipstick on me and messed up my hair. Thankfully, Jared and Madoc had seemed too rushed to notice yet.

"I want to race the Boss!" I can hear Dylan as I head over to where she stands on the track.

Jared climbs out of the car she's standing next to and hands her the keys, probably having just pulled it into position for her.

"Enough," he bites out. "We're not changing the plan this late in the game."

"I've been asking you for months. I'm better in that car!" she argues.

Jared closes his eyes, pinching the bridge of his nose and looking exasperated. "Okay, let's try something new." He opens his eyes back up and looks straight at me, not Dylan. "Quinn," he says. "Dylan can't drive the Boss, because she wants to race the Big Loop. The Big Loop has tight twists and turns, and she needs a lighter-weight vehicle if she wants to have any chance of handling that track." His tone is sarcastic, and I can feel Dylan tense next to me as I fight not to laugh.

"Not only will she lose if she races with the Boss," he goes on, "but she'll also probably take out every other car, trying to make those turns. Now, can you please explain that to my daughter in a way that she understands, because every time I try it's like I'm talking to a wall?"

And then he shoots Dylan a pointed look before turning around and walking away.

Dylan just stands there silently until I glance at her out of the corner of my eye. "So you got all that, right?"

"Shut up."

I snort, and she folds her arms over her chest, pouting.

"You're just nervous, and you want a familiar car," I soothe, turning toward her. "You'll be fine."

"Yeah, better listen to Daddy like a good little girl," Kade teases. He and his brother walk around us to stand in front of her.

"Leave her alone, Kade," Hunter says.

But Kade just shoots him a cocky grin and turns his eyes back on Dylan, lowering his voice. "She can handle me."

Hunter shakes his head, while Dylan stares at Kade, looking defiant. He's always pushed her and teased her, and she always rises to meet the challenges he throws down. Like he sets the pace and she needs to try to keep up.

I don't like the way he eggs her on and constantly makes her feel like she needs to prove herself.

I doubt his twin likes it, either. They often fight, and Dylan's usually not far from the root of the problem.

Kade twists around with a gloating little smile on his face and walks to the bleachers where his friends are sitting. A girl hops down from the stands and slinks her arms around his neck, and he holds her hips, kissing her long and slow and putting on a nice show for everyone.

I wince, turning my eyes away. I've absorbed enough family bedroom knowledge for one day, thank you.

But then I see Dylan staring in his direction, her eyes pained.

Hunter watches her and then shakes his head, turning around to leave.

"Hunter?" she calls, stopping him.

He spins back around, looking agitated. "Yeah, what?"

She fidgets with her hands and stares at him, wincing a little. "I'm nervous."

He breathes out a quiet laugh, like he understands completely.

Walking up to her, he pulls his iPod out of his jeans pocket and yanks out the cord to his headphones that hang around his neck, and hands her the iPod.

"War playlist," he instructs. "Track five."

She lets out a relieved breath and smiles. "Thanks."

He nods, letting his gaze linger on her for a moment. Reaching out, he tips her chin up. "You're Dylan Trent. They're scared of you. Don't forget that."

She gives him a shaky smile and inhales a deep breath, squaring her shoulders again. "Got it."

He turns and heads to the bleachers, sitting next to Hawke, on the opposite side from Kade and his friends. Hunter is on the football team with Hawke and his brother, but he always sits apart, separate from everyone else.

"So how's that book going?" Dylan asks.

I glance over at her, remembering she left off after the kitchen floor scene.

She'd missed a lot, and my mind turns back to everything I've read tonight.

I'm confused about my mother and father's relationship. I keep trying to remember how they are now, solid and happy. It's hard to wrap my head around how much of a life everyone—my parents, Jared, Madoc, Jax—had before I was born.

My mom and dad eventually got their shit together. I've yet to finish the book, so I'm not sure how. But I hate their stupid choices and having to readjust everything I thought I knew about them. Also, I still have no clue who sent the book to me—or why it's important to them that I know the backstory to my parents' marriage. Is someone trying to stir shit up?

I also hate how I felt everything Kat was feeling. The uncertainty, the fear, the desire to stay with what's familiar even if you're miserable . . . the powerlessness.

I can relate.

"She's so weak," I finally admit, noticing the hint of self-hate in my voice. "She scheduled her entire life around him. Barely existed without him or had any interests or hobbies outside of him. He held her entire happiness in his hands."

Dylan leans back on her Silvia, the car her dad is making her race tonight, and stares ahead.

"It's not so unusual, is it?" she responds in a thoughtful tone. "How much we invest in wanting one person's love? In wanting them near and for them to think of us?"

I notice she's looking over at Kade's group, and it occurs to me that maybe I'm not the only one relating.

"No, it's not unusual," I agree. "I think too many people give others too much power over them. But if they're not missing you or thinking about you or wanting to be near you, then it's time to realize you're worth someone who does."

We stand there, the chaos of the crowds and music around us a distant hum as the conversation hangs in the air.

Lucas clearly forgot we all existed back here, and Kade uses Dylan like a pet puppy, enticing her to learn tricks for his amusement.

Dylan shivers and blows out a breath. "Well, that was deep," she jokes and turns to me. "All right, you're with me, right?"

I laugh. "No. I have zero interest."

I don't like the way she drives even when she's not racing, so she can do this without me riding shotgun.

"No argument," she protests. "No one will tell your dad. I promise."

I dart my eyes to the two drones hovering overhead.

Dylan follows my gaze. "Oh, yeah," she grumbles. "I forgot about those."

Jax thought drones would be a great feature to use for overhead shots and video, as well as an easier way to capture what went on out on the off-roading tracks. While I could avoid the GoPros on the cars, the drones would get shots of who's inside the cars, and my dad would eventually get wind of it.

"Clear the track!" Zack Hager, one of the track managers, booms over the speakers.

A flood of people disperses, clearing the area and heading to their preferred vantage point: the bleachers, their cars, or behind the fence. Music blasts into the air, and the huge digital clock counts down from thirty, letting the racers know they should be in their cars when it hits zero.

"Well, here I go." Dylan exhales a heavy breath and smiles excitedly.

I brush her chin with my fist, fake punching her. "Here's looking at you, kid."

She bumps my hip with hers. "Stay gold, Ponyboy."

I always laugh at our customary farewell, quoting *Casablanca* and *The Outsiders*, respectively.

She climbs into her race car, a tricked-out Nissan Silvia that was part of her father's collection, as I leave the track and position myself behind the chain-link fence.

Normally Jared prefers American muscle, but he was forced to broaden his horizons when he became such a big deal.

Madoc stands at my side with Fallon and their daughter, A.J., on his other side.

There are three cars lined up on the track, and I don't recognize the other two drivers, but they look young, so it should give Dylan a decent chance. They likely won't have much more experience than she does.

Engines fire up, and I feel the high-pitched whir vibrating underneath my feet.

"Any of this getting you excited?"

I look at Madoc, the ever-hopeful light shining in his eyes. "Like turned on, you mean?"

"No!" he bursts out, looking disgusted. "I mean like, do you finally want a car, so you can stop mooching off family for rides? Look at them." He waves his hand toward the track. "They're so hot. Don't you want that?"

"Pay him no mind," Fallon says, peeking around him. "He's about to orgasm."

I laugh, holding the waist-high fence with both hands. Exhaust pours out of the cars, the red stoplight shines bright in the warm evening dusk, and my stomach starts to flip a little. Dylan must be so nervous.

"Just go ride with Dylan," Madoc suggests. "Get a feel for the car."

"There's drones everywhere. You know Dad will find out."

"Dad dealt with me racing," he points out. "He can handle you doing a ride-along."

"She's not interested, Madoc," Fallon scolds. "Leave her alone." *Thank you.*

But then Madoc spits out, "She doesn't know what she is." And my smile falls at his harsh tone. "Her entire life has been played out from the palm of his hand since the day she was born. She can't make a decision without running to Daddy for his input."

My eyes flare.

"Madoc!" Fallon whisper-yells.

I jerk my head to face him, glaring. "What did you just say?"

He shrugs, a challenge in his smiling eyes. "I said you're a wimp."

That's it!

I storm back onto the track and head straight for Dylan's car. I open the passenger side door and turn to look at Madoc, shooting him my middle finger, because he's an invasive, interfering butt-nugget who needs to learn how to shut up.

Everyone in the vicinity starts laughing, Madoc included, and I dive into the car, anger raging beneath my skin.

Dylan stares at me with her eyebrows raised in a question.

I breathe hard and pull the seat belt down over my head, the shoulder straps descending in a V in front of me as I fasten it.

"I have places I want to travel and recipes I haven't tried. Stay on the road and don't kill me in this thing," I warn her.

But she just frowns at me. "Roads? Where we're going we don't need roads."

Oh, whatever. I roll my eyes at her *Back to the Future* reference.

She chuckles and plugs in the iPod. "War playlist," she says to herself, navigating the touch screen on her radio. "Track five."

The screen reads "'Stronger' by Through Fire," but as soon as the song starts, Dylan's door opens.

Jared leans in, looking at his daughter and holding out a necklace of some sort. It's some kind of charm or something on a ribbon.

She smiles and reaches out slowly, as if shocked. "Thanks," she says, her voice small.

He nods and gives her a half-smile, and then reaches over, pulling on her and my harnesses, making sure we're locked in. Kissing her forehead quickly, he closes the door.

"What is that?" I ask, watching her hang the charm on her rearview mirror.

"It's my mom's thumbprint," she answers. "It was a craft she made when she was little. My dad had it with him in every race for good luck."

The charm looks like an oval piece of clay no bigger than a quarter, and in the middle is a small fingerprint pressed into the piece, like a fossil. It hangs on a tattered, light green ribbon that looks ages old.

The announcer's voice shouts over the speakers outside, and I tense, hearing the crowd begin to go wild.

It's time.

Dylan squeezes the steering wheel, twisting the leather in her tight fist as she focuses out on the road, and the music starts to get going.

Outside, the engines rev over and over again, and Dylan begins rocking to the song Hunter gave her, her eyes narrowing and getting zoned in as she looks at the road like it's her bitch.

I gulp, feeling her engine rev underneath me, and when I glance at the cars on our left and right, the windows are tinted so dark I can't see a thing. *Shit.* A steel band wraps around my stomach, and my heart's in my throat.

Fuckin' Madoc.

The red light changes to yellow, the engines roar, and screams hit my ears, and then . . .

Dylan shoots off, and I slam back in my seat.

"Oh, my God." I damn near choke on my breath.

We race down the track, Dylan punching into third and then fifth, skipping second and fourth altogether, and I'm breathing hard, scanning the track for the other drivers.

The car to our left is only a hair behind, and the car to the right is head-to-head. Dylan jerks the steering wheel to the left, rounding the first turn, and then charges ahead, winding to the left and then the right for a few minor curves as she slams into fifth. The car on the right falls behind, but the white Honda on the left pulls up head-to-head with us.

The lights on the track dart past us like stars at warp speed, and I grab hold of the safety bar with one hand and my seat belt strap with the other.

A tight right lies ahead, and I glance at Dylan, seeing the muscles in her arm flexed and her jaw locked shut.

Is she going to slow down? We'll flip at this speed!

"Dylan."

The Honda pushes harder, not backing off, and it looks like it's trying to take the corner with us.

"Dylan," I warn again. She needs to slow down.

But instead, she punches into sixth, growling, "Screw this." And she slams on the gas, going faster as the music screams at us and fills the whole fucking car.

"Hell, yes!" she bellows. "Thank you, Hunter! Whoo!"

"Oh, my God!" I scream and cover my face with my hands, because I can't look.

My body vaults to the left as she turns right, the torque dragging us around the turn, and I scream as I keep my eyes squeezed shut under my hands.

I feel the car tip, and my head hangs to the side as an army of butterflies swarm in my stomach.

"Holy shit!" I burst out.

The car straightens, and I feel the tires on my side find the ground again as I jerk my head to look behind me. The other two cars are behind us now, the blue one way back.

Adrenaline floods my body, and I can feel every single hair on my arms stand on end.

I laugh, the rush of emotion too much to contain. "Go, go, go!" I urge her.

She smiles at me, and I turn the song on full blast, as high as it will go.

She takes the curves quick and smooth, rounds the next left and right and swings around the last quarter of the track.

The white Honda creeps up on her again, and all of a sudden something hits her driver's side window. We jump and Dylan swerves as we jerk our eyes to the window. She struggles with the steering wheel, trying to gain control of the car again.

"What the hell?" she growls.

A white glob of what appears to be wet paper sticks to her window, slowly falling off in little chunks.

"Asshole," she yells and presses the button, rolling down her window.

"Dylan, don't."

But she does it anyway.

The guy in the car next to us, young, with black hair and a cocky grin, snarls at her. "Weston sends its regards, Pirate bitch!"

I groan. *Really?*

Dylan turns her eyes back on the road and shifts into sixth again, speeding up.

"Dylan! Slow down!" I yell as she comes up to the last turn.

"No!" she growls, mumbling to herself. "Piece of shit asshole. This is a Falls track. He doesn't get to push us around."

Weston is one of Shelburne Falls High's rivals, and they only come over here to start shit. Them and St. Matthew's, a private school near Chicago. Sometimes the two schools even partner up to give our Pirate football team hell and anyone who goes to Shelburne High, for that matter.

"Yeah, go ahead and try to be your daddy, baby," the guy eggs her on. "You fall short!"

"Haven't you heard?" she shouts out the window at him. "I'm a mama's girl!"

And she speeds up even more.

"Dylan!" I yell, clutching the safety bar.

But she hits the corner, tries to turn, but the Honda's on the inside, not backing off. His turn widens, and she barrels into the brush, forced off the track. I spot his car, flying into the grass as well, and we bounce in our seats as we hit the rough terrain. The car skids to a halt, both of us lurching forward, against the harnesses as the car stalls.

My shoulder burns from where the strap rubbed, and I breathe hard.

"Oh, my God. Are you okay?"

I look over at Dylan, but she's already tearing off her seat belt and charging out of the car.

I fist my fingers several times, taking inventory to make sure I'm okay before I unfasten my belt, too.

Following her out of the car, I see everyone, a crowd of people, running down the track toward us.

To our right, the Weston asshole is crawling out of his heap, rubbing his head.

Jared rushes up and takes Dylan's face in his hands, scanning her head and body. "Are you okay?"

She's breathing hard, still shaken, but she nods.

Jared steps up to me. "You okay?"

"Yeah."

Madoc, Jax, Tate, Fallon, and Juliet follow, fawning all over us, checking our limbs for any bruises or scratches, a crowd of people surrounding us so tightly I can barely breathe.

Jared approaches the Weston kid, getting in his face. "If I weren't the adult, you'd be on the ground right now," he threatens. "Get the hell off this track and don't come back. You're banned."

The kid turns his face away, scowling as Jared leers over him.

"Dylan, are you okay?" Hunter steps up, pushing through the crowd.

But then I hear Kade's smooth voice off to the side. "Well," he says, grinning as he approaches the Weston guy. "Lucky for me, I'm not the adult."

And he throws a punch in the guy's face, sending the kid reeling back and crashing into Dylan. Both of them tumble to the ground, Dylan crying out as she lands on the gravel lining the track.

"Ow, shit," she cries.

"Kade!" Hunter yells at his brother and scrambles through the tight crowd to get down to her and pull the guy off her. Helping her up, Hunter turns her arm over, checking out the scrapes.

But Kade didn't even notice. "When you come to the Falls," he warns the guy, bending over to grip his collar, "bring backup, you fucking idiot."

"Enough!" Madoc grabs his son off the guy.

Kade drops the kid, and he and his friends sneer down at him.

"Everyone off the track!" Jax hollers, trying to push everyone back. "Now! We need room!"

Jared stares down at the Weston kid, planted on his ass. "Get your car, and get out of here, or I'll have it towed."

Everyone starts to disperse, and I check out Dylan's arm, making sure she's okay. The scratches are red and angry, but she's not bleeding.

As soon as nearly everyone is gone, Hunter lashes out at Kade. "What the hell is the matter with you?"

His brother just sneers. "Oh, why don't you grow a set, huh?"

Kade's friends snicker and laugh, but then Kade's eyes lock on Hunter's hands on Dylan's arms, and Kade pushes them off her. "Let her go. She's fine."

"Stop it," I finally chime in.

"Hunter, I'm fine," Dylan assures. "It's cool."

"See." Kade smiles at his brother. "She can handle it."

Hunter shakes his head, anger written all over his face.

"And the night's just getting started," Kade points out, looking around to his friends. "Road trip to Weston, anyone?"

The guys smile, mischief gleaming from their eyes, and I rub my hand down my face.

Hawke hooks an arm around Kade's neck, both of them staring at Dylan. "Under a Black Flag We Sail," he reminds her, reciting the Pirate motto.

"Hell yeah," one of the guys adds.

Dylan stares at Kade, his challenge clear. Weston deserved a retaliation, and was she game?

Hunter looks to her, narrowing his eyes. "Dylan, don't."

She glances at him before looking back toward Kade, and I see it in her eyes. The conflict. She knows what's right, but she wants what's wrong.

"I can take care of myself, Hunter." And then she steps toward Kade, Hawke, and their friends.

CHAPTER 10

"Hey, you all going home?"

Fallon pops her head up from the trunk and nods. "Yeah, we'll do some s'mores and let the kids catch fireflies. Try to shake off what happened tonight. Might need some wine, too." She laughs. "You want to come with? Madoc can drop you home later."

"Sure."

I'd already texted my parents, letting them know I was with Madoc and the rest of the gang and that I might crash at his house tonight.

I help Fallon load up a cooler, lighter now that she'd drained the melted ice. Opening the back door, I grab my bag and take Lucas's hat off the strap, turning it around in my hands before putting it on.

The truth is, I can blame my dad for holding me back as much as I want, but there are other things that keep me in my stalemate. That keep me nervous to leave for college in the fall, afraid I'll miss something back here. That keep me weak and invested in things that probably don't deserve my attention.

I clear my throat. "So how's Lucas doing?" I ask, trying to sound casual. "Have you talked to him much?"

"Only as far as work goes," she replies, pushing up her black-framed glasses. "When our firms cross paths and such. He just . . ." She pauses, thinking. "Established his own life out there, I guess. Madoc talks to him, though. He refuses to let Lucas get away."

I'm sure. Madoc likes to see his family grow, not shrink.

"I wonder what keeps him out there," I cage, knowing exactly what I was hinting at. "I guess he must like it. You don't miss him?"

"Of course, I do," she rushed to reply. "But . . ."

"But what?"

She finishes securing A.J.'s seat belt, closes the car door, and shrugs. "I know he'll come home," she states. "Everyone comes home. He left for a reason, and we might not completely understand it, but he obviously wants distance, and I'm respecting that. He knows we're here when he's ready."

"Well, he shouldn't assume everyone will just wait for him."

But Fallon frowns, studying me. "Who's waiting?"

I slow my hands, seeing the wheels in her head turning as she probably wonders what the hell I'm talking about. *Yeah. Who's waiting, Quinn?* No one else is putting their life on hold for Lucas Morrow.

I finish pushing the seat cushions into place in the trunk and quickly grab the picnic blanket off the ground. "I'll take this to Tate."

And I walk away, as fast as I can from her stare.

Tate is standing near her car, having just finished placing her sleeping son into his seat. I hand her the blanket that I recognized was hers.

"Thanks." She tosses it in the backseat.

"You all going to Madoc and Fallon's or going home?"

"Home," she replies. "James has a doubleheader tomorrow, and

I promised your brother 'cuddle time' tonight if he's going to be forced to sit through two baseball games tomorrow."

She did the air quotes around "cuddle time," and I laughed to myself, knowing what that meant.

"Tell Jared, racing is a sport, too," I correct. He found sports like baseball, basketball, and football boring, and while he wouldn't really be considered an athlete, there's skill and sweat in racing. He was into sports, just not ones that required running. Or standing.

Or fighting with other guys over a ball.

But he made every effort to show up for his kids. I think I respected him more for that. He put in the time, watching events that were tedious to him, because he really loved his children and wanted to do everything to support them.

"It's not hard for him to do things he doesn't like for his kids' happiness, is it?" I ask. "Probably because he had such a rough time with our mom. He knew what kind of parent he wanted to be. And what kind he didn't want to be."

She stops and thinks about it for a moment. "I'm sure that had something to do with it."

It's strange to me that he doesn't see our mom like I do. I understand it a little better now, but I always knew there was a divide between them. He's good to her, and they talk, but he's still the first one to pull away when she hugs him.

"Does he love her?"

He would lie to me and say yes. Tate would know the truth.

"I honestly can't answer that," she tells me. "There's a lot Jared doesn't talk about. He and Katherine kind of grew up together, and he definitely could've had it better as a kid. A lot better. But . . ." She pauses, finding her words. "I think he also realizes that everyone does things they regret, and while she'll never be able to erase the mistakes she made with him, she's not making the same ones anymore. She's been a great mom to you, she's a wonderful grandmother, and she's there for Jared when he decides he needs her."

Yeah. I guess that's all true. She's nothing with me like she is with him in the book.

"Why are you asking about this?" Tate brushes my hair behind my ear.

I shake my head, reaching into my bag and taking out *Next to Never*.

"This book is messing with my head." I hand it over to her, letting her see it.

She studies the front and back cover and opens it up, scanning a random page. "So strange."

"Yeah, I can't figure out who wrote it. I asked Juliet, since she's the only writer I know and she wouldn't lie to me, so . . ."

Tate continues reading a part, her expression turning thoughtful. "Hmmm . . ."

"What?"

She inhales a deep breath and closes the book, handing it back to me. "It's very personal, isn't it? Like whoever wrote it actually lived it."

What?

"What do you mean?"

She pushes off the car and stands up, looking at me. "Occam's razor," she says, referring to the scientific theory. "The simplest explanation is usually the correct one."

The simplest explanation. I let my eyes fall closed as realization hits.

Of course.

KAT . . .

"Jared!" I shouted up the stairs. "Dinner's ready!"

I rounded the bannister, bumping into the accent table along the wall. "Ow!" I whisper-yelled.

I dashed back into the kitchen and took the milk out of the refrigerator, pausing. Does he drink milk? Probably not.

Well, he should drink it, anyway. I plopped it down on the table,
blinking away the blur in my eyes.

The timer on the stove finally beeped, and I grabbed a pot holder
and opened the oven, taking out the frozen lasagna. I set it on top of
the stove, knocking down a pan on top. I jumped right as it hit the floor
at my feet.

"Hey."

I spun around, seeing Madoc Caruthers standing in the entrance
to the kitchen. It still unnerved me, seeing him around my house. Not
because I knew his father a lot more than he knew I did, but because
he'd hate me for his mother's sake if he ever found out about my past.

Jared would hate me, too.

"Hi," I finally forced out, turning back around. "I didn't know you
were here."

"Jared's changing," he explained. "He said I had to leave the room."

Ooookay.

I threw the dishcloth over my shoulder and took a sip of my wine.
I was still in my work clothes—a burgundy dress—and walking around
barefoot as I rushed to get dinner done. I'd gone out with some friends
after work—a few drinks—but I'd cut my plans short, trying to make
an effort and be home.

"Okay, are you staying for dinner?" I asked.

"Uh . . ." He glanced back at the stairs, and I could hear Jared
pounding down the steps. Madoc turned back to me. "It looks great,
actually, but I think we're heading out."

"What?"

Jared swept into the kitchen and opened the refrigerator. "We already ate," he informed me.

"Jared?" I threw the cloth down, anger creeping up. "I canceled
my plans to be home."

"I should thank my lucky stars." He tipped back the carton of orange juice, gulping it down.

"That's enough," I miffed. "Madoc is welcome to stay, but you are sitting down and eating. You're not going anywhere."

He tossed the carton back into the fridge, wiping his mouth with the sleeve of his hoodie. "Jax called, and he needs me. I'll be home late."

Pivoting around without so much as a look in my direction, he headed out of the kitchen, Madoc following close behind.

"You know, you could make an effort here," I said, not caring that his friend would overhear. "My entire world does not revolve around you."

Jared laughed. "Did it ever?"

And he opened the door, walking out, and Madoc closed the door behind them.

I stood there, staring at the door and listening to his car engine roar in the driveway before he sped off down the street.

He just left. Like anything I had to say didn't matter.

God, he hated me. He didn't even fight with me anymore. He. Just. Didn't. Care.

I rushed for the freezer, taking out the bottle of vodka inside. The clear alcohol swished in the chilled container like thick oil, and I threw off the top, not seeing where it landed.

I took a swig of the bottle, tears wetting my lashes as I squeezed my eyes shut. He doesn't hate me.

I took another drink and groaned, savoring the warmth of the alcohol coating my stomach. Tomorrow will be fine.

And I started sobbing, taking gulp after gulp after gulp, because I knew I was lying to myself.

There was no coming back from this.

I dragged my feet into the living room, carrying the nearly empty bottle in my hand, then I collapsed on the couch. The sweet oblivion fogged my brain so much, I saw Jase smiling down at me. He kissed the corner of my mouth, under my ear, and the corner of my eye, whispering in my ear.

"Katherine?"

The world shook, and I jerked, feeling like I was falling.

"Katherine, wake up," a male voice said, and I felt a fist squeezing my stomach as the nausea rolled like a wave through me.

I shoved at the hands, convulsing. "I don't feel good. Leave me alone."

I heard footsteps walk away and then come back before hands grabbed me and flipped me over. Something was shoved into my mouth, and I felt fingers press against the back of my throat. I gagged, feeling the pressure of everything coming up from my stomach as I coughed and heaved.

"No," I grunted, but it was too late.

Everything I'd drunk came pouring out, and I grabbed the small garbage can in front of me, emptying my stomach, coughing and sputtering as my gut wrenched. The vomit burned my throat, and I heaved again, feeling like someone was twisting a knife into my stomach.

"Oh, my God," I gasped, wiping my mouth on my sleeve. "What are you doing?"

I coughed, spitting out any remnants from my mouth. Blinking through the tears in my eyes, I finally noticed James, Tate's dad, standing above me.

"Jared's been arrested," he said.

I stopped breathing. "What?" And I scrambled to grab my phone on the end table, swiping the screen to check for messages.

There was nothing. Not even a missed call.

"He called you?" I asked, turning my eyes on him in question. My son didn't call me?

James simply handed me a towel to clean myself up and walked around me, toward the front door. "I called a judge I know at home. He assigned Jared a bail instead of waiting for court in the morning. Hurry up. I'll drive you."

Ten minutes later, we walked into the police station, my gross hair tucked into a ponytail under a baseball hat, and I'd changed out of my vomit-stained clothes and into a pair of jeans and a T-shirt.

It was past midnight, and James hadn't been able to tell me how long Jared had been here. He'd left our house around six, I think. Maybe it was earlier? I shook my head, trying to clear away the fuzz and fogginess of the night. The alcohol and the vomiting had wreaked havoc with my balance, and I couldn't stop the tips of my fingers from buzzing.

The station was quiet and nearly empty, but I spotted Madoc sitting on the chairs. As soon as he saw me, he rose out of his chair.

But I shot out my hand, stopping him. "I don't want to talk to you. Go sit down."

His face fell a little, but he sat back down and kept quiet. In all honesty, I knew Jared had most likely gotten himself into this, but the last possible person I wanted to see, other than Jase Caruthers, was his son right now.

Stepping up to the counter, I called to the female officer standing by her desk.

"Jared Trent is my son," I told her. "Where is he?"

"He's fine," she answered, approaching the counter and looking like this wasn't at all urgent for her. "He's in the back. Bail is fifteen hundred. Pretty cheap for this, actually." She sounded unhappy about that. I guess James's judge friend did us a favor. "You can pay it with the cashier."

And she jerked her head to the side, indicating another counter at a window down the hall.

"What happened?"

"He attacked a man named Vincent Donovan, apparently the foster father of his brother?"

I let my eyes fall, thinking. "Uh, I think so. I don't know."

Jared had a half brother named Jax, whom he met the summer I let him visit his father when he was fourteen. I wasn't sure who his foster parents were, though. I'd never thought to reach out.

The boy was only a year or so younger, and my suspicions must have been right. Thomas had been screwing around while we were still together. In fact, the boys were so close in age, Thomas must've gotten her pregnant not long after Jared was born.

Jax's mother split early on, and since Thomas was in jail, Jax was in foster care. I thought about taking him in, but I obviously couldn't parent the one kid I had, so that was out of the question. Right now, anyway.

"Well," the officer explained, "he claimed the man was abusing his brother, so he retaliated. The victim has three broken ribs and is in surgery right now for internal bleeding. He should be fine. Luckily."

"Victim," I sneered, repeating her term as I tried wiping the dizziness out of my eyes.

Who else rushed to protect Jax when that asshole hurt him? Jared, that's who.

And who rushed to protect Jared when his father beat the shit out of him two years ago?

No one.

I moved my arm and accidentally knocked my purse to the floor. James bent down to snatch it back up.

The clerk pinned me with a stare. "Are you drunk?"

I squared my shoulders and glared at her, taking my purse back from Tate's dad.

"My son is a good kid," I told her, ignoring her question.

She nodded, looking sarcastic. "I'm sure you did your best."

She turned and walked away, and I stood frozen, left with no words. What was I going to say? *You're wrong? I don't have to explain myself to you?*

Because, you know, Kat, your son's sitting in a cell, and you had no idea where he was or what he was doing. He stays out at all hours; he could be drinking and driving or getting someone pregnant, and he does whatever he wants for one simple reason.

He can. He barely has any parents, and that is something you do have to answer for.

We walked down the hall to the cashier, while Madoc remained quiet, but I could tell he was watching me. I paid the bail, barely able to sign the papers, because I was shaking so hard.

"It'll take a while to process," the clerk told me. "You can wait in the chairs."

"What happens now?" I asked.

"Well, your son will be given a date to appear in court. You'll need a lawyer."

I closed my eyes, exhaling a small cry as I turned away. "Lawyer," I repeated, whispering to myself. "This isn't happening."

"I can call my dad." Madoc approached. "He's in the city, but he can be here in the morning. He'll be able to get Jared out of this."

"No," I shot out. "Thanks, but I'll handle this."

He just stood there for a moment, looking like he wanted to argue but thought better of it.

All of us walked to the chairs and took our seats, Madoc giving me space and sitting a few chairs down.

James leaned forward, his elbows on his knees. "I don't know which judge his case will be assigned to, but I can talk to the one I know and see if I can work something out," he suggested. "It's his first offense, and I know he's a good kid."

I nodded, giving him my permission, but my mind was already racing ahead. What would life be like in five years?

I took the house all those years ago for Jared. For him to have a better life. But it seemed all my fears were coming true.

Where would we be in the next few years? Would Jared be in college? Would I be married to a man who loved me and curled up on the couch to watch TV with me every night? Would Jared let me hug him?

Would everything be completely different and we'd all suddenly have the perfect life and family?

No. Everything would be exactly the same, only worse. Jared would be in jail, like his father, because I'd abandoned and neglected him, and it was my fault Jared was here.

I took my phone out of my purse, my fingers hovering over the numbers, because I didn't want to go backward, but if this was my one chance to help my son . . .

"I should call Jase," I mumbled, giving in.

"Jase Caruthers?" James asked. "That kid's father, right?"

I glanced at Madoc, his face buried in his phone, and nodded.

James plucked my phone out of my hand and held it securely. "You don't need him," he maintained. "Let me try to deal with this."

"Why? Why do you want to help?"

He looked like he was searching for words. "Because I love Jared," he admitted. "He's a little shit, but I care what happens to him." He handed my phone back. "You don't need Jase Caruthers. You have friends. We'll handle this."

I squeezed the phone, meeting his eyes. Did he know? Jase and I had stopped seeing each other a few months after James and Tate moved in next door. Had he seen Jase there, coming in late?

Christ. What he must think of me.

"Jared's been falling apart for a long time," James spoke softly, careful not to let Madoc hear. "I kept my mouth shut out of respect, because I didn't feel it was my place, but every kid needs at least one person to think that the world rises and sets with them, and I don't think . . ."

I swallowed the knot in my throat, both of us finishing his sentence in our heads.

"Tate was that for him," James pointed out, "but they don't talk anymore, and Jared has only gotten worse. He needs help."

I nodded, staring out at the linoleum floor. And what had I said to him tonight?

My world doesn't revolve around you?

Did it ever?

His words washed over me, and I was fucking paralyzed. All these years I knew what I was doing. To myself and to him. This wasn't some goddamn epiphany, but for the first time I realized that I was more to blame for how he saw the world and how he behaved than his father. He was angry before I let Thomas see him. He hated me before that summer. He'd been pulling away his entire life.

No one should've come before him, and it wasn't that he didn't care that I'd always put myself first . . . No, he didn't even wonder why anymore. This was his life. I was his horrible reality, not his father.

I chewed my bottom lip, shaking my head. "I was his for so long that I didn't know who I was without him." Of course I referred to Jase, hoping James understood. "Why was I so weak?"

"Because we all eat lies when our hearts are hungry," he quoted.

I closed my eyes and allowed the quiet tears to spill over. Yeah. Jase didn't take anything I didn't freely give. And if it wasn't him or Thomas, it would've been someone else.

"I need to get well," I finally said.

"That's easy to say, isn't it?" he retorted. "The truth is, you have two choices here. Jared can stay with me while you're in rehab. Or Jared can stay with me for good."

I darted my eyes up to him.

"And you can leave him for his own well-being while you go off to drink for however long your body allows you stay alive to do so," he concluded.

I covered my eyes with my hands, breaking down once again as I shook with sobs and sank to rock bottom, feeling naked, cold, worthless, and empty.

Oh, my God.

I didn't want that. Of course, I didn't want that! I never wanted to stop being his mom.

But James was right. Jared would be worlds better off with him than he was with me.

While I cried and cried and cried, James remained quiet and let me come to terms with what had to be done.

"I love my son," I told him, wiping the tears from my face.

"Then prove it to him."

CHAPTER 11

KAT . . .

I stood in the next-door neighbor's garage, leaning down and affixing the wires to the new taillight, locking them in place, and popping the new cover back into position. I had no idea what had happened to this car, but when I left for rehab, James had a mint-condition Chevy Nova sitting in his garage. Now the car was nearly totaled, and Jared was over here working on it nonstop.

When I asked, James simply assured me Jared wasn't responsible for the damage.

I had to hand it to James. In the month I'd been away, he'd straightened Jared out and gotten him on track. His schoolwork was done, his grades were slowly improving, and he was making an effort to be civil with me, even if we still rarely spoke.

I did what I could do to bridge the gap. Nothing would fix all the wrongs I'd committed, but I wasn't going to stop trying. One day when Jared went next door in his spare time to work on restoring the car, I inched my way in and asked James if I could help, as well. And now, after a few weeks, Jared and I still weren't friendly, but he accepted my presence and I got to be close to him, so I took what I could get.

Soon, though, I feared the car would be done and he'd find more trouble to get into. Especially when Tate came back from her year abroad next summer. I wasn't sure what happened between them when they were fourteen and suddenly stopped being friends, but maybe this distance would be good for him.

I just hoped that shit wouldn't hit the fan again when she finally came home.

"All righty, that's done," I said, straightening and dusting off my hands on my jeans.

"Here, hold this," Jared requested, his tone clipped.

I walked around the front of the car and took the hose he handed me, the black, grainy grease staining my fingers.

He worked the wrench, tightening a notch.

"Don't make it too tight," I warned him.

"I know what I'm doing."

And so do I. You're making it too tight.

But I wouldn't say that.

Just then, as I knew would happen, the notch snapped, and I heard metal pieces fall down into the engine.

"Damn it," he growled in a low voice before standing up and snatching the hose away from me as if it was my fault.

I remained silent, like I hadn't noticed. "Okay," I said, realizing this was my cue. "I'm going to run and get us all some burgers and stop by Miller's for the bulbs for the dash. I'll be back soon."

He ignored me as usual, and I grabbed the shop cloth, wiping off my hands and sticking it in my back pocket as I left the garage. The weather was turning chilly, but we could still get away with T-shirts and no jackets.

I didn't want to admit it to Jared, because he would think I was try-ing to suck up to him, but getting under the hood of a car again felt really good. It felt like the old me, and I hadn't realized how much I'd tried to be someone else for too long. I was sober, I had a good job that had waited for me to get clean, and my son was safe and healthy.

I might still feel the loneliness, and Jase may still cross my mind every day, several times a day, but I had to be thankful for what was good and keep moving forward. I was still young, after all. I still wanted to do things.

Climbing into my car, barely even blinking at the smudges of grease on my jeans and fitted gray T-shirt, I tightened my messy bun and slipped on my sunglasses, deciding to head to Miller's first.

Jared usually handled any repairs on my car, so he was in here a lot. Me, not since he was small.

"Kat!" Deena beamed, holding out her arms as I walked into the store. "Damn, girl. Where've you been?"

I smiled, stretching over the counter to give her a hug. She'd worked here since her youngest started school, and I knew her boys loved it. They mooched off her discount. I knew Jared raced out at the Loop, but I wasn't sure if he'd ever run into her son, Nate. They were the same age.

"Hanging in there," I told her. I didn't care to mention my stint in rehab, but she probably already knew. We'd fallen out of touch in the past couple of years, but it wasn't a big town, and news traveled quickly.

"Jared is repairing James Brandt's Chevy Nova," I explained. "Do you have bulbs for the dash lights?"

"That's a '71, right?" she asked, probably remembering from all the trips James and Jared had made here already this fall. "You can take a look. If we don't have them, I can order them."

"Thanks."

Walking down the aisles, I scanned the parts and finally found the bulbs I thought they would need. If I was wrong, they were cheap, so no big deal. Seeing the bulbs for the dome light, I grabbed that as well, just in case.

"I can't it make it look like new," I heard a male voice whine. "Not like they do at the repair shop."

I smiled, recognizing Madoc's voice pretty well by now.

He was over at our place frequently, and I'd thought it would be hard to be around him, but he was so unlike his father. So cheerful and happy, always making jokes. Plus, he was Jared's only real friend, and I couldn't take that away from him.

Stepping around the corner, I saw him standing at a selection of spray paints, buffers, and other tools. Jase stood with him, both of them dressed casually, since it was Saturday. My heart picked up pace, but I simply took a deep breath and forced myself to relax again.

"I'm not paying for repairs every time you dent up your car at the Loop," Jase barked. "You can learn how to fix your own dents, damn it. If I knew you were going to be racing with this thing, I would've bought you a piece-of-crap Honda."

"Ugh." Madoc frowned. "I love you so much more when you just give me your credit card."

"Yeah," Jase mused. "Like I've never heard that from either of my wives."

Madoc snorted, breaking out in a laugh, and Jase smiled in turn, sharing the joke with him.

"I'm sorry," he rushed to add. "I love your mother. You know that."

Madoc shook his head. "I'm going to go check out tires."

"You just got new tires."

"I'm just looking," Madoc assured, disappearing around the corner.

I stared at Jase's back as he watched Madoc go, my heart still thundering but my breathing remained calm.

I knew I should turn around and walk away, but a larger part of me knew I could do this. I had to do this. Running, hiding, avoiding anything difficult . . . that was my past. Jase was only as dangerous as I let him be.

He'd made good on my request all those years ago. Other than the phone call after we'd picked up Jared and Madoc at school freshman year, he'd left me alone. He wasn't a threat, and I wasn't going to make him one. Our sons were friends, and I wasn't going to let our past interfere with that. It was high time Jared stopped paying for my mistakes.

We could be civil and move past this.

"Hello," I spoke up.

He twisted his head toward me, standing still as I approached with the two small packages in my hand.

"Hey." His eyes fell down my clothes, and I suddenly remembered that I was absolutely filthy. Awesome. Every woman's fantasy to see your ex with flyaways spilling out of your bun, grease stains on your hands and clothes and probably streaked across your face, too.

"Yeah, I know." I laughed at myself. "I'm a mess."

He swallowed hard and shook his head. "I wasn't going to say that."

I noticed the spray can and a couple of other bottles tucked in his arm, and I gestured to them. "Looks like your boy's costing you about as much as mine is costing me."

"Yeah." He nodded absently, looking like he barely heard me. "I . . . I heard Jared's helping repair James's car."

"Something to keep him busy," I explained, knowing that Jase probably knew about Jared's arrest from Madoc. "He's staying out of trouble now. I'm not sure he's okay, but he's better." And then I looked away, feeling guilty again. "I did a lot wrong with him."

"Yeah, well," he replied, looking somber. "Madoc hasn't been a piece of cake, either. He keeps a lot buried and just puts on a good show."

Yeah, I wouldn't know about that. I always knew when Jared was ready to lose it. But I could imagine it was just as frustrating to try to communicate with a child who lied to you about what they were feeling, too.

"You're doing well?" he asked, moving closer.

His scent drifted over me, and I held my breath, afraid of the attraction for a moment.

"Yeah," I replied. "I'm doing great. I'm a managing partner of the accounting firm now, and I . . ." I laughed at myself, kind of embarrassed, "I got it in my head that I'd try to run a half marathon next spring, so I'm trying to get in shape."

Actually, anything to keep me busy. Anything to keep me from being bored and thinking too much.

Jase held my eyes, and drew in a deep breath.

"And you?" I asked. "How've you been?"

But he didn't seem to hear me. His hand drifted toward me and reached my neck, and I stilled as his thumb rubbed at a spot there.

His chest rose and fell in heavy breaths, and he seemed mesmerized. Pulling his hand away, he rubbed his thumb over his fingers, staring at it. "Grease," he explained.

Flutters hit my stomach, but I steeled myself.

It will never be over. I heard his words in my head. I blinked long and hard.

No.

Opening my eyes, I forced a smile and returned the favor, giving him a once-over and taking in his blue cargo shorts and white polo shirt.

"What are you wearing?" I asked.

His eyebrows pinched together in confusion, and he looked down at his clothes. "Nothing. It's just a . . . golf polo, I guess."

"You don't golf."

"Things could've changed," he shot back, joking with me. "Why? You don't like it? I'm told it's fashionable."

"It's not."

I turned around and scanned the clothing, sifting through the coveralls and aprons, finding the T-shirt selection. I knew Jase owned T-shirts, but they were the sixty-five-dollar kind from Ralph Lauren.

Picking up a gray one that probably only cost ten bucks, I tossed it to him.

"Your shoulders are one of your best features," I told him. "Keep it simple. Women don't want a man who looks like he'd screw them on twenty-four-hundred-dollar sheets, Jase." I mocked. "They want a man who looks like he'd bend them over a kitchen table."

His eyebrow shot up, and all of a sudden he didn't look nervous anymore.

"Remember," I taunted. "They marry the lawyer. They screw the plumber."

He laughed, but his eyes turned heated, and he took a step forward, looking like he'd just been challenged and he was accepting.

"Is that right?" he responded. "Because I seem to remember someone saying how good those sheets felt on her twenty-first birthday." And then he shrugged. "But I guess that was my imagination."

I offered him a nervous smile and began retreating as he inched into my space. Yeah, I shouldn't have joked with him about this. Maybe we could be civil for our sons' sakes, but moving up to banter had escalated things too fast. Those sheets had felt great, but I wasn't ready to remember that right now.

We stood chest to chest, everything from so long ago flooding back to swamp me. His eyes hovering down over me, his smell, the heat of his body . . .

"It comes back so easily, doesn't it?" I mused.

He stared down at me. "It never left."

Reaching out, he held my face in his hand. "I've dialed your number thousands of times," he whispered. "And every time I forced myself to hang up, I wanted to fucking break everything around me."

He leaned in, his shaky, hot breath falling on my lips.

But I turned my head. "I can't."

"I know." He hovered over my mouth.

And then he dropped his eyes, a hint of sadness in them. "I'll always love you, Kat."

I nodded, feeling old tears well up. "I know." I pulled away, forcing a weak smile. "I'm sorry. I shouldn't have teased you. Old habits die hard, I guess."

But not too hard.

I paid for my items and left the store, still feeling the heartbreak, but reassured that I was finally strong enough to walk away.

JASE . . .

The rain pummeled my windshield as I sat in my car, outside her house. Madoc had gone home to work on his car, and I'd been driving around, cruising every street except for Fall Away Lane. I couldn't stand to be home. I didn't want to see my office, my bed, or all the photos on the wall of a fictitious life I'd invented. All the pictures of me smiling through the lies I'd been living for forty-two years.

Stepping out my car, I walked through the downpour, not caring that I was getting drenched as I climbed the steps of her porch.

This was supposed to be my house. The house I was going to live in when I married her, and if I'd had the guts to do what I wanted to do from the moment she was nineteen and slapped me in the face, calling me an asshole, we'd be here with a house full of kids, and I wouldn't hate myself so much.

Sacrifices and decisions aren't hard for good people. For selfish ones like me, they're hard until they're no longer yours to make.

For people like me, we don't truly realize what we want until the choice is taken away. Only then do we know.

I knocked on the door, a knot in my throat as I waited for her to answer. When the door opened, though, it was Jared looking at me. Dressed in a black hoodie and flipping his keys around his fingers as a little Boston terrier stood at his feet, he looked up at me with interest.

"Hey," he said. "Madoc's not here."

"Yes, I know. I'm not looking for Madoc."

His eyes narrowed on me, and I immediately wanted to shrink. I didn't know how he did that, but I half expected him to back me up out the door and send me on my way.

Instead, though, he didn't press. "Mom?" he called behind him. "I'm going to go visit Jax."

"Okay," I heard her reply. "Be careful driving."

Jared tipped his chin at me and left the door open as he walked around me, the dog racing after him and both of them hopping into a black Mustang. I walked into the house, and before I closed the door, I heard his engine fire up. I was sure I had him to thank for getting Madoc into cars and racing.

Or him to blame.

The house was dim, the glow of a few lamps shining in the living room and family room. I continued down the hall toward the kitchen, hearing Kat move around in there. New pictures lined the walls, and I also saw that she had painted the living room and added some new bookshelves.

As I stopped at the entryway to the kitchen, I watched her at the sink, and it looked like she was peeling potatoes.

I slipped my hands in my pockets and took her in, remembering all the times I had just stood and watched her in the past. I loved to see her move around the house, making pancakes or putting laundry away or cooking dinner. I pretended that she was mine and I could stay forever and this was our life.

She moved her foot behind her ankle, scratching it with her toe, and the sudden desire to touch her was almost too much. She'd changed into a clean pair of jeans with a white shirt, and her hair was down.

Turning off the water, she grabbed the hand towel and wiped off her hands before spinning around.

Locking eyes with me, she let out a little gasp. "Jase."

I held her gaze, having no fucking clue what I was doing or what I wanted to tell her, except everything.

I inhaled a long breath and looked down, because I needed to find my words, and I couldn't do that staring at her.

"When I was four," I told her, "I walked in on my father with another woman." I finally raised my eyes, seeing her holding the towel as if frozen in the middle of drying her hands. "I don't remember much, but I still have the image, and for the longest time, I thought maybe I imagined it or it was a dream that had stuck with me." I leaned against the door frame and kept going. "And then when I was sixteen I saw him touch my mother's best friend at a party when he didn't know anyone was looking. My mom knew. She knew everything. And still she constantly put on a brave face, trying to act like everything was fine and we were the perfect family."

Her eyes shifted from side to side, hopefully absorbing what I hadn't shared with anyone.

"I promised myself I would never do that to my family," I explained. "I would never become my father. But then I met you, and I knew. You were the girl I was going to love." My chest tightened, and I had to force the words out. "So I deluded myself. I told myself I wasn't him. That I had good reasons for doing what I was doing. I was keeping my family together for my kid, doing what was best for him. I needed you. I kept telling myself that. I was falling apart, and what we had was special. You were the only one, after all. It wasn't like I was a serial cheater. I wasn't him."

Tears pooled in her beautiful brown eyes, and I was fucking lost. God, I felt weak.

I licked my dry lips and continued, "And then one day, years ago, Madoc answered my cell phone, and it was you calling. I was so angry, I yelled at him. I saw me, four years old, all over again. He couldn't find out, I told myself. He couldn't look at me the way I looked at my dad. He wouldn't understand. I couldn't be a failure to him. He had to love me," I gritted out, pain wracking my body, because I could still feel everything that tore me and her apart.

She clutched the towel in her hands, listening.

"The truth is," I said, feeling my eyes grow thick with tears, "I knew what I should do, what I wanted to do, but I was afraid of being a failure, not realizing I became one anyway."

I rushed forward and held her head in my hands, rubbing circles on her cheeks.

"I should've let Maddie go and been with you and only you," I admitted. "I should've moved you into my house and made you my wife and had you in my bed every damn day." I leaned down, nose to nose as her breath shook with silent tears. "I should've married you years ago, and Madoc and Jared would've grown up with two loving parents."

I took her lips in mine, the pain of sixteen years replaced with the hunger that was always between us. I would always need her because she made me feel alive and she expected more from me than anyone in my life other than my son. She made me want to be better, and while I had always failed her and never fought to keep her, that would end today. I didn't want to wake up to another day without her.

"I'm miserable," I told her. "Seeing you today hit me like a truck. Every day I spend without you, I'm miserable. And maybe it's what I deserve, but I'm so sorry I never gave you what you needed. I'm sorry I treated you badly for so long."

I wrapped my arms around her and pulled her into me, burying my face in her neck and scent, holding her to my body.

"Marry me," I whispered.

"You're already married," she pointed out.

"I left her," I admitted. "Months ago. She's moved out, and I'm working on the divorce. I love you, and I don't want to waste another day."

She pulled back, her hands cupping the back of my neck as she peered up at me. "Why now? After all this time?"

"Because seeing you today was when I realized that I couldn't hurt you anymore," I admitted. "You're stronger, and maybe . . . just maybe . . . I won't be bad for you. Maybe I don't have to feel so ashamed for what I did to you and force myself to stay away."

Her eyes glistened. "I'm not ready."

"Do you still love me?" I asked, barely a whisper. Because that was all I needed to hear.

"Yes."

I kissed her again, long but soft, savoring the feel of her lips and her in my arms.

"When I come back for you, it will be forever," I told her, releasing her and backing away. I had to leave now before I pushed her too fast and made another mistake. "Tell me it's not over."

She held on to the sink behind her, her chin trembling, but then she finally gave me a small smile, and said, "I guess we'll see."

I turned and walked out the door, the feel of her still coursing under my skin.

I'd take that challenge.

CHAPTER 12

Racing into the police station, I hold the door open for Fallon as she ushers A.J. through ahead of her, and we all hurry inside.

They're not hurt. If they were hurt, they'd be in the hospital, not the police station.

After we make it through the second set of doors—heavy wooden ones—I spot Jared at the counter with Tate, while their son, James, sits on a black cushioned chair, playing with one of his parents' phones.

"What happened?" I burst out, hoping he just leads with "they're okay."

Jared turns around, speaking to me but glaring at the cops behind the counter. "They won't tell us," he growls and then speaks directly to a female cop who's rounding her desk. "I want my kid!"

"Jared, calm down," she scolds, sticking a file folder in a tray on a desk. "She's perfectly fine. As soon as Madoc and Jax get here, we'll bring them out."

He shoves at a piece of paper sitting on the counter, sending it floating to the floor, and scowls at her before walking away.

"Don't make me remind you what the inside of my cells look like, boy!" a burly cop with a double chin and white hair barks at Jared from behind the woman.

Jared's eyebrows come together and he folds his arms across his chest, but he shuts up. If I weren't so worried, I'd laugh. After reading and learning what I have tonight, I realize what I don't know about my brothers could probably fill a stadium.

Just then, Madoc and Jax storm through the door, Juliet right behind them, and everyone goes straight for the counter.

"Barry!" Madoc calls to the old cop who scolded Jared.

The man finishes talking to another officer and makes his way over to us. A.J. and James sit on the chairs, playing on the phone. The rest of us are crowded into the counter.

"The kids are fine. No one's hurt, and you can take them home tonight."

"What happened?" Jax speaks up.

"Kade happened," Barry the Cop answers, arching an eyebrow. "Did Dylan have a scuffle at her race tonight?"

Jax nodded. "Yeah, some kid ran her off the track. He won't be racing there again."

"No, I doubt he will," the officer rushes to agree, sounding sarcastic. "Your kids—and I imagine they had more help—dug a wide but shallow grave on Weston's football field. They stole the kid's car, drove it into the hole, and buried it. They even made a nice little tombstone for it."

Snorts go off around the group, and I stifle laughter as Tate covers her amusement with her hand. Jared, Madoc, and Jax struggle not to smile.

Of course they're proud. Of course.

"This isn't funny," the officer bites out.

"It's a little funny," Madoc mumbles, avoiding the officer's eyes like a naughty child.

"Well," Barry goes on, giving Madoc a sinister smile, "let's see how you take this news then. When the boy found out, he and his friends chased them into town, and your kids offered a rematch right here on our city streets. Kade, Hawke, and Dylan, at least," he specifies.

I imagine Hunter was only along to make sure Kade didn't do anything that would get Dylan hurt.

"Things escalated," he continues, "three cars were sideswiped, and your old Boss"—he looks at Jared—"is presently sitting in Ducane's Ice Cream Shop after your daughter crashed it right through the huge bay window. "

"Oh, my God!" Tate bursts out, looking scared.

But the cop holds up a hand. "She's fine," he assures. "Thankfully, the shop was empty at the time, too, so no one got hurt." And then he fixes his eyes on Madoc. "But I've got lots of angry parents calling, Madoc. There were people on those streets tonight."

Madoc drops his eyes, his amusement gone. He, Jared, and Jax all look a little repentant, because they know the cop has a point. It's all fun and games until someone gets hurt.

Someone's life could've been forever changed tonight, because Kade—and I have absolutely no doubt this was all his idea—thinks he's untouchable.

"Now, the boy's dad is Kurt Rhomberg," Officer Barry goes on, speaking to Madoc, "so he's not pressing charges out of respect for you, but he will expect that you take care of the damages to his son's car. As well as the estimated forty grand in other damages your kids caused tonight."

He says the last piece to all of the parents, and Madoc digs his thumb and middle finger into his eyes, rubbing them, while Jared combs his hand through his hair.

"Christ," I hear someone growl under their breath.

Forty thousand dollars. *Shit.* Officer Barry just served a big, heaping dose of reality, and everyone is shutting up now.

"And out of respect for all of you," he says, "I won't take their licenses. But if there's a next time, they'll be riding the bus for the rest of their lives."

Madoc nods, looking contrite, and says, "Of course. Can we see them now?"

"We have them in a room. I'll get them."

"No," Madoc shoots back. "Leave them there. We need to talk to them first."

"Right now?" Fallon questions him.

But he just ignores her. All seven of us trail to the back of the station, A.J. and little James staying with a police officer, as we follow Barry. But when he stops and opens the door to one of the interview rooms, a flood of shouting and furniture scraping against the floor hits us, and all I can see is the cop and Madoc rushing into the room, pulling Hunter off Kade, who's backed against the wall and bleeding from his mouth.

"Oh, my God," Juliet breathes out.

She quickly pushes past me, into the room, and rushes for Hawke, who's bending over with his hands on his knees and breathing hard like he was trying to break up the fight.

We all hurry in, and I close the door behind me as Tate and Jared rush for Dylan, who's standing behind Hawke and looking like she's about to cry while Jax picks up the chairs that have toppled over.

Hunter is panting and glaring at Kade as he tries to yank himself out of his father's grasp. "She could've been killed! You're a piece of shit!"

"Come on, you little bitch!" Kade holds out his arms, begging for more.

"Enough!" Madoc bellows, pulling tighter on Hunter. "What the hell is the matter with the both of you?"

Kade moves closer to his brother, threatening his space and unwilling to back down, but then Jared is there, staring down at Kade, walking into him and forcing him back again. Kade's jaw flexes as he stares up at his uncle, but he finally drops his glare and stops.

Everyone is damn near hyperventilating, but slowly everything starts to calm down. Hunter stops fighting against his father's hold, and Hawke is resting against the wall, looking exhausted.

When Madoc lets go of Hunter, he comes to stand between his sons and looks back and forth at both of them. "What the hell? You both realize that 'mayor' is an elected position, correct?"

The police officer chuckles, and I realize I haven't even thought about that. Everything that happened tonight could hurt Madoc's campaign—not that his career comes first, but it won't look good when Madoc can't even keep his children in line.

"I think we should just take them all home," Tate says, Dylan's face buried in her neck. "It's late."

"Yes, let's sort through this tomorrow," Fallon adds.

But Madoc just shakes his head. "No. Everyone over here." He points in front of the table. "Now!"

I jump, noticing a vein on his temple and his face getting red. I've hardly ever heard Madoc get angry. I've seen him get frustrated in the garage or yell at Jared or Jax, but he rarely gets pissed like this.

Hawke, Kade, and Dylan round the table, standing in front of it, while Hunter lurks behind them, everyone silent.

Behind me, the police officer leaves the room, quietly closing the door behind him.

Madoc stares at the kids, shaking his head. "You know what? You've all had it made," he tells them. "You've had the very best of what we could give you. Loving, supportive, two-parent households, family vacations, phones, iPads, clothes, cars . . . You were spoiled!"

I glance at the others, my brothers and their wives, and see them all listening. No one has a problem that Madoc is yelling at their kids.

"And we knew," Madoc went on. "We knew this would happen, but, for some reason, we couldn't not give you those things. How were we supposed to withhold anything that made you happy? We just thought you'd learn some goddamn humility. We thought you'd learn how to be grateful for everything you have."

Dylan and Hawke are avoiding his eyes, looking contrite, while Kade is still scowling, and Hunter's fists are balled up, both of the twins looking angry.

But they're quiet.

"And we were no better at your age," Madoc continues. "But we did know that some things couldn't be replaced. Not everything is disposable." And then he looks over at Fallon, his voice growing quiet. "You only learn that lesson through loss, and that is something you kids have never known. Not one of you."

He draws in a deep breath and crosses his arms over his chest. "I think it's time you all start learning that lesson. You have two choices," he bites out. "You're too destructive together. Hawke graduates in a year, so let him and Dylan stay put, but my boys can switch schools—"

"What?!" Hawke bursts out.

"No—" Dylan follows, standing up straight and looking suddenly worried.

"That's crazy!" I hear Tate say.

"Or . . . ," Madoc interjects, because he's not done. "You all can take your punishment and build some goddamn character if you want to stay together."

"Yes," Dylan answers quickly. "Don't send them away."

Madoc can't tell Jared and Jax what to do with their own kids, but Dylan and Hawke aren't toxic together anyway. They don't need to be separated.

But I'm sure that, even though Hunter and Kade are destructive together, he doesn't want them separated. They're brothers, after all. And maybe, just maybe, he figures taking them out of

Shelburne Falls and away from certain "distractions" will solve their problems.

Ideally, though, that's a last resort. This is everyone's home, and we all belong together.

"You all owe about forty grand in damages, so what are you going to do?" Madoc asks.

Dylan speaks up. "We'll pay it."

"Oh, you'll pay it," Jared repeats in a humorous tone. "Will that be Visa or MasterCard?"

"We'll pay it out of our college funds and then we'll work to put the money back," she clarifies.

Madoc nods. "What else?"

"Curfew by ten?" Kade offers.

But Madoc just laughs, his chest shaking as he turns to Jared. "That's cute," he tells him. "They actually think they're allowed outside of the house besides work and school." And then he turns to face Kade. "Grounded. The entire summer."

Kade's chest visibly caves, but Hunter remains silent.

"What else?" Juliet joins in.

"Extra chores?" her son suggests.

"Keep going," I hear Tate say, looking at Dylan.

"We'll volunteer at the hospital a few hours a week," her daughter adds.

"And?" Jax folds his arms over his chest.

"And we'll work for free at the summer camp as soon as school lets out," Kade grumbles as the consequences get heavier and heavier.

"And?" Madoc keeps going, looking at Hunter.

But it's Dylan who speaks up. "We'll write letters of apology to the people whose property we damaged and to the city."

"And?" Tate says.

"And we will earn back your trust," Dylan adds. "We're so sorry."

Madoc steps up to Kade, glowering down at his son who doesn't look sorry at all. Just pissed that he got caught.

"Are you?" he questions in a hard voice. "Are you sorry? Because if it's not fair, I can enroll you at Weston on Monday."

Kade looks like he bit into a lemon, but he finally nods, mumbling, "It's fair. We'll do it."

"Not me," another voice speaks up, and Madoc raises his head to look at Hunter.

I pinch my eyebrows together in confusion and shock. *What?*

"I'll pay for the damages and work to replace the money out of my college fund," his son says, "but I'm taking option A."

"What?" Fallon moves forward.

"Hunter, no," I hear Dylan plead, her frightened eyes on him.

Madoc's entire body tenses, and he doesn't say anything as he stares at his son.

Hunter wants to leave. Switch schools. He actually wants to go?

"We'll talk about this at home," Madoc says, turning away.

"There's nothing to talk about," Hunter insists. "You said it was an option."

Kade, who'd been silent, finally turns his head to look at his brother, something I can't place going on in his eyes. "You want to leave?"

For all the arguing and the fighting, Kade doesn't sound happy.

Hunter locks eyes with his dad, his demeanor eerily calm. "I was thinking St. Matthew's."

"That's our biggest rival," Hawke blurts out. "Are you fucking kidding me?"

"Hey!" Jax barks at his son's language.

Hawke looks back down, shutting up.

"I could stay with Grandpa Monday through Friday," Hunter tells Madoc. "It's only an hour away from here. I'll be home on weekends."

But Madoc shakes his head. "You are not living . . . with him."

"So you were bluffing?" Hunter throws back.

Oh, boy.

Yeah, Hunter could enroll at Weston and still live at home, but if he wanted to go to St. Matt's, he wouldn't be able to make that commute every day. He'd have to live with Ciaran, Fallon's father, in Chicago.

And despite the fact that Madoc and Ciaran get along semi-well, Madoc still doesn't want his son living with an ex-gangster.

Hunter pushes off from the table and walks up to his father, dropping his voice. "I need to get out of here," he tells him in a near whisper. "I need something of my own. Please."

My heart goes out to him, because I know what he's feeling. Kade rules the school. He's always the one everyone notices and the life of the party. He feeds off being the center of attention, and Hunter doesn't ever seem to be able to carve out his own niche. He feels out of place and invisible.

I can't see Madoc's face, but I can tell he's staring at his son, not saying anything, probably because he doesn't want him to go, but he also doesn't know how to fix everything that's making Hunter unhappy.

"Fine with me." Kade finally breaks the silence, the hint of pain in his voice that I heard earlier now gone. "Maybe now he'll stop touching my shit."

I close my eyes for a split second. Jesus. He's talking about Dylan. I know he is.

She's the wedge between them.

Hunter's eyes turn dark, and a loaded smirk I've never seen before curls his lips. He turns around, and I'm afraid he's going to hit Kade again, but he simply walks up to his brother, calm and confident.

"I'll see you on the field in the fall," he says, tossing it out like a threat.

Kade straightens, both brothers the same five foot eleven as they glare at each other. "Damn right you will."

Madoc and Fallon say nothing, but I can see their heavy breathing as if they're struggling for air.

I know Fallon and how she thinks.

She'll get the boys home. Talk to them. Everything will calm down and all of this will pass. Hunter will see reason.

Madoc, on the other hand, has a plan for every contingency, but if he's silent, then this was a twist he didn't plan for. He was bluffing about switching schools, and Hunter called him on it. He's not sure what to do, or how to fix it. Not yet.

As we leave the police station, I finally understand how hard it is to be a parent. To watch your kids make mistakes.

They won't learn until they learn, and I know Madoc is struggling. But maybe sometimes the hardest part isn't what to say and when, but rather, when to say nothing at all.

And how to know when it's that time.

I reach down and clutch the bottom of my bag, feeling the book and diary inside.

Talking isn't always the answer.

There are many other ways to teach your kids their lessons, after all.

I'm making my way through the house, toward the kitchen, when I hear the clock chime midnight, and my eyes burn with exhaustion. Today's soccer game feels like so long ago.

Passing the photos in the hallway, I see the ones from my parents' wedding—a charming, small, and candlelit ceremony in a rustic barn north of here—Jared and Tate's wedding—which seems even more special to me now that I know more about their past—Fallon and Madoc—who have no photos from their wedding but instead a great shot of her on his shoulders at the top of Mount Fuji on their honeymoon, arms spread wide and smiles on their faces with the clouds below them . . .

And Jax and Juliet, who finally gave my mother the big family wedding she'd wanted for at least one of her kids.

I hear voices coming from the kitchen, and I head there, knowing I'll find my mother.

"We spent how much in New York?" my father asks, sounding shocked. "Jesus, we didn't go to Paris! What the hell?"

I snort, seeing him leaning over my mother as she sits in her little desk along the wall, both of them studying the screen of the laptop. She's no doubt doing the family bookkeeping, and I hear my dad having the same meltdown every month.

"Don't look at me," my mom says. "I bought one pair of shoes. You spend more money on Fifth Avenue than I do, Pretty Boy."

"Pretty Boy?" he blurts outs. And then he reaches for her, squeezing her cheeks as he leans in and kisses her.

She laughs, trying to twist away from him. "Stop it!"

I take a minute to lean my shoulder into the door frame, watching them.

And I see it. I see Jase and Kat, their playfulness and flirting, the ease and comfort they have in each other. My father and how much he loves her and my mother and how she resembles that girl in the garage, working on his car. The way they complement each other and know when to bend. All of these things I never noticed before.

My dad releases her and starts studying the spreadsheet again. "Well, can we deduct some of this? We talked about work while we were there, right? Just claim the trip as a business expense."

"No!" she protests and swats his hand away from the mouse. "Go away. I don't mess with your case files. Stay away from my numbers. They're all organized."

He smiles and stands up straight.

"Hey," I say when his eyes fall on me. "How's it going?"

He sighs. "Fine. Your mother's a good woman," he muses,

heading to the refrigerator. "She keeps me out of jail by talking me out of tax fraud."

"Damn right," Mom adds. "You make enough. You can pay your taxes, cheapskate."

I watch them, smiling, and wonder what would've happened if my mom had never gotten help. If my dad had never gotten a divorce from Madeline or Patricia. If they'd never stopped trying to hold each other up.

I realize that now.

No one else can make you happy, and putting that expectation on the other person will doom both of you. You don't look at someone and say "*you* can make *my* life better." You look at them and say "*I* can make *your* life better." Be a blessing, not a burden.

I clear my throat. "May I talk to Mom for a few minutes?"

My dad pauses mid-sip, staring at me. "Um, sure." He nods, his eyes shooting to my mom. "You'll tell me everything she says later, right?"

"Ha-ha," she mocks. "She keeps my secrets. I'll keep hers."

"That better not be true." He gives her a scowl, but I can see his grin as he heads out of the room. "I'll be in my office."

Mom types quickly on the computer, pounding the final key with some extra punch, and then turns to me, waiting.

Inhaling a deep breath, I reach in my bag and pull out the book, setting it on her desk, right in front of her.

Her eyes fall on the cover and stay there, no surprise registering on her face at all.

"You had Pasha mail me the book?"

She hesitates, but finally gives a small nod. "I knew you'd figure it out."

Pasha lives in Toronto, setting up Jared's production line, and my mother didn't want me to see the book postmarked from Shelburne Falls. I guess she wanted me to read it before I started hunting down who sent it?

Occam's razor.

Reaching back into my bag, I pull out the diary from her closet and plop it down on top of the novel. "Well, whoever wrote it had to have access to this. You, right?"

I couldn't believe she'd trust anyone else with all those intimate details.

"Yes," my mom admits, turning her swivel chair to face me completely. "Juliet helped me. She didn't want to lie to you, but I asked her to hold the truth, if you came to her, until you were finished with the book. I wanted you to read it first."

The strange look from Juliet makes sense now. She didn't technically write it, but she did know about it.

"You could've told me all of this," I chided. "Did you think I'd hate you? Or Dad?"

"No," she rushes out, leaning over to take my hand as I sit down in the chair at the table. "When I found out I was having a daughter, Quinn, I honestly wasn't happy. I was worried. I was so afraid I'd have another version of me, making the same mistakes, crying over the same types of men, and making bad decision after bad decision to make someone else happy. Someone who doesn't deserve her."

I'm not sure if she's talking about Jared's dad or mine, but I keep quiet and listen, anyway.

"That's the hardest thing about being a parent," she explains. "Living through heartache, bearing your struggles, learning the hard lessons the hard way, and enduring years of climbing a wall only to fall back down and have to start all over again . . ." She holds my eyes, and her voice is weighted with sadness. "The tears, the waiting, the zero sense of who the hell you are, and then one day . . ." Her voice grows lighter and she looks happy. "You wake up, and finally you're exactly the person you've always wanted to be. Strong, decisive, resolute, kind, brave . . . But then you also look in the mirror and you're fifty-eight."

An ache hits my chest, and I can imagine a fraction of what

she's talking about. All those years, all the wasted time . . . She finally grew up but at a huge expense.

"And when you have a child," she goes on, "it's like watching yourself start all . . . over . . . again. You want them to make the most of every moment and be the type of person you've finally become, but that's the cruel joke of youth." She smiles sadly. "No matter what I tell you or share with you or try to teach you from everything I've learned, it won't hit home for you until you've lived it. You won't really know what I'm talking about until you've made those mistakes and learned from them on your own." She lets out a heavy sigh. "And unfortunately, that could take years."

I slide my bag off my shoulder, absently dropping it on the floor. My mom may have been happy with her life and proud of what she'd survived, but her regrets don't end with her.

She worries for me, too.

"I wasn't sure I would ever let you read it," she tells me, looking embarrassed. "Obviously, some of the scenes I wrote would be uncomfortable for you to read."

Uh, yeah. I'll try not to think about the episode in my dad's office the next time I swing by his work.

"But I wrote it when you were little, and I included your dad's side in the story, using his thoughts from some of his old letters to me that I've kept over the years, because I felt his side was important, too. I've just been concerned about you for a long time. I finally decided that if I could show you some things in a way where you could feel them for yourself, then maybe you would learn something from him and me, and what we went through, after all. The book was a way for you to live vicariously—go through the experiences without the costs and consequences."

"Why do you worry about me?"

She leans back in her chair, shaking her head. "Maybe your dad is right. Jared was so difficult, and it was my fault, of course, but raising you has been such an easier experience that maybe I don't know what to do with myself."

Her eyes flash with something, like she's practically lost in thought, and I know she's thinking about my brother.

"Jared was just such an open book," she muses. "If he didn't like something, you knew. If he wanted something, he'd take it. If he wasn't happy, he didn't act like he was." And then her eyes narrow so she can study me. "What do you want, Quinn? What makes you happy?" She leans forward, taking my hand. "Whatever it is, don't wait on anyone else to give it to you. Don't wait for it to just happen. Go get it."

I frown, and it's like I'm standing on a cliff, looking down onto a waterfall and everyone else has jumped—laughing and calling to me to follow—but I'm afraid of the drop.

"It's kind of scary," I choke out. "What if I love you all too much, and I'm afraid of disappointing you?"

"I know you love us," she assures. "We all know, and we love you, too. That will never change." She leans in, trying to catch my eyes. "But does it make you feel good? Sacrificing your own happiness to please others? Honey, if our love is that brittle, then we don't deserve you. A strong person realizes that the only love you truly need in this life is the love you have for yourself. If you have that, it's like armor. No one can stop you. No one else matters."

"So that's why you decided to let me read it," I ask, looking up. She nods.

"But why did you write it in the first place?"

"To learn about myself. To try to make sense out of everything Jason and I went through. Everything we put Madoc and Jared through." She pauses and then continues. "We could say we were young and stupid, but that excuse only lasts so long before you realize that you were selfish and just really big assholes."

I laugh to myself, leaning back and crossing my arms over my chest. "Did you learn anything else?"

A smirk crosses her face, and she reaches behind her to dig in the desk drawer.

Pulling out a small forest green booklet, she hands it to me, and I open it up.

I see several transactions printed, and I can tell it's a bankbook. I widen my eyes, spotting the balance on the bookmarked page. "Oh, my God."

"I learned that it's okay to love and to feel vulnerable and to make mistakes," she says, "but it's not okay to live a trapped life. Never give up your control to someone else."

"Where did this money come from?"

"After I finished the book, I realized a woman should always protect herself. So I gave Jax some of the money I had saved, and the smart investor he is, he multiplied it." She laughs. "Many times."

Oh, my God.

I shoot my eyes back up to her. "Was this your security? In case you and my dad broke up?"

"No," she answers. "It's yours. I didn't really need the savings when I married your dad, so I let Jax create an account, and it's been collecting interest ever since."

"It's mine?" I can't take this. What if she needs it some day?

"As long as you remember, Quinn . . . when you fall in love, take care of him," she explains, "but take care of yourself, too. Make yourself happy. Spend it. Save it. Give it away. Your choice. Your life."

CHAPTER 13

slip the bankbook into my back pocket and make my way down the hall toward my father's office.

My mom had just given me a crap load of money, and I shouldn't take it, but she said it was a gift, and I could do anything with it. Save it, donate it . . . spend it on something.

My heart has started hammering in my chest, and I'm on autopilot, but I just keep going. I'm not sure what's going to happen or what I'll say to my dad, but it's probably going to be something he doesn't like, since why else would I be so nervous?

The hardest part is jumping. I can't retreat, and I can't keep trying to please the world.

I'd hate myself. There's no choice.

Opening the cracked door wider, I step inside and see him standing at the bar against the wall, pouring himself his favorite GlenDronach to wind down before he heads to bed.

"Hey," I broach, my voice surprisingly light.

He twists his head and replaces the top on the decanter, smiling at me. "Hey. I missed you tonight. Were you at the track?"

"For a bit." I nod and walk into the room. "Dylan had her first race, so I rode with her."

His eyebrows shoot up, and I immediately laugh. He may as well find out now before it shows up in his Facebook feed.

"Madoc all but forced me, okay? I'm still in one piece."

He twists his lips to the side, scowling. "That kid, I swear . . ."

Yeah, that *kid*. I almost laugh.

My dad still sees Madoc as a cocky teenager, but I think he understands completely. We're all helpless when Madoc decides he wants something.

Walking over to the large brown leather chairs by the bookcases, he sits down and takes a sip of whiskey. I follow and sit in the identical chair next to him, a small round table between us.

"I'm sorry I couldn't make your game today," he says. "I heard you 'kicked major ass.'"

I snort, knowing those aren't my father's words. "Madoc lies."

Dylan and the rest of the team carry me. I'm simply there to make sure there are eleven players on the field.

But my father corrects me, anyway. "Lawyers don't lie. We invent truth. It's an art."

Yeah, I'm sure. Lucky enough for him, he has clients willing to pay such huge amounts of cash for his "art."

I lean back in the chair, pushing my hair behind my ear and studying him for a brief moment. His gray hair has a good amount of blond left, but while there are wrinkles around his eyes and the lines on his forehead have grown deeper over time, his blue eyes still pierce like lightning in a storm, and his hands are still so strong. I can remember the feel of my little fingers in his when he'd help me cross streets in the big city as a kid.

After all he and my mother went through and put each other through, I understand how he has so much hope for me. I was a long time in the making.

"You really love Mom, don't you?" I say, holding his eyes.

"Of course," he answers and then looks down, seeming lost in thought as he takes another sip. "I can't live without her. I never could."

"What made you finally realize it?"

"When I realized that she was fine without me," he admits. "I'd always loved her, but when she got sober, and she was working and paying her bills . . . doing everything just fine on her own, I realized I had lost her, and the finality of it hit home."

I narrow my eyes on him, still not sure I understand. He wanted her, because he no longer had control of her?

He seems to see my confusion, because he continues explaining.

"I was so arrogant back in those days, honey. I took everything for granted." He swirls the liquid in his glass, staring at it, probably because it's easier than looking me in the eye. "But seeing her turning her life around—happy—honestly, it hurt. It hurt my pride. It hurt my confidence. It hurt my equilibrium. It hurt everywhere."

"Didn't you want her to be healthy?"

He finally looks up at me, his tone turning soothing. "Of course I did. But I guess I thought, though, that if she didn't need me, why would she want me? And all over again, I was in knots. Now that she had choices, would she still choose me?"

And all of a sudden I understand.

My dad had had absolutely no idea what he brought to the table outside of his money and power. He spent so much time and energy taking care of things, providing for her, throwing cash at their problems, that the nature of their relationship had been blurred. He thought my mom loved him because she was young and naïve. Because fear kept her bound to him.

Once she was older, wiser, and stronger, what did he have to offer her except himself? And would she even want that?

"I'd lost her too many times, and now it was going to be for good," he continues. "I couldn't let her go. I finally woke up."

For a long time, my father did what was best for him. Even though he loved her.

But after sixteen years, my mother finally realized that no one was going to save her but her, so she let him go. If he came after her, he came after her. If he didn't, life would go on.

I'm not sure if my mother's plan worked by giving me the book, though. I'll make mistakes, and I'll want things that are bad for me. That goes without saying. It's human nature to be imperfect, after all.

But I have learned one thing tonight. Life moves fast, and the next forty years will be here before I know it. I don't want to wake up at fifty-eight with regret.

I take in a deep breath, exhaling a sigh. "Dad, I suck at soccer," I say, raising my eyes to look at him. "I hate piano, and I don't want to be a lawyer or a doctor. I don't want everything you want for me."

His eyes narrow on me, and he tenses. "Quinn, if this is about Notre Dame—"

"I want to go to Notre Dame," I cut him off. "I think it's exactly where I belong."

I see him relax a little. "Good."

"And I agree, taking a couple of courses here in town this summer is a good idea. Maybe I can finish my degree early."

He nods, still looking nervous like he's waiting for bad news to drop. "I'm . . . glad you think so. But why do I get the feeling that you're about to tell me you met a boy and you're pregnant?"

I chew on the corner of my mouth. Here goes nothing.

"You know the property you own on High Street?" I ask. "The old bakery on the corner of Sutton?"

"Yeah," he replies hesitantly. "I bought it years ago. It was a prime location, so I snatched it up. Why?"

I hold my breath, spitting out the words before I have a chance to second-guess myself. "I want you to sell it to me."

He rears back, looking at me like I spoke another language.

"Just let me say something," I blurt out, holding up my hand. "I've been busy in one way or another my entire life, and I understand that what you wanted for me you wanted out of love. And because I didn't know what else I wanted to do, I went along with everything. The tutors, the extra courses, dance classes, gymnastics, swimming, summer volunteer projects in the rainforest . . ." I list each item on my outstretched fingers. "I did it, because it was better than staying still. Or so I thought. But if I had stopped, I would've had time to think." I lower my voice, trying to get my point across. "I never dream, Dad. I never look forward to anything, because none of it's a passion. Sell me the store. Give me a new summer project and see what I can do."

"You want to start a business?" he asks. "At seventeen?"

"A summer business," I clarify. "For now. And I'm almost eighteen. I promise I won't get distracted. I realize college is important, and I'm going. But I really want this."

"It's not a dollhouse, Quinn." He laughs, sounding flustered. "It's a building with property taxes and health and safety inspections and plumbing problems—"

"And I can do it. I know how to research, plan, and be a problem solver. I can do this. It won't be your problem."

He shakes his head, closing his eyes. "Quinn . . ."

"Dad, please," I implore. "I'm excited. I can't wait to get started." And then I lean in, joking with him. "I mean there are worse ways I could spend my time, right? If I'm buried under this project all summer, I won't be dating, will I?"

He rolls his eyes and sets his drink down, next to the crystal bowl of gourmet jelly beans.

"How do you plan to pay for this?" he questions. "You'll need supplies, renovations, inventory, utilities, and even if you did get a loan to buy the property, I'm not comfortable with you having that kind of weight on your shoulders—"

"I don't need a loan." I pull out the bankbook and toss it on the table.

He stares at it before picking it up and opening it. Quickly scanning the inside, his eyebrows finally shoot up. Probably when he saw the balance.

His eyes dart over to me, all humor gone. "This isn't your college account. Where did this money come from?"

I give a half-smile and stand up, grabbing a jelly bean and popping it into my mouth.

"I think you need to go talk to Mom."

And then I turn and walk out the door.

"That's not the ten millimeter!" I hear Jared yelling when I walk into his shop.

"You told me to get the eight millimeter!"

"The eight won't fit."

"Didn't I tell you that?" Madoc bellows back, and I hear tools clank as I come through the large room.

Jared, Madoc, and Jax are all crowded around a Chevy SS, the hood popped open, no tires, and a missing windshield. Madoc is still dressed in his suit; however, the jacket and tie are gone and his shirttails are hanging out.

"It's okay," Jax tells him, coming up behind him and squeezing his shoulders, trying to calm him down. "Relax."

Madoc shakes his head, pain written all over his face. "My kid doesn't want to live in my house anymore."

"It's a lot more complicated than that," Jared says. "Give him time."

I guess they all came here to blow off some steam after the scene at the station. Under the hood of a car is the one place they find their center.

"Hey," I say gently, making myself known. I'd planned on Jared being here, but I was glad I'd found all three of them.

"How did you get here?" Jax asks, knowing I don't have a car.

I won't tell him I rode my bike at midnight.

Ignoring him, I reach into my satchel and pull out the Internet printouts I gathered at home and hand them to Jared.

"What's this?" He takes the papers and starts skimming them.

"It's a list of event coordinators. Your expo in Chicago is way too much of a time commitment, and one of them will do a much better job than I will."

He narrows his eyes, finally looking up at me.

"I love you guys," I tell them, "but I have other plans for the summer. I'll be around, but I won't always be available. And honestly, the expo is stressful. I'm sorry."

Jared gives a half-smile. "Of course it's stressful. That's why I push it off on you or Pasha," he tells me. "But it's fine. I just like having you around. I'll make do."

He leaves a quick peck on my forehead and folds the papers, sticking them in his back pocket.

Thank God. I guess I should've known Jared would be understanding. He's a firm believer in people doing exactly what they want to do.

I turn to Madoc. "And I will volunteer ten hours a week this summer, but I'm not interning, and I'm not on a schedule, okay?"

He shrugs, looking like his mind is on a million other things. "Okay."

I glance at Jax. "And Hawke can coordinate the fireworks show," I tell him. "He needs some responsibilities."

Jax runs his hand through his hair, looking tired but in complete agreement. Hawke is allowed to roam at his own free will. A little routine wouldn't hurt him, and Jax knows that.

"Are you okay?" Madoc asks.

"Yeah." I nod. "How long are you guys going to be here?"

Madoc sighs, tossing down his wrench. "I'm on my way out. Fallon just texted and Hunter's not home yet, so . . ."

"I'll be here until this is done," Jared answers, gesturing to the car. "Maybe an hour, but now that Madoc is leaving, it should go faster."

"Blow me," Madoc mumbles and walks over to the toolbox and grabs his jacket lying on top.

I jerk my thumb behind me, toward the door. "I'm going to head down the street . . . check something out," I tell Jared. "I'll be back soon. Can you give me a ride home?"

Yeah," he says.

I wait until I'm outside to dig out my new keys.

t's mine.

I smile wide, unable to contain it.

Walking as quickly as I can, I carry the little lamp from my bike in one hand, and the keys my father gave me dangle from the other as I take a right on Sutton, scurrying across the narrow brick lane and into the alley behind the old bakery. While the main streets are well lit, I rush as quickly as possible, because back here, there's nothing and no one. Not even a street light.

My hand shakes as I try to work the key into the lock. My blood is racing, and I inhale a couple of deep breaths to try to calm down. Twisting the knob, I finally swing open the door and immediately paw the wall inside, searching for a light switch.

I'm opening a shop. By next summer, I'll have it ready.

I flip the switch but nothing happens. Well, I guess that makes sense. This place has been shut down for years. I turn on the flashlight and close the door behind me, aiming the light into the room that I can tell already is the kitchen. Three long wooden tables sit parallel to each other while stoves, sinks, a refrigerator, and a cooler door line the walls, along with old aluminum racks holding empty trays.

I walk in further, trying to take everything in, already inventorying in my head the appliances that would need to be inspected, possibly replaced, and all the cleaning that would probably take a whole month in itself. Lifting the toe of my shoe, I lightly shove an empty flour bag out of my way as I push through the revolving door separating the kitchen from the front of the store.

"What are you doing?"

I jump and suck in a breath, spinning around. "What the—" I gasp, flashing my light on Hunter, who stands in the open doorway. "What the hell are you doing?"

He shrugs and steps inside, closing the door behind him. "I was driving around, and I saw you sneaking in the back."

My heart pounds so hard it hurts. I shake my head at him, starting to calm down.

"Madoc's looking for you." I turn and push through the door again. "Where've you been?"

He follows me through, into the front of the shop, but doesn't answer. If his father's looking for him, and Kade is home, then Hunter took the truck without permission. I'm sure he figures there's not much more trouble he can get into after what happened tonight, though.

We walk through, and I flip more switches, checking for power, while Hunter kicks garbage and newspapers with his feet.

There are cobwebs in the corners of the ceiling as well as under the counter, and I can still smell the scent of warm sugar, probably from the remnants of old sprinkles and icing inside the display cases. It will be a wonder if I don't have roaches to deal with, too.

The wallpaper has to go, but I catch sight of the floors, and as I brush away some paper and dust under my foot, I notice that the tile is a Moroccan mosaic pattern. Lots of color and so different from anything else around Shelburne Falls, that's for sure.

That can stay.

I see Hunter finally lean back, sticking his hands in his pocket and resting on a wrought iron table.

"I'm going to buy this place," I tell him. "I'm going to turn it into a pastry shop."

He just stares at me, nodding, and I narrow my eyes on him.

"You don't have anything to say?" I challenge. "No smart-ass remark?"

"You're confusing me with Kade," he retorts. "I think the world has enough shit talkers."

I smile, turning my head away so he can't see. He looks and sounds like he's pissed, but I couldn't appreciate the remark more. He's absolutely correct. Enough talking and bullshit, and I'm thankful for his silence. I don't need anyone else's judgments, concerns, or negative feedback.

And when Jared, Madoc, and Jax have something to say tomorrow when they find out, I'll tell them the same thing. Mind your own business.

Hunter leans down, picking up a chair that was overturned. "You need to make sure you have those Blackberry Swirl Brownies," he says, leaning back down to collect trash and toss it into the bin in the corner. "They're Dylan's favorite. And the Sugar Cookie Apple Cobbler and those Samoa donuts you made with the Girl Scout cookies that time . . ." He trails off, letting out a sigh that sounds suddenly hungry. "I swear, you'll have people lined up out the door."

I watch him as he starts tearing flyers off the wall and throwing them away. I love that he isn't hassling me.

Walking over to his side, I help tear the papers through their staples. "Were you saying good-bye to her?" I ask quietly, not looking at him. "Is that where you were at?"

He's silent, but he doesn't ask who we're talking about. We both know.

"I'm just going to Grandpa's," he tells me. "I'll get a summer job and earn some money before the school year at St. Matt's starts. I'll be home on weekends."

"No you won't." I glance over at him. "You'll make friends. Find reasons to stay in Chicago. We'll see you less and less."

I remember saying the same thing to Lucas nearly three years ago when he said he would be back. He was lying, and I knew it then.

But Hunter stares up at the wall, now bare, looking like he's thinking about more than he's saying. "I'll be back," he assures. And then I catch a small smile curling his lips. "There's Rivalry Week, after all."

Yeah. Rivalry Week.

I shake my head. That'll be fun.

EPILOGUE

The sun begins to dip below the horizon, casting an orange glow over the city, and I stare west, barely feeling the day's warmth soak through my suit jacket.

I hate this time of day. No meetings, no deadlines, no conference calls or site inspections . . . nowhere to rush off to. There's too much quiet, and I don't like quiet.

Looking out over the rooftops of the city, I tip my beer up and take a drink as I let the view soak in. The awe-inspiring designs of the skyscrapers, the day's light reflecting off all the glass and setting the city aglow, the Persian Gulf looming behind me, the domes of the ancient mosques, and the smell of the spices and wares drifting up from the souks . . .

Dubai has been a place for me to sink myself into these past three years. It's been an inspiration, giving me the drive and knowledge to push further and further into new territory of design. There's been so much for me to learn and live up to, and I've been grateful for the noise and distraction. How could I ever go home after living in a place like this?

I set my beer down on the ledge of the balcony and reach into my breast pocket and pull out the compass Quinn gave to me before I left Shelburne Falls four years ago.

I look down at the antique brass heirloom, smiling at the thought of her. She was so innocent and curious, so angry and sad to see me go.

Making her mad at me wasn't something I enjoyed—especially when I couldn't explain to her why I needed to leave—but I had to admit, she was the only one who made me second-guess leaving. The only one who made me feel like I *needed* to stay. It had kind of felt good to know I'd be missed.

I can't help wondering what she'd be like now. She'd be almost eighteen. Nearly an adult.

And here I am, nearly thirty, and still alone, burying myself in my work.

I haven't changed at all.

Flipping open the top of the compass, I watch the disk under the glass wobble on its axis and the dial slowly find its position just slightly past the *W*. Turning my body a hair to the right, I pause and wait, watching as the needle moves again, coming to rest at the exact point between north and west.

And then I look up, fixing my eyes dead ahead, out to the horizon.

"Mr. Morrow?"

I blink and snap the compass shut. Sliding it back inside my breast pocket, I pick up my beer again and turn my head to see Tahra, the housekeeper, standing in the doorway between the balcony and the apartment. An immigrant from India, she comes several times a week to clean up, grocery shop, and cook supper, earning a little extra money in addition to what her husband brings home from the oil rigs.

"Yes, Tahra?"

She smiles, speaking softly. "Your dinner is staying warm in the oven, sir. I'll head home now."

"Thank you," I tell her. "Good night."

I turn back, catching the sun just as it disappears beneath the horizon. The dry air burns my nostrils as I breathe in, but I'm not ready to go inside yet.

"Are you all right?" I hear her ask tentatively.

I twist my head around again, regarding her. "Yes, why?"

She studies me for a moment and then gestures to me with the dish towel in her hand. "You've started standing in the same spot every night, facing the same direction."

I hesitate before responding. "Have I?"

I haven't been keeping track, but I guess she's right. I thought I'd been more restless lately, but if she was starting to notice, then I guess it is pretty obvious.

"If you wish to pray, Mecca is that way."

And I look back up in time to see her gesture to the southwest with a knowing smile.

I grin, shaking my head. "You don't stop trying, do you?" And then I look back out on the last light of the sun shimmering on the city, and I think about what's beyond the skyscrapers and the bazaars and the desert. Beyond Mecca, the Red Sea, Africa, and the Atlantic . . .

"Actually, my home is that way," I finally say, pointing with my bottle and gesturing northwest. "My home is 7,308 miles from this spot."

"That's a long way."

I nod, lost in thought. "Yeah." I pause and then continue, "And even still, nothing is different. She was right."

"Who?"

Happiness is a direction, not a place. Yeah, she was certainly right. The corner of my mouth lifts in a smile, thinking about how smart that kid always was.

Even a young girl, fourteen years old, knew that anger and un-happiness had not one fucking thing to do with where you lived, whom you loved, or what you did with your life. It was all in our heads.

And no matter how much you run, you can't run from yourself, can you?

Amusement fills my chest, and I'm suddenly wondering what she's doing now. What they're all doing. Madoc and his barbecues and picnics and pool parties, making everyone laugh and love him despite themselves. Jared with the sound of his engine filling the neighborhood and Tate and how she always wanted to play in the rain, even as an adult. Fallon and her smart mouth, who always got everyone we worked with to do things exactly her way; and Juliet with her sexy, free spirit. And then there's Jax, with one eye always on the ball and one eye always on his wife.

I wonder about the kids and how they're all grown up and prob-ably wreaking hell, getting their licenses and breaking rules.

Quinn annoyed the crap out of me when she was little, but she always stood by my side, literally, making me feel like one of their own in a group of people that weren't really my family.

Why did I leave home again? I suddenly struggle to remember my reasons, because right now, it feels like what I gave up is a hell of a lot more than what I ran away from.

"Sir?"

My eyelids flutter, and I take in a breath, coming back to the conversation. "Sorry. Nothing. Never mind," I say quickly, dismiss-ing her. "Thank you, Tahra."

"Good night, sir."

But before I have a chance to turn back around, she speaks up again, "If you don't mind my asking . . . if you're homesick, why don't you just go home?"

I drop my eyes, remaining silent. I'm not sure how to answer that, but it's a good question.

Can I go home? Of course. Anytime I want.

So why wasn't I budging?

I inhale a long breath, feeling the welcome heat suddenly hit my cold fingers as I stare northwest.

"Someday," I whisper.

Copyright © Penelope Douglas

PENELOPE DOUGLAS is a *New York Times, USA Today,* and *Wall Street Journal* bestselling author. Their books have been translated into twenty languages and include the Fall Away series, the Hellbent series, the Devil's Night series, and the stand-alones *Misconduct, Punk 57, Birthday Girl, Credence,* and *Tryst Six Venom.* They live in New England with their husband and daughter.

VISIT THE AUTHOR ONLINE

PenelopeDouglasAuthor.com
 PenelopeDouglasAuthor
 PenDouglas